S.W. TANPEPPER'S GAMELAND

episode one
DEEP INTO THE GAME

episode two
FAILSAFE

BRINESTONE PRESS
San Martin, CA

THE GAMELAND COLLECTION

Golgotha (prequel to GAMELAND)
Episode One: *Deep Into the Game*
Episode Two: *Failsafe*
Episode Three: *Deadman's Switch*
Episode Four: *Sunder the Hollow Ones*
Episode Five: *Prometheus Wept*
Episode Six: *Kingdom of Players*
Episode Seven: *Tag, You're Dead*
Episode Eight: *Jacker's Code*

Infected: Hacked Files from the GAMELAND Archive

Velveteen

Signs of Life (*Jessie's Game*, Book One)

*A Dark and Sure Descent:
Being a True Account of the Long Island Outbreak*

Dead Reckoning (*Jessie's Game*, Book Two)
Fall 2014

SHORT STORY COLLECTIONS

Undead and Other Horrors
Insomnia

SCIENCE FICTION

The Green Gyre
Recode T.G.C.A: The Grayson Cole Affair

GAMELAND
Episodes One & Two:
Deep Into the Game & *Failsafe*

Copyright © 2012, 2014 by Saul Tanpepper

Cover and interior art by Ken J. Howe

Design by Brinestone Press Copyright © 2014

All rights reserved.

Brinestone Press

http://www.brinestonepress.com

PUBLISHER'S NOTE:

This book is a work of fiction. Names, characters, places, and incidents either are the product of the author's imagination or are used fictitiously, and any resemblance to actual persons, living or dead, business establishments, events, or locales is entirely coincidental.

No portion of this book may be reproduced by any means, mechanical, electronic, or otherwise, without first obtaining the permission of the copyright holder.

For more information, contact Brinestone Press or the author at:

editor@brinestonepress.com

authorsaultanpepper@gmail.com

ISBN-13: 978-1-500-33349-2

ISBN-10: 1-500-33349-2

10 9 8 7 6 5 4 3 2

rv140626

Contents

Welcome to GAMELAND vii

Episode One: *Deep Into the Game*

Prologue 1

Part One: The Plan. Or Rather the Pathetic Lack of One

Chapter One	13
Chapter Two	23
Chapter Three	28
Chapter Four	35
Chapter Five	46
Chapter Six	49
Chapter Seven	51
Chapter Eight	57
Chapter Nine	64
Chapter Ten	72
Chapter Eleven	75
Chapter Twelve	82

Part Two: Breaking In

Chapter Thirteen	86
Chapter Fourteen	95
Chapter Fifteen	101
Chapter Sixteen	107
Chapter Seventeen	113
Chapter Eighteen	117
Chapter Nineteen	122
Chapter Twenty	129
Chapter Twenty One	138
Chapter Twenty Two	145
Chapter Twenty Three	149

Episode Two: *Failsafe*
Part One: There are No Guarantees in Life

Chapter One	159
Chapter Two	170
Chapter Three	176
Chapter Four	183
Chapter Five	190
Chapter Six	196
Chapter Seven	205
Chapter Eight	208
Chapter Nine	211
Chapter Ten	219
Chapter Eleven	226
Chapter Twelve	231

Part Two: That's Why We Have Contingencies

Chapter Thirteen	239
Chapter Fourteen	242
Chapter Fifteen	248
Chapter Sixteen	251
Chapter Seventeen	260
Chapter Eighteen	266
Chapter Nineteen	270
Chapter Twenty	275
Chapter Twenty One	283
Chapter Twenty Two	286
Chapter Twenty Three	293
Chapter Twenty Four	297
Chapter Twenty Five	303

ACKNOWLEDGEMENTS	307
ABOUT THE AUTHOR	308

Welcome to GAMELAND

Dear Friend, a quick word about GAMELAND:

First, thank you for purchasing this book. It's my fervent wish that this story exceeds your every expectation.

GAMELAND was the brainchild of discussions between myself and my publisher, Brinestone Press, back in 2011. Together, we fleshed out an overarching storyline to be told over the course of several "episodes." Each features a group of recurring characters, has its own theme, and works out its own particular issues. Structurally, the series is modeled after popular television shows (think *Fringe, Bones, The Walking Dead*), with each episode roughly the equivalent of a two-hour program. GAMELAND is, however, wholly unique—, a mix of cyberpunk, horror, suspense and mystery.

These are the first of eight episodes, first published beginning May 2012. They introduce you to the main characters, their foibles and strengths, their world and the issues confronting them. The larger story issues will mature over the course of the series.

If you would like news about the GAMELAND series, just shoot me an email to **authorsaultanpepper@gmail.com**. I also urge you to subscribe my newsletter, the *Tanpepper Tidings*. You'll get updates on new releases, notices about special and exclusive pricing events and giveaways, and will be automatically eligible for contests:

https://tinyletter.com/SWTanpepper

You can also find me on Facebook:

http://facebook.com/saul.tanpepper

I value your opinion and invite you to offer your thoughts on this work. Share it with your friends; write a review. These small acts are more powerful than any promotional tool I may wield on my own. Email me. I want to know what you think and promise you that I will always give your feedback serious consideration.

Now, sit back and enjoy *The Game*. I hope to see you back for the next installments of GAMELAND.

Saul
San Francisco, CA
June 26, 2014

S.W. TANPEPPER'S GAMELAND

episode one

DEEP INTO THE GAME

Prologue

*Seventeen years after the invention of
Reanimation Technology*

It wasn't Reggie's idea to break into Gameland, not initially, though of course he took all the credit. He liked being the go-to guy whenever it was something the five of us could all get behind. He was funny that way — a big brute of a kid with all kinds of brains and good looks and a huge gaping insecurity complex that needed constant attention. But whenever something turned out to be not so good after all, he was usually the first to distance himself from it, claiming he always knew it was a bad idea, right from the beginning. That's just the way he was.

He had a way of picking the bad ideas, which is why we should've just said no.

We were in Micah's basement. He and Kelly were team-playing *Zpocalypto*, which is supposed to be something like *The Game*. Except it turned out to be nothing like it at all. First of all, it was nowhere near as real. There's no VR and the action's totally lame. Plus, the holographics are just so-so. You don't get a good feel for what it's like to be in the actual Gameland, fighting actual zombies, trying not to get eaten. Now I know.

I also know this: Not even those lucky rich pricks have any idea what it's like, the ones who are connected enough to pay for a state-of-the-art cybernetic setup and a Player, *plus* weasel the necessary invite into *The Game*. Arc Entertainment didn't just let anyone play. They only wanted the best.

Like us.

Reg and I were bookending the couch. Ashley was sprawled out between us, her feet on his lap and her head on mine. She was drinking a Red Bull through a straw, the can wedged between two cushions to keep it upright. Reg had chugged his and had tossed the empty at the old milk crate in the corner. He missed, of course, and blamed it on the lighting, which admittedly was piss-poor. Micah's HG setup was old and glitchy, so he had to keep the lights dimmed.

Reg was antsy. He was always antsy, but probably more so then because of the caffeine. He kept asking us if we were finished with our drinks. I'm sure he thought the first miss was just a fluke and wanted to redeem himself. That's how self-deluded he could be. But I'd barely even touched my RB. I like the taste of it, but the stuff gives me a headache if I drink it too quickly. And Ash was purposefully nursing hers just to be a pissant.

I was messing with her coppery hair, twining it between my fingers, trying to straighten the curls and watching them spring back. For some reason it struck me as comical and I kept giggling, even though I wasn't even the slightest bit drunk or stoned. Not like Micah. He was the druggie in the group.

The rest of us got our highs playing games or hacking them. That was our escape from the misfortune of being born into families that couldn't afford to buy a decent entertainment system. My family was once so lucky, but after my dad died and Grandpa was fired from his prestigious command post in the Marines, that all went away. Of course, that all happened fifteen or so years ago, so as far as I could remember we'd always been as poor and out-of-the-loop as anyone else in that room.

I caught Reg glancing over at us — probably envisioning me and Ash acting out one of his perverted girl-on-girl fantasies. I obliged him. Sort of. I reached over and pinched Ash's nose until she slapped my hand away with an inviting shriek. The movement caused her to dig her heels into

Reggie's crotch, which was precisely what I was going for. I saw him jerk in pain. He tried to hide it, but I saw.

"What's so funny, Jess?" Ash asked me, gazing up at me with those brilliant green eyes of hers. They were so innocent looking, but I'd always known how manipulative they could be.

"Nothing," I answered. Then I coughed, trying to hide another snort of laughter.

Reggie groaned out loud. Then, trying to hide his discomfort, he started complaining about how bored he was: "This scene blows, guys," he whined. "You know what we should do? We should break into Gameland."

"We already tried, Reg. Remember?" Kelly replied. He was referring to Ash's and Micah's attempt to hack *The Game* a couple weeks earlier. But I sensed that Reggie was talking about something else altogether, something a hell of a lot more illegal and a shit-load more dangerous.

I watched as Kel's and Micah's zombie hunters searched through a dark warehouse looking for food. I'd never played this level before, but I could guess what was going to happen. There were certain patterns to how *Zpocalypto* was constructed. Once you recognized them, it was a lot easier to survive and advance to the next level. If my guess was correct, they were about to be jumped by a bunch of the Undead at any moment.

"Not *The Game*, dweeb," Reggie barked. "I'm talking about breaking into Long Island itself. We should actually physically *go* there ourselves."

Kelly didn't look up. "Yeah, man. We'll just hop onto the next transit over there right now." He exhaled with disgust when a zombie slipped out of a shipping crate and chomped down on his ankle, immediately crippling him. If he didn't make it back to his antivenin kit within the next few minutes, his character would be dead and return to undo everything he'd accomplished to get this far.

The "antivenin kit" was one of those things that irritated me the most about *Zpocalypto*. First of all, the bite causes an infection; it's not a poison, like a snake bite. They should've called it an anti-infective. Secondly, in real life, if you're bitten, there is no cure. What's the saying? Once bitten, twice dead?

That professor who tried fifteen years ago proved that. The one who everyone says killed my father.

"I'm not talking right this minute, brah," Reggie answered.

"I'm up for it!" Micah said, as he lopped the virtual head off a virtual zombie with a virtual light saber, something the game was obviously not programmed to provide.

Ash raised her head and looked at me in disgust after seeing this. I just shrugged. It didn't surprise me anymore. Micah was always reprogramming the game in his favor.

"But we should try soon," he added, throwing the severed head into his virtual backpack. "Like, this weekend."

"Where'd you get the light saber?" Kelly asked. He sounded jealous.

Micah smiled his shit-eating grin. "I did a little creative recoding yesterday."

"Cheater."

"Well . . . yeah."

"Why this weekend?" I asked, only because I was curious to see how far the boys were willing to take this conversation. Theorizing something as blatantly illegal as breaking into LI was much more entertaining than watching the boys play a game they'd hacked. It was also more entertaining than seeing how springy Ashley's hair could be. Or causing Reggie bodily harm and insult.

"Because in two and a half short weeks, our lives are totally going to be over, girl. That's why."

Micah was referring to the start of our senior year in high school. Well, Ash would technically be only a junior, but she had enough credits to graduate with the rest of us, and probably would.

Just three more weekends before our last year of incarceration. Nineteen more days of parole before we were all swallowed up in that mess of a penal system that masqueraded as a social welfare program. It was ostensibly there to prepare us for the harsh realities of an even harsher world, but it failed to do so on so many levels that it was almost ridiculous.

As far as the majority of kids my age were concerned, school was just another relic of the past. How was studying mid-sixteenth century literature supposed to help us deal with rising sea levels in the mid-twenty first century? How was knowing the sum of the angles of a triangle going to help us in the event of another outbreak? If it wasn't for the fact that getting caught skipping school was pretty much a death sentence, signing years of our afterlife away into conscription, we wouldn't even bother going.

I exhaled, trying to quell the sense of panic and anticipation rising up inside of me. I didn't like to be reminded of time slipping away, of what awaited us on the other side of August. I reminded myself that I had to suffer only one more year of that institutionalized prison, then I'd be free to do whatever I wanted to do. We all would.

Most of us were planning on skipping college and going straight into one of those high-paying jobs as a coder with ArcWare. Kelly was the only one of us giving college any serious thought. He was always the one who had to be different from the rest of us. That's what first attracted me to him, his long view, and it's what I so dearly loved about him.

Out of all the guys I'd ever known, he was the kindest, the most caring. Anyone who knew the Corben family — who knew Kyle, Kelly's little brother — could see that.

On the outside, Kelly wasn't much to talk about: brown hair and eyes, an average build, average looks. A girlfriend probably shouldn't say this about her boyfriend, but he was... forgettable. Nevertheless, he more than made up for it with his earnestness. I'd rather be with a guy who was honest with me than one who was easy on the eyes.

Lately, though, he'd been acting all strange. He was moody, inattentive, distracted. Just once in a while I wished he'd lighten up and relax.

"Wait," he said. "You're not serious, are you?" He jerked his body to the left, then twisted it as he tried to get his player to respond faster in the game, but the cheap sensors were low-res and iffy and it made his hunter look more like one of the hunted, all lurchy and uncoordinated. "You mean, like, actually *break into* Long Island?"

"Dead serious, brah," Reggie replied. He laughed, probably realizing he'd inadvertently made a funny.

Reggie was Kel's opposite. In fact, he was pretty much the opposite of any of us. "Big, bald and brash," Micah always said about him, a stark contrast to his own blond, blue-eyed, befreckled boyish good looks and charm. "A brute with a heart the size of Texas."

And Micah would certainly know about Texas. He was once a Republic good old boy before his parents defected to Connecticut. He always had a smile on his face and a reputation for never hurting a soul. A *living* soul, that is. When it came to zombies, on the other hand, he was a stone-cold killer. The Undead rarely stood a chance against him. He was the best game player I'd ever seen. Probably the best hacker, too.

Kelly wasn't nearly as good as Micah in the gaming department — or me, for that matter — but still a hell of a lot better than most. Better than Reggie, anyway. And while he could hack, he didn't like doing it. He was too uptight for any of that action, though not enough to not hang out with us.

Yet, as different as the three boys were, they were all brilliant, and they all shared the same passion for gaming. We all did, which is what brought us together in the first place. It's what kept us together despite the immense differences in our personalities.

"Why would we even want to go to the Wastes?" Kelly asked without looking away. The Wastes were the places that had been decimated over the past thirty years by rising sea levels. Pretty much every coastal city had such areas, variably referred to as the Wastes or Wastelands. They were urban ghost towns, and LI was just one of many. Perfect breeding grounds for outbreaks.

Reggie shrugged. "Uh, no reason, brah, other than to see if we actually can. To say that we did."

"Sure, why not," Ashley chimed in. "I'll try anything once. We haven't done a damn thing exciting all summer and it's almost over!"

I wanted to pinch her nose again just for reminding me of that.

The more I thought about it, the more I realized how breaking into Long Island — even just *planning* something like it — would liven things up, take our minds off of school and the inevitable dreariness of those long winter days ahead, hunched over a desk in sub-zero classrooms, suffering the slings and arrows of outrageous Shakespeare-inflicted misfortune.

This time Ashley didn't ask why I was giggling.

"Doing something just so you can brag about it isn't a reason," Kelly argued.

"Oh, don't be such a weenie," Reggie retorted. It was his typical comeback whenever any of us disagreed with something he said. We usually let him get away with it because he was so damn big. That, and he actually relished a good argument.

But Kelly wasn't giving in so easily. They got into a heated discussion, mostly focusing on the actual logistics of breaking into what had once been a militarized zone and was now blockaded by physical and electromagnetic barriers.

I was listening with interest, but Ash got bored and made me go upstairs with her. She needed to use the bathroom and the one down in the basement was nasty. But she never liked wandering around Micah's upstairs all alone. She said it felt spooky, like his parents were ghosts watching over her.

When we came back down, it appeared that the argument was over. Micah and Kelly were back to playing *Zpocalypto* and Reggie was asleep on the couch, snoring loudly. He had a smile on his face.

Ashley kicked him. "Hey, perv! Make some room," she said. "Quit hogging the couch."

Reggie opened one eye and his smile widened, but he didn't move. "Where'd you guys go?"

"Upstairs to have hot lesbian sex in Micah's room."

"That was quick."

"Yeah, well, Jessie's super easy to bring to climax."

"Ashley!"

I could feel my face burning. I may have lost my virginity at fifteen, but I was still a bit of a prude about it, especially around her. It was like I needed to balance out her own over-the-top sexuality.

Ash didn't care what people thought. She always just said whatever was on her mind. In fact, I'm sure she said things just to try and elicit a reaction.

I looked over at Kelly, but he hadn't even heard what she'd said. He was too absorbed in the game.

Reggie snorted. He gave Ash a good, long, appraising look, beginning with the thumbs she'd hooked onto the waistband of her jeans, pausing at the low neckline of her more-than-ample breasts, then finally reaching her eyes. Not once did she flinch. If anything, the look on her face grew even more defiant.

"Sorry I missed it," he said.

She glanced pointedly at the bulge in his jeans and smiled. "I'm sure it was just as exciting as you imagined it."

Reggie laughed and pulled up his legs, then swung them over the front of the couch. Ash plunked down next to him with a heavy exhale. He swung his arm over her shoulders, letting his fingers dangle a hair's width away from the top of her breast. Though the two weren't technically together, everyone knew they were doing it. At least whenever there wasn't anything better going on. Or any*one*.

I glanced past my boyfriend to the flickering HG image in front of him. He was back to level eleven — his nemesis. If I were a betting girl, I'd wager he was on his last life and was about to be attacked. Again.

Poor Kelly. As good as he was, he just couldn't seem to make it past this level no matter how many times he tried. But I didn't feel much pity for him at the moment. Sometimes, like right now when he wasn't paying any attention to me, his obsession with the game kind of pissed me off.

"So . . . what'd you guys decide?" Ashley asked. "About Gameland."

I looked over. Reggie's thumb was now resting on the exposed skin of her breast. He was slowly brushing it back and forth. I felt a tingle pass through my own body, then a twinge of jealousy. Reggie was a code geek, just like the rest of us, but at least he had broader interests outside of the games.

Kelly could learn a thing or two from his example.

"Well, actually, it wouldn't technically be Gameland," he told Ash. "We'd just be breaking into one of the Forbidden Zones on LI — an *outer* zone. I think the Gameland arena is more toward the center of the island — that's what Micah thinks, anyway — and it's probably pretty heavily barricaded to keep the Players from getting out."

He was talking about the implanted zombies that were recruited into *The Game*. They called them Players.

"There's still the Infected Undead on the rest of the island," I pointed out.

Reggie chuffed. "Yeah, like there'd be any IUs left after thirteen years. They're all dead by now." He waggled his fingers spookily at me and said, "No brains to feed on."

"You don't know that."

He shook his head. "You're beginning to sound just like your boyfriend. He says it's not doable."

"I didn't say that."

Reggie smiled. He was egging me on, and I'd fallen for it. I should've known. Whatever Kelly said, Reg always tried to say the opposite. And now that Kelly was saying it was impossible to break into LI, it just made Reg even more determined to say it wasn't.

Kelly paused his game so he could tick reasons off on his fingers: "Fifty foot wall around the entire island, electrified razor wire, all the bridges demoed, no-fly zones, biometric mines in the East River, electromagnetic barrier— "

"EM, brah? Really? Chillax. I'm not talking about *hacking* in, I'm talking about breaking in. Remember? The EM's nothing to worry about."

"It could fry your implant," I said.

"Implant, shmimplant."

"There's no way," Kelly insisted. "I'm telling you, it's impossible."

"Maybe there is a way," Micah said, still playing. He was one of those freaky types who could give a hundred percent of his attention to something like *Zpocalypto* or *Warlock Four* and yet still be fully involved in a conversation, even while being stoned off his gourd. I could never understand how he did it. The guy was more than just scary smart. It was like he could partition his brain into distinct segments — one for gaming, one for being wasted, one for everything else — yet still use them all at full capacity. He was like a computer. "I'll give it some thought."

"I know!" Ashley exclaimed. "We'll just sprinkle a little fairy dust on our bodies and fly ourselves in."

"I'll sprinkle fairy dust over your body if you do mine," Reggie said.

I snorted.

He looked over at me. "Every time someone disses a fairy, another zombie gets its wings."

I rolled my eyes, but I was laughing.

"That's just . . . stupid!" Kelly snapped. "Besides, you have to get through Manhattan's restricted zones first. That can be a hassle."

"That's true," I said. I'd gone there on occasion with my brother; he had a special pass. I remembered all the checkpoints and the guards questioning us.

Kelly smiled and nodded at me, thinking I was actually taking his side in the argument. "It's crazy talk."

I went over and plopped down on his lap and planted a kiss on his lips. It wasn't one of our usual hot-n-heavy lip-bruising kisses — I didn't want to start anything — but I hoped it was enough that he'd not take what I was about to say the wrong way.

"If Reggie says he can come up with a plan, then . . . . Well, I'm in, too."

Kelly leaned away from me like I was contagious.

Reggie gave a howl of triumph. "See? Didn't I tell you it was a good idea?"

† † †

That was weeks ago now. How many exactly, I don't know. I've lost count of the days.

Reggie is leaning on me, pushing all of his weight onto the bandage pressed at my side as if he's afraid my guts are going to come spilling out at any moment. Now he doesn't look so sure of himself.

"I knew this was bad," he growls. "Right from the start I knew we shouldn't have come here. That's what I tried to tell you guys."

I look up at Kelly standing outside the glass door looking in — what's left of him, anyway — and I see now that he was right. He was right all along. I just wish he'd tried harder to stop us.

I don't blame either of them, though. I don't blame anyone. Not myself, not even the asshole who first planted the idea in Reggie's brain. We all had our own private reason for coming. That's what really drove us to do it. But would we have come if we knew then what we know now? Would we still have agreed to try?

I don't know. Maybe not.

Then again, maybe.

As I lie here dying, lost somewhere in the Wastes with zombies closing in, wanting nothing more than to feed on those of us still alive, the truth finally hits home: it never really mattered what we wanted or didn't want. Arc Entertainment had this all planned from the very beginning. They wanted us in *The Game*. That's why it was so easy for us to break in.

And why getting out has been such a killer.

I slowly reach behind my back, to the cold metal of the gun tucked into my waistband. I've got one bullet left. Just one. I know it sounds cliché, but I've been saving it for just such a moment.

My fingers wrap around the grip; they find the safety and flick it off. They touch the curve of the trigger, test its resistance. Reggie sees the wince on my face as I pull it free, but he thinks it's just the infection taking hold. He doesn't yet see the gun. All he knows is that the disease is spreading inside of me. He knows the agony I'll soon be going through. He knows the monster I'm about to become.

I cough. "Got any antivenin?" I ask, trying for humor.

He smiles a wistful smile.

I draw the gun out and hold it up. They all see it at the same moment, though it doesn't register with any of them right away what I'm going to do with it. Then, all at once, they know, and they start yelling for me not to do it.

But I don't hear them. All I can hear as I aim and pull the trigger is Kelly — my poor, dear, lost Kelly — whispering inside my head how much he loves me.

I guess he was a better player than I realized.

Part One

The Plan.
Or Rather the Pathetic Lack of One

Chapter One

Two days before breaking in.

Thursday mornings during the summer are set aside for free sparring at the dojang. I've been studying hapkido since I was nine and recently passed my 1st gup black belt. What prompted my older brother Eric to push me into martial arts was the second outbreak, the one that happened down in DC. He thought a little self-defense training might come in handy.

The problem with that kind of thinking is that nobody believes a bunch of fancy kicks and holds is any kind of defense against the Infected Undead. And especially not against those with implants. I'd seen the Omegaman propaganda videos in school and knew the damage they could do to a person when fully under the control of a functioning L.I.N.C. implant. But since the government only just started making them mandatory about ten years ago, there are still tons of people who don't have one yet, just waiting to become an IU in the event of another outbreak.

So, yeah, while guns have their shortcomings, I'd rather have one than not.

Despite knowing all that, I decided to stick with the training anyway. I had other reasons for doing so. For one thing, it helped me manage my anger. For another, it kept the bullies who knew my family's history from kicking my ass.

The first outbreak took place in New York, on Long Island, but I don't really remember it. I was maybe four at the time. Eric says it was terrible. The one in Washington wasn't as bad. The military had some experience dealing with thousands of IUs swarming through cities by then. It's probably why DC was never abandoned like LI was. That, and because the island was already pretty trashed from the flooding earlier in the century. As it turns out, it looks like that flooding may provide us the means to break in.

Ashley pinged me last night during dinner to tell me that Micah and Reg had been working on figuring out a way to access LI without passing through the EM barrier. "They think they've come up with a working plan!" She'd sounded excited, breathless. Despite my own doubts, I couldn't resist getting excited, too.

"And?" I'd asked, trying not to sound impatient. "What is it?"

Eric threw me a dirty look over the table. I ignored him. He's always tried to take care of me like a parent, given how there was a huge gaping vacuum in our lives in that regard, but he's barely able to care of himself, much less me. Even his department-mandated shrink tells him that.

"So," Ash said, "you know how everyone knows about the wall and no-fly zone, right?"

I grunted. It was all common knowledge. Plus the bridges, which were bombed out years back. I thought about mentioning how the East River was heavily mined, but I knew it would just make me sound like Kelly. And besides, it was a moot point anyway. None of us had a boat, or even access to one, so sailing across the river was out of the question. Mostly, though, I just kept quiet because Eric and Grandpa were sitting right there, trying not to look like they were listening, but not fooling anyone.

I turned my back and held my Link tight against me ear.

Deep Into the Game / 15

"Jessie?" Grandpa said. "Dinnertime is family time, young lady. Disconnect, please."

"I'm sorry. This is important. I really have to take this." I got up and slipped out of the kitchen.

"Jessie!" Eric called. "It can't be that important."

I heard Grandpa tell him to control himself, which, of course, led to another argument between them. I never understood the animosity the two shared for each other — frankly, I couldn't care less — except for being aware that it had something to do with my father dying when I was two. Eric had been fourteen at the time, so he still has memories of Dad and all that happened after his death. It really messed him up.

Pretty much everything in my family traces back to that singular event, like it was some kind of Big Bang event or something: my mom's nervous breakdown, Eric's pacifist days followed by his stint in the Marines followed by his creepy obsession with the Undead, Grandpa's scandal and then coming to live with us. I'd never known my father — except by reputation — so I never really felt much interest in learning about him and the circumstances surrounding how he'd died. At least he had the good sense to be murdered before the Life Service law was passed. Not that the government would've had much to work with in his case; from what little I knew, most of his brain had never been found. And without a brain, there's no chance of reanimation.

I hurried down the hall and slipped into the bathroom and closed the door. Ash was saying something about tunnels. I barely caught the tail-end of it.

"What tunnels?"

"Micah thinks he can get his hands on some of the old subway maps and traffic tunnels connecting Manhattan and Long Island."

"From where? How?"

As far as I knew, all of the old plans and schematics had been collected and destroyed after LI was militarized and the wall was built. It was against the law to possess anything related to them. I think it was more an act of denial by the government than one of defiance or security. They probably would've gone in and nuked the place if they could've gotten away with it, if the radioactive ash cloud didn't take out a million more people, making them ripe for reanimation.

"Micah says nothing's ever totally lost, not once it's been in the Stream. There are off-line archives. Someone somewhere is bound to have their own file. Or hardcopy. It just takes a little time to find someone willing to sell the information."

"Where are we going to get the money? And isn't that illegal?"

"Shh!"

I thought about this for a moment, then shook my head. "I'm sure the tunnels are all bombed out or filled in. It wouldn't make sense to just leave them open for zombies to walk through to Manhattan. Otherwise, we'd be seeing a lot more of them, right?"

"First of all, Jess, I think Reggie's right: there aren't any more IUs alive on the island. Second of all, the tunnels were flooded before the first outbreak. Remember? And everyone knows zombies can't swim."

I snorted. Duh. She was right, of course. After that massive ice shelf broke off of Antarctica nearly thirty years ago and caused the sea levels to surge higher by thirty feet, most of the underground transportation networks in coastal cities had to be abandoned. I guess I hadn't really paid very close attention in history class that day.

"What about the tunnel openings?" I asked. "They'd still be above water, wouldn't they? Surely when the wall was built, they would've closed them— "

"The wall was built ten years ago."

"Okay . . . ."

"Don't you see? *After* the second flood. The openings would've been totally underwater already. Micah thinks they wouldn't have bothered blockading them since they'd be covered by a good twenty feet of Atlantic Ocean. Out of sight, out of mind, as he says. What's even better, if they're still open, then we can totally bypass the EM barrier by going *under* it! No walls, no razor wire. It's perfect!"

I shook my head. "I don't know . . . . It sounds like wishful thinking to me. And anyway, the last time I checked, I didn't have gills. And neither do you or anyone else I know."

"Reggie's looking into that."

"Reggie? What's he going to do, rent us a sub or something?"

Ash laughed. "No, silly. The sensors would totally detect something that big, even going through the tunnels. He's thinking a bit . . . smaller, something more personalized."

I asked her what, but she wouldn't elucidate.

It seemed plausible, and yet I still had my doubts. It was almost too easy. If one of us could come up with a solution like that so quickly, then surely others would have already done so as well.

But then I realized why that wasn't likely. Most normal people avoided lower Manhattan like the plague. And even if you had to go there, the closer you got to LI, the harder it was with all the checkpoints you had to cross. Besides, who in their right mind would seriously think about breaking in? No one was crazy enough to actually want to. They called them Forbidden Zones for a reason, not Disney-Arc Land.

I mentioned this to Ash.

"That's where your brother might come in handy," she said.

I knew exactly what she was talking about: Eric's permit. But before I could argue about it there was a knock on the door. "Jess?" It was my grandfather. "Come out here, young lady, and finish your dinner."

"Just a sec," I yelled. "Ash, I got to go." I lowered my voice to a whisper and added, "You know how the Colonel gets."

"Yes sir!" Ash said, giggling. "I'll get right on spit shining my dinner plate with my tongue, sir!"

I laughed and told her I'd think about it, then we disconnected.

When I stepped out of the bathroom, Grandpa was just making his way back down the hallway. He turned and gave me a stern look and told me to go finish my dinner. I was so excited that I almost shouted, "Yes sir!" just like Ash had done.

I love Grandpa, but there's one thing you never do and that's antagonize him. You take your life into your own hands. The only reason Eric gets away with it is because he's just as bullheaded as Grandpa is.

And, honestly? I think Grandpa's a little afraid of him.

† † †

It's a beautiful August morning by the time I leave the house for the dojang. The sun's still low on the horizon and it's not too muggy out. Not yet, anyway. The cicadas are singing in the trees. I almost feel like skipping all the way there.

The studio opens at seven, though I usually don't show up until around eight thirty. This morning, however, I'd been too wound up to sleep in, as thoughts about actually getting to see a part of the Forbidden Zones suddenly take on a more realistic feel to them. I'm earlier than usual — only the third person to arrive — so I'm left without a sparring partner and will have to wait.

Kwanjangnim Rupert is with some guy I don't know, a green belt. They're walking off the mat as I sign in, looking like they've just finished up their first sparring exercises. They go straight into their meditations. I can hear the master talking about *Yu*, the water principle: "The stream flows around and surrounds its obstacles," he quietly says, "and so passes them. Dripping water patiently makes its way through the hardest stone. This is how your strength flows in and through and around your opponents."

I smile privately, thinking about the coincidence that the kwanjangnim's message for today would be about water, since that was all Ash could talk about last night. But while *Yu* teaches us patience and flow, one thing it doesn't explain is how to breathe in an airless environment. If the tunnels turn out to be a valid option, then we'll have to figure out how to get through them.

As far as I know, none of the five of us has ever been scuba diving. In fact, I've never even been snorkeling, except in the neighbor's pool when I was five, but that doesn't really count.

I settle on the bench and pull out my Link and ping Kelly to see if he's awake yet. It sends me straight to his message box, so he's either playing or still asleep.

"Sunbae," Kwanjangnim Rupert calls over at me, startling me out of my thoughts. He walks over and stands before me with his hands on his hips. I exit the app and slide the Link into my bag. I'll try again later or just stop by his house after I'm done here.

"Yes sir!" I shout, as I jump to my feet.

"You're early." He smiles knowingly. I have a reputation for being a late-sleeper.

"I wanted to get today's exercises out of the way, Kwanjangnim."

He gives me a strange look and asks, "What could be more important than your training?"

I quickly backtrack. "I mean, it looks like it's going to be another hot one today. I figured I'd beat the crowds."

"Is this the beginning of a new Jessie?"

The boy looks up from where he's stretching on the mat and his eyes widen. He's tall for his age, blond, big-boned, bordering on heavyset. He has this ruggedness about him, like he'd be a football or rugby player if they weren't illegal sports. He looks a little familiar, but I can't seem to place him. I think he might be in the grade below me, although I know that's not the real reason for my ignorance. Ashley's a grade below, too. The real truth is he's not part of our circle, our gang of gamers and hackers. I don't do much socializing with anyone outside of it. Not even with other hapkido students.

"Ready to spar?" Kwanjangnim asks me.

I nod. "Yes sir." I jump up and stand to one side so he can lead me onto the mat.

"Oh no, not me. Today I'll be talking it easy."

"Why?"

He groans. "I strained my back this morning."

Once more I glance over at the boy. "From sparring?" I can't imagine Master Rupert being injured by a lowly green belt.

"No," Kwanjangnim says. His laughter is thick and contagious. His face gets a little red. "I got hurt . . . . Actually, I strained it getting out of bed." He rubs his back and shrugs. "I guess I'm getting old. Either that or my mattress is."

We both enjoy another laugh before he adds something about going in to get his implant soon. It kills the moment, leaving us standing in an awkward silence before he gestures the boy over.

"This is Sunbae Jacob Espinosa," he says, introducing us. "Sunbae Jessica Daniels."

"Jake," the boy says, offering his hand. Meanwhile, I've bowed, so he withdraws it, even as I raise up and extend mine. Finally, we both clasp hands and bow awkwardly to each other. His grip feels weak, like he's consciously afraid of hurting me.

Rupert laughs at us and says, "Jake's new to the school. His forms are really pretty good. You two can warm up on each other, but for sparring today, no kicks, okay, Jess? Just hands, hits and holds. And try to take it easy on him. He'll be testing for his next belt in a week and we need him all in one piece."

"Bring it!" Jake says, slipping into a sparring stance. Rupert frowns, but I return the challenge with a growl.

"Keep it clean, guys!"

Despite the differences in our skill levels and the restriction on kicks, it turns out to be a good workout. Jake's quick and strong, almost as good as most of the red and black belts I'm used to sparring against. But he's also a bit top-heavy, and I'm clearly a lot more seasoned. After dropping him for the fifth or sixth time, I get him in an arm hold that he can't escape out of.

He calls it quits, saying he's got to leave, but just as my grip relaxes, he spins under me and wrenches my arm. The next thing I know, I'm lying on the floor with his knee on my back and my arm twisted away from me. I can't move.

"That was a cheap shot," I say between clenched teeth.

He lets go and stands up. "Sorry."

When I get up, I think I see a brief flash in his eyes, something powerful. I can't tell what it is. He looks away too quickly.

While I'm packing my gear, he comes over to talk to me. I wait for him to apologize. I'm still a little miffed by the unexpected throw, so I just grunt responses. That sort of poor sportsmanship isn't allowed in here, and if Kwanjangnim

Rupert or any of the other trainers had seen what he'd done, they would've given Jake a severe tongue-lashing.

He tells me he's only been training for about ten months, and I tell him nobody gets as good as that in such a short time, which makes him pause. I might as well have called him a liar.

"I . . . I guess I'm a quick learner," he stutters. "How about you? How long have you been training?"

I give him a good long look before telling him I've been at it for eight years. "Off and on," I say, though it's not exactly the truth. I did miss one summer when Eric took us on a trip to Seattle after he got out of the Marines. "And I started in juniors."

He shakes his head and stares at me, a smile curling his lips.

"What's so funny?" I ask.

"I'm sorry. It's just that . . . ."

I narrow my eyes and wait for him to finish.

"I guess I was a little surprised to see you walk in this morning."

I stare at him. "Have we met before?"

"Um, no. But Ashley Evans talks about you all the time," he explains. "Says you have mad gaming skills. She was my science partner last year in chemistry lab. She's a jacker, right?"

"Jacker?"

"Game hacker. That's what the kids call her and others like her."

I think about this for a moment, then decide I actually like the term. Even though it doesn't apply to me specifically, it does describe the others quite well. "I just play. I don't hack."

He nods, tentatively, and looks around for something to say.

"I have to go," I tell him.

"I really enjoyed you this morning! The sparring, I mean. Not you. That is, you're really good."

"Are you hitting on me?"

He blushes.

"I already have a boyfriend."

His face reddens even more. He looks like he's about to choke. I smile. At least we're even now.

"Kidding," I tell him. "To be honest, though, if it ever came down to it, you'd probably kick his ass."

He laughs. I can see him relax. "And you could easily kick mine," he says.

"In a fair fight, maybe." He's got a good four inches on me and probably fifty pounds. And he is strong.

"I'm sorry about that move back there. The last dojo I was in didn't care too much about etiquette. It was all about skill and strength and speed and taking advantage of our opponents' weaknesses. That's one of the reasons why I transferred here."

"Don't sweat it," I say. "Just don't let it happen again."

Chapter Two

I ping Kelly again on my way out. He immediately connects this time. As I walk past the window I look in. Jake's just standing there watching me leave. I can't see his eyes because of the reflection, but something about the way he's staring makes me a little uncomfortable. It may be totally innocent, but I can't decide whether to feel threatened, creeped out or flattered by the attention.

" 'Sup, J?"

I hurry away, but I can feel his eyes on my back.

"On my way home from practice. Mind if I stop by?"

"Mom's here, but sure. I'm just hanging out, not really doing anything."

"Translation: trying to figure out a way to get past level eleven," I say.

He sighs and tells me I'm coldhearted. "So much for Micah's extra cheater lives. I'm lame. I'm just a lame gamer."

"Self-pity doesn't suit you, Kel."

"Nothing lamer than a poor-ass gamer like— *Wait a sec.... Yes! Woohoo!*"

"You're playing right now, aren't you? You're playing even as I'm talking to you."

" . . . maybe."

Frustration wavers on the verge of anger. I don't know what's going on between us, but lately it feels like he's slipping away. I don't want to lose him, and yet it feels like I am

"It's just the 2D version," he says, trying to placate me. "You know we don't have HG."

"Just save some of that energy for me," I say. It's a desperate move to distract him, make him pay more attention to me. I immediately feel guilty for being so needy, but not enough not to use my coup-de-gras: "I'm feeling frisky."

"Um, I did mention my mom's home, right?"

"Never stopped us before."

I can hear him exhale shakily into the Link, and it brings a smile to my face.

When I get to Kelly's house, his five-year-old brother Kyle answers the door. He gives me a big smile and a hug, which I enthusiastically return with change: an extra loud zerbit on his neck. He runs away giggling.

"Better watch it," I warn Kelly, when he wanders down from his room. "Looks like you've got some competition."

"What? Kyle? Robbing the cradle now, are you?"

"No one will ever replace Kyle," I answer. "Not even you. No, I mean at the dojang. There's this new kid. I sparred with him this morning. I think I embarrassed him when I suggested he was hitting on me."

"Was he?" Kelly asks.

"Easy there, cowboy," I reply, but even I'm not so sure what it really was that happened. "Jake couldn't land a real hit, much less a figurative one, unless I let him."

Did you? Let him, I mean."

"Really? Don't be like that, Kel"

He sighs. "So . . . Jake, huh? Do I know him?"

"Doubtful. He's a junior. Not a gamer or hacker. Seems Ash does, though. He was her science lab partner last year."

I take Kelly's arm and lead him back upstairs.

"Keep the door open," his mother yells up at us from the kitchen.

"Morning, Mrs. C," I shout back.

We keep the door open — barely — but we don't exactly behave. Even an open door doesn't stop us from getting in some serious make-out time. And it sort of makes things a lot more exciting, too, knowing someone could walk in on us at any moment.

By the time his mother calls for Kelly to come down a half hour later, my whole body's tingling and I feel like I'm about to explode. Kelly has this glazed look in his eyes. I don't know who's in more agony, him or me.

We straighten our disheveled clothes and hair before going downstairs.

"What are you kids up to today?" Mrs. Corben asks innocently.

"Going over to Micah's," Kelly answers. He looks over at me, sees the look on my face and shrugs.

If Mrs. C notices this, she doesn't say anything. Instead, she looks her son up and down and then says, "Walk over. You could use the exercise. You're starting to get a little flabby."

"Mom! I'm not getting flabby!"

"Mm hmm. And what exercise have you gotten lately? Outside of VR, I mean."

I stay out of this conversation. I know anything I say will just come off sounding suggestive in a way that would make me look slutty.

She throws him an apple from the bowl on the counter and tells him not to stay too long. "Your father'll be home early tonight and he wants to talk to you about colleges."

Kelly grunts.

After I drop my sparring gear off at home and get a quick shower, we head out to Micah's.

"He pinged your Link while you were in the bathroom," Kelly informs me. There's a dark look in his eyes. "Did you talk with him last night after we left or something?"

It's not like Kelly to be jealous of Micah, but after my teasing him this morning, I figure he's probably a bit more sensitive than usual. That's what the make-out session was supposed to take care of.

I shake my head and tell him about Ash's call during dinner.

Kelly grumbles. "This is all just a waste of time. You know that, don't you? An exercise in futility. There's a reason they sealed that place off, and I'm sure they didn't just do a half-assed job about it."

I shrug. "So what if you're right? Even if it turns out to be impossible, it still beats just sitting around watching you play *Zpocalypto* all the time."

"I don't play it all the time!"

"Dude, you're totally obsessed with it."

"I just want to pass this level is all. What's wrong with that?"

I squeeze his hand as I stop, swinging him around to look at me. "*Then* what, Kelly? Level thirteen? Fourteen? When does it stop?"

He gives me a resentful look.

I sigh with frustration. "Last year you told me you didn't just want to be a code jockey. You wanted to go to college and become something more. Why else would you suffer with those academic geeks in the college track at school instead of being in the trade track like the rest of us?"

He shrugs.

I'd feared that his entering the college track last year would put a strain on our relationship, since it meant we wouldn't get to see each other as much during school, but it actually didn't matter. It wasn't like we saw much of each other during classes anyway. The real strain actually started over the summer, feeling like a repeat of last year.

"Now look at you," I say. "All of a sudden you're eating and sleeping and drinking that stupid game! You were the one person that the rest of us looked to as a reminder that there's more to life than games and codes. But now it's like you're addicted."

"Me?" he exclaims, yanking his hand away from mine. "You're accusing *me* of being obsessed? You're the one who's obsessed. You and Reggie— "

"Reggie's just a friend, Kel!"

" —and all the others. How could you even consider going into Gameland?"

"It's not Gameland, Kelly, and you know it. Reggie didn't mean to say Gameland. It's just LI, and it's just for fun— "

"It's not just for fun! This is serious. Micah's all over it like flies on dog crap! Stupid Reggie for even bringing up such a dumb idea. He's had some bad ones in the past, but this one takes the cake."

"Stop screaming at me."

He raises his hands to his head and stumbles off like he's hurt or something. I suddenly just want to kick him, to send him sprawling, to knock some sense into his brain. But to do so would be to violate all the principles of discipline I've ever been taught in hapkido. We never attack out of spite or anger.

We only fight to diffuse those emotions and to defend ourselves.

But the thing is, I know he's right. We are obsessed with games. All of us. And why shouldn't we be? Look at all the things my generation grew up with that we can't control: global warming, a fractured government that has pretty much given up doing anything useful, the Undead. Why wouldn't we want to escape into a world we can manipulate? The worst consequences in a game are having to go back to the beginning and starting all over again. You can't do that in real life. When you die, you just keep playing.

It's telling that we're most obsessed with games where we have to fight the dead, since what we most want is to live and feel. We want to *experience* life. But we can't. Our lives are so full of rules and restrictions. Nobody ever pushes us because pushing goes against everything we're taught. "Go to school," they drone. On and on like it's a mantra. "Become like everyone else." Sometimes it feels like we're just going through the motions.

That's why we play. It allows us to escape.

And the worst part about it? Games are such piss-poor substitutes for life — flat and two-dimensional, even in HG — that they only make us want more. We want to do something dramatic, something that we can feel. Like break into LI.

Kelly stomps off, leaving me behind. How could he not understand?

I sigh and follow along after him.

Chapter Three

Ashley is talking to Micah when we arrive in his basement. "Any hacker worth her salt," she's saying, "should be able to access the old government systems." She looks up and nods at us, then goes back to typing.

"What're you doing?" I ask.

Micah waves us over. "We're trying to get into the military's old computers in the Forbidden Zones on Long Island."

"How? Are they even still running?"

He shrugs. "That's what we're trying to figure out right now. Reggie thinks they probably kept them operating for non-essential functions like environmental control and such."

"Environmental control?" Kelly asks. The contempt is thick in his voice. He hasn't looked at me once since storming off, and it just makes me even angrier at him. "What the hell do they need that for? UIs don't need air conditioning."

Micah raises his hands. "Don't look at me. Ask Reg. This is his show. I'm just here to provide services."

"Looks like they're up and running," Ash chimes in. "I can see their identifiers — IP addresses, I believe they were once called. Hello, little computers, this is Granny knocking on your firewalls. Let me in, let me in. Ooh, what crude encryption you have!"

Kelly shakes his head in disgust.

Ashley's playful grin turns into a frown. "Micah? Does it seem like a lot of traffic's going through those nodes?"

Micah leans over. We all do, but it's scrolling too fast for me to make anything out. He shrugs.

"It's a lot of data for basic maintenance programs, but you know how inefficient the old codices were."

I grow bored of watching it. "Speaking of Reggie, where is he?"

"Yo."

I turn around just in time to see him coming out of the bathroom zipping up his fly. I roll my eyes. He smiles his shit-eating grin. Thankfully he doesn't say anything stupid, like, "I left you a present in there." I don't think I could bear his grade-school humor this morning.

"Okay, assuming you can find a way in," Kelly says, leaning over Ash, "wouldn't they have upgraded to iVZ?"

"The systems were put into place before ArcTech even existed," Micah explains. "I don't think they would've bothered with iVZ codex. Too much hardware to transfer over and convert."

"Exactly," Ashley agrees, nodding. Her fingers fly over the keyboard. Type scrolls madly across the screen. "Which means we're talking about accessing pre-Stream databases and programming. What they called the Internet way back when. Piece of cake."

"Which means," Reggie pipes in, "nobody's watching it anymore."

"We *hope* no one's watching it."

"Why bother?"

I remember talking to Grandpa about the internet age, which preceded the ArcTech systems that he helped put into place before he "retired." He was the commander of the Omegaman Forces, back when reanimation was first developed and zombies— initially called Zulus— were put under computer control using the L.I.N.C.s, which are similar to the latent individualized neuroleptic connections that all living citizens are supposed to get now. L.I.N.C.s are what connect us and our handheld Link devices to the Stream.

I reach my hand up to the back of my head and feel around until my fingers find the tiny scars. I got mine when I was three, even before it became mandatory. I remember Eric didn't want to get his. He argued that it was just another example of government intrusiveness, of thinking it knows what's best for us. But Grandpa convinced Mom and she signed the papers, so Eric had no choice. He was eleven.

They say the implants are there to prevent what happened during the outbreaks— so they can shut us down if we ever get infected— but it's pretty obvious the program has some serious flaws to it. How do you guarantee a hundred percent of the population is compliant? You can't. Look at Master Rupert: he's got to be in his fifties, and he still doesn't have his implant.

I lower my hand and say, "If it's pre-iVZ, then don't you need a physical uplink? There's no more wireless towers anymore, right?"

Grandpa had said that everything back in the first couple decades of the century either required a physical connection — which they called 'wired' because information was passed in the form of electrons through actual circuits — or radio waves — which they called 'wireless.' But all the wireless transmitters were disassembled years ago and replaced with EM towers. Electromagnetic signals are much more efficient and a trillion times more secure.

I remember him telling me how the old defcon management system was totally susceptible to hacking, and that it was a miracle nobody ever went in and triggered a bunch of missile launches. In fact, that's why ArcTech was first created, to design better, more secure computing systems. ArcTech's intralink VZ and the Stream replaced the Internet years ago and, along with it, the Cloud, which turned out to be a huge disaster. And although many have tried to hack into iVZ — including a few right here in this very room — nobody's ever been able to do it. The encryption is just too good.

Micah holds up a cable, which I can see he's spliced into the guts of yet another piece of equipment, which I immediately recognize as highly illegal: an old tablet computer. "What's the saying about necessity?" he asks.

"It's the mother fucker of invention," Reggie replies, and he and Micah slap palms.

Ashley suddenly yelps. She reaches over and yanks out the wires.

"Hey," Micah cries, but then we all see the look on her face.

"There was some fishy code flashing by in there. I think it was trying to track us so I severed the connection."

Getting caught hacking a government system — even an old one — would get us into serious trouble, enough to probably add six or seven years to our Life Service commitment.

It reminds me of the close call we had a couple weeks ago when Ash and Micah tried hacking into the VR part of *The Game*. They'd spent a solid three days down here, barely sleeping, feeding on nothing but Red Bull and Little Caesar's pizza. They said it was a hundred times harder than anything they'd tried before. Heck, maybe a million times.

Most of the programming developed and used by ArcWare is open source. Even so, they always embed a few black boxes within the games to keep things interesting, cryptic code that somehow adapts the game to a player's habits and skill level. Gamers and hackers alike love that they do it. Otherwise, what would be the fun in playing or hacking into them?

Not *The Game*, though. That's a whole different animal. *The Game* is protected by an ArcWare-developed code called iVZ, short for "intralink virtual zeality." It's got one of the most sophisticated firewalls any of us has ever seen, and a proprietary base code that none of us could ever hope to break. It's light years beyond military grade. In fact, iVZ powers the government. Hack into *The Game* and you'd practically have the tools needed to hack into the national defense system.

It was Ashley who first proposed the idea to crack *The Game*. She'd built this crude translator for ArcWare programs. That's how we found their back door. How she accomplished that is beyond me — I'm not a hacker like she and Micah and Reggie are. She's hacked into more of ArcWare's black boxes than anyone I know. She said she used what she salvaged as sort of a Rosetta Stone to come up with her translator, a frankensteinian piece of software built from bits and pieces of scavenged code.

"It's a heuristic program," she tried to explain to me, apparently oblivious to the fact that my eyes were quickly glazing over. I prefer nascent coding, creating programs. And I stick to the standard languages, like andro, Khartoum-four and MesmerZ. Going in specifically to crack a program isn't my idea of fun.

"Heuristic means it teaches itself," she went on. Of course I knew what heuristic meant, but I didn't bother to correct her. "The program essentially runs on a loop of testing, evaluating, refining and retesting, becoming better and better as it ages."

Whatever. I never, ever thought it would work.

But it did. Sort of. Between her and Micah's mad coding abilities, they got as far as copying the software's architecture before the program shut them out. Architecture is Micah's specialty. He loves thinking about game structure and could stare at it all day long, drooling like a puppy at how clever some of the programmers can be.

I remember Ash pinged everyone when they made the breakthrough. We all went running over.

I got there just in time to see Micah's screens lighting up with error messages Then everything went totally ape-shit.

"Yo, there's suicide switches everywhere, y'all!" he shouted. We stood in awe and watched, making sure to stand out of the way as he hammered at his keyboard. It was fun just watching him. He and Ash were hopping from console to console, the whole time shouting at the top of their lungs. Then: "Not another—" Micah screamed. "No, no! Aw, shee-it!"

Everything went blank. The game had locked them out. Wouldn't even let them log in with new fake identities, blocking us all out, in fact. It was as if it suddenly knew everything about us, could track us even if we jumped Streams. It was a huge disappointment, of course. We'd gotten a glimpse inside *The Game*, but we'd almost gotten caught, too.

"Easy peasy," Ashley says, as she holds up the tablet in triumph.

"You got the maps?" Micah asks. "Lady, I could just kiss you!"

"You wouldn't be able handle it. You'd spontaneously combust!"

"What maps?" Kelly asks, impatiently.

"The tunnels," I say. "Weren't you even listening this morning when I told you about it?" I know I'm just taking out my frustration on Kelly, but I can't seem to help myself.

He frowns at me, then shakes his head and repeats the question.

Ash holds up the disemboweled tablet. What we see on the pixilated screen is an old drawing of the transportation system of Long Island. She points to a pair of lines connecting lower and eastern Manhattan to LI. The first is labeled BROOKLYN BATTERY TUNNEL. The second, QUEENS MIDTOWN TUNNEL.

"Schematics are embedded. Which one do you want to check out first?"

We all look at each other without speaking. What we're seeing is highly illegal to possess, much less study. Then we're all speaking at the same time.

"The Queens," Kelly announces, when the rest of us have quieted down. "Let's look at that one first."

Ash opens the embedded file and begins to read:

"*Opened in 1940, the Queens-Midtown tunnel connects the Borough of Queens on Long Island with the Borough of Manhattan. It consists of twin tubes carrying four traffic lanes and is 6,414 feet long.*"

"Over a mile," I murmur. I don't know what I'd been expecting, but it certainly isn't something quite as long as that. "How're we going to get through something a mile long and filled with water?"

"Scuba," Reggie says.

"Whoa!" Kelly turns to Reg. "Getting a little ahead of ourselves, aren't we? Nobody here knows how to scuba dive. Besides, we don't even know if the tunnel's still accessible."

"Yeah, well, the other tunnel's even longer," Ash says, busily reciting facts from the other file. As if it makes any difference. One mile or ten, scuba gear or not, Kelly's right. If the tunnels aren't open, we might as well be talking about swimming through concrete.

By rights, they should all be filled. Or at least gated. And for all we know, they could be caved in. It's a hundred years old, for chrissake. And despite Ash's assurances to me last night, I still seriously doubt they'd just leave the openings unblocked.

Micah asks where the Manhattan opening for the Queens tunnel is.

Ashley taps the screen. "The old midtown," she says. "Between what used to be East 34th and 35th Streets." She opens another file. Nods. "Yep. It's totally underwater."

"Okay, then," Kelly says, holding up a gaming controller. "Now that that's resolved, how about we— "

"Check it out?" Reggie says, straightening up. "Good idea. I mean, we won't know for sure what it looks like unless we see it for ourselves, right?"

Ash turns to me. "Did you bring it?" she asks.

I nod and pat my Link. "Uploaded it last night, after Eric went to bed." Kelly frowns at me like I've betrayed him.

"Woohoo!" Reggie shouts. "Road trip!"

Chapter Four

The five of us pile into Micah's beat up old Ford. It's so ancient that it even has a docking station for the old Apple iCorp storage devices rather than getting music from the Stream.

Micah drives. Reggie takes shotgun. The rest of us sit in back. We head down Route 95, which is the quickest way to Manhattan, even though it means having to pass through about a half dozen checkpoints, including the ones at each interstate border crossing.

After about twenty minutes, we pass through the first. The guard looks bored. He scans our Links and doesn't speak.

I see the abandoned Teterboro Airport off in the distance. The moss-covered hangars poke out of the water like giant eggs that never hatched.

Finally the guard waves us through. He doesn't even bother to ask where we're going.

"There's the Meadowlands," Reggie says, pointing off to the side a minute later, and I think about how the old football stadium looks like a giant concrete nest to go with the eggs.

"Don't you mean the Swamplands?" Ashley remarks, making us all laugh.

This leads to a discussion by the boys about the banned sport of football, with Reggie arguing that they should bring it back and Kelly saying it was a brutal sport that has no place in our world today. I want to slap him and ask what place zombies have in our world, and isn't the television show, *Survivalist*, or *The Game*, on which it's based, just as brutal? But I don't. I feel like we're already treading on thin ice today.

We come to another checkpoint just before crossing the new elevated bridge that will take us into Manhattan. Here, the guard asks us where we're going and what we're doing. "School project," Ash pipes up. The guard gives us a doubtful look and she quickly adds, "Summer school."

"College track," he says, sneering, but he scans our Links, then asks if we all have implants. After recording our IDs, he lets us pass.

"School?" Reggie asks, once we're clear. "Really? That's the best you could come up with?"

Ash laughs and shrugs and says she just got nervous. "You know me. I don't think well under pressure."

Soon we're zooming right over Central Park. Looking down is enough to make anyone queasy, but Reggie sticks his head out the window and howls like a wolf. The wind whips the spit from his lips, and I'm suddenly glad I'm sitting in the middle of the backseat. If anyone gets sprayed, it's Kelly, but he doesn't say anything. He just sits there glowering out the window.

I elbow him and give him a smile. He sighs and offers me a half of a smile back, his way of forgiving me. He relaxes, resting a little more of his weight against me. For his reward, I give him a kiss on the cheek.

"Get a room, lovebirds," Ashley groans. But of course, this just makes us laugh and want to do it some more.

I'm practically sitting on Kelly's lap when the road curves right and begins its gentle decline toward south Manhattan.

"Another checkpoint," Micah announces. "I quickly plop back into my seat, wiping my lips with the back of my hand. I reach down and squeeze Kelly's thigh and he nearly jumps through the roof of the car. I can't tell if he's so tense because of me or because we're getting closer to LI.

And we are close. I can smell the ocean. Water surrounds us all around, canals wending their way through and around the old skyscrapers, most of them abandoned now, crumbling. It's our own version of Italy's Venice. Of course, the real Venice is long gone now, buried under thirty feet of Mediterranean Sea years before I was even born. A diver's paradise.

Not that any of us'll ever get to see it.

We pull up at the checkpoint and this guard, after giving Micah's car a good looking over, flatly tells us no access. "This is a commercial district," he states.

Ash points to me and says I have a permit. I flash him my Link with Eric's permit on it and he inspects it for minute before handing it back. "Remember the curfew," he says. We all nod dutifully and promise to be out of New York long before dusk.

Despite all the restrictions and the hassles of the checkpoints, the roads are crowded with business people. So are the waterways. Water taxis ferry people around, drawing white trails in the deep blue. Despite all the flood damage on this side of the East River, despite the proximity of LI, Manhattan still somehow manages to be a bustling city. It's still the financial center of the universe, even though New Merica has essentially isolated itself from the rest of the world.

But then, every so often, I catch a glimpse of the stark gray walls of LI rising up across the water, looking like a giant alien ship or a prison.

How do these people work here every day knowing what lies on the other side of the river, not two miles away? How can they look out over it and see that wall every day and not give it a second thought? It's so close. Or do they just pretend it's not there?

After the first outbreak, thirteen years ago, the military went in to control the Infected Undead and evacuate the living. Certain parts were declared disaster areas. They set up barriers and controlled access, preventing people from moving back in. These eventually became known as Forbidden Zones. But the zones kept growing, getting larger and larger, spreading out until, eventually, they began to connect with each other. The flooded Wastelands were now truly lost, leaving only the higher points of land free, isolated pockets on which the last stubborn islanders remained.

The government said sealing the island off was for the protection of the living from the Undead. But Eric once told me the truth was quite different. It was to protect the Undead from illegal poaching by people who didn't think it was right to let the Undead roam free.

"The government considers zombies assets," he told me. "Even those without implants. After all, each one could take the place of a living soldier who won't have to go into combat."

But nobody knows if anyone ever went in and implanted any of the IUs. It seems unlikely.

Congress passed the Life Service Law almost ten years ago. Now, every single person is legally considered government property after death, not just the ex-criminals, and not just the ones that made up the Omegaman Forces. Although the law has since been challenged several times in the Supreme Court, the politicians and the judges are too spineless to strike the thing down. And, honestly? Nobody except a few rights activists really wants to. We may not like the idea that we'll become one of the Undead someday and have to pay our dues to the government, but it's better than going back to the old ways, when living people fought wars and cleaned sewers.

The road finally reaches its lowest point, which is still about sixty feet above water level. It's where the experts say sea level will be when all the arctic ice finally finishes melting. They say that won't happen for another hundred years, but that's what they said forty years ago before the first major ice shelf broke off and raised sea levels by thirty feet.

"Times Square," Micah calls out. We all look to the right. The place is a dump, abandoned and disintegrating. "We should be just about parallel with the tunnel now. A few more blocks to the south and we'll be there."

Traffic has thinned out quickly and is now almost nonexistent. We come to one last checkpoint. Here, the guard is all business. We sit silently as he checks our Links. He takes each one and scans it, then does the same with each of us, making sure our Links match our implants. He spends a lot of time with Micah's until, finally, Micah asks for his Link back. He messes with it for a moment before returning it to the guard.

"It's been having problems lately," Micah says. "I think it's time for an upgrade."

The guard frowns for a moment, stares at the screen, then at Micah. His jaw clenches and he takes in a deep breath.

"This is an inner zone," he says. "What's your reason for coming here?"

This time, when Ashley explains that it's an extra-credit project for summer school, he just stands there tapping his thumb on his own Link, waiting for us to come clean.

"We swear it," Ashley insists. "It's part of our community service commitment."

"And the NCD permit? How does that fit in?"

"My brother works for the department," I explain. "Eric Daniels? You probably know him."

The guard just stares.

"We're doing a survey in conjunction with the police department. It's on . . . ."

"Potential sources of outbreak transmission," Kelly says.

The guard sighs. "Zombie freaks. Okay. Just don't go anywhere restricted. Heed the signs. Don't get in any trouble. Fines are doubled in an inner zone. And remember the curfew."

We all breathe a sigh of relief as he waves us through.

"Outbreak transmission?" I ask Kelly, once we've pulled away.

"I had to say something. You guys were totally boffing it back there."

"Thanks," I say. "I knew there was a reason I kept you around." I lean over and grab his face for another kiss.

"Aw, sheesh," Ash complains. "Not again."

We stop at a traffic light, and dutifully wait for it to change, even though there are no other cars around. I glance down and see an empty water taxi stand just outside the old Grand Central Station. A bunch of obsolete train cars had been hoisted onto the rooftop platform and converted into high-priced restaurants and hotels. They all stand empty and rundown now. Grass sprouts out of every corner and crack.

"Take a left here," Reggie says, checking his Link. Micah turns on his blinker, making Reggie snort and shake his head.

After a few more minutes, the buildings thin out, become shorter, squatter. Then the vista suddenly opens up. We all exhale as one as the dull gray desert of the East River spreads out before us, as if it's the most wondrous thing we've ever seen. In truth, it kind of scares me.

"According to my Link," Micah says, "we're almost where the opening should be. Just a few hundred feet ."

We all look down, but of course there's nothing to see. It's not like there's going to be a blinking sign pointing the way: *Access to illegal tunnel to LI.*

Micah pulls into a deserted parking structure and stops the car. We're the only ones there. We get out and follow Reggie, who's got his Link held in front of him like a divining rod. After a few minutes, we reach the end of building and he points out about a hundred feet. "Should be right about . . . there."

All I can see is a big gaping pool of water, roughly three hundred feet wide. It stretches out for at least a quarter mile until we lose it in the distance.

"Look! You can see the sides of the entrance ramp there!" He thrusts his arm to the right and, sure enough, we can see part of the ancient roadway surfacing a few hundred feet away, looking like the tongue of sleeping beast hanging out of its wet mouth. He swings his hand in the opposite direction and adds, "So, that walkway there should be the old overpass covering the mouth of the tunnel."

Ashley pulls out the reassembled tablet and boots it up. The thirty or so seconds it takes feels like forever. Old tech, I think to myself. How did people ever have the patience for it? Makes me realize how lucky we are to be constantly connected, constantly on.

When it's ready, Ash opens an old photograph of the tunnel entrance and we all crowd around to see. The resolution's horrible, but now we can see the familiar landmarks. The walls look to have been constructed from hewn stone. The tunnel opening stops approximately twelve or fifteen feet below the top of the overpass. Now, only the upper five or six feet of the structure are above water, but there's a muddy high tide line just below the surface of the road.

"Must be connected to the river here," I say.

Micah nods. "Half of lower Manhattan is."

There's no water in the photo, of course, just ancient cars going into and out of the tunnel.

"Shall we try and get closer?" Micah says, extending his elbow to Ashley.

She twines her arm around his and answers, "We shall." They're acting like this is all a game. I'm actually feeling a little giddy myself.

Micah, Kel and I follow. We go down a couple flights of stairs and reach a sidewalk that surrounds the building. To the left is a loading platform for watercraft. It's probably less than fifteen years old, but it looks much older. To the right, the walkway arches out past the edge of the building.

Kelly holds back. "Seriously, guys? What are we doing? So we get closer. Then what? How're you going to know if the tunnel's open?"

"We draw straws," I joke. "The winner gets to go swimming."

They all look at me. But I shake my head. "Except me. I left my medicine at home."

It's got to be one of the lamest things I've said in a long time, and a really bad excuse to boot. Reggie laughs at me. He shakes his head and says, "Nobody's going swimming. We're just scoping things out today. I just want to see how close we can get. Next time we come back — tomorrow, maybe, or Saturday — we'll be better prepared."

"Prepared for what?"

Reggie raises his eyebrows at Kelly. "Duh. A little exploratory work."

This clearly doesn't please Kelly. He drags his feet while the others follow Reggie. I lag behind to walk with him.

"What's this all about?" I ask him, when the others are out of earshot. "Why are you acting like this all of a sudden?"

"What do you mean, Jess?"

I roll my eyes. I don't know what else to say that won't make things worse, so we walk along for a few more minutes without speaking. Then he elbows me and gives me a wry smile. "I can't believe you forgot your inhaler. Tsk, tsk. What's the Colonel going to say?"

"Grandpa doesn't know." I shove him playfully. "And he doesn't need to find out, either."

I've used the inhaler my entire life. I'm supposed to carry it around with me all the time and puff on it three times a day, so it's become almost habit. But I do forget on occasion, and when my grandfather finds out, he gets all OCD about it and interrogates me for like the next week. *How am I feeling? Have I taken all three doses? Do I feel sick?*

Most of the time I can honestly answer that I'm following my regimen, but sometimes I forget. Like today. I'd forgotten to take it out of my gear bag this morning and left it at home.

I shrug and tell Kelly that we'll be back soon and I'll just take a dose then. "It's not like I'm going to drop dead if I don't. It's just an immunity booster."

The truth of the matter is, I'm not exactly sure what it's supposed to do. I've always been told by the doctors that it's to help stave off infections, but they've never really clearly explained what's wrong with me that I should need it.

Sometimes I hate having the inhaler; it makes me feel weak and vulnerable. Other times, though, I'm glad for it. Like, for example, whenever I want to get out of having to do gym class, I just hold it up and complain that I feel like I'm coming down with something. It's a lot easier and less embarrassing than saying I'm having menstrual cramps.

We reach the end of the walkway. Ash and Micah have stopped and are leaning out across the railing. They're looking down into the darkness below us. "The opening's right here," Ash says, even though there's no way she can possibly see it. "Does it look to you like it's open?"

I look down, but it's too dark and the sunlight keeps bouncing up and into my eyes. I try to lean further over. Before I realize what's happening, there's a flash of color off to the side, a splash, and water sprays up at us. I stumble back gasping and wiping it from my face.

"What the hell was that?"

"Dude!" Reggie exclaims. He's got a huge smile plastered over his face. "Kelly is what happened, that's what. Crazy mother fucker. What'd you say to him to make him jump, Jessie?"

"Kelly?" I shout, running back over to the railing and looking down, but there's nothing to see. "I didn't tell him to jump, you idiot!"

This shuts him up.

"Don't just stand there! Do something!"

But nobody moves. Nobody wants to jump into that murky water. We all wait and count the seconds.

Thirty heartbeats pass. Then forty.... Fifty....

Sixty.

"Kelly," I moan.

A minute and half is gone just like that and now I'm really starting to get scared. Ashley's eyes have grown wide, too. She's got her fingertips in her mouth. She's chewing on her nails. Even Reggie and Micah are beginning to look a little nervous.

"It's barely two minutes," Micah says. "I can hold my breath for two minutes. Hell. I could hold it for three if I needed to."

But all I can think is that it's Kelly we're talking about, not Micah. Kelly's not conditioned for holding his breath.

"How long?" I ask. Nobody answers. "*How long!*"

"Three minutes."

"Kelly!" I scream. "*Kelly!*"

Then everyone's yelling, shouting his name. Reggie's peeling off his shirt and getting ready to climb onto the railing. Micah begins to kick off his shoes. But we're all interrupted by a shrill whistle coming from man in a dark green uniform. He starts running toward us.

"You there! You kids! Stop right there! There's no swimming here."

Reggie's standing on the first rail, leaning his knees against the top rung, looking like he's going to jump in anyway. The cop blows his whistle even harder and waves his EM pistol frantically at us. Now he's about a hundred feet away.

"Our friend fell in!" Micah shouts. "He fell in! It was an accident. We need help!"

The cop reaches us, his feet slapping the sidewalk. He's panting and I'm sobbing by then. So's Ashley.

"Our friend fell in! We have to save him!"

"You can't go down there," the cop says. He's an older man, graying at the temples. His face is rough and scarred. He shoves his pistol back in its holster but keeps his hand on it. "It's dangerous. Bad currents. Can't you see the signs?" He points.

"But our friend—"

Just then there's a watery gasp from below us and Kelly's head pops up. His face is blue and his eyes are bulging. He scrambles to grab onto something, but the edge of the overpass is too far out of reach. The cop bends down under the railing. He leans over and extends his baton.

"Grab onto this, young man."

Kelly gets a hold of the baton, but he's too weak to pull himself up. Reggie joins the cop. He reaches down and grabs both of Kelly's arms and he lifts him out of the water like he's nothing but a stack of wet laundry. Kelly shoots up and manages to grab the lowest rail.

Reggie slips out from underneath and quickly repositions himself over the railing. "Hold on!" Kelly hurtles over it and smacks down on the walkway, where he collapses in a wet, shivering heap.

I rush over and wrap my arms around him. He places his face in the crook of my neck. His skin is cold and there's a scratch on his cheek that's just starting to pink up with fresh blood. I notice he's hiding it from the cop.

"There's no swimming here," the officer repeats. "I could have you arrested." He gives us a stern look and keeps it on us a few seconds longer than necessary. We all know what that means. An arrest like this would go on our permanent record and add time to our LSC, time that would, without a doubt, get front-ended.

He sighs and shakes his head. "What are you kids doing down here anyway? This is no place for young folks like you to be. You should be at home enjoying the summer break."

We all look around at each other. Finally, Ashley manages to say, "School project?"

The cop snorts. "Right, like I'm supposed to believe that."

"We were just looking for some privacy," Reggie says. He sidles up to Ash and wraps his arms around her.

The cop sizes them up for a moment — giant Reggie and diminutive Ash — then he looks at me and Kelly. Finally his gaze settles on Micah and we can all see that he's figuring out the math. His eyes flit around, as if he expects to see another person to be hiding somewhere.

But he just shakes his head again and tells us the next time he comes by we had better be gone. "This is a class B zone," he tells us. "Only authorized individuals are allowed in here. It's not a . . . . It's not a motel."

He turns on his heels and walks away, much to our surprise. He doesn't even bother to scan us.

"Class B?" Reggie whispers in disbelief. "Man, we are so lucky he didn't bust us."

Class A would be the East River, of course. The penalty for trespassing there wouldn't be arrest or LSC years. It would be vaporization by one of the mines.

When the sound of the cop's shoes on the pavement fades away, I turn back to Kelly and shake him. "What the hell were you thinking jumping in there? You almost drowned!"

He slowly raises his eyes, but he doesn't look at me. It's Reggie he stares at, his eyes dark and penetrating. "Well, Reg, you wanted to know if the tunnel's open. I got your answer." He takes in a shuddering breath and looks at the rest of us.

"Blocked?" Reggie asks.

Kelly shakes his head. He shivers again and says, "Open. All the way through."

Chapter Five

"How do you know?" Ashley asks. "How could you possibly know it's open all the way through?"

"Currents," Kelly replies, pushing me away a little. I think about the cop mentioning currents and realize he's right. In order for there to be currents, the tunnel must be open.

"They're actually pretty strong down there. It was almost like getting sucked into a drain. Lucky for me, the current was pushing me back out, otherwise . . . ." He doesn't finish. He doesn't need to.

He coughs, spits. "I ended up grabbing onto some old wiring or something and pulling myself along the ceiling. I went as far as I could before I ran out of air and needed to turn around."

"That was some crazy-ass shit, man," Reggie says.

Kelly locks eyes with Reg and doesn't answer. After a few seconds pass, he combs his dripping hair away from his forehead with his fingers.

"I thought I'd just let the current push me back out, but then my shirt got caught on something." He lifts his arm to show us the tear under his left sleeve.

I don't know why the next thought pops into my head, but suddenly I wonder if the cop happened to notice the rip. Why that would matter I don't know, but the whole encounter strikes me as odd, forced. Why would he just take off like that without even scanning us? And what does Kelly know that he'd want to hide the scratch from him?

Kelly laughs weakly and shakes his head. "I sort of panicked, thinking it was one of those sewer gators you always hear about."

"Urban myth," Micah says.

"I guess I freaked out. I lost my air. I tried to kick. Whatever it was holding me tore away. I felt my shirt rip and the next thing I knew, I was shooting back out with the current. Good thing too, because I don't think I'd have made it out if it was even another second or two. I'd probably have inhaled a gallon of water and sunk straight to the bottom."

"What do you think it was?" Ashley asks. "That snagged you, I mean." She has this worried look on her face. We can all see what she's thinking, but nobody wants to say it.

Kelly shrugs. "Loose panel or something. Maybe a jammed log or a pipe. I don't know. It was too dark to see. There's got to be a ton of crap washed down into there, just not enough to block the flow entirely. The current's definitely strong enough to move a lot of water, so there's got to be spaces wide enough for a person to swim through."

I lean back and study Kelly and wonder why he's suddenly stopped being so resistant.

"Or maybe it was a zombie," Reggie jokes.

He suddenly laughs and slaps Kelly on the back and makes appreciative sounding noises. "Just kidding, brah. But, man, that was totally off-the-wall, what you did."

Everyone nods, but I'm still furious.

"Why?" I scream at him. "You're the last person I would've expected to do something stupid like jump into the river!"

"It's not the riv— "

"I don't care what it is! You could've drowned."

He shrugs and sighs. "Maybe that's why I did it," he says, studying my face. "I don't know. Maybe I just realized that you're always right about stuff and I'm wrong and such a stick in the mud all the time. I just figured I'd see for myself."

"You could've lied about it," Micah quietly says. "You could've told us it was gated or something. We wouldn't have known any better."

"Believe me, I thought about it. But while I was struggling to untangle myself, I don't know, I guess I just thought, *really?*" He looks at Reggie. "I still think it's a bad idea, though. Nothing changed my mind about that."

Reggie shakes his head.

"Besides," Kelly goes on, "there's the other tunnel, the Brooklyn Battery. If I told you this one was blocked, knowing you guys, we'd just end up going over there and checking that one out. Am I right?"

A couple of us shrug and murmur our agreement.

"Guys?" Ashley says, interrupting the boys. "I hate to break up this little discussion, but maybe it's time we cleared out of here. I don't know if that cop was serious, but I don't want to find out. He said he'd be back, but he didn't say when."

Reggie and Micah help pull us to our feet. Despite the warmth of the day, Kelly is still shivering. The scratch on his cheek has stopped bleeding, but now it's puckered out white and angry-looking on his pale face. He lifts his shoulder to wipe it away, wincing, and a fresh thin line of blood appears.

"Don't do that," I tell him. "You'll only make it worse."

"How'd it happen?" Micah asks as we walk back to the car.

Kelly shrugs. "Like I said, it was dark. Whatever it was that snagged my shirt scratched my face too, I guess."

I take a closer look. There are three parallel scrapes, each separated from the other by about a half inch. They look like claw marks. Only the middle one is deep enough to break the skin. "Just make sure you put some antibiotic on it when we get back," I say.

"Yes, Mom," they all chorus.

I frown at them. "Hey, it may not be the East River *per se*, but it's still pretty nasty water."

Chapter Six

I wasn't worried about Kelly getting some nasty bacterial infection. I was worried about him coming down with something worse.

Ash's grandmother, Junie, used to joke about how, when she was my age, having unprotected sex could kill you. She passed away last year, quite unexpectedly. She could remember a time before the implants, before zombies. Back when diseases like AIDS and diabetes and cancer worried people. She'd laugh her bitter laugh because she knew things are a lot worse now, when there are diseases that don't just kill you, but raise you back up again.

"I hope they put me into *The Game*," she started saying to us, shortly before she died.

"Don't joke about it," Ashley told her.

"I'm serious, girl." Of course, we all knew it was highly unlikely she'd get her wish. Only the freshest and fittest of the recently deceased ever get recruited to be Players. "And think of the money it would bring the family."

"We don't need the money," Ash told her. But even I knew that wasn't true.

"But that's not why."

"Then why, G-ma? You know the lifespan of a game zombie is only a few weeks. Months at best, depending on your Operator." She shuddered; I knew she was remembering some of the scenes we'd watched on *Survivalist*.

"What they're made to do in *The Game* can be pretty brutal."

"I've seen that program, dear. I know. That's why I think it would be better. I'd rather spend my Life Service commitment doing that." G-ma Junie closed her eyes then and sighed, nodding. "A few brutal weeks. Who cares? I won't even know because I'll be dead. And if I'm dead, I want to be *dead* dead, not standing in some remote border outpost as a deterrent to trespassers or strapped to a bomb in Mexico. I just want to be laid to rest."

Of course, nobody gets 'laid to rest' anymore. They don't do burials. Everyone gets incinerated. *After* their LSC is completed.

Since her G-ma's death, Ashley has been talking more and more like that, too. "I'd rather just go quickly in *The Game*, even if it's to act out some sick fantasy of some sick rich fuck. Better that than be put to work cleaning sewers for three years or pulling guard duty. Although getting blown up would be a quick way to go, don't you think? I could be an Omega."

I remember once how Eric told me we probably won't have to worry about reaching our LSC age.

I knew he wasn't talking about a cure, or a change in the laws. He was talking about another outbreak happening, a real bad one. Global in reach, total in nature. An outbreak that wouldn't be quelled like the others.

There wouldn't be anyone left to quell it.

Chapter Seven

Kelly's clothes have stopped dripping by the time we get back to the car. We stop and wait for him to dump the water out of his shoes and wring his socks and shirt out. While we do, we see the cop from earlier walking past us down below. He's clearly checking to make sure we're gone, but he doesn't look up, so he doesn't see us.

Micah complains about his seat getting wet, so we just hang around and talk about nothing much while Kelly dries off some more.

"Do you really think we could do it?" Ash asks. "Do you think we could actually get to LI?"

I look out in the direction of Long Island, past the edge of the parking structure, out past the tunnel opening. I can't actually see it because there's another building in the way, but I can feel it out there. I shrug. Nobody answers.

Micah and Ash eventually drift away with their heads bent over the tablet. Reggie seems uncomfortable around us, so he trails along after them.

I turn to Kelly and smack him on the arm. "You scared the crap out of me, Kelly Corben."

He inhales, clears his throat. "I didn't jump, Jess."

"What? You fell?"

"I was pushed, Jessie. Somebody pushed me. I'm pretty sure it was Reg."

"He wouldn't do something like that!"

"How can you be so sure?"

"He's your friend, Kelly. *Our* friend. He's not— "

Kelly wraps his goose-fleshed arms around me and I squirm from the coldness of his skin and his clamminess, but he holds me ever tighter and won't let go. "Maybe you're right," he says. "Maybe I just slipped."

But he doesn't sound at all convinced. He sounds like he's humoring me. But I'm not amused. I give him another long, hard look.

He closes his eyes and leans his head back against the wall. I want to smack him again, but how can I? Something deep down inside of me knows what he said is possible. He and Reg have always been competitive. Micah's always been the alpha male in our gamers' club. The other two accepted that long ago, leaving open the question of who was second.

Boys! I think. Why'd it always have to be about power?

Thankfully, Micah returns a moment later. He asks where Ashley and Reggie are. He's ready to leave.

"I thought they were with you."

He shakes his head. We're all thinking the same thing.

"Idle hands do the devil's work," he mutters, rolling his eyes. "I wonder where Reggie's hands are idling right about now." He holds them out, illustrating exactly what he means so there's no question.

"That's disgusting! We're in a parking garage."

He laughs as he opens the car door and leans in to push on the horn. I stifle the urge to tell him to stop. He doesn't even seem to care that we're not supposed to be here.

"Ash!" he shouts. His voice echoes in the otherwise empty structure. "Reg! Come on, you pervs. Time to go!"

Two or three minutes later, the pair comes jogging over. Ashley's face is flushed, and Reggie's got his usual smile plastered on his face. Before any of us can say anything or tease them, Ash frowns at us and says, "Don't even think it. We kept our clothes on. We were just doing a little scouting."

We get back into the car. Kelly sits in the front this time, since he's still damp and nobody wants to sit next to someone who smells swampy. Ashley gets the hump this time in back, between me and Reg. I sit behind Micah, but I study Reggie's face for any indication he did what Kelly says he did. But there's nothing there.

"The cop makes a regular pass," Ashley says after we're back on the road. "We watched him. He does a circuit of some kind. It looks like it takes him almost exactly sixty minutes to do it."

I give her a questioning look.

"And what did you guys do?" she asks me, pretending to act all innocent.

"Not much," I say, but I steal another glance at Reg. He looks over at me, the same inquiring look on his face as Ash's. It's impossible to read him.

Kelly scratches his head. "Doesn't it seem strange to you that there'd be a cop patrolling? On foot? I mean, why? Nobody's going to be wandering around down there. The place is deserted."

"*We* were."

Micah's shoulders lift and fall as he drives, but he keeps his eyes on the road. Kelly frowns. The question remains unanswered, though not forgotten. It's just that none of us knows if there is an answer.

After that, the conversation drifts. We pass through the checkpoints and the guards don't even bother to scan our Links. Going out is a hell of a lot easier than going in. One guard checks the trunk of the car, but that's the most any of them does. Does he think we're carrying illegal contraband or something?

Micah drops me and Kelly off at my house. Nobody's home, so we take a risk and jump into the shower together while Kelly's clothes get washed.

We begin soaping each other down, but as much as I want to mess around, it's clear Kelly's mind is anywhere but on sex. We quickly rinse and towel off. I throw the clothes into the dryer while Kelly sits in my room wrapped in a towel and my robe.

"You look cute," I tell him. He looks over distractedly and turns back to his Link. I go over and peek over his shoulder. "What are you doing?"

"Looking up whatever I can find out about LI. You know, history and stuff."

"You know nothing that's on the public Streams is reliable."

He nods. "Still, better to be prepared."

"I thought...."

"What?" He looks up expectantly.

"Nothing."

The sanctioned history claims that the wall was first built around the island to stop the spread of infections. But the outbreaks kept on happening anyway. The government says it's because of sabotage, but that's not what most people believe. Some of the more recent outbreaks have been as far away as Seattle and Los Angeles. But they don't get much play on Media. They've been small, a few hundred cases at the most, and quite easily contained. In fact, there was nothing like the panics caused by the ones on the East Coast. It's like we've gotten used to them happening. Nobody even bothers to be worried anymore. We've all become desensitized.

There are a ton of theories circulating about how the outbreaks happen. Some people believe they're caused by mosquito-borne transmission. There's rumors that the original genes used to make the first Zulus came from a virus called dengue, which was spread by mosquitoes.

Grandpa says that's impossible. He says dengue was eradicated after the plague of 2012 by this scientist who blocked the virus' ability to replicate inside mosquitoes. The scientist's name was Stephen something— Archangel, maybe — I can't remember, and there's nothing about it on the Stream.

Other people think the infection can be transmitted through the water. That's why I didn't like Kelly getting scratched today. I know it's just being paranoid, since zombies don't last very long in water. But you never know. Maybe the zombie germ does.

The truth is, nobody knows for sure how it happens. They don't even know what causes the disease in the first place.

Except maybe the government, and they're not talking.

"Why'd they move the Omegaman training facilities off LI?" I ask Kelly. "After the second flood, I mean."

"Well, the island was pretty much a lost cause," he answers, reciting history that both of us supposedly learned years back. I've since forgotten so much of it. The explanation sounds familiar, but it also sounds too convenient, like a lie. "The Army Corps of Engineers went in and walled it off and evacuated any people still alive."

That was the official account. Unofficially, I've heard there weren't any of them left.

"Grandpa says the Marines moved the Omegaman training facilities to Washington State seven or eight years ago. He says they were just going to let the remaining IUs keel over."

Most zombies just sort of run out of energy after a while, contrary to the old stories about them. Without human flesh, they'd last maybe a year. After a dozen years, the place would essentially be free of them.

About four or five years ago, Arc Properties went in and reclaimed some of the zones. They said they were going to do a survey. While they claimed to have found a few active zoms, the ones they did find were so slow that they were harmless. Of course, nobody cared a whit by then. Nobody wanted to go and re-inhabit the island.

Year before last, Arc Properties converted one of the zones into a new type of gaming arcade, which they called Gameland. They imported a whole new crop of fresh zombies as Players.

"Arc," Kelly spits. "Bastards." It's the only time I've ever heard him say anything bad about the company. It comes as such a surprise now because for the past couple of years, the rest of us talked about joining the company after high school and Kelly was actually pretty supportive of it, even though he had different plans.

"What, Kel?"

He shakes his head bitterly. "Rich bastards. All they care about is money. Did you know it costs a million bucks to buy into *The Game*? And that's not even for a good zombie, but an older one, probably with a first gen L.I.N.C."

I frown, wondering where this hostility is coming from and why he's all of a sudden talking about Arc and *The Game*.

"People who have that kind of money should use it for good instead of just throwing it away. If I were that rich, I'd make sure Kyle got treated."

I lean away from him.

His eyes clear. "Sorry, Jess. I guess I'm just a little tired after everything that's happened today."

He gets up and fetches his clothes from the dryer. "Think I'll head home."

Chapter Eight

Ashley pings me that evening. Thankfully, she waits until after dinner this time. Grandpa and Eric are at each other's throats again in the kitchen. At the moment, Eric's shouting and Grandpa's sitting there with his trademark military composure, which only seems to infuriate Eric all the more.

I close my bedroom door, muffling their voices.

"What's up?"

"Reggie wants us to meet at his place," Ashley says. "Can you come?"

"Right now? Um, I guess. What's this about?"

Stupid question, of course. There's only one thing it could be about.

"He's figured out how we can do it."

I snort. "Right."

"Just be there, okay?"

As soon as she disconnects, Kelly pings me. "You hear?"

"Just got off with Ash, but she didn't give any details, just told me to meet her at Reggie's."

"I guess they got equipment."

"What equipment? Scuba gear? How?"

I slip into my sweater and sneakers as Kelly explains.

"Apparently Ash knows this guy whose uncle owns a shop on the edge of town."

"A dive shop? Really? I don't remember any dive shops around here."

"Not so much a dive shop as a military surplus store."

I pause to think. "Are you talking about Eppy's over by the old hospital?"

"I guess. I stopped by Micah's on the way home. He said they were going to meet with this guy Ash knows. They invited me to go with them."

"Did you?"

"Reg was there."

I can tell by the way he says it that he still believes Reggie pushed him over the railing down in lower Manhattan.

"So?"

"Anyway, I had to get home and help out with Kyle. But Micah pinged me just over an hour ago and said they got everything we'd need, even wetsuits." He paused. "Apparently there's a catch, though."

"Yeah, money, that's the catch."

"Maybe. Micah didn't say, just told us to come to Reggie's tonight."

"Wait, you knew about this an hour ago and you didn't tell me?"

"Well . . . . I didn't want to ping you during dinner."

I grumble, but I know he's right. The last thing he'd want to do is interrupt my supper for a second day in a row, especially if he and the others hope to get me to come out afterward.

"Stop by and pick me up?" he asks.

"Yeah, give me about ten minutes. I think Grandpa and Eric are still arguing downstairs, so I'll try and sneak out. Otherwise, I'll have to think of something. I can't just say I'm going over to Reggie's."

"Tell them you're going to Ashley's then."

"That's like two miles away. Eric'll offer to drive. Then what?"

"You'll figure it out."

"I always do, don't I?"

Eric is still ranting in the kitchen, going off about some plan to expand the duties of his department at work. He's standing at the sink and flinging soapy water around as he washes the dishes, his back facing the doorway. "As if I don't have enough paperwork to do already!"

Grandpa's sitting in his chair leaning back. He's got his hands laced behind his head and he isn't moving. Just as I'm about to turn the corner, his chair turns and he looks at me. He doesn't say anything, just looks.

"I'm, uh . . . ." I point at the door. "I'm going over to Ash's. Me and Micah and Reggie and . . . Kelly. They're picking me up, so I don't need a ride."

He just sits there while I mess with the strap on my backpack. Finally he says, "Don't forget your medicine." Then he turns back around. Eric isn't even aware of what's happening behind him. He's still talking a mile a minute.

I slip out into the night and hurry over to Kelly's as fast as I can, afraid that if I turn around, I'll see my grandfather standing there watching me.

"That was quick," Kelly says.

"Yeah, well, things at my house are a bit explosive right now. Sounds like there's something going on down at the police station."

Kelly looks over. "Is everything all right?" He means did stealing a copy of Eric's inner zone permit cause any problems.

I shake my head and say, "It was something about having to do more work."

"Wonder if there's been another outbreak." He tilts his head like he's thinking.

I shrug. "I haven't heard anything about one."

My brother works in the Necrotics Crimes Division. Basically anything to do with offenses committed by or against the Undead is his responsibility. It's generally agreed that NCD is the suckiest job on the force, but it fits Eric's personality to a tee.

"Can we talk about something else?" I ask, and Kelly nods.

Ten minutes later we're standing on Reggie's front walk. We hear a low whistle and see Micah standing in the shadows beneath some tall bushes. He waves us over. "This way. We're in back."

"Why all the secrecy?"

"Reg's mom."

Kel and I both nod. Mrs. Casey is the nosiest woman on the face of the planet. If she got a whiff of what we were planning, she'd be on it like a bloodhound on the trail of a killer.

We circle around the house to the garage. Reggie's father had it converted years ago into a retro game room. There's a pinball machine and some ancient video arcade games, a pool table with worn felt and a ping pong table. It's totally lame, but the older generation seems to like it. That's why we hang out at Micah's instead, even though his basement is musty and the couch sags and smells like dogs and stinky feet and the downstairs bathroom should probably be condemned. Or at least fumigated.

"Hey guys," Reggie says, meeting us at the door. He's smiling. He hands me and Kel one of his father's beers and waves us in. I see that Micah's already got a bottle and that it's nearly empty. "I hope your weekend's clear, because we're shooting for Saturday. Whoever can make it, that is." He looks pointedly at Kel. "Right now there's four of us."

Kelly stops. "Four?" He looks over at me. I give him a quick shake of the head to indicate it doesn't include me. "Who's the extra?"

Reggie gestures with his beer behind us.

We turn just as someone says, "I am."

Stepping out from behind Ashley is a boy. I recognize him immediately. His name is out of my mouth before I realize it: "Jake?"

Kelly does a double take.

"The kid from this morning?" he says. "This is the guy who was hitting on you at karate?"

Jake raises his hands. "Whoa, wait a minute. I wasn't— "

"What are you doing here?" I exclaim.

"Wait," Kelly says. His face is starting to turn red. "Let him finish what he was going to say. I want to hear this."

I frown my displeasure, silently willing him to drop it.

"You two know each other?" Ashley asks, as she swings around Jacob to stand between him and Kelly. I can tell she's amused by this unexpected development.

"No, they don't," I say. "Not really. And I just met Jake this morning."

Ashley turns to him, raising her eyebrows. "You didn't tell me— "

"Jessie gave me really good a workout," Jake says, glaring back at Kelly.

Kelly takes a threatening step forward. I pull him back. "It was nothing," I say. "We sparred. At the dojang. There weren't any other students around so I— "

"No one else was around, Jess? You didn't tell me that."

"We weren't alone, Kel! Rupert was there." I turn to Ashley, eager to change the subject. "I don't understand, Ash. How did Jake get involved in our little . . . outing?"

"He knows about LI. Everything. And Jake was my lab partner last year, so . . . ."

I narrow my eyes. Ash always hated science. And yet I seem to remember she got an A in the class, though. "*Just* your lab partner?"

She shrugs and doesn't take the bait. "Look, guys, we needed equipment. I got it for us. That's all. There's no conspiracy, no *quid pro quo* here."

"Fancy words," Kelly grumbles.

"So your uncle owns Eppy's?" I say. "You're *that* Jacob Esposito? Little Jacob?"

Jake nods. "Nobody's called me 'Little' in a while."

"I remember you!" Kelly says. "Little punk on the playground, always picking on the smaller kids. What'd you, like, grow a foot over the summer?"

"Something like that."

Reggie comes over and manages to get between us all, somehow spreading us all apart to a safe distance. Kelly's still glaring, but the look in his eyes is not as hateful as it was a moment ago. Now it's filled with distrust.

"It actually works out having Jake join us," Reggie says. "He's a rescue diver and his uncle has all kinds of scuba gear. He's agreed to let us borrow it."

"Well, actually, it won't be scuba gear. And Uncle Joe doesn't know."

"In exchange for what?" I ask.

Jake looks around at the rest of us. "For inclusion in your little party, of course. I thought that was clear. I want to be included."

I narrow my eyes. "Why the hell would you want to break into Long Island? Don't you know it's illegal?"

"I do. And why would you?"

"Because we're hackers," I say. "Mostly anyway. Isn't that what you called us this morning? Jackers? That's what we do."

"Maybe. But hacking isn't the same as physically breaking into a Forbidden Zone." He shrugs. "That's where I can help.

I've done all sorts of survival training. What can I say? I'm more of an outdoorsy type." He pauses. "Computers, on the other hand, well, that's just not my thing."

"And now there's an even number," Reggie says, giving Kelly a look.

"Why is that so important?" he asks.

"The first thing they drill into your brain in survival training is that you partner up," Jake answers. "You can do threes, but it's best to have twosomes, especially in a dive group. You both watch each other's back." He glances at me, and I don't know if it's just my impression, but that hungry, animal-like look is back in his eyes. I feel Kelly tense up next to me, even though we're not physically touching.

"And anyway," Micah quickly adds, "once we told him we needed the equipment, it's not like we could exclude him."

"You'd squeal on us?" I ask.

Jake pauses just long enough before shaking his head. There's little doubt what he'd do.

I sigh and throw my hands up in the air. "Fine."

"I'm not fine with it!" Kelly shouts. "I don't trust this guy as far as I could throw him."

"Don't go then," Jake counters. There's just a hint of a grin at the corners of his mouth.

"If Kelly doesn't go, then I don't go."

Jake's grin falters.

"Guys," Ashley says. "Don't be like that. Jake can partner up with Micah." She gives Micah a wink.

Suddenly I'm not thinking about Jake and Kelly, but Micah. This new question enters my mind. In the year or so that I've known him, have I ever seen him with a girl? I mean, other than just hanging out with me and Ash. Micah's always been the spare tire of our group, though it never felt like that big of a deal. There was never any jealousy at all.

Reggie raises his bottle for a toast. "Tomorrow, Jake's going to give us a quick lesson on diving using this special gear he's getting for us. Tonight, we plan. We need to figure out what to take. I'll look at the tide charts, all that stuff. Then, assuming the currents are right, we'll shoot for Saturday morning."

"Tides are on a roughly six-hour cycle," Jake adds, "so that'll give us a few hours to hang out before we need to come back." It bothers me how much he's inserted himself into the plan. And into our group. It doesn't feel right.

"Don't worry, Jess," Reggie says, misreading the concern on my face. "We'll have you back home long before dinnertime."

Micah and Ash clink bottles with him. I raise mine too, but don't drink. I notice that two other bottles are missing: Jake's and Kelly's.

I sigh unhappily, feeling as if my pent up excitement and worry are at war with each other. We're really going to do this. Or at least try.

But I'm not so sure I want to anymore.

Chapter Nine

"The oxygen rebreather was developed by NASA about a dozen years ago," Jake explains, holding the odd-looking mask up so that we can all see it, "and further adapted by the Navy for short-term underwater use."

It's just after eight o'clock in the morning and we're at the Page Mill levee and, except for some fishermen a few hundred yards away, we're all alone. The fishermen don't even bother to glance over at us. They look like they're well into their second case of cheap beer, and by the sounds of their singing, it doesn't appear they really care if they catch anything.

"Where's the air tank?" Ashley asks.

It's such a stupid question that I just know it has to be a set up.

Jake smiles. "I'm glad you asked that, Ash. By the way, I hope you don't mind my saying, but you look really... nice today." He turns to me and adds, "You both do."

Kelly makes a sound of disgust and looks away. Ashley beams. Of course she looks nice, she's wearing a skimpy white Ronnie Marx two-piece bikini that really highlights her red hair and green eyes. Not that any of the guys are looking at her hair or eyes. They're checking out the other assets that suit is also highlighting.

I look down at my own outfit, a pair of dingy oversized gray workout sweats. Underneath, I've got on a relatively modest rainbow-colored two-piece with French-cut shorts. Suddenly I feel like a shapeless blob.

"Thank you, Jake," Ash says, tossing her hair.

"What a loser," Kelly murmurs, too quiet for anyone else to hear, and for once I have to agree.

"As I was saying, the rebreather was developed to take the place of an oxygen tank, but primarily for use in short-term situations and tight spaces, such as between airlocks and docked vehicles."

"Are we traveling through any airlocks?"

Jake's eyes narrow. "You could say the tunnel is one long airlock."

"Just not in outer space."

"No." He clears his throat and continues. "The cartridge is perforated to allow pressure equalization. It's essentially a cage protecting an inner Mylar sack that contains a catalytic converter — beads linked to a chemical that converts cee-oh-two back into good old fashioned oh-two."

"Ah, good old fashioned oxygen. It's so much better than the new fangled stuff."

I snort and hip check Kelly. "Just ignore him, Jake. Go on."

"The rebreather wasn't intended for underwater use, but the Navy has been employing them successfully for strategic missions, rapid insertions and near-surface operations in confined spaces. They're a lot less bulky. Inert gasses, such as nitrogen are simply passed through the matrix, maintaining a proper balance and concentration relative to oxygen. That way your brain doesn't think it's either oxygen-deprived or in surplus. And that's important because either of those scenarios will cause you to faint. I probably don't need to tell you what happens if you faint while under water."

"Maybe you should explain it anyways," Kelly shouts. "You know, just in case Ashley hasn't figured it out."

I slap his arm and tell him to behave. Ashley gives him a dirty look and Reggie chuckles. Micah just sits and stares at Jake, whose confidence has all but vanished.

He disengages a canister from the hose attached to the mask and holds it up. It's about the size of a tub of Cheezy Cheeze. "There's enough chemical converter in one of these to last roughly three hours, give or take. Ample time for us to get through the tunnel and out the other side. But, just in case, each of us will carry a spare on our belt. They're sealed. All you have to do is insert into the hose and twist."

Just in case of what? I think. I don't want to be underwater for more than hour. Then I wonder: How long does it take to swim a mile?

"Why not just use scuba tanks?" I ask.

"You have to be certified to get the tanks," Jake answers. "And it's illegal to rent them out to uncertified divers."

"Isn't what we're doing already illegal?"

"Look, guys," Micah says, inserting himself in front of Kelly, "it's either the rebreathers or we don't go. Jake's uncle would definitely notice six dive tanks missing. But these?" He holds one up. "They're cheap and disposable. They've got cases of them in the store."

"What the hell for?"

"Military surplus," Jake says. "Uncle Joe bids on closed crates at auction. He gets whatever he gets. You'd be surprised what people will come into the store to buy."

"We'll also pack a third set in a waterproof pack for the return," Micah says, steering the discussion back to the trip.

"Talk about overkill," Kelly whispers.

"Better safe than sorry," Jake replies.

"Who put you in charge anyway?"

"Kelly! Stop it! Please."

"The rebreathers work just like the old fashioned masks. Bite down on the mouthpiece and inhale. You also exhale through the mouth, but instead of the waste gas bubbling into the water and going to the surface, it goes into the bag and gets recycled."

He tosses the rebreather into a box and comes up with a pair of goggles.

"Now, with scuba, to clear your goggles of leaks, you'd normally exhale through the nose. With these systems, you don't want to do that because . . . why? Anyone?"

"You'll lose your air?" Ashley quips.

"Exactly. The canisters don't create oxygen, just recycle it. Lose it and it's gone. So unless you have gills, I'd suggest you pay attention. These goggles are equipped with their own clearing mechanism."

He points to a silver cartridge inserted into the elastic headband. It's about the size of a large hotdog. "This is highly compressed air. Just push the button on the top . . . here . . . which releases a puff, thus forcing any water out the bottom. You can get as many as twenty puffs, but then that's it, so make sure your goggles are a good fit. They should be tight and well sealed. Otherwise you'll be looking out through water goggles for the rest of the dive."

"Speaking of the water, are we actually going to get in it today?" Kelly asks. "Or are we just going to sit here and listen to you?"

Jake's ability to ignore Kelly reaches its limit. His face flushes and he fumbles the mask. He was so confident last night, so confrontational, that I almost don't recognize him now. It sort of worries me, because it makes me wonder if he's a little bipolar. There's enough emotional drama in our group without adding his baggage to it.

"I, um," he stutters, "was going to say it's time to get — uh, to put on the equipment." He quickly turns and picks up a box behind him. "There's another crate in my van with wetsuits, weight belts, and fins. Everyone gets a set. I took a guess on the sizes." He looks at Reggie and adds, "Although some might be a little tight."

Reggie grins and turns to Ash and says, "The tighter the better." She slaps his arm and sticks out her tongue. But then she thrusts out her chest at him and laughs.

"Let me know if you need any help getting it on."

"Let me know if you need help getting it off," Ash counters.

The rest of us are used to this, but Jake's face turns so red that I'm afraid he's going to spontaneously combust or something.

To distract himself, he launches into a lecture on fitting and prepping our goggles. The spitting part to keep them from fogging up amuses Reggie, of course. He makes a show of hocking a nasty loogie into the lenses, much to Ashley's disgust.

We don't get to use the rebreathers right away. Rather, Jake has us snorkel around a bit near the shore so we get used to being in wetsuits and flippers and being neutrally buoyant, which I seem to be having trouble with.

At first I have too much weight on my belt and keep sinking. I quickly grow tired from trying to keep myself at the surface. It's frustrating, especially since nobody seems to be noticing. Kelly's ignoring me as he paddles around twenty feet away, as if he can actually see anything in the murky depths below us now that we've stirred up all the mud. Finally I give up and waddle ashore to take some of the lead weights off.

"Here, let me help you," Jake says, startling me. I'd thought he was still in the water. He yanks my belt and it falls from my waist. Holding one end up, he threads a pair of one-pounders off. "You don't need as much weight because you've got so little body fat."

I know what he's thinking. Although I'm not flat-chested, I'm definitely not well-endowed, either. And he obviously hasn't seen my fat ass.

But pointing these things out to him isn't going to make things any better. We're already stressed enough.

He reapplies my belt, checks to make sure it's snug, then waves me back toward the water. "Just let yourself relax," he says confidently.

Without Kelly standing right there, his nervousness has vanished.

I look out over the surface of the lake to where the others are still paddling around and find Kelly's faded blue swim trunks and his lily-white legs. He hasn't even noticed I'm not there with him. So much for buddying up.

After the belt adjustment, staying at the surface turns out to be so much easier. Diving down to the bottom and coming back up for air takes very little effort, too. It's only ten or twelve feet down and, with the flippers, only three or four quick kicks before I'm there. Once I get to the bottom, I relax. My body just sort of sits there, swaying gently with the movement of the water, neither rising nor sinking. It's just as I imagined being weightless would be like.

After a brief break and a light snack, we try out the rebreathers. Ash immediately gets into trouble with hers, complaining that she keeps forgetting and exhaling out through her nose, which means she has to surface to get a fresh lungful of air. I can see it in everyone's eyes: What we're doing isn't just dangerous, it could be fatal if we don't pay attention.

After about the fourth or fifth time this happens, Micah lays into her. He tells her there won't be air pockets inside the tunnels. The frustration is written all over his face. He's worried about her, but I can see that he's only trying to scare her into remembering. "You need to remember not to exhale through your nose, Ash," he practically shouts, "or else you'll be in deep shit."

"I'll try," she says. Her lip quivers. I want to go over and protect her, but I know it's for her own good. She needs to try harder.

"No," Micah snaps. "Don't *try*. You *have* to remember. Do whatever you need to do to remember, even if that means sticking corks up your nose."

Ash glares at him and we all stop and wait for it, the inevitable outburst. I can tell she's close to breaking. If there's anything I know about her, it's that she hates appearing weak. That's why she's always got this tough-as-nails exterior. Inside, though, she's fragile.

But then she snorts and laughs. "Anyone got any ABC gum? You know, already been chewed? I can stick that up my nose." And the tension melts away.

After another twenty minutes, during which Ash stays completely submerged, Jake takes us to the other end of the levee. There are some ruins, giving us a chance to explore a little while practicing moving around and through obstacles.

"Make sure you always know where your partner is. The idea is to get used to swimming while watching out for each other. And remember, we're not here to become underwater salvage experts or anything. No wandering off."

He hands us each a waterproof flashlight and tells us to follow him. We all obey, grimly glancing around at each other, yet barely able to restrain our excitement. Even Kelly's eager to give it a go. There's a glint in his eyes that wasn't there earlier, despite his initial reluctance. I smile tentatively at him. He takes my hand and asks me if I'm having fun yet.

"I am now." And I give his hand a squeeze. We quickly kiss, then splash into the water. We're the last pair in.

The ruins are surreal, nothing like anything I've ever seen before! I mean, they're only an old two story commercial structure that happened to be built on a low point of land before the flood, but still. For the first time, I really begin to appreciate the old buildings and stuff we lost when the waters rose and covered the Wastes. Whole worlds of forgotten places where, just a single generation before us, people lived and worked and played. They slept in these buildings. They made love and they . . . .

They died.

My heart falters. I wonder if anyone died in here. Or drowned. I wonder if a person who had drowned would return. What would a zombie do after reanimating underwater?

We emerge from the one ruin and float over to the upper story windows of a second building. All of the glass has been broken out, most likely by the rising waters themselves, but maybe also by scavenger divers and thrill seekers. Nothing's left inside. All the old furniture and fixtures are gone, leaving just an empty shell, which is now caked with mud and lake debris and storm wash.

Jake guides us through the rooms. I feel like I'm in the belly of a sleeping beast. Then a big, black hole opens up before us, an elevator shaft, gaping like the beast's gullet. We crowd around him as he enters it.

He waits until we're all there, then he shines his light down and we hover over the darkness that fills the space below like heavy water. We all look at each other and wonder the same thing: What's down there? Jake's beam of light gets soaked up before it hits bottom. It looks like a bottomless pit. Anything could be hiding in it.

He signals, flips over, kicks and begins to descend. Almost as effortlessly, Micah does the same and follows. Then go Reggie and Ash, just as smoothly, and I think that Jake was right, this is a lot easier than I'd expected. Kelly tugs on my arm and we head down.

The shaft continues for what seems like forever. I can feel my ears popping from the pressure. Some of the others can feel it too, because they're puffing out their cheeks to clear our ears as Jake had shown us earlier. We rest for a moment until everyone's ready again. I notice that Kelly keeps drifting upward and kicking himself back down. I make a note to remind him to use more weight tomorrow. I don't want him to have to waste energy keeping himself down.

Suddenly, a thousand bubbles of air dance their way past me. I look down and see Ashley's panicked face. Her flashlight, now forgotten, drifts down into the inky darkness as her hands flutter near her mask. Now I can see her trying to suck air out of a canister that's mostly empty. Her eyes widen and she starts to kick herself up. She shoves Micah aside. But I can already guess that she'll never make it out in time. We're too far inside the building.

Jake shoots past us and grabs her leg. She kicks and kicks, but he doesn't let go. I feel Kelly brush past me, aiming for Jake, thinking he's trying to keep her from saving herself. But before he reaches him, Jake has yanked Ash's goggles off and is holding it below her face. His thumb pushes the blue clearing button and a rush of air surges out and envelops her head. I see her open her mouth. She stops struggling.

After a moment, Jake gestures upward and we begin to surface. I take one last look down into the depths, to where Ashley's flashlight has settled on the bottom of the shaft, its beam stabbing weakly into the unseen chambers. Then I follow.

"I can't do this," Ashley gasps, as soon as her head pops up out of the water. "I can't. I'm sorry."

Reggie swims over to her and grabs the front of her wetsuit and pulls her close to him. "You can," he says. "You're tougher than the rest of us put together, Ash. You're tougher than me. You can do this."

She looks around at us and we all dutifully nod. None of us wants her to back out now, least of all me. I don't want to be the only girl in the group. But I'm also worried, and not just for her. I don't think Reggie truly understands how difficult and risky this will be.

But to me it's clear. Our margin of error is thinner than the edge of a razor.

Chapter Ten

After returning from our practice dive, we laze around in Micah's basement. Micah's halfway through a bottle of his parent's scotch. Kelly's back to playing *Zpocalypto* and Reggie and Ashley have disappeared.

Jake's there, but he's sitting on a folding chair on the other side of the room, watching from the shadows. Kelly reamed him on the way back for not telling us we could use the air in the goggles in an emergency. Jake claimed he was going to, that he wanted to drill into our heads not to rely on it, but it's clear that Kelly doesn't believe him. "What else have you forgotten to tell us?"

"Nothing."

The tension is thick in the room, and I can tell Kelly's just waiting for another excuse to say we're all nuts for trying this. I'm relieved when Ash and Reg return and she grabs my arm and drags me upstairs to find something to eat.

I look for anything with protein, but all I can find is an open bag of stale peanuts. I take a handful and start munching on them. Meanwhile, Ash digs into a carton of mint chip ice cream.

"Want some, Jess?" she asks, holding it out so I can see how badly freezer burned it is. I shake my head and mumble something about keeping my girlish figure. Sugar and I don't play well together. A moment on the lips, as they say, forty minutes on the treadmill. With my metabolism, even three solid hours a week of high intensity hapkido training can't keep an ounce of chocolate from turning into a pound of butt-lard.

Ashley, on the other hand, seems to be able to subsist almost exclusively on a diet of sugar and caffeine. She never exercises, much to my amazement, and yet never seems to gain a pound. Granted, the girl isn't exactly skinny to begin with, but neither is she fat. Her five-foot-five, hundred and twenty pound curvy frame is one hundred percent energy. She burns more calories just breathing for five minutes than I do over an entire tourney weekend.

"Besides, it looks too much like zombie flesh," I tell her.

"Mmm, yum," Ash replies, and we both laugh, even though it's obvious why zombies happen to be on my mind. "You'd think Micah's parents would have more food around," she complains. "At least not expired food. Even the milk in here is old and chunky. What does Micah eat, anyway?"

"Duh. Take out," I say, pointing to the overflowing trashcan.

I've never met his parents. Micah says his father is constantly away on business and his mother is constantly out of the country visiting relatives in Texas or Arkansas. According to him, she's pretty useless.

I know all about useless mothers, have had plenty of experience with one myself, but it seems to me that Micah's really only half correct: If his mom is useless, then didn't that make his father just as bad? He's never around either.

I'd once privately mentioned this to Kelly, but he just changed the subject. Of course, he'd had his hand stuck up my shirt at the time, so I couldn't be sure his response actually counted for anything.

"Honestly," I said, as he struggled with my bra, "has anyone ever seen his parents?"

"Really, Jess?" he complained. "You really want to talk about Micah now?"

"Not him, his parents."

"They're real. Don't worry about it."

There's certainly enough evidence supporting their existence: the pictures hanging on the walls and sitting on shelves, the female hygiene products in the bathroom (yeah, I'm nosy, so just shoot me). Micah's an only child so they can't be anyone else's but his mother's. Plus, the packages addressed to them that I occasionally see sitting around on the counter.

Ashley gazes mournfully into the empty ice cream carton. "Think we should make a run to the grocery store?"

I shake my head. "It's almost dinnertime."

She shrugs, then sets the carton carefully down on top of the trash bin, being careful that it doesn't topple the unsteady heap. I'm tempted to go over and gather the top of the bag and take it outside, but I know Ash would just tease me about being so motherly.

She grabs my hand as we head back downstairs. "I'm nervous about tomorrow," she says. But before I can respond, we're back downstairs, and I can sense she doesn't want me to say anything about her confession. Still, I squeeze her hand to let her know that I understand and feel the same way.

The party breaks up shortly after that.

"Meet back here by seven tomorrow morning," Reggie tells us. "High tide peaks at four, so we'll have till about ten to take advantage of the outgoing current. That means we should be suited up and in the water by eight thirty. Nine, at the absolute latest."

Chapter Eleven

I don't sleep a wink all night, so I'm dragging when I finally get up at five thirty the next morning after checking the clock a dozen times over the space of about ten minutes. A cold shower doesn't even help. I don't feel rested at all. I just feel jumpy.

The house is quiet when I creep down the stairs. Eric's already gone to work, his lone breakfast bowl in the sink waiting for him to wash it after his shift at the police station.

Grandpa doesn't eat breakfast. I don't know if he ever did, now that I think about it. I can't ever remember him doing anything but going out to the back porch for a smoke, his extra large mug of coffee in his hand, steaming into the air. Rain or shine. It feels like such an old habit that it makes me wonder if he's always done that, even back when it would snow. It's been twenty years since Connecticut was cold enough to get any. I bet he did.

I learned long ago to just leave him be. He doesn't like company when he goes out to the railing. He just stands there looking out past our backyard and all the other backyards in the neighborhood. Looking south. He never talks about what he's thinking. He never shares his secrets.

What does he see?

I don't know.

But he's not downstairs yet, so I grab myself some cornflakes and juice and sit down at the table to do a quick check on the Media stream.

Then I raid the cabinets.

I look for anything that won't get ruined if it gets wet: granola bars hermetically sealed in plastic, a bunch of emergency waters in disposable bag containers, a couple oranges. I'm busy packing them into my backpack when I hear someone's throat clear.

"Mom?"

She stands at the entry to the kitchen looking miserable, like a hangover that just won't end, and I realize that pretty much sums things up with her — has pretty much summed them up for the past fifteen years. Her hair's a mess and her nightshirt is stained and worn and has holes in the collar. She smacks her lips unappealingly, then scratches the underside of her left breast.

A shadow shifts behind her and some guy appears and brushes into the kitchen. He slaps her ass and grunts. It's a different guy than the one she brought home yesterday afternoon.

Hey! I want to scream at him. He looks like the wife-beater type, but I could probably take him easily, knock him down a few rungs. "Never be the aggressor," Master Rupert's voice councils me. But my anger shouts even louder: *Don't treat my mother that way.*

She grunts, and I think, *Why do I even bother?* If she doesn't care about herself, why should I?

"What're you doing, honey?" she asks me. The man, thinking she's talking to him, mumbles something about beer.

I sigh. "Just getting some snacks for later." I stare daggers at the man's back, but they bounce harmlessly off. "I don't know if I'll have time to come home for lunch. In fact, I may be late for dinner."

She slips from the wall, tilting like gravity can't make up its mind today which way to pull. She seems to fall into the kitchen. For a split second I expect her to land splat on her face, and my heart almost stops. But she catches herself. She manages to limp to the table and sink into a chair.

Meanwhile, Mister Penis-du-jour is bent over in front of the fridge, probably confused by the milk jug sitting directly in front of the incomplete six pack of Hudson River Pilsner. Micah calls it Piss-ner and refuses to drink it. It's that bad.

"Did you hear me?" I ask. "I might not be home for dinner."

"Okay, honey."

I give her a chuff of disgust before I snatch my backpack from the chair and whirl out of the room. As I do, I hear the top of a beer can pop open. Then a second. The front door slams behind me as I flee.

Kelly sees me from his bedroom window before I turn up his front walk. He intercepts me with a whistle. I tilt my head up and blink against the bright sunlight reflecting off the glass.

"Be right down, J," he whisper-shouts.

I stand in the coolness of the porch overhang and wait. It's already warm. The temperature is supposed to peak at just under a hundred today, and humidity is high. Just another average August day in Greenwich, and the thought of slipping into that cool water actually takes the edge off the fear gnawing at my gut.

The door creaks open and Kelly slips out. He gently closes it behind him, acting as if the soft click of the latch is as loud as a gunshot. I give him a questioning look and he exhales through his pursed lips. He gives me a quick shake of the head. I notice dark circles under his eyes.

When we get to the sidewalk, I ask, "You couldn't sleep either?"

"It's Kyle," he says. "He's finally sleeping now, but he had another rough night last night."

I nod. Kyle's had a tough go of it. He had kidney failure when he was barely two and almost died. He managed to get a new one, but he's always sick. He often has these spells where he spikes a fever and screams as if he's in terrible pain. Nobody knows why. The only thing that makes it stop is exhaustion. But he's a light sleeper and even the slightest disruption can rouse him, starting it all over again.

I can see the strain of this most recent episode on Kelly's face.

"Are you sure you want to do this?" I ask. "I'll stay home with you instead of going. They don't need us."

He turns to me, but the look on his face isn't one of relief. Instead, he shakes his head and says. "No, I'm going." Then he adds, "Someone's got to pay the bills." I know what he's referring to, just not what he means. It's such a random thing that all I can do is simply dismiss it, chalking it up to his fatigue.

The financial strain on the Corbens has been almost unbearable for them. Kelly's dad works two jobs and his mom stays home to care for Kyle. Kelly has offered to start working a part time job — he's also hinted that maybe he should go work for ArcWare after graduating — but his parents are adamant about him going to college.

He hoists his backpack onto his shoulders and together we head over to Micah's.

"What'd you bring?" I ask.

"Lunch. Water. A few . . . other things."

I nod. "Me, too." But his pack looks much heavier than mine and I wonder what 'other things' means.

He sees me looking over. His eyes soften and he says, "It's a surprise."

"A picnic in zombieland? How romantic."

He laughs. "Not exactly."

Micah, Ash and Reggie are already waiting for us when we arrive, a few minutes after seven. I throw my pack into the trunk along with the rest of the gear: a couple other backpacks and a pair of large duffles.

" 'Bout time you guys showed up. Thought you were going to back out."

Reggie gives Kelly a long, meaningful glance, waiting for him to reply. But Kelly doesn't respond. He opens the back door of Micah's car and slides in. I notice he's still got his backpack tucked under his arms.

"Not much of a morning person, is he?"

I roll my eyes and tell him to cut Kel some slack, that Kyle had a rough night. Reggie's aware of the deets — they all do — and he immediately backs off. I'm glad. It just feels like so much of my effort is being spent on pretending everything's fine between everyone to have to pile the Corbens' situation on top of the mix.

I push in next to Kelly. He's got his Link out and is scrolling through it. I peek over his shoulder and see the ArcWare logo flash by.

"Go back," I say.

"What?"

"What was that?"

"Nothing. Just dumping a bunch of old messages."

"Are you applying for a job at ArcWare?"

"I said it was junk, Jessie."

"Can we go, folks?" Micah says, calling over to Reg. "We need to take advantage of the outgoing current. It'll switch directions around ten. I don't want to be fighting it."

Ash and Reg pile into the car. Once more I'm relegated to the middle of the back seat, but it's just a short drive out to the edge of town, so I don't mind. We're meeting Jake behind his uncle's store. From there, we'll head down to Manhattan.

When we arrive, Micah slowly drives around in back, where we see Jake's van with its door popped open. All the windows of the whitewashed building are barred and there's spotlights shining everywhere, even though the sun's up.

After he stops, we all tumble out but leave the car doors open, as if we're afraid of making any noise, setting off any alarms. Micah whistles and Jake slips out the heavily-screened metal door of the store. It bangs shut, making us all jump.

"Uncle Joe's at an auction up in Albany," he shouts down at us, grinning. "There's nobody here." He draws us around to the van and shows us the booty he's gotten for us. "We'll divvy it up when we get there."

Looking at the hodge-podge of equipment, I suddenly realize how little planning we've actually done for this trip. Other than the diving part, that is, and figuring out when to go and come back. And even that now seems pitifully inadequate. For such a dangerous proposition, you'd think we'd be better prepared. It's like we're all in denial. It's been such a surprise how easy everything has happened so far, relatively speaking, that nobody wants to tempt fate by questioning our good fortune.

But now I take the opportunity to bring up the possibility of encountering zombies. I know the others don't believe there'll be any, but still. "Shouldn't we bring weapons?" I ask. "You know . . . just in case."

Reggie wraps his arm around my shoulder and says, "You're a black belt, aren't you? Isn't that considered a lethal weapon?"

Kelly rolls his eyes, but I have to give him credit for not freaking out about Reggie's arm. It seems he can only be jealous of one guy at a time, and right now Jake gets the honors.

Jake holds up a bandolier and pulls a sick-looking knife out of a sheath. "We'll each get one of these." Then he pulls a couple of longer blades from one of the packs. "I've also got a couple machetes, if anyone wants one." He runs his thumb along the edge so we can see that they're not very sharp.

I shudder, and both Ashley and Kelly shuffle uneasily next to me.

Micah steps forward. "We won't need them. They're just going to be extra weight and get in the way. Besides, we'll only be there a few hours. Four tops. We get in, take some pics for proof that we were there, do a little exploring, pick up a couple small souvenirs and . . . ." He pauses and looks at each one of us. I can smell alcohol on his breath, but he appears to be perfectly sober. "Remember, we need to leave there by three o'clock at the absolute latest."

"The Colonel," I say, sighing. "Yeah, I know."

"Actually, I was going to say because of the currents."

"And the curfew," Kelly reminds us.

"Who's the Colonel?" Jake asks.

"My drill sergeant grandfather. He's got it in his mind that I have to be home every night for dinner. He runs the house like he's still a general and we're his Omegas."

Jake frowns in confusion. I wave it off. "It's a long story."

"Bottom line," Micah says, trying hard to get us back on track, "we're not there to take heads. Right, Reg?"

"Aw, why not?" he pouts. "I was all itching to kick some Undead booty!"

"There aren't any, remember?" Micah says. "But in the unlikely event that we do see any, I'm pretty sure they'll be so worn down and slow that you could sneeze on them and they'd fall over."

"Speaking of sneezing," Kelly says, turning to me, "did you remember to bring your inhaler?"

"You're as bad as Grandpa," I say, but when I pat my pockets I realize it's not there. I remember taking it out right after breakfast for the first of my three daily puffs, but then . . . .

Then Mom and her creepy new boyfriend happened. I must've left it on the counter.

I wince, waffle for a moment, then shake my head. "Can we make a quick detour at the house?" I ask.

Micah's face sours.

"I already missed two doses yesterday, plus this morning's."

He checks the time on his Link and grumbles. "We're already running late. Why do you even need that thing? I don't think I've ever seen you have an asthma attack."

"It's not for asthma," Kelly says. He sounds like he's had to explain this a thousand times.

"Then what the hell is it for?" Reggie asks. "Vitamins?"

"I just need it, all right?" I snap. "Please. It'll be quick."

Micah sighs. "I'll run Jessie and Kel over to her house. We'll catch up with the rest of you guys at the parking garage. You can start getting the equipment ready for everyone. If we leave now, we should only be about fifteen minutes behind you."

"How is Jake going to get through the checkpoints?"

Jake points to the back bumper. "It's got interstate tags for commerce. Uncle Joe uses the van when he does deliveries."

"Okay then," Reggie says. "Are we good?"

"I just need to lock up," Jake answers. He reaches for Kelly's backpack. "Want me to take that?"

Kelly swings it out of his reach. "I got it."

He doesn't notice the curious look Jake gives Reggie, but I do, and it makes me wonder once again why Kelly's being so defensive. But Micah tells us to hurry up and get in and even before I've got the back door closed, he's spraying gravel.

Looking back, I see Ash and Reg climb into the van while Jake heads up the steps to lock the shop.

Chapter Twelve

"**Finally!**" Reggie yells at us as we drive into the parking structure. His voice booms through it, sounding eerily hollow.

I had pinged the others to let them know we were going to be later than we'd expected because Grandpa decided to give us the fifth degree and the guards were hassling us.

Apparently the guards also hassled Jake. They'd torn the van apart, searching it. But they found nothing, and finally accepted his explanation that the equipment was for the store.

Kel and I tumble from the car. "Is it too late to go?"

Micah walks over from the rail. He shakes his head. "The tide's still going out. We should be okay."

"The direction of the current will change in about an hour," Jake says, checking his Link. "If we don't leave now, we'll be swimming against it."

This snaps us all to attention.

Ash comes over and hands us our wetsuits. "I've been watching for the cop," she says. "Same as the other day: there's just one on patrol." She looks at Reggie, who tilts his head at her and gives it a quick shake.

He says, "It looks like they're on the same sixty-minute schedule. He comes, hangs around for about ten minutes, then leaves. His last check was twenty six minutes ago, so . . . ." He checks his Link. "We've got about twenty minutes to get suited up, grab our gear and get under water before he returns."

"I still think that's odd," Kelly says. "Why patrol? And why with such regularity? They might as well announce to the world, 'If you want to do something illegal here, you got about thirty or forty minute window to do it in.'"

"Bureaucracy," I say. But something about it troubles me too.

Ashley opens her mouth to speak.

"Enough jibber-jabber," Reggie quickly says. "We need to hurry to make our window. Otherwise we'll have to wait till tomorrow."

Jake has already arranged the gear. Luckily, I've thought to wear my swimsuit under my sweats. The guys did too, but Ashley hesitates. Then she shrugs and strips off her shorts and tee shirt, right down to her undies.

Jake stares openmouthed until Reggie slaps him upside the head. "Give the girl some privacy."

Out of the corner of my eyes, I see Kelly smile.

I go over and block the boys' view.

"I can't believe you forgot your swimsuit, Ash." A part of me wants to believe it was an honest mistake, but I can't help wondering if she did it on purpose, like she's hoping she won't have to go. She pretends embarrassment, but then doesn't even try to be discrete.

"Well, you forgot your inhaler," she counters. I snap my mouth shut. Her actions haven't put the trip at risk. Mine have.

After the suits, we don our knife belts and hoist the waterproof backpacks onto our backs. Each one contains a pair of oxygen rebreather cartridges, light sticks, food and water and any other stuff we've brought. An extra cartridge is Velcroed onto our weight belt, along with a flashlight and another light stick. Each flashlight is attached to us on a short tether, so if we drop it, we won't lose it.

Kelly's off to one side, his back to us, transferring what he brought into the sack he's been assigned. I want to go over and see what he's brought, but I know he'll be upset if I do. He already told me once it's a surprise, and I don't want to ruin whatever it might be. Every once in a while, he gets a little romantic streak in him. Doing something special on LI would definitely give us something to remember.

Jake finishes getting geared up before the rest of us. He passes around our goggles and masks, attaching the cartridges as he goes. "Kelly?" he says, tapping him on the shoulder. Kelly spins around as he stands, his eyes flashing. "Number three, right?"

"I'm three," I say, reaching over for it.

After our practice dive yesterday, Micah put numbered tags on the masks and goggles so we won't have to readjust them. They're in order by our first names.

Jake stares at me for a second before slowly handing me the mask.

"Everything okay?"

"S-sure"

He drops Micah's and Reggie's equipment in their laps. They're busy discussing last minute details. They mumble thanks before resuming.

"No prob."

I glance over at Ashley, remembering how much of a fright she gave us toward the end of our dive. But she looks as cocky as usual, as confident and assured of herself as ever. Maybe it's the way the suit clings to her body and her awareness of the boys' hypersensitivity to it. I don't know, but if she has any of the self-doubt left over from yesterday, she's definitely not showing it now.

Micah packs the last few things in his sack. I notice the old tablet computer and a few other electrical gadgets. I don't bother to ask what he plans on doing with them as it seems pretty obvious. He wants to find an old terminal and see if he can hack directly into the iVZ infrastructure using one of the old nodes.

Whatever. I doubt we'll have enough time to find a working node, much less figure out a way turn it on, if it isn't already, *plus* physically splice into it.

He checks his Link and announces that we've got nine minutes at the most before the next patrol. It'll take us three of them to get down to the walkway, leaving us only six minutes of leeway.

"Ready?" he asks. "Last checks. Let's make sure everyone's good to go."

We buddy-check to make sure there aren't any loose belts or straps and that everything that needs to be sealed is sealed.

"Everyone got their Links?"

We all dutifully hold them up. They're strapped to our wrists so we won't accidentally drop them.

Micah holds his up and says, "Smile." Then we're all snapping photos of each other and laughing. Already I'm dripping with sweat and thirsty from the dry heat of the approaching day.

"Okay, enough of that. Let's go."

We shuffle off after Reggie, looking like a pack of upright seals that happened to get tangled up in a bunch of equipment. Kelly and I trail along in back. I look over and give him a smile. He smiles back, then turns his determined gaze forward again.

Then, before we know it, we're standing at the railing pulling on our flippers.

Nobody hesitates. We're all climbing over and are perched on the other side looking down into the water. None of us wants to think about what we're doing for even a second longer than we already have, because to do so would be to realize the insanity of our plan.

Micah takes a quick look around, then slides into the water, doing a perfect scissors kick that barely makes any noise or splash. We all follow, trying to imitate him.

A moment later, we pop back to the surface: six black lycrene-covered balls bobbing in the water. The coolness of it feels so good on my exposed skin. I was seriously starting to float inside my suit, standing out there in the heat. Everyone else looks just as relieved.

As one, we spit into our goggles, polish and rinse them, then slide them over our faces.

Micah signals to Jake, who slips his mask into his mouth, then his head sinks into the water.

Within seconds, the rest of us join him. The world and the hot sun and the noises of the dry August wind all disappear.

Visibility is about thirty feet. Light sticks begin to glow. A beam of light stabs the murkiness. Then, one by one, five more join it.

At nine thirteen a.m., we slide into the gaping mouth of the Queens Midtown Tunnel.

Part Two

Breaking In

We didn't so much break into Gameland as sneak in, although putting it that way might suggest it was a piece of cake. While it was easier than it should have been, there were more than a few problems, beginning almost as soon as we set off for LI. But each time trouble arose, we pushed even more doggedly on. I've lost count of how many times we should've turned around. At least a dozen. We should've cut our losses, but we didn't. Not once did any one of us even try to force the issue. We just kept right on going.
    Stupid.
    Of course, it wouldn't have mattered. Even before we slipped into that water, it was already too late to turn back.

Chapter Thirteen

Everything grows eerily quiet as the tunnel envelops us in inky blackness. The canned sounds of my own breathing and the ghostly inhales and exhales of my friends around me seem loud. Every once in a while, there's a *click* or a *tap* or some strange rattling noise. The sounds echo all around us, coming from everywhere and nowhere, telling us nothing about what might be making them.

My eyes quickly adjust to the gloom. Five other glow sticks bob about me, looking like pastel St. Elmo's fires: yellow for Micah and Jake, green for Ash and Reg, and red for me and Kel. Six flashlight beams pierce the underwater twilight and illuminate a surprisingly open passageway.

Several of the flashlight beams converge on a vertical divider, separating what was once the southbound and northbound tubes. Micah had mentioned this earlier, and by prior consensus we all kick to the right.

We've gone maybe a hundred yards in — it's hard to tell exactly how far since there's a definite push provided by the current — when my Link pings. I look down at the glowing screen and see it's Ash:

<< U OK? >>

I quickly type back while keeping an eye out for Kel's light next to me:

<< YES. U? >>

<< :o} >>

I type:

<< SO KUL >>

There's a pause and I glance up and try to identify which spot of green light up ahead is hers. Then, I get another ping.

<< :o) >>

I smile to myself and show the messages to Kelly. He nods and gives me a thumbs up, then urges me to catch up with the others.

We encounter our first obstacle about ten minutes later. It's actually not an obstacle, but it does make us stop. I don't see it at first. Kelly puts his hand on my arm and gestures ahead, shining his light.

It's a school of fish, small ones, thousands. Maybe millions. They move like a silver fog, and the water is so thick with them that it seems as if they're a single organism. We float there, entranced, until Micah waves at us and points to his Link, reminding us that we're running out of time.

The next obstacle, about twenty minutes later, nearly forces us to turn back.

It's a huge pile of garbage — boards, pipes, furniture, tree trunks, tires — all dammed up against the hulking carcass of an old bus. Everything's bleached to a universal gray-brown by layers of silt and mud and slime. The windows of the bus are opaque, hiding whatever might be inside. Seeing it, I wonder why there aren't more vehicles down here. I've seen all kinds of objects on the floor of the tunnel, but very few automobiles.

I get an urge to go down and inspect the bus — a sense of adventure, or maybe nervousness at not knowing what's inside — but once more Micah shakes his head. He points forward and I know he's right. We're not here to explore. Maybe if there's time on the way back we can. Of course, by then it won't matter so much. After LI, an old empty bus won't seem so new and exciting, even underwater.

Jake finds an opening against one wall, about half way up. It's roughly six feet wide and just as tall. The current is strong here, so we're careful as we wend our way through it, cautious of any sharp edges and loose objects that might cut us or fall on us.

The path through seems simple enough at first. Some sort of large metal frame appears to be both holding everything in place and preventing it from filling the opening. We grab it for handholds and actually have to "walk" our way through, since the current is quite strong.

Near the other end, we reach a mass of twisted wire and chain link fencing.

I look up just in time to see Reggie's hand slip. He crashes into Ash and together they slam into what looks at first glance like a solid wall. But their impact causes something to shift and pieces of garbage begin to rain downward. Something hits the cage above us, producing a loud *thong!*

We stop.

A large wooden dresser appears out of the darkness above. It tumbles down, heading straight for Ash. Reggie pulls her out of the way at the last second, and the dresser goes rolling lazily into the darkness below, where it lands with a muffled crash.

When the current washes away the mud and silt we've disturbed, I can see two yellow glows hanging in the darkness ahead. My Link pings. It's Ashley telling us she's okay.

Kel and I let go of our perch and slide through the end of the opening and out past the garbage dam. We time our kicks to avoid hitting anything else, twisting and turning past the unstable rubble. Micah and Jake are already ahead of us and closing in on the others.

Once the way ahead is clear, I send her a message back:

<< WAY 2 STAY KUL >>

I'd worried about her losing her air, but it seems that she's handling everything just fine.

She immediately pings back:

<< ABC GUM! >>

I almost laugh.

The screen suddenly blurs. I blink, but when that doesn't help, I try wiping my goggles, thinking they've fogged up. The blurriness remains. *The fog is on the inside of the lenses, stupid!* My head pounds. I'm starting to feel lightheaded.

I'm dimly aware of Kelly grabbing my elbow, but I can't move. He turns and gestures before coming back to me.

He holds up his Link for me to see:

<< OK? >>

I don't answer.

He shakes me.

Then Jake's there. I feel him yank on my belt. My throat hurts and my eyes are burning. Everything seems too bright.

A moment later, everything clears. The ache in my head is still there, but it's fading. My vision is clearing.

He shows me the used cartridge, then his Link:

<< FAULTY >>

Kelly shakes his head and glares as best as he can through his goggles and mask.

As we leave the pile behind, I wonder about that cartridge. Was it just an accident? Could it really be defective? How many of the others' are as well?

The garbage dam disappears into the darkness behind us. The tunnel ahead is wide and tall and, other than the occasional drifts of garbage along the floor and that one huge pile, it's remarkably uncluttered.

Micah — or maybe Jake, I can't tell which, just that it's someone with a yellow glow stick — shines their light on the sides of the tunnel. We drift pass old traffic signs and ancient graffiti, past the tendril remains of old wiring and pipes. Light fixtures dangle from the ceilings and walls, looking a little like the tropical moss that hangs from the trees along the south Connecticut coast.

A sudden burst of bubbles draws my attention to my right. We all hear it, stop and turn to look. It's Kelly and he appears to be struggling with his mask. In a panic, I swim over to him. His hands drop just as I reach his side. He frowns, waving me away. Then he points to his goggles. Relief washes over me as I realize he's just clearing them of water.

Our Links all ping at once:

<< EVERY1 OK? >>

It's Jake. We all give him a thumbs up. I can't really tell with the masks over our faces, but the look Jake shoots Kelly doesn't seem like concern as much as hostility. It's like there's this electric current running between them. But I still can't understand why Jake would harbor such feelings toward Kelly. Or is it just that he's sensing Kelly's jealousy? I don't know.

The look between them lingers a moment longer, then we're off again. I give a kick of my flippers and propel myself through the group. I want Kelly to catch up with me. I want to be in front for a while, instead of always in back and following.

Also, as long as I'm in front, I won't feel like I have to keep turning around and shining my light into the darkness, fearing that something is going to come out after us, a large fish or an alligator. Or shark. It's silly, I know, but I can't help it.

Even though there's this fear, it's not that bad. More like a shadow of fear, or a memory of it. There's obviously a sense of wariness and caution, just not the alarm I'd expect considering the risks we're taking. Maybe our excitement is neutralizing it. Or maybe it's the lack of sleep. I don't really care.

I keep kicking, feeling the strength in my legs. I know it'll be an effort for Kel to keep up, but I don't slow down. My Link pings. I ignore it.

I can feel my pulse beginning to pound inside my head. Out of the corner of my eye, I see a beam of light closing in, then the red glow of Kelly's chemical stick. He reaches out. His hand brushes mine, but I keep moving. That's when I sense the change in the water.

I slow. Then stop. Kelly slides up next to me. He holds his hands up, giving a wondering gesture. I look behind us and see that the group has spread out: two blue glow sticks between us and the two yellow ones further back.

I realize I'm drifting toward them. That's what Kelly's trying to tell me.

I raise my Link and quickly type:

<< TIDE RVRSING >>

I send it to everyone.

I can see the glow of five more Link screens, twinkling as they close the distance. A flurry of messages scroll across my screen, coming from Ash and Jake and Micah:

<< HOW FAR 2 GO? >>

<< WE'RE OK >>

<< NEED 2 HURRY >>

The others reach us, motion for us to stop for a moment. Micah types into his Link and sends it out to the group:

<< STLL TYM. OVR HLF WY. STY STDY >>

I can always tell when he sends a message because he hates using vowels.

He looks at me and gestures, as if knowing my thoughts. I nod, slowly and exaggeratingly: We need to push harder now or else struggle later. I thrust myself forward into the waiting darkness ahead. I can feel the others close behind.

I soon find myself pulling away from the group again. The sound of Kelly's breathing grows fainter behind me. I slow down to let him catch up, but it's Jake who reaches me first this time, Kelly close at his heels.

Kelly's breathing hard. The current is definitely strengthening, though it's not too bad. Yet.

I hear another rush of bubbles, and we all stop and wave our lights around until they find Reggie clearing his goggles. Ash and Kelly take the opportunity to clear theirs. I want to warn Kel to save his air, but I'd only be telling him something he already knows.

My mask is tight against my skin, sealed with Vaseline, as is everyone else's. A little water has leaked in, not much. I go ahead and raise my thumb and find the button just above the bridge of my nose and push.

Pressure on my eyeballs. My ears pop, then there's a sudden snap and my goggles slip away from my face. Everything around me suddenly goes blurry. I wave my hands around trying to find them, but I can't see anything. I drop the flashlight and its beam swings around before dropping to the end of its tether.

Air bubbles burst from my nose. Instinctively, I try to pull them back in and suddenly I'm coughing, choking. My lungs constrict. The air leaves my mouth, but not into the canister. It bubbles past my face and is quickly lost above me. Now my lungs are empty and so is my canister. I can't even find my goggles to use the compressed gas.

My ears are ringing, my throat constricts. I want to open my mouth and inhale and my mind screams at me, *No! No! Don't do it!*

I feel hands on me, on my arms and legs and head. Then my goggles are pushed into place against my face while another hand presses on the back of my head. There's an explosion of air and my vision clears. My lungs are beyond bursting.

The hand behind me forces my head down and another set of goggles is there. I'm not sure how many releases it takes before I realize there's air rushing up and into my face. I open my mouth and gasp, taking in putrid river water and air and I cough and gasp and cough some more and I feel like I'm drowning and going to die.

The air suddenly stops. Luckily, I've recovered my wits a little and my lungs are full. I feel my mask getting shoved into mouth, but I still can't see because of the hands holding the goggles into place, trying to fix the broken headband.

I reach up and try to push them away, but they stay. I bite down and exhale explosively into the canister, then inhale just as quickly. The air tastes stale in my mouth, but it takes the edge off, so I repeat the cycle again and again until the dizziness leaves my head.

Finally, the hands holding the goggles move aside enough so I can see the Link held up into my field of vision. I blink and the screen comes into focus:

<< UR MASK BROK >>

I nod. *No shit.*

The words scroll up and a second line of text appears:

<< OK NOW? >>

I nod again.

<< CANT FIX. TRY 2 HOLD URSELF >>

The text slides up.

<< OR GO W OUT >>

I reach up with both hands and push against the mask. I need them to see. The other hands fall away. Now I can look around me, though my own hands limit my peripheral vision. I see the concerned faces gathered in a circle around me, treading water. Without letting go of the goggles, I manage to hold a thumb up and everyone nods and reciprocates.

They pull away, all except Kelly, who lingers a moment longer. Despite how little of his face I can actually see, what isn't distorted by the goggles and mask, it's obvious he's worried. He holds up his Link so I can read it:

<< DONT DO THT AGN! >>

He leans forward and plants his lips on my cheek. The kiss is cold, but it sends a surge of warmth through me.

He slips beneath me and retrieves the flashlight on the end of its tether and flicks it off, knowing I can't hold it myself now, not without letting go of the mask.

Jake slides into view, gesturing that we need to go. I'm not sure how far we've slipped back in just the few minutes that have passed, but it puts us further away from our destination. Once again, I'm holding the others back.

Embarrassed, I let the others go ahead of me. I hold back a moment, wondering if we should turn around and head home. I won't be able to swim very fast with my hands like this. And dispensing with the goggles so I can doesn't seem like much of an option, either.

Kelly tugs me forward, his hand on my elbow. Despite what I've just gone through, he doesn't even ask if I want to go back. It pisses me off. But already the rest are moving on, and I know he has no choice but to follow.

Neither do I.

Chapter Fourteen

My arms ache. My back is stiff. My legs are burning. And still we swim on.

If not for Kelly's hand on my arm, I don't know how I'd make it, since I can barely steer with just my feet. Even with him guiding me, I feel like I'm fighting against some invisible force that wants to turn me around. I'm moving as much sideways as forward. I try to correct my trajectory by twisting my body, but it doesn't help much, just makes me all the more exhausted.

The yellow and blue glow sticks pull away from us, begin to fade in the distance and the murk. I kick harder. My breathing grows ragged. My body's not used to this particular kind of exercise.

I can hear Kelly beginning to strain, too. Then, without warning, he jerks me to the side. His hand slips off of me and I'm bathed in blackness as the beam from his flashlight winks out.

Kelly?

I twist, but all around me is nothing but black ink and midnight loneliness. I strain my eyes through the goggles. They leak. I push them hard against my face.

Kelly!

But then the beam from his flashlight flickers on. It's way off to one side. It swings around, jerks, then sinks down to the floor. I wonder if the tether somehow came unattached from his belt.

I spin around, kicking to get myself turned, and my flipper connects with something that feels like it has some give to it. I cringe, thinking I've just kicked my boyfriend in the face. But when I extend my legs, there's nothing there.

The light below me changes. I see the faint outline of a figure holding it. The beam swings up and stabs at me. I swing my feet around and once again I feel a momentary resistance behind me.

A bubble of air escapes from my mouth. Water squirts into my goggles.

Kelly?

The light catches me square in the eyes. But then I feel a firm hand on my leg. I realize one of the others has come back, and I relax and wait for whoever it is to come alongside me. Without my hands, without my flashlight, I feel helpless.

The grips tightens, begins squeezing. I grunt when it starts to become uncomfortable. A second hand grabs my other leg.

Kelly's flashlight jerks back and forth below me, coming closer. He's swimming back up. I reach behind me to push the person off — guessing that it's Reggie by his strength — but when I turn to look, it isn't Reg. It's nobody I recognize.

The man's hair floats wildly about his pale face, and his eyes are gaping black holes. His mouth yawns at me and his teeth are yellow and ragged. He pulls himself toward my body. A tongue lolls out. It takes my mind a moment to process that he isn't wearing a wetsuit or a mask or goggles. *That's not possible,* I think, before realizing I'm in the grip of one of the Undead.

Air slips from my mouth and nose. My body contracts. The movement draws the thing even closer to me. The grip has hardened. It feels like a vise. It burns my skin as I kick desperately at it.

One hand lets go, reaches forward. I kick and scream inside my throat, but the hand finds my upper calf. The second hand releases me and somehow manages to grab me just above my knee. I slap at them with the goggles and kick. The zombie leans in to bite me.

But the grip slips on the slick material of the wetsuit, and it slides down my legs. For a moment I think I'm free. But then the hands catch on my flippers. Icy cold fingers wrap around my bare skin and begin marching back up my legs. I can hear the monster's teeth clacking together as it extends it rotting neck and mouth toward me once again, desperate to feed.

Then, suddenly, the thing jerks to the side. The motion pulls me along with it. I see a flash of silver and the weight on one of my ankles falls away. The hand is still gripping me, but it's no longer attached to an arm. I kick wildly, sobbing. Slowly the grip weakens and eventually the hand falls off. The blood seeping from it is thick and oily, staining the water black.

But this only seems to make the zombie angrier. It bats its oozing, jagged stump at me and begins to pull again. There's another thump from the side, another flash of silver, and I see Kelly's knife embeds itself deep into the zombie's neck. He wrenches it free and the wound tears open, revealing a tangled mass of atrophied muscle and veins and the thick cord of the monster's blackened gullet before the water clouds up with its gore. But still it doesn't stop coming.

By now I'm flailing my entire body in a panic. The goggles are gone. I'm kicking and it's not making any difference. I barely manage to remember to bite down and breathe through my mouth into the cartridge. It feels empty.

I remember the knife in my belt. I reach down and pull on the handle, but it won't come free! More air leaks from my mouth. The monster's stump hammers at my flipper.

No! No, no no nononono!

Somehow, my fingers find the snap holding the blade. They flick it open. I pull the knife free and try to bend over. Now the zombie is behind me, just out of reach. I twist desperately and hack blindly at the space near my foot.

More air escapes out of me. I'm feeling it in my lungs now, the lack of air. I'm feeling it in my throat. I'm feeling it behind my eyes and in my head and it screams for me to breathe, to open my mouth and take in a huge breath of air.

Blackness pushes against the edges of my vision.

The knife! Use the knife!

A pinprick of light forms in front of me. Grows. It's warm and whispering comforting things at me: *Breathe now, it'll be all right.*

I'm dimly aware that I'm still hacking, but my movements feel weak and pitiful. The blade connects with something rigid, jarring my arm, rousing me momentarily.

The monster twists and clacks. The knife is nearly wrenched from my hand. I feel the grip on my ankle loosen for a fraction of a moment before tightening again. *I've hurt it!*

I yank the knife free and hack again. There's more resistance, then the weight drops away.

I let the knife go and kick to get away from the body of the monster I can't see, the remaining hand still attached. Blinded by darkness and oxygen deprivation, my eyes burning from the filthy water, I reach down to pull it away.

The fingers are like plastic bands. I pry desperately at them. My stomach revolts, but to be sick now would be fatal. I finally manage to loosen the hand just as a bright light begins to fill my vision. *Kelly*, my mind prays, but deep down I know it's not him. The whiteness is in the space behind my eyes. It's my brain shutting down. The whispers grow loud inside my head.

I feel something caress my face. I open my mouth and water flows in. I cough, sputter, and open it again. I inhale just as another balloon of air envelops me. Kelly forces the mask into my mouth and holds it there, pinching my nose, willing me to breathe into my canister.

After a few minutes, I open my eyes. He holds me like that for several more minutes, until the black light inside me and the whispers fade away.

When I'm ready, he points the beam of his flashlight down into the darkness below us. I can't see much without the goggles. I don't know if he's showing me the zombie; I kick to get away, but he holds me until I stop struggling.

Once more he points the light down, then at his face, then at me. He means that we need to go down and find my goggles.

Still shaking from the encounter, still weak from lack of oxygen, I try to follow. He goes slowly, waiting for me.

When we reach the floor, he begins to search, sweeping his light back and forth. The floor is littered with objects washed in over the years. It all just looks blurry and shapeless to me.

I begin to think it's hopeless when his light reflects off something shiny. Kel dives down and comes up with my knife. He pushes it back into my sheath. Then he goes back down.

After a few more minutes of searching, he returns, shaking his head. He points to his own goggles, offering them to me. I tell him no and gesture that we need to go. We're completely alone. There's no sign of the other four. They haven't even noticed we're not with them anymore.

Kel grabs my hand and together we rise toward the ceiling. If the current wasn't pushing at us, forcing us back toward Manhattan, it'd be easy to mistake which direction we need to go. We angle toward the nearer end of the tunnel, not sure if maybe we aren't making a mistake anyway.

Within minutes, a point of light appears in the darkness ahead. It swings around like a strobe and grows quickly stronger until it fills the tunnel. I shield my eyes. A second beam joins the first. We swim hard for them. Finally, I see two yellow glow sticks dangling just below the light beams. Micah and Jake pull up beside us, gesturing frantically. Micah holds up his Link.

I reach down and pull mine up to my face, holding it close to my eyes to read. There's an old message there from Micah and it reads:

<< WHR R U? >>

I delete it and a second message pops up from a minute or so later:

<< ANSR PLZ! >>

Micah quickly types in a new message:

<< FASTR! >>

Anger fills me. There's no wondering whether we're okay. No asking what held us up. No apology for leaving us behind. I was attacked by a fucking zombie! I could have been bitten!

Excitement flashes in his eyes. He jabs his thumbs once more at his screen. My Link receives his post:

<< NRLY THR >>

I want to cry. I want to scream and kick and hurt someone, but I'm suddenly exhausted. Numbness overwhelms me. Kelly gently prods me forward and I follow. I can feel myself drifting into shock.

Sometime later — seconds? hours? I have no idea — I sense the blackness of the tunnel begin to weaken. I start to see the faintest details: seams in the walls, objects lying on the floor below. Even without goggles and a light I can see. We've reached the end of the tunnel. It begins to arch upwards and light breaks over us in ever stronger waves. We've done it. We've officially broken into LI.

And yet I'm too shaken to celebrate.

A moment later, we pop up out of the water. At a minute before eleven in the morning I get my first glimpse of a city that was abandoned to the Undead.

Chapter Fifteen

Reg and Ash join our floating circle. Everyone's speaking all at once, asking questions, laughing, yammering, demanding where the hell we were and what took us so long. They don't realize anything terrifying happened down there.

Jake notices my missing goggles and asks about them. He seems more worried about them than he is about me, but that may just be me being oversensitive.

Neither Kelly nor I answer any of their questions. Kelly brusquely waves them off, growling that we need to get me to land. I'm grateful for his strength. I'm grateful that I don't have to say anything or even think. I wouldn't be able to string two coherent thoughts together, must less words.

My shaking has grown much worse, as if my body knows that safety is within reach.

Or knowing that I'll have to face that horrible experience aging on our way back. I don't know if I'll be able to do it. Or how.

I'm faintly aware of Micah talking. He's telling us that the overpass where we've surfaced is too high to climb. It rises six feet over our heads. The wall extends to both sides, stretching about a hundred and fifty feet before turning back toward us. We spin around. The water reaches into the distance, fanning out wider and wider as it reaches the horizon.

Reggie points to a place where the chain-link fence has been pushed from its poles and now dangles into the water. It's only thirty feet away.

"We can climb that," he says.

He sounds as tired as I feel, and now I can see the fatigue on everyone else's face, the strain. And maybe a little disappointment, too. I don't know what they were all expecting — I know what I was before my underwater encounter: Pristine buildings, a preserved city. But all I see here is bleached out structures that look run down and dirty.

The place is a ghost town. But, thankfully, it appears to be just as abandoned as Reggie had claimed it would be.

Or maybe that's why they're disappointed.

Kelly pulls me toward the fence. I let him. I can't seem to find the strength to move, so I just drift. Where does he find the energy? I look over at him and notice that he's straining his neck above the surface. He's scanning for any signs of trouble on land.

Despite having to tow me, Kelly's the first to reach the fence. He makes sure I'm holding onto it before he peels off his flippers and tosses them over. Then he climbs up. The fence sways and clangs, sounding too loud in the eerie quiet.

"Looks clear," he says, after a quick but thorough look around. The rest of the group begin to clamber up. Kelly reaches down and helps me. My arms are shaking so badly that I can barely hold on. I still have my flippers on. He practically has to drag me up.

I immediately sink to the ground. Everyone else is peeling off their equipment and unzipping the tops of their wetsuits. The sun is baking us, but I'm shivering.

Kelly doesn't bother with his equipment. He finds an abandoned car on the tunnel overpass and climbs up onto its roof. It's covered in dust and rust and tufts of grass. It creaks and rattles. He cups his hands around his eyes and scans the horizon. Reggie is the first to notice his odd behavior. He chuckles.

"Check out the brah! Already looking for IUs. I told you before there won't be any."

Kelly's eyes flash and he jumps off the car and rushes over. He slams Reggie in the chest and screams, "No zombies? Then what the fuck was that down there?" He points at the tunnel and everyone looks, confusion clouding their faces.

"Where?"

"In the goddamn tunnel, asshole! Where the hell were you?" Kelly turns to each of the others, glaring. "We were attacked by one down there! Jessie could've been . . . ."

His eyes suddenly grow wide and he rushes over to me. "Were you bitten?"

I shake my head.

The others are watching all of this in shocked silence. Then Ashley leaps to her feet and points at Jake and Reggie. "I told you guys we should've told them!"

Kelly's eyes narrow. "Told us what?"

Reggie sweeps over and stands between them. "We didn't know, Ash! How could we have known it was a zombie? It was too far away. We still don't know!"

Ashley ignores him. She peers around Reggie to speak directly to Kelly. "We saw one. And don't tell me it wasn't a zom either, Reg, because I know what I saw! Back there. Damn it, I knew it was a zombie, but you said it was just some homeless guy who fell in the water!" She hits Reggie on the chest.

My head snaps up. "What?" My throat hurts and my voice croaks. "You saw a zombie and you didn't think to warn us? You didn't ask, *Where the hell are Kelly and Jessie? Maybe they're in deep shit?* You just left us back there!" My voice has risen to a screech. I'm nearly in tears by now. "What the hell were you thinking? I almost got bitten! I almost fucking drowned!"

Nobody says anything for a moment, then Jake says, "It wasn't in the tunnel."

As if *that* excuses why they left us behind.

Kelly whirls on him. He's shaking with rage and sputtering almost incoherently. Finally a single word explodes from his lips. The f-bomb shatters into a million pieces across the city. In the distance, a flock of pigeons lifts off the ground before settling back down again a moment later.

Jake is clearly shaking. "It was while we were waiting for you in the garage. When Micah took you back to get Jessie's medicine."

"What the hell are you talking about?" Kelly screams.

"Keep it down, guys," I say. But the words somehow dry up in my mouth and flutter away like dust.

"I told you," Ashley cries. She hurries over to where I'm kneeling on the hot asphalt. "I told you we should have told them what we saw." She points at Jake again, thrusting an accusing finger at him. "But you just kept agreeing with

Reggie. Why the hell would they call in NCD for a homeless guy?"

NCD?

"They called in Necrotics?" I stammer. "Was it Eric?"

Jake backs away. Reggie glares around himself looking like he wants to punch someone. Then he suddenly bends and picks up a chunk of rock and heaves it far out over the water. The splash sounds clunky and doesn't even echo. "We didn't know for sure what we saw," he mutters. "And, no, Jess, your brother wasn't there. At least, we didn't see him."

"Now we know why the cops patrol down there by the tunnel opening," Kelly says. "They're checking for swimmers."

Reggie shakes his head. "No! You said it yourself, Kel. If they were so concerned about breaches, why wouldn't they just block the opening?"

Nobody speaks. It's a valid question, one we've all been wondering for days now. Why make it so easy for zombies to get through? For that matter, why make it easy for people, too?

"It wasn't a zom," Reggie concludes. "It couldn't have been."

"Then why call NCD?"

"Swimmers?" I ask, shaking my head. Logically, I know zombies can't swim. In the water they're just as helpless as logs, drifting with the currents. But the one that grabbed me sure felt like it had taken lessons.

Kelly waves his arms helplessly. "Well, what else are we going to call them?"

"Floaters," Ashley says.

"The one that attacked us wasn't floating. It was like it was waiting for us."

"It wasn't waiting for us, Jess," Kelly says, but even I can see the doubt in his eyes. "It just happened to be there, I think."

I swing my head to Ashley. My neck feels stiff and creaky. "You actually saw them pull one out? Before we left?"

"What we saw," Reggie quickly answers for her, "was a cop dragging a body out of the water. A *dead* body. It wasn't moving, so, no, I seriously doubt it was a zombie. Besides, even if it was a zombie, it was dead. Don't you get it? It was totally dead. We had no way of knowing there'd be more in there. *Live* ones."

"He used a hooked pole and dragged it out onto the walkway," Ashley mumbles. "We watched as he pinged someone on his Link. A couple minutes later, NCD came in a van and carted it away."

"They didn't even use gloves!" Jake insists.

"What the hell does that prove?" Kelly snaps. "That doesn't mean it wasn't a zombie!" He grabs Jake's tee shirt and pulls them together until their faces are inches from each other. My mind screams at Kelly to be careful, but all I can do is moan. Jake doesn't fight back. "Everyone knows it takes more than skin to skin contact to pass the infection! It takes a bite. Of course he didn't wear gloves!"

"But, water— " Jake begins to argue.

"Bullshit!" Kelly's eyes shift over to me. Everyone's looking at me now, wondering if I swallowed any water down there. They have to be thinking I might've been infected. "Wearing gloves doesn't mean shit, you idiot!"

Ash hugs me closer. "Don't worry," she whispers into my hair. "G-ma Junie was wrong about that. Water can't transmit the infection."

I know she's just trying to cheer me up, to help me get past the attack in the tunnel, but it doesn't help.

I push her away and lean over to one side. The remains of my breakfast cornflakes and all the river water I swallowed come pouring out of me. Ash jumps back, not wanting to get splashed. The others watch in horror, afraid to get too close to me.

When I'm done, I feel a lot better. I get weakly to my feet and say, "We're wasting time. It must've been a fluke. There aren't any more zombies here, obviously, so let's do what we came for and get the hell back home."

I've lost all my enthusiasm for this game. I'm not having fun anymore.

The rest glare at each other for several more seconds before finally nodding. They busy themselves finishing stripping off their gear and stowing it. Ash and I leave our wetsuits on, keeping them unzipped to the waist.

While they're distracted, I pull my inhaler out of my pack. I take a long, deep hit. Then a second.

Just to be sure.

And I pray to God that G-ma Junie was right about the disease not being spread by water.

Chapter Sixteen

Reggie decides that we should all stash our diving equipment inside the trunk of the abandoned car Kelly had climbed on earlier.

"But keep your knives with you," he recommends. So we strip away the rest of the gear from the bandoliers and rebuckle them on our waists.

He opens the front door and reaches in and pops the latch. We all lean away, as if expecting something to come crawling out at us. But the trunk is empty, save for a spare tire, a single men's shoe — size nine and a half — and an umbrella. He tosses in his pack, mask and goggles. We each follow suit.

Micah's off to one side, messing with his Link and mumbling to himself. Reggie goes over to get his gear, but Micah waves him off. "Give me a sec."

"Ooh," Ashley says. She reaches into the trunk and pulls out the umbrella. She has to struggle a bit to open it up, and when she does, the fabric is so dry and flimsy that it immediately begins to disintegrate. Black flakes rain down on her head. What's left of it looks like a month-old sun-baked carcass: just the ribs and a few flaps of skin-like fabric barely hanging on.

Her silliness makes me laugh, and my laughter signals to everyone that it's okay to relax. I lean over and whisper in her ear that I'm glad she came.

"What should we do first?" Reggie asks, pouncing on the uptick in our moods.

Kelly glances over at me. His face is still filled with concern.

"I'm fine," I say. "Really. I'm actually up for a little distraction." I pause and add, "Just, a little, though. And promise me no more zombies. If I never see another one as long as I live, I think I'll die a happy woman."

"But then you'll have to be one," Jake says with all seriousness.

Everyone gives him a dirty look and his face flushes deep red.

"Are you always this clueless?" Kelly asks.

"Uh, guys?"

We all look up. Micah's off about fifty feet away, standing and staring off into the distance. He slowly turns to us, then raises his hand and points.

We all get up and walk over.

About a quarter of a mile away is a solitary figure. It doesn't move.

"Is that what I think it is?"

We strain our eyes, but it's too far away to tell. "Looks like a tree," Reggie says. "Or a statue."

"Or maybe it's a homeless guy," I say.

Jake reaches into his pack and withdraws a pair of binoculars. He trains it on the figure and adjusts it.

"Sorry, Jess. It's a zom. Naked. It's skin . . . ." He shivers. "Now I know what standing outside in the sun every day for thirteen years will do to you."

"Is it . . . dead?" Ashley asks.

"It's not moving."

He scans with the binoculars all around us before announcing there aren't any more.

"We'll just keep an eye on it, then," Micah decides. He comes over to me and asks if I'm okay. I nod.

"I don't know about the rest of you," Ashley says, "but I'm starving. I think we should eat."

"Beef jerky?" Reggie jokes. Everyone groans. But then he pulls a Slim Jim from his pack and laughs. "I was sort of hoping we'd see one just so I could do this."

"You really are a disgusting pig."

I grimace and clutch my stomach. It's still a bit touchy. "Not for me."

Kelly pulls out a Red Bull and opens it for me. "At least drink something then."

"It's warm."

"Drink."

I notice that nobody teases him for mothering me.

When we're done eating and resting and Jake has confirmed that the zombie hasn't moved in the last twenty minutes, Ashley jumps up and exclaims, "Pictures! We need pictures."

She whips out her Link and hands it over to Micah, ignoring Jake's outstretched hand. Jake gets this embarrassed look on his face and pretends he was reaching for something else. I can't help but feel a little twinge of guilt for him. He's trying so hard, but he's so obviously not figured out how to be a part of the group. I doubt he ever will.

Ashley plucks the umbrella from where she dropped it and starts parading around with it over her shoulder. She twirls it and says, "I feel like one of those flappers from a hundred years ago."

"More like a hundred and twenty years ago," Kelly says.

"Dude, do you have to be so freaking — I don't know — *literal* all the time?" Reggie says, then quickly adds, "Just messing with you, brah. Chillax."

Micah snaps a couple pictures of everyone in various poses, including a few zombie poses that strike me as both amusing and vaguely unsettling. Then he announces that he's got things to do.

"You guys go ahead. I'm going to try a few quick computery things. He pulls the old tablet from his pack, and a tangle of wires trails out.

"Still think you can hack into iVZ?" Ashley says.

Micah shrugs. He presses a button on the side to boot it up. "It's worth a try."

I frown. "Why? It's already coming on noon. We've only got a couple hours or so before we should get ready to leave."

"Um . . . because." He looks around us, as if it's obvious why. "We couldn't get into *The Game* before, but now that we're inside the ArcTech firewall . . . ." He shrugs and points to a spire in the distance. It's one of many that rise from the top of the wall every quarter mile or so. They're supposed to prevent implanted zombies from breaching the perimeter by frying their L.I.N.C.s if they cross it. It's also there to keep hackers from breaking in. Hackers like us.

Because of the intervening buildings, we can't actually see the wall at the moment, but we can see the EM towers poking up above the buildings. The air around them glimmers, almost as if we're looking through water. I know it's just an illusion, but it sure seems real.

Micah taps a few things on the screen and holds it up for us to see. It shows a map of where we're at and a cluster of tiny red dots. He zooms in and the dots assume labels. We all gasp.

"Hey, that's us!"

"You hacked our implants?" Ashley cries. Her hand instinctively reaches behind her head, as if she could block whatever connection Micah has made to it.

He shakes his head. "Actually, not directly. It was easy to hack your Links, and from them get your L.I.N.C. numbers. Once I had those, I coded in our implants into this old tracking app and embedded it within a geolocator." He points to the tower again. "The signals ping off the towers within range and triangulate back to me."

"Subtitles, please?" Jake says, looking bewildered.

"It means he can track wherever we go," Kelly says.

"W-why?"

"Wait a minute," I say. "Does that mean *anyone* can track us? At any given moment?"

Micah frowns at me. "Like the government isn't tracking each and every one of us already?"

"So, they know we're here?"

Micah shakes his head. "No one outside the wall can track us in here. The EM masks our signal, preventing anyone on the outside from seeing anyone inside. That's why nobody can hack the Players' implants. The only way to connect with them is through ArcWare's iVZ codices, which are tuned specifically to their nodes." He points to the EM spires. "And I'd be willing to bet you there's a node in each and every one of those towers."

Jake's still looking totally lost, but the direct implication of Micah's hacking is easy for the rest of us to calculate: another chance to access *The Game* and actually play it.

"It's simple, brah," Reggie patiently explains. "If you break the iVZ programming language, you can read *The Game*. But you still need to be able to connect to the Players. That's what the tracker does. That's basically what the ArcWare codex does. It's just a device. Anyone could build one, but without being able to speak its language, it would be useless. ArcWare uses a proprietary coding format written in interweaving layers, but now that we're inside, the entire language architecture is completely exposed."

"Meaning?"

"Meaning after we return," Reggie exclaims, "we'll be able to build a descrambling device and play *The Game*!"

Micah holds up his hand. "I still need to see if I can actually find and track Player signals. That's why I needed to hack your L.I.N.C.s. First, to prove the concept, then so I can subtract them out as background."

"I don't care about *The Game*," Jake declares. "And I don't want you tracking me!"

Micah chuckles. "I'll wipe all your numbers after we get back. Don't worry. It's only temporary."

Reggie slaps him on the back and says, "What are you doing standing around for, then? Get moving!" He rubs his hands together. "I can't wait to get back and wreak some havoc on some real zoms. No more *Zpocalypto* for this guy."

Ash's face lights up too, at the prospects. Even Kelly looks a bit more excited than a moment ago.

But something bothers me. If Micah is able to hack and track the Players' implants, then obviously the next step is learning how to control them. That's essentially the point of all this. So, if he's able to do that, what's to stop him from doing the same to us? Other than his promise not to, I mean.

I try to dismiss the thought. He said he'd get rid of our implant numbers. Besides, if it were even possible, then surely someone would've tried it already. As much as I distrust the government, they wouldn't allow something like that to happen, would they? Our implants are supposed to be inactive until we die. That's what the *latent* part of their name means.

Nevertheless, I keep my thoughts to myself. I don't want anyone else thinking it, or worrying over it. Or getting any ideas. Micah's not the only one of us with the skills to accomplish such a thing.

I turn around to retrieve my backpack and find Jake watching me. Our gazes lock. There's worry on his face. Despite his admission of technical ignorance, somehow I suspect he's made the connection. The same thoughts and fears are going through his head, too.

Chapter Seventeen

Micah repacks his bag and heads for the closest EM tower. "I'll ping everyone once I get in," he says. "And I'll send your Links the app so you can track each other, too."

"I don't want to track us," Jake says, still protesting. "And I don't want anyone to track me!"

"Think about it like this, Jake: This way, we'll be able to see any implanted zoms too. Not saying there are any here, but wouldn't you want to know if there were?"

"Lot of good it does us." He points at the lone zombie and says, "You still can't track the them. IUs don't have implants."

Micah shrugs. "IUs are harmless." He shoots me a look and winces. "Well, maybe with one or two exceptions. We still don't know if that one was a rogue escaped from one of the work details back on Manhattan, right?"

Jake frowns, obviously not convinced. "How about some company then?" he asks. "Besides, you'll be safer with someone watching your back."

Or watching over his shoulder.

"No, but thanks, Jake. You'll just distract me. Don't worry. I'll be fine. Go have some fun. You'd just be bored if you came with me." He checks his Link. "Let's plan on meeting back here around . . . two. If not sooner. Ping if anything comes up. We should leave by two thirty so we don't have to fight the current again."

Ash and Reggie are standing off to one side whispering to each other. I'm about to ask what they're planning on doing when she giggles and slaps his arm. Reggie glances over at us and grins.

"Ash and I are going to check some things out," he says. He looks around and his gaze stops in the direction of an old Holiday Inn. "Over there."

"Want some company?" Jake asks, again.

I roll my eyes. *He really is that clueless!* Then again, could Ash and Reg really be that horny? We've got a couple hours to explore the abandoned city and they're going off to mess around. *Really?*

Reggie shakes his head. "Naw, brah." He wraps his arm around Ash's shoulders. She looks so small standing next to him. "I think I can handle this alone."

Ash cocks her head up at him and smirks. "A bit overconfident, are we?"

Jake realizes too late what they're talking about. He turns to me and Kelly, his face red.

"No," Kelly snaps, before he can say anything.

"Why not? I said I was sorry about the zombie thing back there."

Actually, he didn't. But while I may be willing to let that slide, Kelly clearly isn't. "I don't remember hearing any kind of apology from you," he spits. "And even if I did— "

"Kel." I frown and tell him to cut the guy some slack.

He sighs and says, "Fine, you can tag along with us. Like a little puppy. It's not like I wanted to spend a little *alone* time with my girlfriend or anything."

"Really?" I say. "That's what you want to do?" I jut my chin out at Reggie's and Ash's receding figures. "Is that all I am to you is a sex toy?"

"That's not what I meant! I got something else in mind." He pats his pack. "But don't ask, because as I said, it's a surprise."

"Ooh, I can't wait."

He rolls his eyes.

There's a cluster of high rises due south of us a couple blocks away. Kelly points in that direction and says he wants to see how high up off the ground we can get. "Maybe we can see over the wall from one of the windows. Wouldn't it be cool to get a pic of Manhattan from here?"

"Pictures? That wasn't the type of surprise I was expecting," I say, but he just smiles like he already knows that.

Jake looks doubtful. "Shouldn't someone stay here and make sure our stuff is safe?" he asks.

"Safe from what? Look around you. Do you see anything that's going to mess with our equipment? Pigeons?"

"Zombies?"

We all turn and look at the solitary figure in the distance. It still hasn't moved.

"Are there two?" Jake says, squinting.

"Shut up."

"No, seriously." He lifts the binoculars and looks through them. "There are two of them."

"Let me see," Kelly says.

He looks for a moment, then shrugs. "There's two. But maybe the other one was standing behind the first and moved a little. At that pace, they'd reach us in, oh, about six weeks."

Despite what happened in the tunnel, I have to laugh. Besides, Jake's concern is misplaced. What would a couple of zombies want with a bunch of diving equipment? The only thing that drives them — drives their 'life force' or whatever you want to call it — is human flesh.

"It'll be fine," I say.

"On second thought," Jake says, "you guys go on. I think I'll just hang out around here."

"Yes!" Kelly says.

"Kelly, no."

He frowns at me.

"Safety in numbers. Remember? Jake should come with us."

"He *wants* to stay here."

"I don't think it's such a good idea, Kel."

"You didn't say that when Micah left, alone."

"Micah can take care of himself."

"And Jake can't? He's a big boy." Kelly smirks at him. "He seems to think so, anyway."

This makes my anger flare again. "Why are you acting this way, Kelly? It's Jake, not Reg! Or Micah." I whirl around to face him. "I don't know what's going on between you and Jake, but you both better knock it off!"

"I didn't do anything," Kelly complains.

"No, but if it weren't for Jake, you wouldn't even be here. You're being a thankless prick."

"Prick? I didn't even want to come here in the first place!"

"Hey, guys," Jake says, "I'll be fine. Really. You don't need to argu— "

"We're not arguing!" Kelly shouts.

"Stop shouting," I say. "You want the zombies to hear us?"

He laughs and makes a show of waving his arms and shouting. "Hey! Hey! Look! Brains! Come get some."

"Quiet!"

"Like your shrieking earlier wouldn't have drawn their attention?"

"Shrieking? You make it sound like it was over nothing."

"Guys! I— "

"You shut up! You weren't even there when I was attacked," I scream.

"You know something?" Kelly says, throwing his hands up in the air. "Fuck this. I can't take it. Stay here with Jake the Flake for all I care. I'm outta here!"

"Kelly— "

He stomps off.

I know I should run after him, but I also know that's what he wants me to do. This is all about him and Jake. It's about their false idea that I'm supposed to make some imaginary choice between them. I don't know why he's become so moody over the past couple of weeks, but it's really getting on my nerves.

"Fine!" I scream at his back. "Fuck you, too! And I *will* stay with Jake!"

I'm sorry as soon as it comes out, but then he turns back around and gives me this look. There's a darkness in his eyes that I can't ever remember seeing in them before. And sadness.

I expect him to yell back at me. I expect him react in kind.

But all he does is shake his head.

"I'm sorry," I want to say. I open my mouth, but nothing comes out.

"I'll be back in an hour," he says. "Or two."

Then he turns around and walks away.

Chapter Eighteen

"So who's G-ma Junie?" Jake asks.

"What?"

"I heard Ashley mention her to you earlier."

I flick a pebble from the railing into the water. It makes a soft plunk and sinks away. The sun's baking my back and my shoulders are starting to burn. Now that I've dried off I'm starting to sweat. I consider taking off the wetsuit completely, but I just can't be bothered.

"Ashley's grandmother," I tell him. "Was, anyway. She ... died. This past spring."

He nods. "I didn't know."

I turn my head to stare at him, wondering why he'd assume he would. All he was to Ashley before this was her lab partner. It wasn't like they were friends or anything. And after this little jaunt of ours, it's likely she'll drop him like shoddy programming. I just don't see him continuing to be a part of our group.

On the other hand, I'm beginning to wonder if any of us will be able to go back to the way we were before all this. Kelly and I are drifting away from each other, faster and faster it seems. Meanwhile, Reg and Ash are looking more and more like a full-time couple, squeezing the rest of us out of their lives.

Even if we continue to hold it together, I just can't see how Jake might fit into the new scheme of things.

"What happened to her?" he asks. "Do you know? Where'd she get sent?"

I hear her voice again inside my head, telling me how she'd rather be a Player than be stuck on guard duty or sewer cleanup.

Probably the last words she ever spoke to me were that very wish.

I take in a deep, shuddering breath and peer out over the water. Except for the sound of the wind and birds, the whole place is quiet. Disturbingly so.

It's so hard to believe that in just a short dozen or so years, this entire island has gone from being overrun with thousands of the Infected Undead, killing the living, turning them into thousands more, to being this deserted. But it has. It's now just a pathetic, empty wasteland. Well, almost empty.

It makes me wonder why nobody has come to take the island back.

Actually, somebody did, didn't they? Arc Properties came, the big conglomerate of companies spanning every major industry there is. ArcTech. ArcWare. ArcBio. But what they wanted wasn't to bring the living back to this place. It was to fill it with more of the Undead: new zombies, stronger and fresher and faster, *implanted* zombies that can be controlled. Players.

What people are willing to do in the name of profit.

The Gameland arcade, at least according to Micah, is thirty miles east of us, centered on a place called Jayne's Hill. That's where the transmission tower is, the island's highpoint. But how he could know all that when the exact details are a secret is beyond me. Regardless, we're miles outside its boundaries.

I clear my throat. It's dry, so I take a drink from my collapsible water bottle before answering Jake's question.

"Her parents think she got sent to some remote place up in North Dakota. That's where they're guessing, anyway. I hear they use a lot of CUs there for border patrol."

"CUs?"

"Conscripted Undead. Or Controlled Undead. Depends on who you ask. Zombies with implants."

He nods. "When I go, I think I'd rather be one of the Omegamen."

I look him over for a second. "Yeah, well, die young and easy — a bullet to the heart or from massive internal injuries from an accident or something — and you can pretty much count on it. Or commit murder. That's the fastest way to become an Omega. You'd make a good soldier."

He smiles and straightens himself a little bit. "You think so?"

I roll my eyes.

"It's everyone's obligation to serve," he lectures me. "Just think how it would be if we had to send the living into battle."

I don't say anything. I know the arguments by heart. All too well, in fact. It doesn't help being related to the person who first proposed that the government militarize the zombies they'd created. Grandpa considered himself a hero for envisioning an end to all wars. But in the end, it broke the country apart and lead to its total isolation from the rest of the world.

"You don't get a choice," I tell him.

"They should at least tell you where they send your deceased relatives for their conscription."

"You know how the government is about sharing that sort of information. People would just want to go see them or . . . ." I let the thought drift off.

Or try to put them down.

"Unless you're highly connected, you can just forget about finding out. And if you're that connected, you can probably afford to buy out your LSC and be incinerated right away."

Jake turns around and leans his back on the railing. He makes like he's stretching, but out of the corner of my eye I can see him looking around. He stares off in the direction of the zombies for a moment.

"I suppose it could be worse," he says, lifting the binoculars to his eyes. "The idea of getting blown to bits somewhere in China or Texas gives me the creeps." He shudders. "At least if you're a sewer cleaner or a guard there's something to incinerate after your three years are up."

"Yeah, turkey jerky," I say. He gives me a strange look and I add, "You said it yourself: that's what happens to a zombie after standing out in the hot sun for a few years."

"The Undead don't know heat or pain."

"Maybe not."

"One of them's gone."

He hands over the binoculars and I look. "Probably crawled back into its hole. The other one hasn't moved at all."

We stay there like that for several minutes. The next time he speaks his words both surprise me and explain a lot: "I totally had a crush on you last year."

I turn to him, trying to keep my face neutral. Trying not to look surprised. I don't know if I succeed. "Look, Jake," I say. "You're a nice guy, but . . . ."

He waits. I want to tell him he's not my type, but it's such a cliché. And, besides, why would he tell me this now? Kelly and I had a little fight is all. It's not like we broke up, leaving an opening for Jake to step into.

I sigh and shake my head. "You wouldn't like me as much if you knew me better. I can be a total bitch sometimes."

"I don't think you— "

"How about we talk about something else for a while?"

He swallows, but the way he holds my gaze makes me feel like I'm the villain.

"You ever know anyone who got sent to *The Game*?" he asks after several more minutes pass.

And so we've come all the way back to G-ma Junie again.

I hand him back the binoculars and say, "They don't usually last very long." I know it totally doesn't answer the question. "A few weeks at most."

"I've seen Players on *Survivalist* leave *The Game* after only one day. God, that's got to be so embarrassing."

I can see why people would want to become Players. At least then a portion of the winnings goes back to the family. The longer you stay in, the more money you get. That's why Operators — gamers who control CUs — are willing to pay top-dollar for the best, the freshest, and the strongest zombies. Even if they have to obtain them illegally.

"Do you think it's true?" Jake asks, as if he can see inside my thoughts. "Do some people sell themselves into *The Game*?"

I shake my head. But once more it makes me think about G-ma Junie. I know it's just my own suspicious nature, but it was like she was there one day, a young fifty-three-year-old woman with a good eleven years left before her LSC, and then, the next day she was gone. Just . . . gone. And what's more, Ashley's parents suddenly seemed to have some extra money.

How else could she have ever afforded a Ronnie Marx bathing suit?

But, no. I can't believe something like that. I just can't see G-ma Junie as a Player. No Operator would ever buy someone as old and worn out as she was.

I shake my head. "No, I don't think so," I finally reply.

Chapter Nineteen

Two more zombies have joined the first. We watch them, fascinated by their incredibly slow, patient waltz. We wonder what they're doing and why they seem to congregate in that one spot. What's there? Did an animal die there or something? Do they even eat wild animal meat if they can't get human flesh?

"It's like they're having a meeting or something."

"Yeah, discussing the weather. 'Hey, Bill, how ya feeling today?' 'Same as always, Frank. A little stiff.' "

Jake snorts.

"They must draw each other by their movement and sound."

"I guess we're too far away for them to notice us then."

I nod and squint at their tiny figures. They seem to appear out of nowhere, then disappear again, as if melting into the ground. But it's just an illusion, a trick of the distance and the shimmering air burning off the concrete.

Another half hour passes and the group has grown to a half dozen. We decide to call them a herd, although I actually prefer flock.

I try to tell them apart, but I can't; they're all burned a rich dark brown and are little more than skeletons.

Then we get the first ping from Micah:

<< IN! TRYNG 2 FND CUS. SNDNG APP >>

Jake and I install the program on our Links and open it. A map of the surrounding area pops up on our screens.

"How come I'm only tracking me?" Jake asks. He tilts his screen so I can see.

I look over, then down at my own screen. There's only a single red blip, and when I tap it, my name's the only one to appear. "Me, too."

I'm in the middle of sending Micah a note when my Link pings. Micah's already realized the problem:

<< SML GLTCH. WRKNG ON IT. PTNCE >>

"Glitch, right. In other words, 'Don't bother me. I already know.'"

Jake nods. "One of the others must've noticed it, and said something to him."

"Too bad. I'd really like to see where they are."

He clears his throat. "I'm sure he's fine. Kelly, I mean."

I know who he means. Yeah, I'm worried about my boyfriend, but I'm also worried about the others. I don't reply to Jake's attempt at reassurance, though. There's no way he could know if they're safe or not. In fact, his words only make me worry more.

"I should've gone with him."

Jake picks up his pack and says, "Come on. Let's get out of the sun." He glances nervously at the zombies, even though they're too far away to see with any clarity. "I'm broiling out here, and I'm not even wearing my wetsuit."

He heads for the closest building in the opposite direction, an old fossil fueling station. Perched over the collapsing structure is a big plastic sign on a long pole. Its bottom corner is shattered. The plastic is bleached and faded, leaving only the hint of the red and yellow logo. The remaining letters spell out HELL.

We duck under the canopy built out over the fueling stands, but the shade provides little relief from the heat. The air feels just as stuffy and dry and stale. There's not even a hint of a breeze. Jake kicks aside some trash to get to the door.

I'm surprised that all the glass in the windows and doors is still intact, but then I remember how quickly the infection overran the island, and how quickly the military came in and evacuated it. There'd be no one left to loot and ransack, nothing but zombies, and the IUs wouldn't bother with glass unless they were trying to get through it to someone still alive.

The irony doesn't escape me that the living can be so much more barbaric than the Undead.

Jake pulls a rusted metal trashcan loose from a tangle of wires and other debris. It scrapes along the cement. Underneath is a nest of spiders and mice, which scamper in all directions after being so rudely evicted. We take a few minutes to stomp the bugs dead.

"It's a tumble weed," he exclaims, holding one up by a branch. He tosses it out onto the cement apron, but it just falls, settling onto its bottom.

"I think you need wind for it to actually tumble."

He smiles, then yanks on the door. "Locked. So much for—"

The glass explodes and Jake jumps back, yelping.

I kick the remaining shards loose and duck underneath the push bar inside.

"You could've warned me, you know!" he yells at my back.

"Sorry. Now we're even."

"For what?"

"For playing dirty in the dojang. For not saying anything about the zombie back in Manhattan. For being such an asshole to my boyfriend."

Anger flares on his face for a moment. But then something flickers over it and the tension drains away. He grumbles a few words under his breath and follows me in.

It's dusty and dark inside, a dull twilight that even the bright sunlight outside can't seem to break. The shelves are still fully stocked, but there's nothing worth taking. Everything's at least a dozen years past its expiration date or brittle or mouse-eaten. Even the liquor looks questionable — not that I'd want it, even if I were a drinker. Just the thought of consuming anything that's been sitting in zombieland for twelve years makes my stomach want to revolt.

We wander up and down the aisles, stopping to check out the old magazines. Yet another relic of the past. Everything's digital now. Gone are the days of printed material, forced by the demise of the old postal system.

The covers of the magazines on top are nearly completely faded away, just the ghosts of images barely visible. I slide one out from behind the others. The colors are still vivid, having been protected from the air and the light.

"Here you go." I toss it to Jake, who deftly snatches it out of the air.

"*Playboy!*" He drops it like it's contaminated.

I reach down and pick it up. "You know how much you could get for this back home?"

Soft porn magazines like this were banned nearly a decade ago. There are Streams where you can find pornographic images, but it's dangerous to do so. Getting caught labels you a sexual predator and can add years to your LSC. A lot of magazines like this one, as well as others that had absolutely nothing to do with porn, like *Scientific American* and *Popular Science*, were blamed for the moral corruption of our society, which in turn was blamed for causing the zombie outbreaks. Puritan logic.

"They're illegal," he says.

"Yeah duh. Since when did you become such a prude?"

He shrugs. "They catch you with one of these . . . ."

"Yeah, yeah. They take another year or two or ten away from you. What does it matter anymore? They always find ways to add years. I don't remember you being so worried about it when we came here. What do you think they'd do if they caught us? Do you think they'd just chuckle and say, 'Nice try. Don't do it again, kiddies.'?"

He sighs, then picks the magazine up off the floor. "Real paper," he mutters, rubbing it between his fingers. "Snow."

The cover shows a tall, buxom, waif of a woman with skin as white as a two-week old zombie. Her lips are the brightest red I've ever seen. She's standing in a simulated pine forest, strategically placed snow-laden boughs covering her private parts. Barely.

I reach over and flip it open to the centerfold and read. "Miss March: Tatiana Lovinescu. God, what a name. Sounds like Titty Loving. 'This all-natural Romanian beauty boasts a bounteous—' "

Jake pulls the magazine away. He gives me an embarrassed smirk before shoving it into his pack.

"You really are a prude, aren't you. I'll bet you're still a virgin."

His face goes crimson, but he doesn't answer. Instead, he turns and heads for the exit. "It's too hot in here."

I chuckle as I follow him out. Just as we reach the door, there's a thump from somewhere deep inside the store. We both stop.

He turns. Did you hea— "

"Shh!"

I lift my Link and thumb the screen to wake it. The app Micah sent comes to life, but it still only shows my little red blip and nothing else. Jake does the same with his, but gets the same result. Micah better get the tracker working soon or else it won't matter.

"What do you think it was?" he whispers.

I wait a moment, then swivel on my toes and head back to check out the noise.

"*Hey!*"

I gesture for him to be quiet.

The store is arranged in four separate aisles running front to back. I make a full circuit of the inside, taking an indirect route to the back, but nothing seems amiss, not until I reach the end of the furthest aisle and see a bunch of cans lying on the floor. Cans that weren't there before.

I try to blink away my panic. My blood is roaring through my head, sounding like a freight train. A zombie could be moaning right behind me and I wouldn't be able to hear it.

I look up into the mirror in the corner of the ceiling. From where I'm standing I can see nearly all the aisles. I slowly creep forward until I reach the fallen cans. Nothing moves.

I pick one up. The label slips off and whirls to the floor. It's all faded and half eaten away by mice and bugs. It's got to be stew or beans or dog food. Rust discolors it and it smells of mouse urine.

Reggie's voice speaks in my head. "Of course it smells like urine here," he'd once joked, after Kelly complained once too often to Micah about the sorry state of the basement bathroom in his house. "That's because you're in here. Get it? *You're in* here?"

Several more cans litter the top shelf, their labels similarly peeled or eaten away. Boxes of some other foodstuff sit nearby, holes chewed into their corners. Cream of wheat.

They're completely empty. When I touch one, the shelf rocks and two more cans roll to the floor.

"Jessie?"

"I'm fine," I shout, straightening up. "It's cool. Just some cans that fell off a loose shelf back here. Probably mice." I toss the can I'm holding onto the floor and head toward the front door again.

The entire episode has set me on edge, though. I walk back, keeping my body rigid and my eyes trained straight ahead of me, even though I want to turn around and look behind. Even though it feels like I'm being watched. I don't want to appear frightened; I'm not sure which of the two Jakes will appear if I do, the overconfident one or his scared helpless twin.

The few steps it takes to reach him feel like miles, and my scalp tingles and my blood pounds and I'm sure I'd jump out of my skin if just one more can of dog food happened to fall off the shelf. Thankfully, it doesn't.

When we get back outside, I breathe a sigh of relief. He checks the time. "They should be back soon."

"What's your rush?" I ask, but I'm eager to see Kelly again, despite the way we'd left each other.

Jake reaches down and sweeps the broken glass off the step and sits down. "Might as well stay here in the shade before heading back over."

I pull out my Link. "I'm just going to ping the guys and see what they're up to. You should check on those zoms."

But he doesn't. He sits there watching me. From where he's sitting, looking up, I know he's got an unobstructed view. I'm wearing nothing else on top but my bikini top.

Despite his confession earlier — or maybe because of it — I pretend not to notice. Let him stare. It's nice being noticed for once.

Don't be like that.

It should be Kelly sitting there, not Jake.

It's not his fault.

My Link pings at me as I'm thinking these things, startling me. I jump and almost drop it.

"It's Kel," I say, and relief and guilt both wash over me at the same time.

"He coming back?"

"Yeah."

"What are you going to do when he does?"

"What do you mean?"

He fiddles with his own Link. "It's just past one. We don't have to leave for another hour and a half or so."

I type in a reply as I consider the question.

"I don't know. I hadn't really thought about it. I guess I was so wrapped up in seeing if we could actually come here that I never thought about what we'd do once we did."

But then I do think of something.

"Maybe we could find an old bookstore. You know how long it's been since I held a real book in my hands?"

"Books?" He shakes his head. "More contraband."

I finish my text and send it:

<< HURRY BCK. MISS U. SORRY >>

My Link pings almost immediately. It's Kelly again. I open the file, expecting a text message, but instead it's a photo. Seeing it, I nearly burst into tears. It's a picture of the surprise he was talking about.

I turn my back on Jake so he can't see me crying.

Jake gasps.

I turn just as he stumbles to his feet. His face is ash white.

"What's the mat—"

He grabs my arm and spins me.

My face grows numb and I drop my Link in shock. Not thirty feet away are at least a dozen Infected Undead. They lurch forward, heading straight for us.

And the spookiest thing about it is that they're making almost no noise at all.

Chapter Twenty

"**Back inside!**" Jake hisses.

"Are you crazy? We'll be trapped! We need to run for it!"

Their numbers have already doubled, as more of them stagger around the corners of the building, closing the gaps.

I grab Jake's arm and twist him back around, but he resists. He dives through the broken glass door in a panic, kicking my Link out of reach as he does.

I watch it skitter to the feet of the closest zombies. They don't even bother with it. Their feet grind it into the pavement. But Links are manufactured to withstand pretty much everything short of a nuclear bomb, so I know it won't break. Still, Kelly's photo is on there. I take a step toward it before Jake grabs the sleeve of my wetsuit dangling down.

"Jessie!" he screams.

"No, let go!" But by the time I've recovered we've lost any chance to escape through them. Now they're three deep and pulling in tighter. I might be able to burst through them, but I can't risk getting scratched or bitten. I let Jake pull me inside.

He runs to the nearest aisle and wrenches the metal shelf from its bracket. Items crash to the floor. He carries the shelf over and slips it between the door's push bar and the frame.

"That's not going to hold them!" I scream, but he ignores me and goes for another.

The first zombies are banging on the corners of the display windows, edging their way closer. The glass thuds, making dull, hollow noises. Those in front get pushed down by those behind. Their hands whisper over the glass, sounding rubbery and dry. A single moan rises from them, triggering all the others. The sound quickly grows.

One of them stumbles against the glass. Its skin is so shriveled and brown that it looks like bark. It opens its mouth and its teeth and tongue are as black as licorice. Its head hits the ground and pops like a puffball beneath the feet of the approaching horde.

"We're trapped!" I shriek. "We need to find another way out. Jake, listen to me!"

By now he's wedged three of the shelves into the opening. He pushes a fourth sideways, locking them all into place.

The zombies fill every spare inch of the window and have reached the door. They rattle it. The metal creaks and groans. They slap feebly on the glass, but there are so many that the glass vibrates. It bulges inward, then back out, as if it's breathing. More zombies push against the ones in front and the glass bulges in again, crackling.

I slide behind the counter and tear through the dusty trash and mouse droppings underneath. There in the darkness I find exactly what I was hoping for: a pistol.

I yank it free. Its cold edges are rimed with flakes of reddish powder, gritty beneath my fingers. A shiver runs through me. But it's not blood, it's rust. Dust and cobwebs fill the muzzle. A quick check of the chamber tells me it's loaded. I don't have time to inspect the magazine. I pray it's full and that the rounds inside it are still good.

When I was nine, my grandfather took me to the shooting range, defying my brother's vehement wishes that he wouldn't. But Eric was only seventeen then, a self-proclaimed pacifist, and Grandpa was a lot more imposing of a figure than he's become since then.

"Your brother may be a spineless idiot, Jessie," he told me then, "but I know you're not. You need to learn how to fire a weapon. You need to know how to defend yourself."

Call it whatever you want — irony or spite, or maybe even resignation — but right after Eric graduated from high school, he went and enlisted in the Marines. He volunteered to fight in Mexico and got sent with the Omegamen to China. Now he wears a gun on his hip. Granted, it's an EM gun, but still. He's not the young man I remember growing up knowing. He's . . . changed.

But Grandpa still calls him spineless.

"Did Mom say it's okay?" I'd asked him, hoping against hope that he wouldn't answer. Or if he did, that he'd lie. I was breathless with excitement at the idea of firing a real gun, but I knew it was my duty as a daughter to ask for my mother's permission. Of course, I could never remember a time when she'd ever actually taken that role seriously, but I still felt an obligation to give her the right to refuse something like this.

I'm not so naïve anymore.

Grandpa must've seen the look on my face because he said, "It's okay, young lady. Your mom's fine with it. I already asked her." I didn't challenge him. We were both complicit in a crime that was not of our own doing.

It wasn't until many years later that he'd tell me it was the same gun my father had fired the night he died. I don't know that it would've made any difference to me then. I doubt it.

I wrench open a drawer and look for the box of the remaining rounds inside. There has to be one. You can't just buy a few bullets.

"Jessie!" Jake yells.

The moaning and banging from the front of the store has grown even louder, more insistent, spurred on by the racket Jake made before and continues to make now.

I take a quick look toward the front. The metal shelves are just thin sheets of aluminum and already they're beginning to buckle against the weight of the zombies pressing against the door.

Jake flies past me and disappears past one of the displays near the back. I hear a door slam open, then the telltale sounds of bathroom stall doors being flung wide. Somewhere in the back of my mind I'm thinking what a crazy-ass time it is to be taking a dump.

"What the hell are you doing?" I scream, still searching for the rounds.

"There's a window in here!" Then, "Shit! They're outside in back, too. We're surrounded!"

"Get out here, Jake!" I scream, alternately searching and checking the windows. The only thing that's saved us from being overwhelmed is the zombies' weakness. They're slow and desiccated, weakened by years of not feeding. Their movements are stiff and jerky. Or at least they were. They seem to be waking up.

It's the noise! Stop making so much noise!

I need to find that box of spare rounds.

"There's a back door here," Jake shouts. "Christ, where the hell are they all coming from?"

Draw them to the front!

How?

I spy the cash register. The bullets are probably in the back of the drawer.

I try to open it, but without electricity, the thing's locked tight and won't budge.

There's a fire extinguisher sign in a back corner. As I hurry over to it, I hear the first splinter of glass from the front, a sharp report, followed by snapping sounds. I fling my head back. It's just a crack, but the windows won't hold for much longer.

I pray that my hunch is right.

"Jake, get the fuck out here! I need you!"

I find the extinguisher, but the object I really want is hanging on the wall next to it: an axe. I yank it free from the mount and sprint back to the front.

I don't even slow down. I raise the axe over my head as I run and bring it down on the register. It crashes into the counter, missing the target by half a foot. I curse just as the window explodes inward. Glass rains down on the horde as the Undead tumble inside, slicing several of the zombies. But it doesn't stop them. It doesn't even slow them down.

The first ones trip and fall. The ones behind begin to climb over them, but they're pushed down by the third wave. The growing mound of Undead acts as its own speed bump, buying me precious seconds.

I wrench the axe free from the countertop and bring it up again before slamming it down on the register. The ancient machine chimes and caves in, but the drawer stays closed. Two more quick swings and it finally pops free. But now the first zombies are less than ten feet away. I raise the pistol, cock it and squeeze the trigger with one hand while the other yanks the drawer fully open.

Coins and bills shower to my feet. The gun goes off, rocking me onto my heels.

My hand is shaking so badly that the shot goes wide. A hole opens up in the chest of a zombie further back. The bullet passes easily through it and shatters the unbroken window, unleashing another torrent of the walkers into the store. The zombie I hit rocks backward and falls. It's quickly overrun by others.

"What the hell was that?" Jake screams from the back.

I aim and the second shot finds the forehead of the closest zombie. Its head explodes in a powder. The skull shatters and the thing collapses. I get off two more shots and drop two more of them before I see Jake out of the corner of my eye, skidding up the aisle.

"This way!" he screams, pinwheeling his arms.

I manage to fire another three rounds, but only one zombie goes down. The noise is making them go berserk. Their moans are shrieks of desperation and their movements are much more focused.

"You can't shoot them all!"

I know he's right. There's no way I'd even be able to reload the clip, even if I had a thousand rounds. They'd be on top of me in a second. And my shoulder already burns from the recoil.

How I wish I had an EM gun.

I duck quickly down and sweep my hand over the floor until it encounters an object with some heft to it. I lift it and shove it into the elastic waist of the wetsuit without looking. Then I grab the axe in my other hand and run toward Jake, knocking a withered zombie in a faded too-large muumuu out of my way. She tips and falls in slow motion.

"I'm coming," I shout, and I pray Jake's not just planning on barricading us in the bathroom.

He's standing beside a metal door, one hand up to stop me, his eyes glued to the tiny opening.

"Jake, you better have a plan, because they're fucking coming!"

He reaches down and grabs something off the floor. It's a tire iron. The other hand holds a—

"Is that a toilet plunger?"

"Yeah." He kicks the door open.

I don't have time to say anything else before we're rushing out into the bright sunlight.

There are only a handful of zombies in back now, the rest drawn to the front by the gunshots. They turn as one as we skid out onto the loose gravel behind the store and begin their advance. They're moving frightfully fast, faster than the ones we first saw in front.

I step around Jake and with a quick shot from the pistol dispatch an Infected wearing the still-recognizable remains of a tattered business suit. Like the others inside, its head explodes in a fine powder, not the spray of gore I keep expecting. A strange powder that lingers in the air before slowly drifting back to the ground.

"What the— ?" Jake exclaims. "Jesus, that's sick!"

"Jesus is dead and he ain't coming back! Now move!"

Another zombie quickly takes the place of Business Suit. I swing the axe one-handed like a sword, not caring if I hit the thing with the flat side or the edge of the blade. Instead, the spike sinks into the monster's face. It falls, pulling me down with it.

Jake reaches over and grabs me, keeping me from falling right onto the blade, but knocking me in the head with the plunger. He swings his other hand at another zombie. It spins around.

He swings again, and the plunger strikes it on the shoulder with a dull *thwop*, accomplishing absolutely nothing. The zombie reaches out. Jake thrusts straight at its face. I expect to see the plunger stick, but the zombie tumbles over backward instead.

"Really?" I shout. "You couldn't find anything better? A toilet brush, maybe?"

"Closest thing to a *dahn bohng* I could find," he says, referring to the short sticks some fighters use in hapkido.

"I prefer the long staff."

"You're doing just fine with that pistol!"

I stumble back to my feet. He points to an opening and we sprint for it.

His backpack bounces up and down and from side to side, making him look awkward. He twirls his plunger and tire iron like batons.

The zombies that were heading around the sides of the store have changed direction and are now staggering toward us. Jake heads for the widest space between them, then suddenly veers off in a new direction.

"Where are you going? Our gear is the other way!"

"Yeah," he puffs. "Exactly." And I realize he's right. We need to lead them away, not toward it. Otherwise we'll never be able to leave.

The Holiday Inn rises up before us. I wonder if Reggie and Ash are still inside. They should've finished by now and come back already. Do they even realize what's going on out here? How could they have not heard the gunshots?

And then I envision them in a hotel room, unaware that it's filling with zombies, the sounds of their lovemaking attracting them from other parts of the hotel.

"Where'd they come from?" I pant. "Jake? Jake, stop! We can't just keep running around like this. We need a plan. And it has to include the others."

He slows, nodding, but doesn't stop. I jog to keep up with him.

"We might be running directly into even more of them."

He puts on the brakes and I plow into him.

"Jesus, Jake!"

"I don't know where they're coming from, Jessie." But there's something in his eyes, an accusing look. He thinks this is my fault.

"They heard the glass breaking."

"It's not your fault, Jess."

He takes a moment to assess our situation, turning in a full circle. Other than the zombies swarming the refueling station, the place still seems empty, but now we know we can't trust this perception.

The zombies we can see number at least fifty by now. They've turned and are heading toward us, as if we're magnets.

There are so many of them. So many, and they showed up so suddenly. Where were they hiding? And why? Were they just trying to stay out of the sun? Were they . . . planning?

I can't believe I'm even entertaining such thoughts. The Undead don't think.

"Jake?"

He's staring at the Holiday Inn. "That's where Ashley and Reggie went, isn't it?"

"Yeah, and that's why we can't go there. We'll lead the zombies right to them."

"What if they're—" He stumbles backward, swearing and shaking his head as some variation of the thought I'd had moments before comes to him. "I hope they didn't come from inside there."

"You need to ping them," I say. I feel naked without my Link, vulnerable. Helpless. "We need to warn the others."

He glances back at the zombies, his eyes still crazed with fright. "Shit," he repeats, but he nods and pulls out his Link. As he does, he starts walking, cutting off to the right and toward more open ground. "Keep an eye out for me, Jess," he says, gesturing with his free hand. He babbles almost incoherently into the Link.

"They're getting closer, Jake. We need to move."

"Okay," he says, slipping the Link back into his pocket.

We start jogging again.

"You told everyone?"

"I tried Micah. No time to key in anyone else."

"You spoke to him? Is he coming?"

"He wouldn't accept. I left a message."

"Damn it!"

I notice we're heading for the tower, the same one Micah said he was going to earlier. It's at least a quarter mile off, far enough away that we'll easily lose the zombies before we arrive.

I'm not sure this is the best plan, however. I don't like having my back up against the wall — literally — and we don't know if there are more zoms in front of us. On the other hand, we need to lead them away, anywhere, just not toward the gear.

And we need to do it quickly, because it now looks like there are close to a hundred of them.

Chapter Twenty One

Jake's Link pings just as we reach the first row of taller buildings. They look like warehouses. We slip around the corner of one and find the street deserted. It's a row of shops. Wouldn't it be ironic if one of them was a bookstore?

We stop to read the message:

<< ON MY WY >>

Jake quickly tries to open a voice line, but Micah doesn't answer.

"Come on, man!" he grunts, pacing anxiously. "Why won't he accept? Damn it!"

He's practically screaming with fright. I try to calm him down. The last thing we want to do is to draw out even more zombies from wherever they might be hiding. "Just leave a message. We need to keep moving."

"Stay there, Micah," he tells the recorder. "We're coming to you."

"Stay there?" I say. "No! He needs to come back. We need to get back to the equipment and leave!"

Jake pockets his Link. "Not with those things just standing there!"

He brushes past me to peek around the corner. "Damn it. They've stopped. Stupid things. They're just shuffling around in random directions now."

I look for myself. From the relative safety of our hiding spot, I can rest a moment and get a better look at them. Their clothes are faded and hang on them in rags. If they have any at all. I notice how weathered they are, dry and dark and timeworn, barely much more than skeletons. The plastination of their flesh from the infection is obvious. The Infected Undead, victims of the outbreak thirteen years ago, the ones the military left behind. Chocolate, sexless, men and women and children. Chocolate monsters.

I put my hand on his shoulder. "Jake—"

"We've got to draw them away from the tunnel," he says, shaking my hand off. Before I realize what he's doing he's back out in the middle of the street, waving his arms and shouting. "Hey, you! Over here! We're over here!"

"Jake!" I whisper, darting out and grabbing his tee shirt. "What the hell are you doing? Stop it!" I check behind us to make sure the street is still empty.

He ignores me and shouts even louder. He jumps and waves and screams. The urban canyon we're in begins to fill with moaning sounds. They echo all around us, amplified by the closeness of the buildings.

Stiff as wooden dolls, the zombies turn and make their way toward us.

From a distance, they all seem agonizingly slow. But now I can see that this is wrong. Not all of them are slow. Some move faster. But that's not the only difference. They have a waxier sheen to their skin and their muscles don't seem as atrophied. They have the same aimless shuffle as the rest, but their steps are longer. Their legs swing just a fraction of a second brisker. Their movements are more precise, more... focused. Fresh zombies? But how?

I don't know, but these are the ones we need to worry about.

"Let's circle around," Jake says. He grabs my arm and turns me. "Maybe we can find a dead-end alley with a fire escape or something."

"You want to use us as bait to draw them into an alley?"

"You'd rather stand and fight?"

I shake my head. "I'd rather just go home."

"Better if we herd them into an alley than leave them scattered about."

"Only one problem," I say. "They're not cows. And they're already too scattered."

"I never said it would be easy." He points to a pair of tall buildings with a narrow space between them. We hurry over, but as soon as we turn the corner we can see that it won't work. The other end is open.

"We're wasting time, Jake," I say. "We need to find the others and get out of here."

We stumble back onto the main street. The first of the zombies are already there, a half dozen lurching toward us, their movements deceptively quick.

"Fuck," Jake pants. "Does it seem like they're getting faster?" He backs away.

"Just run," I say, but he's right. They are fast, and getting faster.

We both turn into the alley and run. When we reach the other end, we turn again, angling perpendicular to the tower and the tunnel as best we can. Our footsteps slap against the road, echoing off the buildings, sounding like clapping.

"This way!" I hiss, reaching out for Jake's arm and turning to the right. His shirt slips from my fingers and he continues straight down the broad road. "Jake!"

He spins around. His eyes are wild, but he follows me. This constant swinging of his between lucidity and panic is driving me crazy.

"We need to get back," I gasp. "We can't worry about Micah. He'll catch up to us."

He looks at the gun still in my hand. "How many bullets do you have left?"

"I don't know." Then I remember the box and pull it from my wetsuit.

"Paperclips?"

"Shit!" I throw the box away. It breaks open and bullets spill out, scattering across the pavement. "Damn."

Jake hurries over and starts to pick them up.

"No time!" I yell. "Leave them. Even if we can just grab the gear and get it into the water, that's better than waiting. It's our only chance!"

New footsteps echo around us, someone running. We both look up in time to see Micah sprinting past us on the street ahead. He doesn't see us.

"Micah!"

But he's already disappeared.

"Shit. *Micah!*"

Micah's head reappears around the corner. He looks up the road in the direction he just came from and makes a snap decision. He sprints toward us. "Get out of here!" he screams. "Go back!"

The moaning is growing louder. The street behind us suddenly fills with walkers. "Run," Micah shouts.

Jake and I spin around. The zombies crowd into the street, lurching madly at us, moaning and shrieking and clacking their rotting teeth.

"Shit! Aw, shit!"

"Calm down, Jake," I tell him. "You need to calm down."

"We're trapped!"

Yeah, whose fault is that? But I don't say it. I push him toward one of the buildings.

Lifting my arm, I bring the axe down on the display window of a bridal shop. The gowns inside are yellowed and dusty. When the glass shatters and falls on them, they tear easily and flake to the floor.

"What the hell is it with you and breaking glass?" Jake screams.

"Just get inside!"

Micah reaches us. He doesn't hesitate. He vaults over the high brick sill of the display window and into the store. Glass crunches under his feet. He stops, turns, and reaches down to help us in.

Jake hesitates.

"Get your goddamn ass in here," Micah growls at him as he pulls me up.

I don't stop to help. I head for the back of the store, looking for the emergency exit or loading door or whatever the hell they've got. It's our only chance to evade the zombie horde.

I hear footsteps behind me.

"I cut myself on the glass," Jake wails, holding his arm. Blood seeps through his fingers. It looks like a nasty gash, but I can't worry about that right now. "Why'd you pick this shop? The one next door had a bigger window."

I don't have time to explain it to him. I kick down a door marked "Employees Only" and find what I'm looking for. There's an emergency exit across the room, but I see that it's secured with a chain and a padlock.

I swing the axe behind me.

"Give her some room, dummy!" Micah shouts, pulling Jake back. The axe barely misses Jake's head as I bring it forward in a sidearm chop.

The blade pings off the chain. I try again, but the chain still holds.

Micah grabs my arm. "Give it to me. From the front of the store, the sounds of moaning and breaking glass come to us.

Jake goes over and tries to barricade the inner door.

Micah lifts the axe with both hands and brings it down on the latch that holds the chain to the jamb. It bends. He tries again, taking smaller, more precise swings. Finally it shatters and falls away. He hands the axe back, then reaches over and pushes the door open.

The alley is narrow. It's also open on both ends, but it's empty and there aren't any zombies in sight. We edge out of the shop. We could very well be trapped, but at the moment it's our only option.

Micah lifts a board from the ground and wedges it against what's left of the doorknob, locking the zombies inside. Then he pulls out his Link.

"What the hell are you doing?" Jake shrieks. "Calling for a pizza?"

"Just keep an eye out!"

I do a quick scan. There are no windows in this alley, no way to easily break into another building if we find ourselves trapped. And the fire escapes are well out of reach above our heads.

"This way," Micah whispers. He puts his Link in his pocket and leads us toward the street he was running down earlier. "We'll probably have to take a few out," he says. He glances at the gun in my hand. "But there shouldn't be as many as you had chasing you. What the hell did you do? Wake the entire island up?"

I give him a look of such frustration that he quickly turns away and starts running up the road.

He's light on his feet, almost as quiet as a cat. For someone who spends ninety percent of his free time in his basement getting drunk and hacking games, he's surprisingly athletic.

We reach the end of the alley and peek around the corner. A few zombies are milling about. Apparently these are the "slow" ones.

"Felt like a hundred of them before," he says. "Nowhere as near as many as were chasing you." He smiles. "Must be that perfume you're wearing." He pauses, then adds, "Jake."

"I'm not—"

I interrupt his protest. "Where the hell *were* they? That's what I want to know. And what woke them all up? Was it noise?"

Micah shakes his head. "Couldn't be. I didn't make any. But when I stepped out of the tower I was totally surrounded. Damn things were all over the place, like they knew I was there. Scared me so badly I just ran right through them. That's when you pinged me, Jake."

"Did you get scratched or bitten?"

He shakes his head.

"Shouldn't we be moving," Jake hisses, "instead of just standing here making small talk?"

Micah takes another look around the corner. "Wait another minute and see if the rest of them clear out."

He pulls his Link out again, reminding me that I'm still missing mine. I just hope there's a chance to go back to the fueling station so I can get it.

"The others should be there by now," Jake says. "Did you let them know what's happening? Is that what you're doing?"

Micah shakes his Link and frowns. He taps the screen. The frown turns into a scowl. "Has anyone pinged either of you?"

I shake my head and quickly tell him about losing my Link. Jake checks his, then shakes his head, too. "Nothing."

Micah looks up in the sky, as if the answer to whatever is bothering him is written there. "I can't reach them. I hope they're okay."

I swallow my panic. "The road's almost clear," I tell them. "Wait just a couple more— "

But then a horrible grating noise comes from behind us in the alleyway. The board Micah had wedged into place snaps and flies off, spinning into the air and hitting the opposite wall. The door swings open, vomiting zombies into the road.

"Go!"

Chapter Twenty Two

"They're there!" Jake shouts. "I see them!"

He's outpaced us and is now sprinting along a good hundred feet ahead of me and Micah. I want to tell him not to get too far ahead, but I'm too out of breath. Even Micah's beginning to gasp. But Jake's still running like he could go on like this all day.

"There's Ash and Reg!"

Alarm bells ring inside my head. *Where's Kelly?*

"They've already got their suits on."

Now I'm glad I left mine on.

Micah and I top a small rise and now I can see the others. They haven't noticed us yet. But just as I'm about to warn Jake not to shout, he calls out.

Kelly appears from around the back of the car. The trunk's open and he's already fully geared up, even though we hadn't planned on leaving yet. Then I see the bodies of a dozen zombies scattered about them and can guess what happened.

"Jessie!" He starts running toward us.

I wave him back. "Get the gear!" I yell, but my voice sounds too small. My throat is dry. Out of the corner of my eye, I see movement. The slower zombies that had been tracking us earlier are now emerging from between the buildings where we first entered the row of shops. Directly behind us are the faster ones.

"Get the gear!" Micah echoes, though a lot louder.

The three at the car turn and gather the rest of the equipment. Jake is the first to reach them and he quickly grabs his wetsuit. Micah and I reach them moments later.

Jake's struggling to get his legs in. Reggie screams to let him help. Ashley runs over to Micah with his suit while Kelly comes to me with my mask.

"Hurry up, Jessie!" Kelly shrieks. I want to slap him. What does he think I'm doing?

I'd started pulling my arms into the suit even before I got there. They slip easily on.

Jake's yanking at the second leg, screaming in frustration. His suit doesn't want to go on. I realize it's because his suit is still wet but he's not. He hasn't even broken a sweat. "Get some water!" I scream at Reggie. "Wet down his skin."

The closest zombies are about a hundred feet away now.

I zip my suit up, then shift the gun from my other hand. I aim at the closest zombie and squeeze the trigger. The gun clicks.

"Shit! Where's my mask?" I toss the gun away, but keep the axe.

Kelly hands me my mask, along with his goggles. I push them away. "They're not going to fit me!"

Reggie scrambles back up from the water's edge. He hurries over to Jake with his hands cupped, but the water spills out before he gets him. The two of them start fighting over how to get the suit on Jake. Reggie just starts shoving parts of Jake's body into places inside the wetsuit where they don't belong. Jake's shaking with terror now, useless. Even from where I'm standing I can see that his suit is twisted. He'll never get it zipped up. Reggie tries anyway. He gives the zipper a massive tug and it rips.

"Never mind," I scream. "Get into the water!"

Kelly has taken my axe and run over to the first zombies. He takes two out and is working on a third. They seem to appear out of nowhere, swarming, their moans filling my ears.

"Kelly!"

He throws the axe at another and sprints back, snatching our backpacks from the ground and hurling them out and over the water. "Let's go!" he yells, as they splash down.

Ashley and Micah are already climbing down the fence. Ash reaches the water first and plunges in, pushing her gear and flippers ahead of her. I snatch my flippers and head for Jake and Reggie, who are still stupidly struggling with the suit.

"No time! Into the goddamn water!"

I grab two more pairs of flippers as Kelly gets their packs. Everything gets hurled over the railing. Reggie kicks at a zombie while pushing at Jake, who's practically sobbing by now and babbling. The zombie gets back up and comes at them again, but it has to push past several of its comrades.

Reggie swings the spare equipment bag at them, bowling them all down.

I grab Jake and yank him away just as another zombie reaches for him. Its blackened fingers close over empty space. Its momentum trips it, but it doesn't stop coming.

"Wrong way!" Jake screams.

"You're going over!"

I grunt and push him over the railing. He flips in mid-air, then splashes into the water.

A hand rakes my back. Instinctively, I step away, even as I reach back, grab, and pull. I use the attacker's own weight against itself. But I realize only too late what I've done as the zombie follows Jake over the railing. I try to pull it back, shouting, "Lookout!" But its arm rips from its socket with a dry popping sound.

There's a splash. Ashley screams. Or maybe it's Jake.

The next zombie lurches at me, but then Kelly launches himself at it and it flies off to one side.

"Go!" he shouts.

"Not without you!"

"I'm coming."

And we vault the railing.

The surface comes up fast. It's a roiling, chaotic mass of water and air as Jake kicks himself away from the zombie. Micah is slashing at it with his knife. Reggie is swimming over, but without flippers he's moving too slowly. Our gear bags slowly gather against the wall of the overpass, pushed there by the breeze and the waves that everyone's thrashing is making.

"I'll help Jake," Kelly yells. "Get your flippers."

I swim over and find them. I've just managed to get the second one on when there's a splash right beside me. I look up and see a zombie tilting over the railing right over me.

"Jessie!"

I kick away from the wall just as it falls, narrowly missing me. Then it seems to be raining zombies as more and more of them tumble over the railing in their attempt to reach us.

Some sink immediately, while others bob near the surface. They thrash. Their moans turn to gurgles as their throats fill with water.

"The gear!"

"Forget the gear," Reggie says. He's got his flippers on now and is swimming Jake's over to him. "We need to go! Now! Look!"

Dozens of the Infected Undead now line the overpass. The line presses forward. A dozen bodies fall and another line takes its place.

"Shit!" Ash screams. "Oh, my fucking god where are they all coming from!"

Jake has finally managed to get the rest of his gear on and has gathered with the others about thirty feet from the overpass. I'm still off to one side, separated from them by twenty or so feet of water and several floating zombies leering at us.

"We need those spare canisters," Reggie roars, holding up his mask, but he doesn't move to get them. Nobody does. To do so would be suicide, since our bags are floating against the overpass. There's no way any of us can reach them. "These still have the used ones!"

"You didn't switch out the canisters?" Jake screams. "What the hell were you doing?"

"Never mind that," Kelly says. "Which bag are they in?"

"We can't!" Micah shouts. He turns to Jake. "You said these last about three hours, right? Well it took us half that to get here. I hope for our sake you're right."

He then shouts over at me to stay put. "We'll meet underwater." Then he instructs Kelly to swim over to me. A minute later, Kelly surfaces a few feet to my right. He grabs my hand.

Micah checks his Link one last time and curses. "Where'd the time go?"

"I don't care," Ashley says. "I'm going now!"

We all nod in agreement. It's now or never.

"But this time," Kelly shouts, "we all stay together."

Chapter Twenty Three

We meet underwater and join hands. The scene around us is surreal: A panoramic movie of zombies drifting down into the darkness below. They lurch and twist at us, looking like dying earthworms dropped into a child's bucket. They remind me of autumn, of rotting leaves sinking into a lake.

Then I remember the old video stream Reggie found one day while searching through some archived footage from the first part of the century: people falling from a burning building, plummeting to the ground, dropping, dropping, until the whole building collapses into a ball of dust that reaches to the clouds and turns the sun red.

"Is this real?" I'd asked, horrified at the images. "This can't be real."

Ashley asked her G-ma Junie about it and G-ma Junie told her to hush and never bring it up again. "Destroy the video. It's illegal to speak of things that happened before."

We slip between the falling bodies. It's easy to evade them. They can't swim. They only drift down, and then they slip along the bottom as the current catches them.

I remember the one that attacked me on our way in. It had acted differently. It seemed like it knew how to swim. But maybe that's just how I'm remembering it.

Is it still alive? Is it lying on the bottom of the tunnel somewhere, unable to move because of its severed spine? How long could it stay there like that? Forever? Would the fish eat it?

The pile of zombies directly beneath the overpass is so large that they continue to rain down. The seething mass writhes and splashes, bodies disengaging themselves as the zombies struggle against one other. We don't stick around to watch. We swim quickly past them and they ogle back at us, looking almost resentful, their mouths gaping and their tongues lolling out. Their eyes black with death, full of longing and hunger.

Earthworms, I tell myself. *That's all they are.*

Except earthworms don't want to eat you. At least not while you're still alive.

The current gently pushes us forward. Already it's very weak, suggesting it'll turn soon. We'll end up fighting it again the closer we get to Manhattan.

We enter the same tunnel we came through earlier. Between the six of us, only two flashlights remain. Reggie holds one as he leads the group into the darkness. The rest of us form a chain, each holding the hand of the person in front: Reggie, Ashley, me, Kelly, Jake, and finally Micah in back. He holds the other flashlight. We push ourselves to the limit, kicking hard with our flippers to get away from that terrifying place.

I'm thirsty and tired, faint from hunger. My feet hurt and my knees burn from all the running we've done. My arms ache from swinging the axe. I can't see very much, and what I can see is blurry.

But I don't want to see. I keep my eyes closed and concentrate on kicking and for once I'm glad that Reggie is the one leading us out. He's always been the physically strongest among us.

We arrive near the place where the zombie attacked me. I only know this by instinct. Or maybe I imagine Kelly's grip tightening on my hand. I keep my eyes closed. It makes the time pass quicker. Soon. Soon we'll be home. I never want to come back.

I concentrate on my breathing — in and out and in again — timing my kicks to keep the rhythm going. The beat becomes a part of me, a part of my own living rhythm, until I no longer have to think about it.

Images gradually creep back into my mind, so slowly and stealthily that I don't realize it at first. The zombies in the store, the way their heads exploded like sacks of flour, like they were so old that they'd completely dried up inside. How could they still be . . . alive?

The ones that attacked us after we'd returned to where our gear was hadn't been like that. The faster ones. One of the zombies Kelly had beheaded had made a wet squelching sound when it fell. A thick, deep red fluid had oozed from its neck. It was a fresh zombie.

I shudder.

Reggie stops a couple times, both times asking us via Link if we're all okay. Kelly notices that I don't have mine and gives me a curious look. I shrug and hold out my empty hands. He types something into his screen, then shows it to me:

<< LOST? >>

I nod. He shakes his head. I'll need to figure out how to explain it to the Department of Citizen Registration when we get back. The questionnaire for a lost Link is over a thousand questions long.

The second time Reggie stops, I notice the drag on us. The current has stopped pushing at us. And while it isn't yet pulling us back yet, the lack of assistance combined with our fatigue is slowing our progress. We've depleted our energy reserves.

I'm especially beginning to feel it, since I didn't eat earlier. My legs cramp. There's a stitch in my side. Any adrenaline I'd been running on has long since evaporated away.

Micah gives Reggie an impatient look and gestures at him to keep going. We quickly reform our chain and carry on. We don't know how much longer our cartridges will last. Once more, I close my eyes and let the others guide me.

The minutes pass. Then I feel Ash and Kelly release my hands. I open my eyes, thinking we've reached the end. But everything's still dark, except for the two beams of light, spreading out.

I push myself toward the source of the closest one. Jake's face emerges from the gloom. I grab his hand and hold on. He stops and looks at me, confused, tension filling his face.

He holds up his Link and types:

<< BLOCKED >>

He reads my frown immediately, since I have no goggles to distort my eyes. Gripping my hand once more, he points downward with the light. Below us is the faint outline of the rear of the old bus we'd passed on our way in.

I look up again. The debris dam looms over us, tall and massive. It stretches all the way to the ceiling and spans the tunnel from one side to the other. A large tree trunk pokes through it, its stunted roots looking like a gorgon's head, a nest of unidentifiable flotsam trapped within its tentacles.

Jake swings the light over to the side. I'm barely able to make out Kelly and Reggie. They're at the opening we used earlier, but now it's blocked. I can see them trying to move something. Ash and Micah hover nearby with the other flashlight. Reggie must have given Jake his light to locate another opening.

I urge his hand to point the beam over the surface of the logjam once more, looking for another way through. Below us, a stream of mud eddies out of a narrow gap beneath the bus. In just the few seconds we hover there, the cloud spreads up to meet us.

A new alarm rises up inside of me: the current has shifted.

Jake realizes this too. He yanks the light away and swings it back up at Reggie and Kelly. They've got a corner of what looks like a box spring mattress and are pulling at it, trying to pry it loose. Jake makes an urgent noise with his throat, but we're too far away for them to hear it. I begin to kick my way up toward them.

I reach Ash just as I start hearing a soft plinking noise below us. I look down and see Jake urgently banging the handle of his knife on the flashlight, trying to alert the others. Ashley hears it and turns, inadvertently shifting the light in Micah's hands away from Kelly and Reg.

Just then there's a low grinding noise, massive and ominous. I feel it in my bones, and I sense, rather than see or hear, the pile beginning to shift, the low grinding of several tons of material moving against itself, pushed forward by the strengthening current, unrelieved now that its only opening has been obstructed.

Jake makes that urgent sound in his throat again, but Kel and Reg don't hear. He swims past us and stabs them with his light. They keep working on pulling the mattress free.

Now I see the first fingers of muddy water beginning to surge past them. I grab Ashley's arm and pull her away.

Her eyes narrow at me in confusion. She pulls back.

A loud metallic moaning sound comes from the bottom of the pile. The bus lurches. Ash makes a sound in her throat. I gesture that the boys need to hurry.

Jake reaches Kelly and pushes him away. They begin to wrestle with each other. Reggie turns and stares as if they're crazy. His body stiffens. He watches them do their slow motion fight for a moment before he tries to separate them.

Something shoots through the small opening. It wraps around Jake's head. He tears it away and tries to see what it is, but it slips from his hand and disappears into the gloom. Kelly takes the opportunity to move away.

I wave my arms, but they don't see me. Jake grabs Reggie and points down, but Reggie can't see what he's pointing at; it's too dark. Behind them, the mattress bulges out. Jake points again and waves his hands in a sweeping motion. Reggie shakes his head. Jake gives up and tries Kelly again.

Behind them, the mattress twists. Suddenly, it shoots out of the gap, hitting Reggie in the back. A bubble of air escapes his mouth and his mask sinks away. For a moment he looks unconscious, but then his head whips around and his hands go to his throat.

I dive downward into the darkness, not knowing where I'm going, only moving by instinct. I sweep my arms around until I feel something light brush against the back of my hand and I stab at it until my fingers wrap around the tube connecting the cartridge to Reggie's mask. It seems like a miracle, but I'll take it. I turn and kick my way up.

Reggie is still struggling. He's drifting away toward the darkness, but nobody else sees him. Kel and Micah are moving to the opening. They see that it's clear again. Jake swims up to them, still gesturing.

A series of thumps comes to us from all around. They echo dully and ponderously, sounding like they're coming from the other side of the heap. A loud scrape follows. Everyone stops what they're doing to look around. Everyone but me and Reggie.

I swim desperately toward the gloom, towards Reggie's fading ghostly shape. I get one last glimpse of his eyes just before he disappears: they're wild and bulging behind his goggles.

I hear the sudden release of air and I know Reggie's using the air in his goggles. There's another release. Then a third. How many more before it's empty?

I need to find him.

Kelly's suddenly there, pulling me back toward the opening. He spins me around. I see Micah hanging onto the edge of the metal cage, kicking against the current, casting his light inside to see if it's clear all the way through. The mud swirls through in thick clouds. But the current looks too strong. Even if it's wide enough for us to swim through, how can we?

I push Kelly away and turn. I kick into the darkness.

Then the light turns toward us. I see Reggie up ahead, his hands clasped over his mouth, his cheeks bulging. His eyes lock on me, and the mask in my hand. He kicks weakly, but he's still drifting further away.

I finally reach him. He clutches me desperately. Even starving of air, his grip is like steel. I thrust his mask into his face. He takes it and exhales explosively into the canister, then inhales. The canister wheezes from the force of his breathing. I fear he'll burst the bag inside.

In he breathes. Out. Repeating the cycle as I try to tow him back toward the heap. But it's against the current. It's like towing a boulder through quicksand.

Reggie recovers enough to help me. Finally we reach the opening. Items are falling all around, tumbling down around us or being swept up in the rush of water through the gap.

Kelly's got his Link out. He flashes the screen at us:

<< 2 DANGERUS >>

He points back the way we came.

Ashley shakes her head. She grabs for Kelly's arm and misses, tries again, grabs his ankle. I can see her shaking her head vehemently at him and pointing in the other direction. There's no way she's going back to Long Island.

I feel Reggie push against me. He's still shaking, but stronger than he was even just a moment before. His recovery is amazingly quick. He grabs the edge of the metal cage and pulls himself into the opening.

The urgency is clear in Kelly's eyes, but Ashley takes the opportunity to jockey her way into the gap. The current pushes her back and she somersaults. But then a hand shoots through the opening and grabs her, turning her around. The gap shifts; the cage begins to crumple.

Micah grabs me and shoves me toward the opening. Then Kelly follows me. I pass Reggie inside, wedged in a tiny recess. He helps us through. Just in front of me, I see Ashley's flippers disappearing out the other side.

Something flutters past my face. Then something else drags across my arm, scratching me. I kick and strain and grab onto anything that'll keep me from sliding back. I'm acting on adrenaline. We all are. There's nothing else left.

I push and pull and kick. Then I shoot through the opening and find calmer water. Ash returns with a pole. She pokes it through. Kelly grabs it and pulls himself out.

There's a loud rumble and everything shifts several feet. Ashley loses her air and lets go of the pole. I take her place while she recovers.

Just as the entire debris pile shudders, Micah emerges. There's a loud crack and a rumble and the cage collapses upon itself. Micah's flashlight gets ripped from his hand. It tumbles away, then winks out. Complete darkness descends over us.

Someone grabs me. A Link screen glows, showing me Kelly's face. He pulls me clear of the pile.

Jake! my mind screams. He never made it through.

Kelly points. I catch a glimpse of Ash holding her Link before her, the mask now back in her mouth: she's trying to put her goggles on. Micah's helping her.

I don't see Reggie or Jake.

Then Reggie appears in the faint glow of Ash's Link. We join them, clustering close together.

<< JK? >>

We all shake our heads.

Reggie types:

<< CANT STAY. CANSTER FAILNG >>

Kelly shakes his head. He points at the pile and begins to swim toward it. But then he stops and turns. He pushes his mouthpiece deeper in and sucks. Panic rises in his eyes.

I can also feel it. I don't know if it's just because Reggie mentioned the canisters failing or if it's actually happening, but I'm suddenly feeling light-headed, just like I did on the way over. There's a dull pressure behind my eyes and I fight the urge to breath deeper and faster. How many more breaths do I have left?

I snatch Ash's Link and quickly scroll through it to find Jake's contact. Pictures of people flash by, some I recognize, others I don't. One goes by so fast that it doesn't register at first, someone I know. Someone Ash shouldn't.

Then there's Jake's image. I ping him.

There's no response.

Micah grabs Ash's hand and pulls her, but I won't let him. I try Jake's Link a second time.

Still no response.

Now we have no choice. We'll all die if we stay. Even if we leave now, we might not make it.

Then Ash's Link lights up.

<< DON'T LV ME >>

Micah shakes his head. There's no way through the dam. Jake's on the other side, but he can't reach us. And we can't reach him.

Ash crumbles, but Reggie grabs her arm, shakes her, points frantically. *We need to go!*

We form a chain again. I take one last look back, hoping for something, some sign that Jake has found a way through. I think I see a flash of light. I stare for a moment, but there's nothing but darkness.

We swim on in total darkness. I can't know if I'm crying because my tears just melt into the filthy, salty water. And yet I do know. I'm crying because we've left Jake behind.

And yet I swim on.

One by one, our cartridges fail. We share the rest between us until all we have left is the one unused one that Micah still had on his belt. And still we haven't reached the opening.

We each have to be wondering, with the five of us using it, will it last?

Reggie guides us with his hand on the wall of the tunnel. We pass the one mask between us: front to back to front again.

And then, just as it begins to fail, the darkness in the tunnel lightens just a tiny bit. I'm half delirious by then, starved of oxygen, exhausted, grieving. We all are. But it's not the light of the tunnel opening we see, it's the light from Ash's Link receiving one final message:

<< IV GONE BAK >>

We each see it, but we don't stop to think about it. Survival is paramount — *our* survival. It's the one thought we all share and can't argue about.

But now a second thought settles in, a doubt, waiting for the first moment when it can capture our full attention: How can we just leave Jake behind? How could we live knowing we did?

We can't.

We have to go back.

S.W. TANPEPPER'S GAMELAND

episode two

FAILSAFE

Part One

There are No Guarantees in Life

Chapter One

"No Jessie."

It's the first thing out of Kelly's mouth, the moment he breaks the surface on the Manhattan side of the tunnel and joins the rest of us already there. As in: We're not going back.

Here I am gasping, coughing, choking, holding onto anything my fingers can wrap around. They feel like rubber. The water clutches at me like the hard, ropy hands of the Undead. And he's telling me *no*? The last thing I need is for someone — *anyone* — to tell me what I can or can't do.

He takes in a huge, rattling breath — it sounds so like his brother Kyle during one of his fevers, wet and drowning, sounding of death. "Don't even . . . think about it, Jess."

How can he be so selfish after we've just escaped with our lives? Already he's trying to protect me. Already he's trying to keep me from saying out loud what is painfully obvious to us all. What we've done. What we're guilty of doing. What we will do if we don't go back.

But his attempts to prevent that from happening only make it that much more wrong. We have to go back. We have no choice.

I knew Kelly had fallen behind in that last fifty or hundred feet. Once the tunnel opening came into view, we split up from one another, dropping any last pretext of sticking together, no longer tethered to each other by our last remaining functioning rebreather cartridge. It was dying anyway, we knew it. We knew we were dying, too. Until we saw the opening.

Each of us racing to get to the surface.

None of us caring who was first or last.

Just wanting to get there.

Thinking about nothing but that precious air, so close and yet just out of reach.

Except for Kelly. How could he even think about me like that? Doesn't he even realize how close he came to drowning down there?

Of course he does. That's why he's telling me no.

I wonder, would they have dragged our bodies out with a pole like they do the zombies that drift through the tunnel from LI? Would they have unceremoniously separated our heads from our bodies — the only guaranteed way to stop the Undead — thinking we were one of them? Would they have then wrapped us up in plastic sheeting and sent us to the incinerator?

"It's out . . . of our hands now," Kelly pants.

I can see him treading water right in front of me. I can hear him pleading, and somewhere deep inside my mind I know what he's saying. But it doesn't register, not right away.

Until it finally does — not *what* he's saying, but his denial of what we did and why I know we have to go back despite the hell we just went through. We left Jake behind to die.

No. It's worse than leaving him behind to die: we left him to become one of the Infected Undead himself.

What if it was me?

"We have to, Kelly," I say, choking.

While there's still time. While there's still a chance to save him. He doesn't deserve to die.

We'd fooled ourselves into thinking Long Island was deserted. That's what Reggie kept saying anyway, and we all believed him. We wanted to believe there was no risk. Or very little. Nothing we couldn't handle. We all just accepted that the IUs — the Infected Undead — from the outbreak thirteen years ago had died off from not having anything to feed on once the island was evacuated. We were wrong.

We saw a few zombies shortly after breaking in, way off in the distance just standing there like statues doing nothing. But even then we refused to believe they were any danger to us. They seemed like no threat at all.

Even after the attack in the tunnel.

God, we were stupid! *I* was stupid.

We were just supposed to go in and take a few pictures in the Forbidden Zones. That was the plan. It was an adventure, something to impress our fellow classmates when school started again in a few weeks. A couple hours on the island, maybe do a little exploring, bring back some souvenirs. Like the ancient copy of Playboy magazine Jake had. On *real* paper. Contraband.

Micah, of course, had other plans, but that's Micah. He's always been obsessed with games and hacking. Reg and Ash. Me and Kelly. Just there for the thrill of it. Except for Kelly. He'd argued against it from the beginning, and now he's telling me we can't go back.

A few hours, that's all it was supposed to be. Then we were supposed to come back. *All* of us.

They came out of nowhere, the Infecteds. Dozens of them. Hundreds, it seemed. I thought we'd never escape.

Where the hell had they come from? How the hell could they act so goddamn coordinated?

We were separated. I'd gotten in a fight with Kelly and was hanging out with Jake. Reggie and Ashley were off doing their own thing — having sex, most likely, at the abandoned Holiday Inn. Like if that's not some weird fantasy, I don't know what is. But they didn't know about all the IUs. And it's Ash and Reg, so it shouldn't have surprised me.

Micah was alone, off near the wall trying to hack into the ArcWare codex. They attacked him, too.

We'd barely made it back to the tunnel opening when it seemed like the entire island's population of Undead was on us. No time to prep for the dive back. No time to switch out our rebreather cartridges. It all happened so fast that we had only the gear we'd been carrying around with us or managed to quickly snatch from the stash in the car. I'd thrown our packs with the spare rebreathers into the water, but the

Undead had fallen in, keeping us from retrieving them. It was my fault.

I can still hear the sickening slap of their bodies hitting the water, the sounds of their thrashing and the guttural moans as they desperately tried to get to us, even as they were sinking. But zombies don't drown.

If only we'd thought to change out our used air rebreather cartridges when we first arrived. The ones that were still on our masks had maybe an hour's worth of oxygen recycling capacity left in them. Ninety minutes, at the outside. Thank God we still had those, at least. But what other choice did we have? That and a prayer that none of them would fail early like the one I'd had going over.

We made good time coming back, at least at first. We probably would've been all right if it weren't for the delay. There was a blockage in the tunnel caused by storm wash that had gotten wedged against the hulking carcass of a sunken bus. The boys finally managed to clear a way through, but the current flowing into the small opening was too strong and the entire thing began to collapse on itself. Jake was left on the other side, unable to get through.

The air cartridges began to fail shortly afterward. We were only halfway back to Manhattan. We couldn't even try to save him. If we'd stayed, we all would've died.

We were forced to share the remaining functioning cartridges between us. One by one they failed. We were swimming nearly blind by then, guided only by the wan glow from the Links. And having to share cartridges made the going even slower.

Luckily, Micah still had an unused cartridge on his belt. We ended up passing it between the remaining five of us for the last quarter of a mile or so. Nobody had to say it, but I'm sure we all knew: if Jake had made it through with us, that last cartridge almost certainly wouldn't have lasted long enough for any of us to reach the tunnel opening. It was failing before we saw daylight. I don't even know who had it last.

Ashley's crying now. Quietly. Hiding it. Her back's turned. Even now, after all we've been through, she can't let anyone know she's anything but tough as nails. She's so freaking concerned with making sure we don't see her break down. I wish I could cry, but I can't. Maybe it's the shock, maybe disbelief. Maybe it's also joy. I'm glad to be alive.

Kelly turns to the others. He bobs in the water without holding onto anything, and he pleads for them to agree with him. But Reggie's eyes are still glassy and his face is slack with shock. He's staring at the sky, his mouth open like he's a little bird and he's trying to eat all the air out of the sky. Micah just looks . . . .

I can't really tell. The look on his face seems almost angry. I've never seen him look like that before.

Ashley gives an audible sob and snoggers. She makes a nervous, choking giggle. The unexpected sound seems to wake us all up.

"Look, guys," Micah quietly says. "Let's just . . . . Let's focus on getting out of the water first — getting out of *here*. We don't know when that cop will be coming around again. If he sees us, it won't matter what we decide to do later. There won't be any going anywhere except straight to a Life Service hearing."

Micah's right. The cop who patrols this area would know we'd lied to him the last time we ran into him. He'd know we weren't working on some lame school project or senior year community service thing. Not that he'd believed us when we told him that before. You could see it in his eyes: he believed we were just a bunch of hormone-crazed teenagers looking for a good place to make out.

One glance at our wetsuits and gear and he'd know we weren't there for sex. Well, maybe the kinkiest kind.

How many years would they add to our Life Service Commitment for breaking into a Forbidden Zone? Five years? Ten? How many more would they tack on once they figured out we'd not only gone to LI but then left one of us there, most likely to die? Another twenty?

Thirty years off the top of our life expectancies. That would make us middle aged already.

"This way," Reggie says, guiding us to the closest wall.

The moment Ashley's on solid ground, she falls to her knees and starts wiping away the water dripping off our bodies and onto the walkway. "Have to dry it," she says. "Have to hide it." She's becoming delirious. But her efforts only end up making a bigger mess.

"We can't worry about that right now," Micah quietly tells her. He gently pulls her to her feet and urges her up the walkway toward the parking garage where his car and Jake's van are parked. He turns one last time to Kelly and says, "We'll talk about it once we're back home and we've had a chance to clear our heads a little."

But Kelly doesn't wait. As soon as we're out of sight of the tunnel, he turns to me and says, "I know what you're thinking, Jess. The answer's still no. Leave it to the officials."

"Kel's right," Reggie says as he shrugs his way out of his wetsuit. It surprises me a little to hear him agreeing with Kelly. They rarely ever agree on anything, and even when they do, Reggie usually ends up arguing the other side, just to be difficult.

A look of surprise and distrust flashes across Kelly's face. He still blames Reggie for everything that's happened. He still thinks Reggie pushed him over the railing here days before. It was how we ended up knowing the tunnel was still open, even after all these years after LI was declared off-limits. Would any of this have happened otherwise — the trip, losing Jake — if we hadn't found that out?

Maybe.

I don't know what to believe anymore. I believe Kelly thinks he was pushed, but I can't picture Reggie doing something like that. He's big and strong and certainly capable, but he's more of a talker than a doer.

I make my way over to Ashley. She's still just sitting there. I reach over and grab her Link out of her hand and wake the screen. Jake's last message is still there. I hold it up for the others to see. "He was still alive after the passage collapsed. He said he was going back. He made it. I just know it."

"You don't know," Reggie says. The fear is clear in his eyes. He just doesn't want to admit he's chickenshit. He's the largest of our group, the strongest, and yet he's like a little kid sometimes. I almost tell him so, but Micah speaks first.

"That's why we have to go back," he says.

"Thank you." I hand the Link back to Ash.

"And then what?" Kelly asks. He angrily swipes his wet hair out of his face. "The place is swarming with zombies. And, okay, let's assume Jake's cartridge lasted him the whole way back — I doubt it, but let's just say it did — how's he going to get out of the water? You saw how many there were. They'd surround him in seconds. He'll be attacked." He shakes his head. "And so would we. No, Jake's . . . ."

He doesn't want to say it out loud. He doesn't have to. We all know it's very likely Jake would be bitten. There were just too many IUs.

"I don't care," I say. I refuse to believe he'd let himself get taken that easily. "He'll find a way. If any of us could, it's him."

Kelly slaps the side of the van in frustration. The obvious jealousy on his face just makes me even angrier. He has no reason to be jealous.

Well, maybe a little.

"Maybe *you* wouldn't make it," I say, knowing how hurtful I'm being and yet not really caring. "But Jake's had survival training."

"What the hell is it with you two anyway?" Kelly shouts.

Micah tries to quiet him down.

"It's not like that, Kel," I say. "There's nothing between us."

The worst part about it is, it's a lie: Jake was hitting on me, back at the dojang where I train in hapkido. At least, in his own awkward way, he was. And I'd been flattered. But then I had to go and mention it to Kelly afterward. I knew even before I said it that it would bother him, but I . . . .

What?

I'd wanted to hurt him.

He'd been acting strangely for a couple weeks by then, ignoring me, becoming moody and distracted. I just wanted him to pay some attention to me.

Is that why I'm so adamant about going back? Because I want Kelly to be jealous? Am I really that selfish and petty?

"I wish you'd explain it, then," Kelly pleads. "Because I'd really, really like to understand why you're willing to risk your life for this guy."

"He's a friend," I say. "And it's just common decency. We can't just leave him behind."

"We can't risk our own lives again, Jessie," Reggie quietly says. "Not without proof."

"And how do you expect to get it without going back?"

Reggie doesn't answer. He knows it's a classic catch-22.

"You'd do it for Ashley," I add. "Even without proof."

He gawps for a moment, but then closes his mouth. At least he knows the truth when it hits him square between the eyes.

"Please," Ashley sniffs. She's still shaking like a leaf, but she's managed to compose herself a bit. "I know we got Jake into this mess, but can we just drop it for a little while? I just can't think about that right now. We almost died back there."

And that finally shuts us all up.

Micah breaks into Jake's van by recoding the electronic lock with his Link. We dry ourselves off as best we can and change back into our street clothes. Nobody says anything about the lock. We all just accept it as a matter of course. We're all used to Micah's wizardry with just about anything that has a chip in it. His hacking abilities are so much better than any of the rest of ours.

Nevertheless, it's this very ease with such matters that reinforces my earlier worries about him.

It was while we were back on the island. We found out that he'd hacked into our implants. He said it was a necessary step in his plan to hack ArcWare's codex, the remote zombie controller used in *The Game*. For hardcore electronic gamers, *The Game* is the ultimate challenge. But only the rich and well-connected ever get the coveted invite. They're the only ones who can afford the minimum buy-in price, which includes an implanted zombie — Player — and ArcWare's cybernetic set-up with which the Player can be controlled. There was no way any of us would ever get to play. Not legitimately, anyway. We were just too poor.

A few weeks ago we'd tried hacking in, but the program ended up being far too sophisticated, even for Micah. The firewalls are too complex and the coding language too arcane.

We got discovered — at least by the program's built-in safety mechanisms — and it locked us out.

Micah insisted that all he'd need to complete the job was a backdoor into ArcWare's codex. A physical hack, in other words. But that could only be obtained from the *inside*, from the other side of the wall surrounding LI, past the EM barrier that protects the Forbidden Zones.

We were all secretly counting on Micah to be successful. Once he had access, it was supposed to be a cakewalk to reprogram any gaming device to take control of any Player in Gameland. We would be able to play *The Game*.

And the hack to our implants? Just a necessary step that permitted him to subtract our L.I.N.C. signals from any other signals he hoped to pick up while we were there — the Players, in other words. The Controlled Undead. The zombies that those rich prick gamers bought and used to play *The Game*.

It was obvious that Jake had been upset to learn his implant had been hacked. He wasn't a gamer or hacker like the rest of us, so couldn't truly appreciate the implications like we did. He was along simply for the adventure. But Micah had given everyone his promise that he'd wipe all our numbers from his program once we got back. I intend to make sure he does.

After we save Jake.

"What do you think his family's going to do when he doesn't show up at home tonight?" I ask. "They'll report him missing. The van, too. If the cops find it here, it's just a matter of time before they trace it all back to us. The checkpoints have a record of us coming here. That's why we need to go back. The longer we wait, that harder it's going to be to explain."

"There's no family," Ashley says. "It's just him and his uncle. And Joe's going to be in Albany at least until tomorrow."

"I'll deal with him if I have to," Micah says.

"How?"

He shrugs. "I'll figure something out. Him and the checkpoint records, too," he adds. He doesn't elaborate and nobody asks. None of us want to know what he's planning, especially since that kind of hacking borders on criminally insane. We just want everything fixed.

"There's also the problem with my lost Link," I say. I'd dropped it while trying to get away from those first Infected Undead at the refueling station. It happened right after Kelly sent me the picture of the surprise he'd been planning for me. "How're we going to get through the checkpoints without it?"

"They only scanned us coming in," Reggie says hopefully. "Maybe they won't check going home."

"You *think*."

"Jessie, please."

But I'm not done. I lean over the back bumper and pull one of the plastic packing crates to me. It holds a dozen more of the disposable rebreather cartridges, still unused.

"If we go back now, we could be home — *all* of us and my Link — by morning. Then there won't have to be any 'fixing' by Micah."

Kelly takes the cartridge from my hand and tosses it back in the crate. He pushes the box back into the darkness inside the van. "Nobody's going anywhere tonight except home."

Micah nods. "As much as I know you're right, Jess, Kelly's got a point. We need to rest, recover. We're all exhausted, not thinking straight. If we attempt to go back now — despite all our good intentions — we'll all just end up zombie meat."

"Besides," Reggie adds, "the tunnel's blocked, remember?"

It's a lame excuse and he knows it. There's the other bore of the tunnel. There's no reason to believe it's blocked, too.

But I don't argue. I'm suddenly so bone-weary, struggling just to keep myself from collapsing right there in the parking garage, that I give up. The truth comes crashing down on me: there's no way any of us would be able to swim the length of a mile-long tunnel for a third time that day — much less turn around to make the return trip. We all need to get some sleep and a warm meal inside of us. Even as well-conditioned as my body is from hapkido training, it isn't used to what we've all just been through.

Kelly grabs my arms and draws me to him. "I promise, Jessie, we'll talk it over first thing in the morning."

"It'll be a short talk then, Kel. Just long enough for me to tell you that I'm coming back." I look around at the rest of them. "With or without the rest of you, I'm coming back. Jake would do the same for us."

Micah nods. "But first sleep and food."

"Okay," Kelly whispers. "You win."

He pulls me to him. I rest my head against his chest, pressing my ear right over his heart, and listen to what it tells me. I know in that moment that he's lying. Once we leave this zone, he knows I won't be able to come back. The checkpoint guards won't let me through without my Link. And who knows how long it'll take for me to get a replacement.

But I won't let that stop me. I will come back in the morning. Even if Micah has to hack into every goddamn Link and Stream to do it.

Even if I have to walk.

Chapter Two

The ride back home is quiet and thick with tension. I sit and stare out the passenger window of Jake's van as Kelly drives. Reggie and Ash are with Micah in his car.

The abandoned skyscrapers of lower Manhattan yield to the derelict, but still occupied, skyscrapers of central Manhattan and New Wall Street. We cross the Hudson and work our way north along the fringe of New Jersey. Nobody points out the old football stadium this time. Or the ghost town of the Teterboro Airport. Or anything. We only see our nightmare.

We breeze through all of the checkpoints. None of the guards scans us, just as Reggie had predicted. They do, however, search both vehicles and warn us about the curfew before letting us through. Exactly the same as last time.

While we sit and idle behind Micah's car at one of the checkpoints, I overhear Reggie asking one of the guards what they're looking for, but the guy won't say. He's all business. They all are. I wonder what there could possibly be in New York that anyone could want to smuggle out. Playboy magazines?

Kelly pulls up to the curb at my house. He sits for a moment, fiddling with his Link, almost certainly wondering if he should ask about the picture he'd send to me on the island. Can he sense how much I want to avoid answering him?

He leans over me to kiss me goodbye.

I turn away. I get out of the van and go inside the house, leaving him sitting at the curb. I don't feel anything, neither guilt nor anger. I'm totally numb by then. I don't even stop when Mom passes me in the hallway. She actually looks halfway sober, which is an improvement. She says something, but my mind refuses to translate it. I just go straight up to bed and crawl beneath the covers.

Eric calls me down for dinner later. I go down and eat and come back upstairs. It's like a dream I'm watching. I lie down and squeeze my eyes closed. I just want to sleep.

But no matter how tired I am, no matter how worn down, I just can't stop thinking about Jake.

Hours pass. Finally, I get up and wander downstairs. The house is dark. I find Mom's Link on the table and sit staring at it for several minutes. Before I realize what I've done, Kelly's voice comes through it.

"Jess? Is everything all right? Why'd you ping me? I saw it was your mom and thought something bad happened."

I blink and stare at his worried face on the screen for a moment, wondering why I'm talking to him. Didn't I leave him behind?

"Are you . . . home?" he asks.

"Kelly?" I hear myself say. Like listening to someone else speaking, except in my own voice. "Can you come over? We need to talk."

He hesitates a moment, then nods. "I just put Kyle to bed. He's feeling a little better than he was this morning." He peers through the Link at me, studying my face. I know he's searching for something there, guilt or relief. But I don't know what he sees. I don't even know how I feel. "I'll be right over."

Five minutes later, he's knocking on the front door. I expect my mother to get it, but the house is silent and I realize I'm the only one still awake. Mom's almost certainly gone out, otherwise she'd be in front of the TV watching *Survivalist*. She's forgotten her Link again. She does that a lot.

I wonder if Grandpa's gone out, too. Probably. He comes and goes as he pleases, sometimes at odd hours, and never tells me where he's going. For an old retired guy six years past his life-expectancy — owing to a rare LSC waiver from the government because of his previous service to the country — he keeps himself busy enough. He's always here for dinner, though, always reminding me to eat right and take my medicine, which I do now, since I forgot earlier.

"Grandpa?" I call down the hall, quiet enough not to wake Eric, but loud enough that if Grandpa's awake, he'll answer. But the house remains silent.

I open the door and Kelly comes in and wraps his arms around me as soon as he sees me. I breathe in his smell. He's showered, so it's mostly just the strong scent of soap. But he's there, too, his particular scent, faint, familiar, comforting. I hold him tight. Then we're upstairs and in bed and my skin feels two sizes too small. He's in me and all I want to do is lose myself in the moment. I want to forget everything: my anger at the world and this feeling of helplessness I've carried around inside of me for as long as I can remember.

And when it's over, he lies beside me. He combs my hair away from my face, breathing with me, his exhales flowing over me like water.

"I love you so much, Jess," he tells me. "I don't ever want to lose you."

I close my eyes. He knows how much I hate when he says things like that, especially right after sex. But I know he isn't like that. He says what he feels deep down, not what's just right there on the surface.

"You won't lose me," I say. "I promise."

I hear him take in a breath and hold it. The word promise holds so much meaning for him right now — so *many* meanings — that I know he's wondering exactly which of those meanings I intend. He lets the breath out. It caresses my cheek and my skin tingles.

"A promise is not a guarantee," he says. It sounds like a line from a song. I almost groan.

"There are no guarantees in life," I say. But as soon as it's out, I regret even thinking it. I want to pull it back inside of me again.

"I wish I could tell you how much you mean to me, Jessie," he says. "How much you mean to all of us."

I pull my head away to look at him better. He holds my cheek in his hand, rubbing his thumb across my chin. He looks deep into my face. At first I just see myself in his eyes, my sun-bleached hair, my narrow face. Then I feel myself slipping into the muddy depths of his brown eyes, losing myself in him.

"You're our rock, Jessie."

He laughs a little when he sees the look on my face. "What I mean to say is, you're so well-grounded, so . . . so solid."

I shake my head. "Me? You're the one who's going to become someone someday. You'll go to college and make lots of money and—"

"And marry you."

I sigh and turn my head away, but he gently pulls it back.

"You care about us all. Even people you barely know."

He's talking about Jake.

I shake my head. "You're the one who cares deeply, Kel. Not just for me, either. Look at Kyle. Look at everything you do for him."

I feel him tense up against me. The line of his jaw hardens and he doesn't meet my eyes for a moment. He's always found it hard to talk about his brother. He's convinced that if they just had a little money they could fix Kyle. He might be right, but it's a moot point at the moment. That's why he pushes himself so hard, so he can go to college, so he can have money. That's why his parents push him, too.

"I'm not like that," he whispers.

"Yeah, well, I'm not as solid as you think I am, either," I say. He knows about my temper. He knows that's one reason I take hapkido. It's cheaper than counseling, anyway, and probably a hell of a lot more effective.

"I feel like I've barely kept things together lately," he says. "If it wasn't for you, I probably would've given up a long time ago."

"Don't say that, Kel."

"It's true. I mean, we're all graduating this year and you're so sure of yourself, going to work for ArcWare—"

"*We serve the people*," I joke. "That's not being sure, Kel. That's facing reality. College isn't for me."

"Yeah, well, I'm not so sure about it being for me, either."

"If anyone can do it, you can. Certainly not Reggie."

Kelly laughs and shakes his head. "I look at him and, I'm sorry, but all I see is a little kid wearing a man's body. He wants to be liked so badly, to be accepted. He wants to be in charge, but he's too scared of responsibility. You're not. You're fearless. I still can't believe how well you dealt with all that shit today."

"I'd rather not think about that."

"And Ash," he says, going on. "I thought for sure she was going to crumble to pieces. Literally. She's like Reg in a lot of ways. She wants to be grown up, but she's got a lot of growing up to do."

"Growing up's overrated."

He nods and rubs my lips so gently with his thumb that it sends shivers through my body. Desire for him overwhelms me. I can't believe just an hour ago I was so tired I was ready to pass out, so fragile I thought I'd crumble to pieces. I can't believe just a few hours before we were trying not to die.

Jake's face flashes before my eyes.

And now . . . .

Now I never want to leave this bed. Or Kelly. Or this moment.

"And then there's Micah." Kelly sighs. "I mean, he's definitely got it going on. But what exactly it is he's got, I don't know. He scares me sometimes. He's so damn smart and capable that I often wonder what the hell he's doing with his life, sitting in a dark, dank basement playing video games. Getting high and drunk. Hacking government computers, or at least trying to. He's self-destructive. I'm afraid he'll end up dragging us all down with him. I wouldn't be surprised if he gets conscripted by the time he's forty. Probably a lot sooner."

As soon as he'd said the part about being scared of Micah, I had gasped. I didn't think anyone else felt the same way about him as I do.

"But you," Kelly continues, not noticing, "you just keep chugging along."

"Chugging? Really? That's the best you can come up with to describe me?"

"You know what I mean. You are our base, Jessie. You're the one who holds us all together. We all rely on you to keep us focused. That's why I did what I did in LI. That's why I do what I do now. And why I'll continue to do what I need to do so I won't lose the people I love. I'd rather die first."

"You won't lose me."

"I know. You promised."

I don't answer. I know he's waiting for me to bring up marriage. But how can I tell him it's the thing I so dearly want when I have all these tiny little doubts — not about us or him, but of me? I'm so afraid if I tell him yes that it'd be like he's settling for something less than he deserves. How can I tell him that?

We make love again. It's awkward and hesitant this time. And yet despite that, it still feels right. Maybe that's what matters in the end, that it doesn't always have to be perfect. It just has to feel right between us. Maybe that's how he knows for sure.

Maybe that's all I need to also be sure.

Afterward, when our breathing has slowed and our hearts have once more settled back into their comfortable rhythms, I finally yield to exhaustion.

"I love you, Jessica Anne Daniels," he whispers into my ear, even as the welcome darkness flows over me, consumes me. "I need you."

I want to tell him Jake needs us, too." But my lips are numb with sleep. His words and my thoughts melt into my dreams. It's not until the next morning, when my dreams are shattered by Ashley's frantic banging on my door, that the full impact of his final words hits me:

"That's why I have to let you go."

Chapter Three

"He's gone," Ashley tells me, and I know immediately who she means. "He took Jake's van. He's gone back to Long Island. Alone."

By all rights, she should sound frantic, but she only sounds relieved. She thinks Kelly's going means the rest of us won't have to. It means *she* won't have to.

She nudges my foot with her toe as I stand there numb with shock. "Hey, girl, you still with me?"

"This can't be happening," I manage to gurgle. I feel like I'm suffocating beneath a mountain of sand. "Kelly wouldn't do a fucked up thing like that. He told me . . . . He said he was going to let *me* go."

Even as I say it, I realize that's not what he meant. He wasn't saying I could go back to LI to save Jake. He was telling me he was letting me go for good. By sacrificing himself. but the last thing I want is for him to let me go!

The betrayal is especially painful after our night together.

"*Let* you go?" Ash says, incredulous. The old Ash returns in a flash, defiant and indignant, fiercely self-reliant, yet hopelessly dependent. "Since when do you need his permission?"

"I don't, damn it! That's not what I meant." I rub my face, trying to wake myself. "Son of a bitch! I'm going to kill him!"

"You, kill? Ha, right! You have a hard time killing bugs."

"I killed zombies."

"That's different. They're not alive. Besides, Kelly's just trying to protect you. You know that, don't you?"

"I don't need to be protected!" I slam my fist into the wall by the door. Somewhere, in the back of the house, I hear a chair squeak. I sense Grandpa leaning forward at his desk, tilting his head and listening. Fine, let him hear. I don't care! "It's Kelly who needs protecting. I can take care of myself!"

Ashley glances nervously into the depths of the house. She grabs my arm and leads me upstairs and into my bedroom.

She sits me down, then goes back to close the door. I pop right back up and start to pace.

"Listen, Ash, are you sure?" I ask her. "Did you actually talk with him?"

"I stopped at his house on my way over this morning," she tells me. "He was gone and his mother asked if I knew whose van was he driving. What could I say? I said it was a friend's he was helping out. I think she knew something was going on. She was acting all nervous and kept asking me questions. She kept asking about you and if you knew anything. I got away as soon as I could and pinged Micah, but he wasn't answering."

"What about Reggie?" I doubt Kelly would say anything to Reg, but Ash's answer surprises me.

"Turns out he spoke with Kel about a half hour before. Said Kelly had pinged him from the road and told him to make sure we all just sat tight. He said he'd be back sometime this afternoon."

"Reggie knew and he didn't say anything to anyone sooner? He didn't ping me?"

"He couldn't."

I wince. Without my Link, I'm shut off from the world.

"He could've told me in person."

Ash shakes her head. I can see it in her eyes, the knowledge that Reggie's a coward. He was all too willing to let Kelly go and take all the risk himself. Just like her. At least she had the guts to tell me in person.

For the first time I wonder if Kel was right about Reg pushing him back at the tunnel opening the other day. He can be so selfish sometimes, so immature, letting others do the heavy lifting.

"Kelly told him to wait a couple hours. He said he had to do it, to go by himself. He mentioned love."

"Love? He said that? To Reg?"

"Said it was his responsibility to take care of the people he cares for."

This just makes me even angrier. How can he speak of love and then lie to me like this? "The people he cares for? He doesn't care about Jake any more than you or Reggie do."

"I care for Jake!"

"Then why didn't you go? Huh?"

There's a moment of silence as she looks away in shame. "Kelly said he had more reason than any of us to go."

"He won't put this on me!"

"Actually, he mentioned Kyle."

Kyle? Is that what he meant by love and responsibility? Somehow it hurts even more knowing it isn't me.

I sit down on the edge of the bed and press my thumbs against my eyelids. I don't want to believe what's happening.

"What do you think he meant by that, Jess? What does Kyle have to do with Kelly going back for Jake? Is this some sort of big-brother thing?"

I push even harder. I start imagining my thumbs thrusting deep inside my brain. What would it feel like? Would it hurt? Tiny little micro supernovas explode behind my eyelids.

"Jessie?"

The problem is, it's all starting to make sense: Kyle and the strange way Kelly'd been acting lately. The mysterious message from ArcWare on his Link last week.

I feel like I'm suffocating.

Inhale and hold.

I wish I was wrong, but somehow I don't think I am.

Exhale.

Kelly's inability to focus lately and his sudden obsession with *Zpocalypto*.

Hold. And inhale again.

It's all coming together, all the pieces. I just can't see how they all fit.

I drop my hands and the white stars behind my eyelids slowly fade away. When they're gone, I look up at her.

I ask her for her Link, and she gives it to me. Once again I see Kwanjangnim Rupert's face streak by as I scroll through her contacts list. I'm dying to know why she has him on her Link, how she knows him. But I can't think about that right now. First I try and ping Kelly. After a moment, I get sent to the messaging app, so I leave a quick request to ping me back as soon as he gets this. Then I disconnect.

On a whim, I next try pinging my own Link. I immediately get the following message:

<< CLIENT DOES NOT EXIST ON THIS STREAM >>

I show Ash the message. She shrugs and says, "Your Link's on the other side of the EM barrier, outside the Stream. At least we know they won't be able to trace it there."

"I tried Kelly and got his messaging app instead of this. It means he's still here. If we leave now, maybe we can catch up with him."

She pulls away. I can see the terror in her eyes. But somebody needs to think about how terrified Jake must feel . . . .

I hear Mom talking to someone downstairs. Another disposable boyfriend, no doubt. But when no other voice responds, I realize she must be on her Link. I dismiss her from my mind. A moment later she knocks at my door and says that there's a message for me on the house Link and asks if I can take it.

I get up and pull the door open. She sees Ashley sitting on my bed and mumbles a hurried hello before handing me the Link and slipping away. I guess I should be happy that she still has enough self respect to be aware of how horrible she looks to my friends.

"Kel?" I say, not bothering to first check the identification code.

"This is a call for . . . Jessica Anne Daniels," a mechanical recording states. "Is this . . . Jessica Anne Daniels? Say 'Yes,' if— "

"Yes."

There's a moment of silence, then the recording asks me to verify my home address, which I do. "This is Connecticut Citizen Registration. You have filed a missing personal Link device report and have requested a replacement. An appointment to interview you and to formalize your application process has been set for nine-thirty this morning in our main office in Hartford. You may take the free eight o'clock transit bus number seventeen from your town's administration hub. You should expect to be with us until approximately three o'clock in the afternoon. If you are identified as being in need of a latent individualized neural connection, you will be required to sign a surgical release and to remain for the implantation procedure and follow up observation for twenty four hours. This appointment cannot be rescheduled. Say 'Repeat,' if you'd like this information repeated."

I don't, even though my head is buzzing. I get the necessary details: address, room number, penalties for missing the appointment and falsifying information. All the while my anger grows and grows until it feels like a living thing inside of me. Ash waits until I disconnect and have finished swearing up a blue streak and throwing stuff around my room before trying to say anything.

"Ugh," she says, trying to be supportive. "I remember the CR office in Hartford. It's in that big, ugly, stupid looking skyscraper. The inside is absolutely dreadful."

"Thanks," I manage to mutter through clenched teeth. "That makes me feel much better."

"Yeah, a whole day of sitting in a hot, stuffy Citizen Registration office answering the same hundred questions being asked ten different ways."

That's not actually why I'm angry.

"Still not helping, Ash."

"But why did you report it? I thought you were going to wait. Kelly and Jake might still bring it back."

"It was Kelly who reported it, not me!"

She looks confused.

"He wanted to be absolutely sure I couldn't go back to LI."

Ashley chews on this for a moment. "Well, it worked. You're stuck here, girl."

I wave her off. "This pisses me off! He has no right to tell me I can't go and then to go and do it himself!" I'm pacing from one end of the room to the other, too angry to care, even when I realize I'm doing exactly what I hate about my brother when he gets agitated. I'm so upset I'm actually seeing red. "God damn him!"

Ash pings Micah and tells him the latest. She has the volume turned down and is talking low and close into the Link. I can barely hear her. I can't hear Micah's replies. From what I can gather as I prowl the room, he doesn't sound too happy with what Kelly's done.

She disconnects. "He says to just go and get your replacement Link. The rest of us will deal with Kelly and Jake." She checks the time. "You better hurry if you're going to catch the transit."

I finish dressing and pick my clothes from yesterday off the floor. They smell of sweat and stinky river water. I know I must smell like it, too, but I don't care. Where I have to go today, I doubt anyone will care.

Ash gets up off the bed and walks with me out of the room and down the hall. I dump the dirty clothes into the hamper and head downstairs.

"Aren't you going to fix your hair?" she asks.

I notice for the first time how hers is perfectly brushed, shampooed and shiny bright.

"Screw it."

I'm still holding the house Link, so I scroll through the menu until I find the account page. I thumb the hotlink for Citizen Registration and wait for the automated voice to walk me through the options. I know the recording said the appointment couldn't be rescheduled, but it's worth a try.

No such luck.

I grab a water pouch and head for the door. Ash trails me. "What are you going to do now?" I ask her.

She shakes her head. "See if I can find Micah. Maybe try and finish translating the new codex, I guess."

I give her a sour look. They should be focusing on Kelly and Jake, not some stupid program.

She must see it on my face, because she adds, "We'll do what we can, but I'm not sure there's much we can do. The coding will keep my mind off things."

"Make sure Micah erases our implant codes from the program when he's done."

Ash frowns, then slowly nods. She walks with me to the transit stop.

"The ride up to Hartford's an hour-long," she says. "I'd go nuts without a Link. What are you going to do?"

Something I barely remember how to do anymore.

"Pray," I say. "Pray Kelly gets home safe with Jake."

"They will."

"I hope you're right. Because when he gets back, I really am going to kill him."

Chapter Four

I arrive at the Citizen Registration office over on Fifth Ave in downtown Hartford a few minutes before the building opens for business, so I sit in the dwindling shade beneath a struggling maple tree and try to stay cool. I watch as workers pass through the doors under the stone archway that announces Carcher Plaza. They thread their way through the security screening area in the lobby and disappear further inside the guts of the place.

Ashley's right. The building is about as big and ugly as you can find in Hartford. It's actually three buildings fused together by glass and metal and concrete. The central tower, right in front of me, is a monolithic structure of yellow stone with an uninspired grid of small windows. The placard next to me says the building was named in honor of some guy named Edwin Carcher, a real estate developer from around the turn of the century. The picture of him amuses me, with his plastic-looking hair and the two beauties on his arms. The building in the picture sparkles. In real life it just looks run down and neglected. Just like everything else these days.

The story that goes along with the picture says Carcher made billions selling coastal property. He got out just before the first floods hit the coastal cities nearly thirty years ago. After the waters receded, he bought all the property back at rock bottom prices, developed it again and sold it to the next generation of developers at a steep markup. Then the earthquake hit Europe and sent tsunamis across the Atlantic. Everything got swamped out again.

The writer of the story seemed to think that Edwin Carcher was some sort of prophet, that he was able to time his purchases and sales so perfectly that he must've somehow known. Maybe he was a prophet. Maybe he knew when disasters would strike. You'd think after the second time people would've stopped buying from him.

There's quite a large crowd gathered by the time it opens to the public, people appearing out of nowhere, off transits from other parts of the state. It's almost like the zombies on LI.

When I think this, a buzz of nervousness thrums through my body. It feels strange to be standing here with this secret, knowing where I was yesterday and what I saw and what happened. Nobody else here has any clue what it was like. Anyone who was there for the outbreak is either dead or became an Infected Undead. A lot of them are probably still there.

The doors finally open, and we all filter into the lobby. It's slow going, since there's only one security checkpoint and we all have to go through it. When I finally get to the front, the guard scans my implant and asks for my Link.

"I'm here to report it missing."

Several people glance over at me, looks of surprise on their faces. Nobody loses a Link these days. It's too much of a hassle to get a new one. Plus, it's hard to imagine life without one. Our Links connect us to the world. Without them, functioning is so much harder. Also, losing a Link places you under intense scrutiny for weeks afterward.

The guard leers at me and snarls when he asks, "Lost or stolen?"

I choose an answer that hints at both and neither at the same time. "I was at the park and it must've fallen out of my pocket. When I went back to find it, it was gone."

"No one would pick up someone else's Link," a little old woman standing behind me declares. She looks like she could be eighty, but I know that's not possible. Everyone gets conscripted at sixty-five. Unless they have a waiver that is, like Grandpa. Maybe that's it.

"Did you try tracing it, honey?" she asks. "That's how I always find mine, when I can't remember where I put it."

"Yes. But it wasn't traceable."

"Oh. Oh dear, then. That doesn't sound right."

"Sixth floor," the guard tells me, rolling his eyes. "Room eighteen. Off the elevator and to the right. Now move along." He gives me a sour look as I pass through the screener. It beeps once, signifying that it has detected my implant and registered it. Behind me, I hear the guard ask the old woman what she's here for.

"To get my implant," she answers.

"Age?"

"Sixty five next week."

"Cutting it close, aren't you, mother?"

I don't hear her answer.

"Link, please," the guard says to her. I hear the scanner beep — a different beep than mine. Then he tells her, "Twenty-third floor. And, mother? Thank you for your service."

I hang back so I can ride the elevator up with her, but she sees me and cuts into the restroom. I don't know who's in worse shape, her or me. She's got a week to live. Me, depending on what happens with Kelly and Jake, it's possible I could have even less than that. Unlikely, but possible.

I wait for the elevator and no one gives me a second look until I push the button for the sixth floor. Then they all seem to shy away from me a little bit. It makes me wonder how they could know. It makes me worry *what* they know.

When the doors open for my floor, I step stiffly through them. The people part for me as if I'm contagious. I find myself on the worn carpeting in the sixth floor elevator lobby, conscious of all the stares on the back of my head. No one follows me out. It's just me. The doors close with a *whoosh*.

The hallway is empty, undecorated, stark and too-brightly lit with a bluish tinge. The lights flicker in sync, as if there's a faulty wire somewhere. The walls are painted a neutral cream color to offset the blue, turning them a glaring white. There's only one other door, so it's not like I have to think about where to go.

As I step toward it, I notice the small, black, inverted dome of a security camera in the farthest corner. I wonder who might be watching me.

My footsteps on the carpet get swallowed up, so there's not a sound. Nothing moves. Even the air seems reluctant to carry a scent.

The door is closed. It's just a plain metal slab, painted blue and lacking windows. A large plastic number 618 is glued to the outside.

There are no instructions, no button to push, no speaker. I consider knocking. Instead, I try the doorknob. It turns.

The room inside is dark, but a light blinks on. It's small, barely eight feet on each side. The walls are as bare as the ones in the hallway. There are no other doors, no windows. All I find is a single desk with a retractable screen. I move to see it better and it flickers on, showing me only the familiar ArcWare logo floating in a sea of blue and their catchphrase underneath: *We serve the people.*

"Have a seat, please."

The genderless voice comes out of nowhere, neither loud, nor soft. A chime sounds, presumably confirmation of my identity by some scanning device.

"The interview will proceed momentarily."

I sit at the desk and stare at the screen. The screen stares back.

There's a beep. Then, "Personal Link replacement. Please provide appointment code."

I recite the code I was given this morning by memory: "Gamma four alpha dash alpha thirteen."

I wait. Nothing happens for a moment. Then:

"Please state your full name."

"I'm sorry, I—"

"Incorrect response. Please state your full name."

I say it. The voice begins asking me for my vital statistics — age, date of birth, parents, L.I.N.C. implant number. Then it stops again.

"This is your second personal Link replacement."

I don't say anything. I'm not sure if it's a question or a statement.

My first Link was lost when I was thirteen. I'd barely had it for a month by then. Eric had just been discharged from the Marines and wanted to take me to Seattle. He didn't explain why until later, but I sort of guessed he wanted to get us as far away from the East Coast as he could, as far away from the

Undead as the government would allow him. Away from the outbreaks.

The South was out of the question, since we were at war with both Texas and Mexico at the time, and the Midwest was one enormous big dustbowl. Everyone said Seattle was still a nice place, a lot like it had been back before Reanimation was invented. Before global warming.

But when we got there, it became obvious very quickly that Seattle wasn't going to be any better than New York or DC. The rising oceans had already wiped out major parts of the city, and a lot that remained was rapidly decaying into Wasteland status. The rain was incessant.

A few days was all it took to convince Eric that we would be just as bad off moving there as we would staying in Greenwich. At least here, we still had the infrastructure in New York in case anything major happened.

He confessed this to me at dinner, thinking I'd be upset that we weren't moving. In truth, I would've been upset if we had. When we got back to the hotel, I realized I didn't have my Link. I was careless and had probably left it at the restaurant. Well, we obviously couldn't leave Seattle without it.

We went straight to the police that night and reported it missing. The process to get a new permanent one at Olympia Citizen Registration was much more streamlined back then. Even so, it still took three days, despite the fact that we reported the Link almost immediately and the police were able to track it within an hour.

They caught the offender, who admitted to picking it out of my pocket at the restaurant. His public defender claimed he was insane, but the judge sentenced him to two months of LSC. He'd already racked up so much time from previous offenses that it put him past his life expectancy. He was immediately executed and his implant activated. We were invited to watch the process, which we weren't allowed to refuse. It was a requirement of the sentencing.

"Given his youth," the judge confided in us just before the lethal injection was given, "he'll be sent to guard the Olympia Power Plant. They had another near meltdown last week, so they'll be needing replacement CUs."

We weren't really supposed to be told any of this, but the judge somehow found out Eric had once been in the Omegaman Corps.

After we were released, Eric took me straight back to the hotel, where we packed up and came straight home.

We got out just before the outbreak hit Seattle.

"Your Link cannot be located in the Stream," the voice says, accusing.

"I don't know what happened to it," I say to the room, hoping they don't have biometric capabilities. They'd know in a second I'm lying. My heart must be racing. "Whoever stole it must've destroyed it."

"Destruction of a personal Link is a class seven misdemeanor," the voice informs me.

"I don't know what that means." Am I being accused of something?

"A replacement fee of three hundred and forty six dollars will be levied in the next taxation cycle. If you cannot pay this amount within ninety days of receiving notice, three hundred and forty six hours will be added to your Life Service Commitment."

One hour for every dollar. I quickly do the math: almost fifteen days.

Eric will pay it, of course.

"The interrogation will proceed shortly. Please direct your attention to the screen in front of you. You are allowed only one break every three hours, during which you are not permitted to leave this room."

Not leave?

"You must complete the entire examination, answering each question as thoroughly as you are able to in the allotted time. Failure to do so will add hours to your LSC. This interrogation will take approximately six hours and twelve minutes, after which you will be free to return to your home. If the examination requirements are satisfied, you will be assigned a temporary Link upon departure. This device will provide you access only to the Media and Government Streams. You must return here in seven days to exchange it for your permanent replacement and for recoding."

"How do I—"

"The examination begins now."

Chapter Five

I still feel naked, even with the temporary replacement Link they've given me. Naked and unconnected.

And wiped out. The examination was grueling. I don't know if it was a whole thousand questions like everyone says it is, but it had to be close. The questions were both on-screen as well as verbal, asked by that faceless, nameless, sexless voice. The same questions over and over again. Backwards and forwards, twisted around, reworded, all trying to catch me in an inconsistency.

I can only assume I didn't contradict myself. I don't think I triggered any warnings. All I got at the end was, "This interview is now concluded. You may pick up your temporary Link in the lobby. Your code is tau one sigma. You have five minutes to exit the building."

I need to pee badly, but I don't stop. I get to the lobby and tell the clerk my code. She hands over the Link and scans my implant. "Return in a week for your permanent Link," she says. She sounds tired. Her eyes don't even seem to focus on me, but rather at some invisible object ten feet behind me and slightly over my left shoulder. I doubt she'd even be able to describe me five minutes after I've left.

The first thing I do after hopping onto the bus back to Greenwich is try to ping Ash with the new Link, but it's just as I'd been told: the interpersonal communication function is disabled. I can't send or receive messages. I can only connect to two Streams: Media and Government.

I flip to Media. Nobody ever connects to Government.

Survivalist is playing. It's the supposedly live feed of *The Game* straight from Gameland, but everyone suspects the footage is both edited and doctored. All in the name of entertainment. For example, there have been times when the video shows rain when there isn't a cloud in the sky, and sunshine when it's pouring down. You'd think Arc

Entertainment would do a better job of syncing something as obvious as the weather.

Despite the show's popularity, I'm not a big fan. Why would I want to sit in front of a screen passively watching someone else play a game when I could be the one playing, even if the games we have access to are poorly rendered renditions with limited possibilities rather than real-time interactive proxies with endless outcomes?

The bus is full for the hour-long ride, and the empty seat next to me is soon filled by a young woman who looks to be in her mid-twenties.

"Ooh," she says, glancing over my shoulder. "Is that *Survivalist* ? I'm hopelessly addicted to that show, but I promised myself I wouldn't watch it at all this week. If I can make it through the week, then I give myself a reward."

"Why would you do that?"

"Because I get hooked into it so easily that I forget the time and the next thing I know I've burned dinner, or it's way past my bedtime, or I'm late for work. My boss has already put me on notice. Twice. He likes me, though, so I doubt he'll fire me."

I lower the Link and give her a half-smile. "I was just surfing." But she looks disappointed and turns away.

I have to roll my eyes. She won't watch *Survivalist* on her own Link, but it's perfectly okay for her to sneak peeks on mine? It's like being on a diet and then sneaking someone else's lunch out of the fridge and rationalizing that it doesn't count.

I shove the thing into my pocket and lean my head against the window and pretend to fall asleep. But the roads are too bumpy and the glass rattles against the window frame. The constant banging is giving me a sore on my forehead, so I sit up and stare at the back of the man sitting in the seat directly in front of me. He has a mole on his neck shaped like an exclamation mark, as if drawing attention to itself.

My thoughts drift and I think about Kelly. I wonder if he's on his way back from LI with Jake. I hope he's safe.

"I've been watching that new Player," the woman beside me says, interrupting my thoughts. "What a hunk. I bet he was a hottie when he was still alive."

I look over at her and frown. She's not in her mid-twenties, as I'd originally thought. More like early twenties. If that.

"Have you seen him?" she asks, raising her eyebrows.

I shake my head. I've heard of people getting attached to Players, but not like that. Maybe that's what people her age do, but to me it's just creepy. I mean, Players are dead people, even if they are reanimated and controlled by the living. No matter how you slice it, it's kind of morbid.

"It's almost supernatural," she gushes confidentially. "He just started playing last week and already people are saying he's going to outlast any Player that ever played *The Game* and anything they might throw at him. He's already taken out over forty other Players." She snaps her fingers. "Like that."

"That's . . . interesting," I say.

"Yup. They say when he was alive, he was one of the world's best Operators himself. It's like he still can *remember* all the ins and outs of Gameland and can control himself."

"They can't remember!" I say, chuffing.

She gives me a pained look, as if I've just insulted her. A couple people sitting close by look over at me. I feel my face get hot.

"I mean, it's probably just that he died young and strong and he's freshly conscripted," I say. "CUs are basically just robots. In fact, if it wasn't for the implants, they'd just go around all the time looking for people to eat instead doing the things their Operators make them do in *The Game*."

"Nobody's denying that, honey. But it sure makes it more entertaining, don't you think, when they're actually worth looking at? I mean, who really wants to cheer on some old, wrinkled, half-decayed zombie all the time?"

Someone across the aisle nods in agreement. The woman leans in closer to me and whispers in my ear. "There's a rumor at work that he was a Volunteer."

She means a person who voluntarily sacrifices himself to get into *The Game* in exchange for money. It's illegal, of course, but I can't remember ever hearing about anyone actually getting busted for it. The rich have ways to skirt the laws. They believe that when the poor make sacrifices for money it only improves society. The poor, of course, believe otherwise.

Still, it makes me wonder how much of the buy-in and the proceeds from *The Game* actually make it to the Player's family. Even a small percentage would seem like a fortune to mine. But, then again, he'd already be rich if he was an Operator. Why would he volunteer?

"I bet he really did," Tanya whispers. "I bet he probably cost his Operator at least three million." She leans away again and says in a normal voice, "But don't take my word for it. You should check him out yourself. I think he's scheduled to play this afternoon."

I nod, slowly. It's disturbing to know that there are people out in the world like her, even if she otherwise seems completely normal.

After a few minutes of blissful silence, she turns to me again. "I really hate this ride sometimes. It gets so depressing after a while. Do you commute, too?"

I shake my head, grateful for the change in subject. I'd prefer to be left alone, but that doesn't appear to be happening. "I just had to go into the capital for... to do something." I quickly ask if she commutes, hoping to switch the focus back onto her.

"Every day. I work in Hartford but live in New York. Two hours one way, every day, six days a week." She brightens up. "But I love my job."

"What do you do?"

She blushes. "Well, not my actual *job* job, which is a recording clerk at ArcWare. I'm talking about my other job. I'm an actress. Well, okay, I'm trying to be an actress. ArcWare's just my foot into the door of Arc Entertainment. And it seems to be working. I have an audition next week!"

She throws her hands up and squeaks. I hate people who do that.

"And what do you do?" she asks.

Me? Oh, nothing, actually. Break into Forbidden Zones. Kill zombies.

"I'm still in school," I say.

"You are? Girl, you look like you're too old for school. I thought you were, like, twenty or something. Like, you and I could be best friends or something. Hell, we could still be friends anyway."

I'm not so sure.

"My name's Tanya," she says, offering her hand.

"Jessica," I reply. I'm starting to believe this ride will never end.

The conversation continues like this for another twenty minutes. Despite her obnoxiousness, I find I actually kind of like her. She seems so carefree. I finally feel comfortable enough to ask her if I can borrow her Link.

She gives me a strange look, so I explain that mine's on the blink. "I think it needs an upgrade." It's the same excuse Micah told the guard at the checkpoint when it didn't sync properly with his implant. A lifetime ago now. "I can't seem to connect to any of the Streams except Media and Government."

The woman smiles and nods sympathetically. "Ugh, Government. So boring. Nobody ever watches that Stream. It's just a waste of bandwidth if you ask me." She hands over her Link.

"I had a defective device a few years ago," she says, "back when I was still living with my parents. It kept sending me messages meant for someone else. I complained to Citizen Registration for weeks, but they kept telling me that the person whose messages I was getting didn't actually exist." She laughs. "Turns out he did, but he was CU. He'd died about a month earlier and was assigned to clean sewers. They found him stuck in a section directly under my parents' house, apparently no worse for the wear."

All I can do is stare at her.

She shudders and nods. "Yeah, I know. I laugh about it now, but when I first found out about this dead person living under us the whole time, I practically freaked out. I even threatened my parents that I'd move out right then, but of course I couldn't. I still had a few more months of school left."

"That's quite a story," I say.

She watches me while I key in Kelly's Link identification. I wait for it to connect. The screen goes blank, then returns with:

<< CLIENT DOES NOT EXIST ON THIS STREAM >>

My face grows numb with shock. Kelly really did go to LI. And he's still there.

"That's the exact same message I kept getting," Tanya exclaims, "when I tried pinging that mysterious person's ID! I remember it now!" She snatches her Link back and bangs it against her palm. "I hope it isn't happening again. Those new rules they put into place for getting a replacement are such a pain in the ass. I hate them. A whole day wasted answering stupid questions."

I force an encouraging smile onto my face, but it feels weak and strained. "Actually, I think I just put in the wrong code."

She looks instantly relieved. "Oh, well that makes sense." She gives a nervous laugh. "For a moment I thought maybe there might be a CU stuck to the bottom of the bus." She laughs.

I try to smile.

"You want to try again?"

I shake my head and push the Link away. "It's just my boyfriend. He can wait till I get home."

She nudges me like we're old friends. "That's right, Jessica. Make the poor bastard suffer! Make him appreciate you more."

I cough uncomfortably and am glad to see my stop coming up.

"Make sure you get your Link updated," she tells me as I get up. "And check out that Player on *Survivalist*. You'll see what I mean!"

Chapter Six

After getting off the bus, I decide to go by Micah's place to see if Kelly has come back yet. I'm kind of hoping to find Jake's van there and Kelly inside playing *Zpocalypto*. But instead of the van, there's another car sitting in Micah's driveway that I don't recognize. I figure it probably belongs to Mr. or Mrs. Sandervol.

I've never met either of them — they're always out of town — so I'm curious to see what they're like. But after today, the last thing I need is to get all wrapped up in the whole 'meet my folks' circus and them asking me about school and future plans and all that crap. I'm not up for acting all normal. Plus, I want to get over to Kel's, so I just hurry on past without stopping.

I see the police car when I'm still a block and a half away. Two officers are just coming out the front door of the house and Mrs. Corben is standing there with her hands clasped together up by her chin. She's clearly upset, and the officers are trying to console her.

I quickly turn up a side street and come home the back way. I don't know what else to do. I can't even ping Ash or any of the others to find out what's going on. All I can do is guess that he's still not home.

"There you are!" Eric barks at me when I walk through the front door. He gets up from the couch and tries to block my way to the stairs. "Where have you been all day?"

I brush past my brother without saying anything. I just want to go up to my room and scream into my pillow.

"What's the matter with your Link?" he demands. "I tried pinging you all afternoon, but all I got was this strange mess— *Hey!* Jessie, I'm talking to you!"

He grabs my arm and twists me around. I shake his hand off of me. I could flip him onto his back in a second, but what good would that do? It would just make me feel like shit and humiliate him. It won't bring Kelly back.

"Jessie, please. What happened to you today?"

"Someone stole my Link," I say. "Okay, Eric?"

"What? Again?" He exhales and shakes his head disapprovingly.

"I'm tired, Eric. I just spent the day in Hartford registering for a new one and the past hour on the transit with some crazy woman with a morbid crush on a Player on *Survivalist*. I'd rather just go lie down."

I turn and head for the stairs.

"Oh, and we're going to be getting a taxation bill for three hundred and forty six dollars in the next cycle."

Eric chokes. I use his momentary surprise to escape into my room so I can think about what to do next, but he chases me up the stairs. He doesn't even grant me a minute to myself. Two seconds after I've shut the door, he's pounding on it. "Jessie?"

"Don't worry," I shout out at him. "I'll pay the stupid bill. I'll figure out a way to get the money."

"I . . . I don't care about that, Jess. Just . . . . Why didn't you tell anyone about your Link? Why did you just go off to the capitol without telling anyone where you were going? There's nothing to be ashamed of."

"I'm not ashamed, Eric. Go away." I flop onto my bed, wondering if it's possible to sneak one of the others' Links so I can talk to someone who knows what I've been through. Ash, for example.

"I would've taken the day off and driven you, you know. You didn't have to take the transit."

"It was fine."

"Damn it, Jess, I was worried about you. We all were. Mom said you got some official ping this morning on the house Link, but then you just disappeared. And when we couldn't get a hold of you, I back-traced the ping to the capital." He stops and waits. "Mom was worried you'd gotten into some kind of trouble or something. She had no way of reaching you. She was frantic."

"I doubt that."

"She was," Eric counters. He sounds hurt, like I'm really blaming him for her being so fucked up all the time. I don't know why he continues to defend her after all these years, after how crappy of a mother she's been to us both. It just blows me away. Especially because he keeps his feelings about our father so private. "She just has trouble showing it, Jessie. You know that."

"Yeah, sounds familiar, like you and Dad."

He doesn't bite. "There's something else, Jess. Were you with Kelly today?"

I turn over on my side, turn my back to the door and wish he'd just go away. But my wish doesn't come true.

"Jessie? Did you two break up or something?"

"No."

"Do you want me to ping— "

"No. I said leave me alone."

"Come on, Jessie. Let's not do this."

"You're the one 'doing this,' Eric! What part of leave me alone do you not understand?"

"Mrs. Corben has been pinging my Link all day. She's been asking about you and Kelly. She said the Stream couldn't find his Link. The same as yours. How does that even happen?"

And there it is. He wasn't really worried about me. It's all because of Mrs. Corben freaking out about Kel and Eric's inability to understand why we weren't on the Stream. Damn cops, always trying to solve mysteries, regardless of whether or not they need to be solved.

"She pinged Mom, too," he continues. "I don't know if she tried Grandpa. I haven't spoken with him yet. He's been out all day."

I highly doubt she would've pinged Grandpa. She's afraid of him. Most people I know are afraid of him.

"She said Kelly left early this morning in a strange van," he goes on. "Said she hasn't seen him since. Was he with you, Jess? Did he go with you to Hartford?"

"I told you I was on the transit, sitting with some whacko."

"Okay, then. So you don't know where Kelly is?"

"No."

"Because she pinged again about twenty minutes ago and was going to call the police. I tried to talk her out of it. I said he probably just lost track of time, but she wasn't rational. I thought he might be with you."

Christ. "I said I wasn't with him."

"Maybe if you spoke with her."

I get up and walk over to the door and open it.

"Fine. But the Link they gave me won't connect to anything but Media and Government."

Eric exhales, like he'd been holding his breath. He's three inches taller than me, and yet he seems smaller, shrunken. I hold out my hand. He reaches into his pocket and pulls out his Link. I wait for him to leave, but he just stands there.

"I need to call Ash and Micah first," I tell him, "see if they know. No reason to make her even more scared."

I close the door. He shuffles around outside it for another minute or so before telling me that dinner will be in less than an hour.

I try Ash first. While I'm waiting for her to connect, I squeeze my eyes closed and try to keep myself from screaming Kelly's name out the window.

"Jess?" Ash asks. Her face is tiny on the screen, but the distress in it is clear.

My mind screams at me to disconnect.

"Jessie? You okay?"

"Are you . . . . Any word from the boys?"

She shakes her head. "Micah said Kel's mom has been pinging him and Reggie all day. She didn't try me. I don't think she likes me. In fact," she says, getting that haughty look in her eyes, "I'm pretty sure she doesn't."

"Maybe it's because of your reputation for corrupting Greenwich's boys," I tease.

"So you're saying she's paranoid? Or, like, overprotective?"

I smile in spite of myself. I don't know why, but just seeing Ashley like this, all indignant, even though I know it's just an act, calms me down. Even if she's really on the verge of crumbling and just hiding it.

"Yeah, something like that."

She twists her face. "I know Kelly's off limits," she assures me. "I'd never do that to you. I'm— Hold on a sec." She turns her head away, disappearing from view. I can't see what she's looking at, but when she returns, she leans into the Link and whispers. "Did she call the police?"

"Yeah. And unless Kelly shows up on the Stream again soon, I have a feeling we're all going to be in deep shit."

She shakes her head. "I tried pinging Kelly and Jake just a few minutes ago. All I got was that same message." She pauses, then asks, "How'd your appointment go?"

"Sucked. Like being stripped naked, slapped silly with a rubber hose and verbally abused by a nun for six straight hours. I couldn't even go to the bathroom."

She turns again. " . . . sucks."

"What do you keep looking at?"

"I'm with Micah."

"I gathered that. Are his parents there?"

She shakes her head, looks perplexed. "No. Why?"

It's like a game with us now. None of us have met Micah's elusive parents. We joke that they don't really exist. But, of course, they do. They're just never around.

"I thought I saw a car in his driveway coming home."

I hear a voice now in the background. Ash turns to listen, then turns back. "We're not actually at his house. I mean, we were earlier. We were working on the codex, but I got hungry so we went out to get some Golden Dragon to bring back."

She rotates the Link so I can see where they are. Micah flashes by, then the view stops spinning. I'm looking down the street toward his house. They're a couple blocks away and the image is tiny, but I can see enough to recognize the cop cars parked outside his house. Their lights are flashing.

"That's not good," I mutter, my worry suddenly multiplying a hundred-fold.

Ash comes back into view. "We thought it might've been from the hacking."

She's talking about the hack last week, when they first broke into the government computers on LI using whatever still remained of the old internet. They were looking for maps of the tunnels. Ash was in the middle of doing a search when she'd quickly yanked the wires from the old tech tablet they were using. She thought someone was trying to track her. But she was sure she'd pulled out before they did.

"They'll probably be coming around to your place soon, Jess," I hear Micah say in the background.

"They don't know anything yet," I assure them. "They're just fishing. And I won't tell them anything."

Ash nods. "I think if we can avoid them till morning — tomorrow afternoon at the latest — then Kelly and Jake'll be back and hopefully they'll leave us alone. And if they do ask about the hack, we should just keep saying it was for a school project."

"Hacking the LI computers? Right," I say. But I know she's right. Once Kelly and Jake are safe, then who really cares about a couple kids breaking into some old, outdated computers? Even the ones on LI. It's not like we're trying to hack someone's personal Link stream.

"What about Jake's uncle?" I ask. "And the van? Did Micah say something to Mister Esposito?"

Micah leans in so I can see him. "Hey, Jess," he says, winking. Same old Micah, even when the cops are pounding down his door he's cool. "I fixed it so Mister E will be staying in Albany for a couple more days." He laughs. "So we're good there, at least."

"I don't even want to know."

"Good girl. It's better that way."

"What if he tries to call Jake?"

"He'll be too busy. I sent him a few . . . presents. Of the female persuasion. Very persuasive females, that is. They'll keep him busy."

"Prostitutes," Ash says, rolling her eyes.

"Where the hell did you get the money to pay for them?"

"Yeah . . . . About that." He shrugs, but doesn't elucidate.

I shake my head.

"Look," Micah says, "right now that's the least of our problems." He glances away. "Looks like they're leaving, Ash. We should get back in there and clean up. Next time they return, pretty sure they're going to want to see more than just the front door."

"Ping me if you hear anything," I say. Then, realizing I still can't receive yet on my temporary Link, I tell them that I'll get a hold of them instead. "I need to talk to Mrs. Corben."

"What are you going to tell her?"

"Got any ideas?"

They don't.

"I figure maybe I'll just tell her Kelly was planning a surprise for me and that I'm pretty sure his being gone has something to do with it."

It's all true. I won't be lying. And hopefully it'll calm her down. At least until nightfall. Then . . . who knows.

I just pray Kelly gets back before then.

That's what I plan on telling her, but when I get off with Ash and Micah, I don't. I just lie there on my bed not moving. I just can't face speaking with Kelly's mom yet.

When Eric calls me down for dinner forty five minutes later, I consider not going, but that would just cause more of a problem. Besides, I haven't eaten anything since breakfast. I need food. Two days in a row of not eating and I'm starting to feel the effects. And assuming Kelly and Jake are back tomorrow and everything's returned to some sort of normalcy, I'll have hapkido. I don't want to get my ass kicked because I'm too weak.

How can I even think of hapkido now? How can I think of anything like that ever again?

Act normal. Micah's last words come to me again. *We'll get through this, you'll see. Just act normal.*

Easier said than done. I just wish everything would go back to the way it was. Maybe it wasn't exactly normal, but at least it wasn't . . . *this*.

I sigh and get up. Grandpa's already at the table, waiting. So is Mom, which surprises me. She gives me a weak smile when she sees me, more than her usual self-pitying smile. At least she's trying, but she looks uncomfortable doing it, awkward. She even did her hair up, and her clothes are clean. More surprises on a day when I don't need them.

"Everything all right?" I ask. I hand Eric his Link back.

"Just have a seat, young lady," Grandpa says. "We're going to have a nice dinner with all of us for once." He looks over at my mom, holds her gaze for a moment. It's a neutral stare — he's a master of hiding his emotions.

"I hear you lost your Link again," he says, after we've sat. It's not an accusation, though it sort of feels like one. "You need to learn to be more responsible." Yup, definitely an accusation.

Mom puts her hand on his arm and says, "Ulysses." She's the only one who ever calls him that. She's the only one who can get away with it. To everyone else, he's simply "The Colonel." Or Grandpa.

He raises an eyebrow at her, just a fraction of an inch.

After the food is dished out and we're starting to eat, Grandpa turns to me. "Where did you lose it, young lady?"

"I didn't lose it. It was stolen."

The eyebrow raises another fraction of an inch.

"So they'll catch whoever has it. I assume they put a trace on it. They'll find it, just like they did that last guy." He stares at me for a moment. "I'm sure no matter where it is, they'll find it."

My face feels brittle, like if I move a muscle, it'll crumble away and show everything I'm trying to hide.

I turn my gaze to Eric, who's also just sitting there, watching me, watching the both of us. I wonder what he's thinking. He has to know something's not right. He tried pinging me. He saw the message. He knows the Link's outside the Stream, meaning either beyond the reach of our communications network or physically destroyed. But why would someone steal it just to destroy it? They wouldn't, leaving only the other possibility.

Speaking carefully, he says, "It looks like her Link's been disabled."

"Strange indeed," Grandpa says.

He stares at me. From somewhere far away, I'm dimly aware of Mom asking, "Why is that strange?" But Grandpa just sits there, thinking his own thoughts. And I sit here wondering what they are.

Thankfully, Eric's Link buzzes right then, startling us out of the moment. I blink and look over.

"My bad. Thought I'd turned the audible alarm off." He looks at his screen and frowns. Then he jumps to his feet. "Damn it," he says. "Got to go. Sorry, Mom."

She smiles tenderly at him, and I think I can see some of the mother inside of her peeking out. "It's all right, dear."

"What's the matter?" I ask.

"It's my boss. He needs me to come in."

"Why, dear?" Mom asks. Now she looks worried. It's amazing the emotions she can suddenly express when she's not numb with alcohol or drugs.

"There's a . . . problem," he says, shoving another bite of meatloaf into his mouth while he simultaneously tries to scroll through his screen and put on his jacket. "Down in New York. They're calling in all NCD within a hundred mile radius."

"A problem? What kind of problem?"

"I can't really say."

Mom gasps. "Another outbreak?"

He shakes his head. "I need to go." He bends down over Mom and kisses her cheek.

"Be careful, honey," she tells him.

"I will. And, guys, not a word about this to anyone," he says, holding up his Link. "It's not made Media yet."

"How can we tell anyone something if we don't know what it is?" I ask.

Grandpa's still looking at me, still watching me. His face is a blank slate. *Almost* a blank slate. Over the years I've learned to read of few of his emotions. The slight tilt of his head, for example, just like he's doing now. I know what it means. He says to Mom, even though his eyes never leave mine, "Well, we know it has something to do with Zulus, don't we? Otherwise, why would they call Eric in?"

Mom winces. She hates that old term, Zulus. Hates it even more than 'zombie' and 'CU' and 'IU.' She hates any reference to the Undead, in fact. But especially Zulu. It was the term in use when her husband was taken away from her.

Eric squeezes Mom's shoulder, then straightens and clips his EM pistol to his belt. "Sorry your birthday dinner had to end this way."

Chapter Seven

I can't believe I forgot my mother's birthday. After all the criticizing I've done about my brother being a jerk, at least *he* remembered.

"It's all right, dear," she tells me after I apologize. She leans over and plants a dry kiss on my cheek, then leaves the dinner table, the food on her plate mostly untouched.

There's no cake. No presents.

I'm a horrible daughter.

And now this. I can't help but feel somehow responsible for what's going on in Manhattan.

In fact, I know I am.

A few minutes later I hear Mom talking to someone in her room. Grandpa and I finish our dinners in silence. If I can just not look at him, maybe I can keep my face from giving it all away. The carefully constructed shell I've plastered there since coming home yesterday threatens to crumble and expose my secrets.

While I'm washing the dinner plates — an excuse to hide my shaking hands — I hear a car pull up outside at the curb. It's not the police, and I breathe a sigh of relief. But then I hear the front door open and see my mother going to out whoever it is, and I suddenly wish it was the cops. At least then she'd stay home.

Grandpa goes off and leaves me alone, much to my surprise. That look he'd given me earlier had hinted at suspicion. I'm almost afraid of what he'll find out in the privacy of his office. He still has friends in the government, despite his rather public fall from grace. One call and he'll know exactly why Eric's going to New York. Or that we were there, too.

I finish the dishes and dry my hands, then sit down at the table and wake the house Link. I tune it to Media and search the sub-streams for news. There's nothing about an outbreak, nothing about Infecteds in lower Manhattan. Nothing at all.

I keep expecting to see a reference to a couple of kids getting caught coming out of the water near the Midtown tunnel. I don't.

Now I'm really worried. My shaking's become so bad that I'm barely able to scroll through the Link.

The closest thing I find suggesting something is going on in Manhattan is a small mention on the financial pages about the stock market getting shut down an hour early this afternoon and the building being evacuated due to an unspecified threat.

These sorts of things happen all the time — terrorists, protestors, random crazies. But this one just feels different. The video capture shows an officer forming a blockade. He holds his hand up to keep the reporter from getting closer. But what I notice is the EM pistol on his hip rather than the standard forty-five caliber police issue. Only NCD officials carry EM pistols. And NCD officers investigate crimes by and against the Undead.

I think it's time to talk to Ash and Micah and Reg again.

"Best you stay home tonight," Grandpa says, startling me. I hadn't noticed him standing just inside the doorway. I wonder how long he's been there, watching me, blocking my way out of the kitchen.

"Stay home? What do you mean?"

"Those friends of yours are trouble. I've kept my thoughts to myself about them in the past, but now I think it's time I say what's on my mind."

"Grandpa— "

"They're not a good influence on you, young lady."

"They're my friends. You don't even know them."

He holds something up. It's my inhaler. "You're not being responsible. Losing your Link, forgetting to take your medicine like you're supposed to. *Three times a day.* How many doses have you missed in the past couple of days?"

I grab it from his hand. "So I forgot. It's not like I actually really need it that much."

"Six missed doses in four days," he says, shaking his head.

"You downloaded my dosing information?" I shout. "You have no right, Grandpa!"

I expect him to get angry, but he doesn't. I've never seen him lose his temper. Just once I wish he would. Instead, he reminds me of the usual crap about the medicine being an immunity booster. And then, when he finishes, he surprises me by adding, "You're special, Jessie. You need that medicine so you won't get sick."

"How am I special?"

But he backs away, leaving the way clear for me to leave. "Someday you'll see. Just . . . stay in tonight, Jessie. It's not a good night for you to be going out."

Chapter Eight

I'm sitting in the darkened living room and Grandpa's in bed asleep when Eric comes in several hours later. I know it's Eric and not Mom, despite there being just the light from the street filtering in through the curtains, because I recognize the sound of his Jeep when it pulls into the driveway. Kelly keeps telling him that he's got bad brushes in the motor, which gives it a sort of characteristic chuffing sound when it runs. Like Kelly even knows what brushes are.

Eric walks in and quietly closes the door and carefully locks it.

I clear my throat.

"Jessie? Why are you still up?" He walks over. The light from the streetlamp shines on his face. It's smudged with dirt.

"Is everything okay?" I ask.

He takes another step into the room, stops, then lays his jacket and holster carefully onto the arm of the chair. He moves through the gloom like a ghost before settling heavily on the couch next to me.

"There's . . . ." He exhales, trying to remember what he was going to say. But then he must change his mind because when he speaks next, it's to ask a question. And not just any question, a shocker: "What do you know about Dad's death?"

I blink into the darkness for a few seconds, trying to process what he's asking. I shrug. "Not much."

I actually have no recollection of my father. He was murdered when I was two. No one in the family talks much about it, though that doesn't mean I haven't heard a lot about it. All through grade school I was tormented by kids who claimed they knew what had happened, had been told by their parents. I'd always just assumed the taunting was the standard animosity that rose up against my family after the outbreaks.

Eric was hounded, too, from what I understood, but by then he was already out of school and the people harassing him were much older and the taunting much more serious. There were death threats. And all because of Grandpa.

He was the man responsible for pushing the whole Undead project with the government. Everything that happened since — the Zulus and Omegamen, the Life Service laws, Forbidden Zones and the war, then Arc Properties and Gameland — traces back to that project. But the truth was, Grandpa had very little to do with all that. He'd already left the government in disgrace by then. And he's never been associated with Arc Properties, not as far as I've ever known. So while he may have been the seed and zombies the tree that grew from it, he'd always disavowed the rotten fruit it bore.

"I know he was killed by an Infected," I answer, "and that he never came back because most of his brain was eaten."

Eric's wince is so visceral, so intense, that I actually feel the couch move. I don't experience the depth of emotions that he does about it, though. I know I should. Emotionally, I should be more sensitive about the whole thing because of who we're talking about, but I can't feel anything. It's like we're talking about a complete stranger. I never knew the guy.

Eric, on the other hand, was ten when Dad died. He has memories. For him, Dad's death is all too real and personal.

"I don't know many of the actual details, either," he admits. "So much of it was classified and Grandpa . . . . Well, you know I can't talk to him. We're like oil and water. That's what my quack shrink says anyway."

I smile in the darkness. I know he's just saying that for my benefit. He knows what I think about psychiatrists. A hapkido master is all the counseling I need.

"And what I remember . . . ." He coughs. "Like you, I've heard a lot about what happened over the years, from people who think they know."

"Yeah," I mumble. It feels strange to be talking with Eric like this, to be . . . bonding. It happens so rarely.

He jumps up, shattering the moment. "Go to bed, Jess. Forget I ever brought it up. It was stupid of me to dig up the past."

"Is it the past?" I ask. Then, when he doesn't answer, I say, "What happened down in Manhattan?"

He gives me a strange look. "How did you know it was Manhattan?"

"That's what you said before you left."

"I said New York."

I'm glad it's dark in the room, otherwise I'm sure he'd see my face flush. "New York, Manhattan," I quickly say. "It's all the same to me."

He grunts, but instead of answering, he turns and gathers up his EM pistol and jacket. He's about to leave when he reconsiders. He comes back over and stops in front of me, hovering, a dark featureless shadow.

"I suppose what I can tell you is what I think'll be on the Stream in the morning: Some of the IUs from Long Island got into Manhattan. NCD's running the investigation, but they've brought in the military to carry out the cleansing operation." He must hear my startled gasp, because he adds, "Don't worry. We're pretty sure we've rounded them all up."

His EM pistol glints in the darkness. It's probably just my imagination, but I can smell ozone, like something burning. I wonder how many times he fired it tonight. I wonder if maybe he used it on anyone still living. I'm afraid to ask.

He folds his jacket over the pistol and says, "We didn't use these tonight. They don't work as well on IUs as on zoms with implants." His eyes unfocus and he shudders. "They issued us shotguns. Blasted anything that moved that didn't have a reflective vest on."

I know how much he hates guns — *real* guns, anyway, with real bullets.

He exhales and rubs his shoulder, wincing. "I'm going upstairs to take a shower to get this stink of me. Then I'm going to bed. You should, too."

I stand up. His words bounce through my head like boulders: *Blasted anything that moved.*

I hope to God that doesn't include Kelly and Jake.

Chapter Nine

The next morning there's still no word from Kelly and Jake.

My nerves are shot.

After last night, I'm scared to death of what might've happened to them. And every time a car drives down the street, I keep expecting it to be the cops.

I didn't get any sleep. I pray they're not hurt. I hope they weren't caught up in the sweep last night. I hope they don't try coming through the tunnel until things settle down. I fear . . . .

I don't even want to think of the possibilities.

"Just act normally," Micah had said. And Ash had added, "Don't give the cops too many details if they talk to you. Keep it simple." It makes me wonder how many times she's been in this sort of situation. Despite her tough exterior, I doubt she has any experience dealing with the cops. Not this kind of experience, anyway. None of us has.

Act normally? How the hell am I supposed to do that?

But there's nothing else *to* do, at least until we either get word that Kelly and Jake are safe, or they show up again. So I grab my gear bag and head for the dojang. I'll probably be useless during my forms, but getting my ass kicked in sparring is still better than sitting around at home waiting and imagining worst case scenarios.

The police drive up just as I head down the front steps, almost as if they'd been waiting for me to come outside. Two officers get out of the car: the first is younger, blond and trim; the other older, graying and sloppy in his appearance.

The contrast is almost cliché, and I can tell just by looking at them that the younger one is going to be all business as he tries to impress his partner, while the partner is going to stand back and let him intimidate me before he comes to the rescue. He'll appear amused, then embarrassed. Finally he'll get impatient and step in with an apology. Good cop, bad cop.

But I get it all wrong: It's the older cop who's bad.

"Mind if we go inside, ma'am?" he asks. "It's a tad warm out here." He sticks a finger inside his collar and adjusts it.

"I'm going to be late for my class."

"This'll only take a few minutes."

We go back inside. I consider offering them coffee, but that would only drag this out longer, and I'm not sure my nerves can handle it. Besides, it's a hundred degrees outside. Nobody wants coffee.

"You wouldn't happen to have any java, would you?"

I give him an incredulous look. "No."

He sighs heavily, like it's a great imposition. He holds up his department-issued Link and says, "We'll be recording this."

"Shouldn't a parent be here?"

"Any reason one should be?" he asks. When I hesitate, he quickly adds, "It's just a few innocent questions about your friend Kelly Corben. He is your friend, right?"

I nod.

"Just a friend?"

"We're seeing each other. What's this about?"

They ask when I saw him last, or talked with him, or heard from him. They don't mention Micah or Ash. They don't say anything about the hacking. It's all about Kel. At least at first.

I give them the vaguest answers I can think of: I saw Kelly a few days before, Saturday; he said something about planning a surprise for me; no, I don't have any idea what kind of a surprise, but that was the last I'd heard from him.

"When my son was your age," Old Cop says, "he and his girlfriend were inseparable, connected at the hip. Literally." He snorts and makes a crude gesture with his hands while winking at his partner, who still hasn't spoken. It surprises me when I see a flash of red touch the younger guy's cheeks. He's the one who actually looks embarrassed.

"We sometimes go a couple days without seeing each other," I explain. "Kelly keeps busy with his things. His brother's sick a lot, and he helps out at home. I try to stay out of his way."

"You don't help out with any of that?"

"It's family stuff. Besides, I have my own life to live. I have classes twice a week, plus sparring another two days." I make a point of glancing at the time on my Link, then reshouldering my bag.

"You might as well put that down."

"I thought you said it would only take a few minutes."

"Have you spoken with Kelly more recently?"

"No." I consider telling him about my temporary Link and how it doesn't connect to the Communications Stream, but I figure that would be in the category of Too Much Information.

"So, the last time you spoke with him was — what? — Friday?"

"Saturday. What's going on? Is he all right?" I try to appear concerned. I mention trying to ping him but getting a strange message. I figure it's information they already have from his mother. "I've never seen a message like that before. And no, he doesn't usually go off like this and not tell his parents where he's going. Or me. Especially me. But then again, I kind of got the feeling he was planning something big for us, him and me. I think he was planning on asking me to marry him."

"That close, eh? Good for him. And you were going to say yes?"

My hesitation is enough of an answer for him. He flips through his Link and says, "We have checkpoint records that show you and Mr. Corben and a couple other kids going down to Manhattan last week. What was that all about?"

I shrug. I'm not sure how I'm supposed to answer this. I've already said too much. And I don't know if they've already spoken with Ash and Micah and Reggie. What would they have said?

"I was just along for the ride."

"Where exactly did you go in Manhattan?"

I shrug. "As far as we could before the checkpoint guards stopped us. We got out, walked around, and then came back. The guards gave us a hassle, but it wasn't like we were doing anything wrong. We were just hanging out."

"And again on Saturday?"

"The same."

"You went to the same place twice in two days because . . . you were bored?"

"I didn't say we were bored."

"So, there was a reason?" He grunts, but doesn't push it. "Your brother is Eric Daniels?" I nod. "The NCD team leader?"

"Yes," I say, hesitantly. I'm aware of how poorly regarded the NCD officers are by the other police officers. They're considered a bunch of misfits and Undead-obsessed freaks. I can't really argue against that. As far as I'm concerned, it's a fairly accurate assessment.

"So you're aware of what happened last night down in Manhattan?"

This is where things get tricky. I don't know if Eric was supposed to keep it hush-hush. He said it was going to be on Media this morning, but all I could find was that travel to lower Manhattan today was going to be restricted and remain restricted for an indeterminate amount of time due to a toxic spill of some sort. No mention of zombies. Typical Media spin. I figured they wanted to prevent a panic.

"He was called down there to help out with something. I think it was a spill of some kind. I would've thought it might have something to do with the Undead, but he didn't say. He left early this morning, before I got up. I didn't get a chance to talk with him."

The older cop rubs his Link on his cheek and regards me for a few seconds. "It was zombies." He studies me carefully to gauge my reaction. I act surprised. "Doesn't it seem strange that there'd suddenly be this trouble with zombies in the exact same place you kids were messing around in just a few days before? And now one of you is missing."

He looks over at his partner. "Doesn't it seem strange to you that, not only is he missing, but he seems to have completely vanished off the face of the Stream?" He shrugs. "Me? I think that's strange. What about you, Hank? You think it's strange?"

The younger cop shrugs. "It's strange, but I can't see— "

Old Mister Fat Cop leans over to me, his face just inches from mine. "I've been on this job for forty years. I've seen a lot of fucked up shit, young lady. I've caught a shit-load of criminals. I've broken a hell of a lot, too. I can tell you that this doesn't smell right. In fact, it smells downright stinky."

If I weren't so scared, I'd laugh in his face and tell him shit usually does stink. Plus, he sounds like the cops from those old shows Micah has bootleg copies of in his basement.

I raise my hands in a gesture of defeat. "I don't know where Kelly is. I wish I did. I'm worried—"

"You don't look very worried."

"Al," the younger cop says.

The older cop inhales slowly. He straightens up, turns and walks to the window and looks out. Then he turns back to me and says, "We're pulling yesterday's checkpoint records. I hope I don't find that you all went back down to Manhattan."

"I was on a transit to Hartford," I say. "And you're wrong about me not being worried. I'm worried sick about Kelly."

The older cop glances down at his Link while I'm talking. He shows it to Al, then abruptly stands up and announces they're finished. I wish I knew what newsflash he just received.

As I show them to the door, the younger cop tries to make nice. "So, you take karate?"

"Hapkido. Eric got me into it years ago. For self-defense."

Shit-Head snorts. "You want my advice, young lady? Teach yourself to fire a gun. That's the only kind of self defense you need." He rubs the forty five on his hip and leers, like it's his dick he's talking about. The asshole probably sleeps with the damn thing in his hand. "That fancy shmancy Chuck Norris stuff won't do you no good, not against the Undead." He chuckles. "Not that you'd ever have any need to use it on them, right?"

He does a clumsy imitation of a karate chop.

I stare back at him with my best blank look, and not because I don't know who Chuck Norris was — I do — but to let him know he's a total prick. Mentioning someone from, like, fifty years ago just shows how out of touch he really is.

"I suppose you've got all kinds of experience fighting zombies sitting at the local coffee shop, is that it?" I say after breaking the stare first. I know even as I'm saying it that I'm treading on thin ice. I lower my eyes pointedly to his bulging stomach. "I heard they like to eat, too."

But he just doesn't get when he's being insulted. "A lot more experience than you, young lady. I was there in the City during the outbreak twelve years ago. You were probably still in your diapers. I hope and pray you never have to meet one of the bastards. Dirty, stinking fuckers. NCDs are just a bunch of wussy necrophiliacs, if you ask me."

He barks out a laugh and claps his partner on the shoulder, who now looks about as uncomfortable as anyone could be. "Oh, excusee my Français. I meant zombie lovers."

I glare as I hold the door open for him.

"Thank you for your time, Miss Daniels," the other cops says. "Sorry to bother you." He taps my Link with his to transfer his contact info. "Ping us if you hear anything."

I nod.

He walks down the steps, then turns. "Will you be around later this afternoon? We may have a few more questions for you."

I shrug, which they evidently interpret as a yes. As they walk down the sidewalk, they hold their heads together, conspiring no doubt about their next move. Good cop and bad cop. Young cop and asshole.

I close the door and lean my head against it

"You didn't handle that very well."

Grandpa's voice startles me. I spin around to find him standing right behind me. I wonder how much of the interview he heard. And that makes me wonder why he didn't come in while the cops were still here. I sure could've used a little help against Fatso.

"Antagonizing the police is always a mistake."

I brush past him. I need some air. And I certainly don't need Grandpa trying to tell me what's right and what's wrong. "I'm late for class."

To my surprise, he lets me go without saying another word.

When I arrive at the dojang ten minutes later, it's all abuzz about something big happening down in Manhattan. I try to stay out of it, though I do listen to what's being said. The theories range all over the place, but a few come uncomfortably close to the truth. At least as far as I know it.

Halfway through one of my sparring sessions, Master Rupert walks past. He catches my eye, jolting me out of my focus. My sparring partner takes immediate advantage of my distraction. The next thing I know, I'm down on the mat with my arm wrenched behind me. The ref grants him the win.

I pick myself up off the floor and hurry away without the traditional bow of respect and thanks. My shoulder's sore and my arm feels like it's been pulled from its socket.

"Kwanjangnim Rupert," I call.

He stops and waits for me, smiling in his usual easygoing way. "Sunbae Jessie. How good to see you. We missed you on Saturday."

"I'm sorry. I was . . . out of town."

He nods and waits.

"How's your back?" I ask, suddenly feeling unsure of myself. How do I ask him about Ash?

He furrows his brow for a moment, confused, then laughs. "Ah, all better. Thank you for asking."

"I'm glad."

His smile wavers and he raises his eyebrows.

"I was just wondering, sir."

"Yes?"

"There's this girl I know. Her name's Ashley Evans. Do you . . . . You wouldn't happen to know her, would you?"

He shakes his head and says, "No, I don't think so. Should I? Is she interested in taking lessons?" I'm not certain, but I think I see a flicker of something cross his face — surprise, maybe, or suspicion.

"Not exactly. It's just that I saw that she had your contact info on her Link."

He shrugs and looks away. "Could be for any number of reasons. Perhaps you should ask her."

I nod.

"Now, if you'll excuse me, I have to prepare for the juniors class."

He turns and leaves me standing there. It's true that the juniors class starts in a few minutes, but it's not like Rupert to treat any of his students with such brusqueness. Do his actions mean anything? Do they conceal a secret, or a lie? I hate feeling that way about a man I've known half my life and have always deeply respected for telling it like it is.

As I ponder what this all could mean, he goes into his office, shutting the door behind him. I watch through the glass as he pulls out his Link and thumbs the screen for a moment before lifting it to his ear. I can see him talking, though I can't hear a word he says. His back is turned, but then he turns and sees me and quickly turns around again.

It's this last bit that troubles me the most.

Chapter Ten

I see Micah's car parked in his driveway when I pass his house going home. It's just sitting there, so conspicuously that it seems strange, especially given all that's going on with the police right now. I go up to knock on his door, hoping everything's all right. Hoping that maybe Kelly and Jake are back and everything's back to normal again.

I barely raise my hand when the door opens and someone yanks me inside. It's Micah. He takes a quick glance up and down the street before closing it again.

"You weren't followed were you?"

"Yeah," I say, confused. "I think I picked up a tail at Vinny's pool hall. But I took evasive action."

"Huh? Vinnie's what?"

I sigh. "What's going on, Micah? I thought you were going to lay low. Your car's in the driveway."

He starts pacing across the room. I've never seen him this agitated before, but there's an excited gleam in his blue eyes. There's worry there, too, but also excitement.

"I wasn't sure if I should go by your place or not. I was afraid they'd be watching it."

"The cops? Paranoid much?"

"I'm serious. Reggie says there's a car parked outside his house. Somebody's watching him." He runs his hands through his curls like he's hyped up on caffeine. If I did that, my hair would be a tangled mess, but his just falls right back into place, looking exactly the way it was before. It's not fair that guys can have nicer hair than me. He probably doesn't even know what bed-head is. "Listen, are you free for the rest of the day?" he asks.

I shrug. "Yeah, I guess. Not like I can go anywhere."

"Well, you are. We're getting out of here as soon as Reg and Ash get here." He checks his Link and shakes his head. "I wish they'd hurry."

I move in front of him so he has to stop pacing. "Hold on a sec. What're you talking about?"

"We're heading back down to New York."

My heart skips a beat. "You can't be serious."

"We're going to get Kelly and Jake."

Now my head really starts to buzz. And instead of the room coming into focus again, it just starts spinning even faster.

"You okay, Jess?"

I fall onto the couch; the springs complain. The air conditioner hums away and a cool breeze blows across my face from the vent in the ceiling, but the room still feels too hot, too close. I think I might be sick. I push him away. I need to think.

"You got a Link, right?" he asks.

"Yeah, but—" I reach into my pocket and pull it out. "Wait, you can't be serious. Are you saying we're going back to Long Island? Have you lost your mind?"

"Ashley finished the hack, Jessie," he says, thumbing through my Link. "Christ, what a piece of crap." He hands it back to me, then kneels down in front of me and grabs my hands. "Ash built an algorithm that could actually parse ArcWare's codex. It ran all day yesterday." He waves his hand. "Doing that learning and adapting shit she's always going on about."

"Heuristic—"

"Yeah, yeah. Whatever. The point is, it works, Jess! She got us into *The Game*! She actually got us in!"

I don't know if it's lack of sleep or food or the overdosing on stress, but I'm having trouble following him. "Are you talking about breaking into Gameland?"

"Yes! I mean, no! I mean, yes, about the hack, not about breaking in." He jumps to his feet and starts pacing again, waving his hands wildly about. He almost hits me in the face on one pass. "I'm talking about being able to see *everything* in there!"

"Damn it, Micah!" I yell at him. "I actually thought you might be talking about going to get Kelly and Jake, but you're just talking about some dumb video game?"

"I'm spewing, I know. Lack of sleep." He hurries into the kitchen and pulls a Red Bull out of the case on the counter and chugs the whole thing warm. "Let me try again. What I've been trying to say is we can see everything inside. Well, almost everything. It's not a video feed, but we can track now. From out here!"

"Still spewing nonsense."

"I *found* them. I found Kelly and Jake. I tracked them with this!" He reaches into his pocket and pulls up his Link. "The location app tells me where they are. We know they're alive!"

My heart starts racing again. I'd had alternating visions of them showing up at my door and in the morgue. Either way, the cops would be with them, taking us into custody.

"So . . . they're still there? You can see that? Why haven't they tried to come back yet?"

"I don't know, but they are coming, Jess, that much I'm sure of. That's what I've been trying to tell you. As soon as Ash and Reg get here, we're going to go meet them."

Excitement and relief wash over me, but then a new thought comes to mind and I gasp in panic. "You need to tell them not to come!"

He frowns. "I couldn't even if I wanted to. It's just a tracking app. It doesn't work that way. We can't talk to them and they have no idea we can see them."

"If they try coming back through the tunnel, they'll be shot! Manhattan is swarming with NCD officers and military right now. Eric's with them. They'll be seen the moment they surface, and I'm pretty sure it's shoot first, ask questions later right now."

Micah's frown deepens. "What's going on in Manhattan?"

I tell him about the call Eric got last night and how he was gone half the night dealing with IUs. "He said lower Manhattan's been invaded. They're coming through the tunnel. Media's buzzing this morning, but they haven't come out and said exactly what it is."

Micah looks shocked for a moment. "I haven't been on Media this morning." He gets up. "Shit. It's because of us, isn't it?"

I nod.

"Aw, Christ. What did we do?" he whispers. "But . . . . Did the zombies come out alive? I mean . . . you know."

"Eric said they had to use shotguns, so, yes, they came out alive."

He exhales heavily.

"I don't think anyone was hurt. And Eric claimed they got them all. But I'm not so sure. I think he was just saying that so I wouldn't panic. You know how protective he is of me. I think that's also why it's not being reported on Media."

Micah nods gravely. "Then it's a really good thing Kelly and Jake aren't taking the Midtown tunnel."

"What do you mean? How else would they come back?"

"They were heading northeast when I last checked this morning. When they came online, they were about a mile east of the Midtown tunnel. They weren't moving and I kind of freaked out a little. But then they did move, so I figured they'd just set up camp or something to wait out the zombies. When I rechecked later, I saw that they were even further away. They'd moved almost four miles. They're clearly going somewhere with a plan in mind. I can't know for sure, but I'm pretty sure they were heading for the other tunnel."

I close my eyes and picture the map Ash had gotten for us before our trip. There were two tunnels: the Midtown, which is the one we took, and the Brooklyn Battery. But the Battery was further south and west, not northeast.

When I mention this to Micah, he shakes his head. "Not the Battery. There's another tunnel — two, actually. They're further north. I think they were heading for one of those."

"I didn't know about any other tunnels."

"Kelly didn't either. Jake told us about them when Ash and I met with him that first day, when we asked him about the diving equipment. But we decided they weren't the best options."

"Are they far?"

"Five or six miles up the coast from the Midtown tunnel. The closest one passes under Randall's Island and comes out into the old East Harlem neighborhood."

"Which is all swampland now, Micah. Nobody lives down that way anymore. And nobody goes there except to fish, old men on the edge of conscription and poor families." I shudder at the thought of the fish they must pull out of the water there.

"Which is a good thing. No one will see us when they come out."

"Fine, but how're we going to get out to the opening? I'm not swimming."

"I still need to figure that out. A raft or something. I don't know how far from the road it's going to be."

I frown. "You said there were two tunnels. Where's the other one?"

"Further north and east, about another mile and half or so. According to Jake, very few people know about it, and it's not on any of the maps we dug up. He said his uncle once told him about it, when he worked as a baggage handler at LaGuardia, which is where the opening is. But they won't take that one. Even if they knew where it is, it's five miles long. The Harlem's only half that."

I whistle. Two and a half miles underwater. Even freshly rested and with the current behind them, it would take almost three hours to swim, the maximum range of the rebreather cartridges. Five miles would be impossible, even with extra cartridges. It's just too long of a distance.

Micah checks the time on his Link. "At the rate they're moving, they'll have reached the opening by now. I just hope they find it quickly." He thumbs his Link awake. "I was just about to track them again when you showed up at the door."

A map of Long Island appears on his screen. He reverse pinches it to expand one section.

I expect to see a pair of tiny red blips, the signals from their implants, but there's nothing, just a schematic of the island and roads that haven't been used in thirteen years. He points. "The opening's right about here."

"I don't see anything."

"That's good news. It means they've found the tunnel and are in it. They're probably directly underneath the wall. The signal there would be blocked."

He hands me the Link. While I stare at it in my hands, he goes over to the fridge. "We've got less than three hours to get there, find some way to float out to where the opening on our side is, and retrieve them."

He hands me a couple water pouches.

For the first time I notice the circles under his eyes, and I realize he's probably been working night and day on the ArcWare hack. All this time I'd thought it was so he could play *The Game*, but it was really so he could find the boys. I feel guilty for doubting him.

"Once they're back . . . ," he says, exhaling heavily, as if he's been carrying the weight of the world solely on his shoulders. He holds up his hands and gives me a weak smile. "Then everything will be okay."

I smile, too, and pray he's not being overly optimistic. I know things won't all be okay. After that cop this morning, just because Kelly and Jake show up again doesn't mean he'll back off. He suspects we're somehow connected with the IU invasion in lower Manhattan. Unfortunately, he's right.

But first things first: Kelly and Jake.

"Come on," Micah says suddenly. He offers me his hand and helps me off the couch. "We can't keep sitting around waiting. We need to move."

"What about Ash and Reg?"

"We'll drive around until we find them."

I bend down to retrieve my sparring bag.

"Leave it."

He grabs my arm and pulls me toward the door. "It'll be fine there. We'll be back in four or five hours."

The heat hits me like a baseball bat when we get back outside. Even Micah winces a bit at the glare. His forehead begins to glisten.

I head for the passenger seat before turning around again. "I forgot my inhaler." He gives me an impatient look, but taps his Link to unlock the front door to the house. "Grab a few more waters on your way out." Then he gets in the car and starts it up to run the air conditioner. "I think we're going to need them."

I go back inside and grab my inhaler out of my sparring bag and slip it into my pocket. As I turn to leave, my hip knocks against the side table. It tips and crashes to the floor, dumping the contents of a drawer.

I reach down to pick everything up. There's a tacky paperweight from the Alamo, one of the few things I've ever seen in Micah's house with any direct connection to his former life as a citizen of the Southern States Confederacy. His family defected from the Republic of Texas years back. He still has the old twang in his voice. We always used to pick on him about it.

There are a few other trinkets, typical odds and ends that people accumulate over time and then lose again in the forgotten nooks and crannies of their lives: an antique yellow and black smiley faced pin, an old digital music player with a silver apple icon, the electronic guts of some other unknown device.

The last thing I pick up is card of some sort. I turn it over and see it's an old fashioned college ID badge, printed on paper and laminated in plastic. Curious, I check out the image of the man on the front. His face is vaguely familiar, but he doesn't resemble anyone I've seen in any of the family photos scattered about Micah's place. I freeze when I see the name underneath: Eugene Halliwell.

For a brief moment I can't tell if I'm actually reading it correctly. But when I blink and check again, it's still there.

Eugene Halliwell, Professor of Immunology, Royce State College.

Micah honks.

I get up shakily, slipping the badge into my back pocket.

I need to know how Micah knows the man who murdered my father.

Chapter Eleven

We spot Ashley and Reg at the corner of Amherst and Fourth. They're coming from the direction of my house. Micah honks and they see us and hurry across the intersection looking relieved.

"Your grandfather said you weren't home yet from karate," Reggie says, getting in behind me. "Hope you don't mind if I say that guy scares the crap out of me. He said we should wait for you at your place, but . . . ."

"Yeah, I know. And I don't mind. He scares a lot of people."

I do, however, suppress the urge to correct him about the karate reference. I've told him a million times that it's hapkido. They're actually very different martial arts. Karate emphasizes strength, meeting force with force; hapkido teaches using an opponent's force against him. The misunderstanding probably bugs me more than it should, like when Kelly calls the dojang a dojo. I guess if they haven't figured it out by now, then it's unlikely they ever will.

"So, Micah filled you in on the deets?" Ash asks.

I turn to her and nod. For a moment I'm tempted to ask her about Rupert's contact info on her Link, but that's less important right now. "I can't believe you actually finished the hack on *The Game*."

She shakes her head. "Just the first step, actually. We still need to incorporate the gaming algorithms into a control device. And it wasn't all me. Micah helped a lot. He's the one who suggested we go back and run a cladistic analysis of the programming structure that ArcWare's been using for their various versions of their games over the years." She shakes her head and laughs at herself. "I can't believe it was as simple as that. Once we had that and Micah's backdoor to the codex he created while we were on LI, it was just a matter of configuring the translator to extrapolate out until the syntaxes aligned."

"Yeah, um, you lost me at cladistic analysis."

Ash leans forward and pats Micah's head. "I thought I was the hidden Markov modeling expert. Turns out Micah's pretty good at optimal nonlinear filtering problems himself."

"Stop!" I yell. "You're making my ears bleed."

"Ash did all the heavy programming," Micah says, ignoring me. "I just suggested a few tweaks. She took them and ran with it."

"I'm with Jessie. Enough with the circle jerk," Reggie says.

"Yeah, we all know who's the expert on gaming architecture. It's only natural you'd want to look at the programming structure, Micah."

"Well, when you put it like that," Micah says, "it sort of takes all the air out of the old ego."

"Ha! Now you know how I feel," Reggie complains. "Jessie's been deflating my ego for years. Long before you ever came along, Tex-Mex."

"Yeah, and yet your ego somehow still manages to fill the car," Ashley teases. "It's probably big enough to be picked up by the Air Defense System."

I give Ash a high five. Everyone laughs. The mood is definitely brighter as we head off the side streets and onto the main roads, as if our inability to do anything about Jake and then Kelly before has been physically weighing us down. Now we're going to get them. That's enough to make us forget, at least for the time being, all our other troubles. We joke and tease like it's old times again.

"Too bad we can't use Reggie's ego to float us out over the Harlem swamps," Ashley says.

"I'm working on it," Micah replies.

"You always say that: 'I'm working on it.' "

"Have I ever disappointed?"

Nobody defends him. There's a kernel of truth to what Ash said. Micah's not the most reliable one in the bunch. That would be Kelly. And with that, the good mood slips away. The car grows quiet, more subdued.

It's the first time I've been on the Old New England Thruway in many years. Apparently, very few people ever use it anymore. Micah says most people take the Bronx River Parkway, since it rests on higher ground.

The inland scenery quickly gives way to the rainforest that lines the coast. It's technically not considered a rainforest — we get too little actual precipitation — but with the constant high humidity, it might as well be. My brother Eric says that back when he was a kid, the temperature rarely reached a hundred in Connecticut during the summers. Now it hovers above ninety for five months out of the year and the number of hundred-plus degree days has grown steadily year over year. We get nearly a month of them now.

Both sides of the highway are lined with moss-covered trees, thick curtains of growth that mask the Atlantic from our view on the left and the inland swamps on the right. Both press against us until we feel like we're drowning.

We cross into New York at the Port Chester outpost, where the guard seems both surprised and happy to see us. He's actually very chatty. So chatty, in fact, that I begin to think he might never let us through. "Going fishing?" he asks. "There's a great rental shack off Locust Point. I take my sister's kids there sometimes. It's so peaceful. Just don't eat the fish. Catch and release, I always tell them."

"Can you rent rowboats there?"

"Rowboats, canoes. Nothing with a motor, of course. You know about the mines right? They're sound and vibration sensitive."

We nod.

"And stay this side of the buoys, you'll be fine."

Finally he lifts the gate arm and waves us on. He smiles cheerily as we drive through. "Use the blood worms," he shouts. "A hundred for a buck. They work the best!"

"We should've come this way before," Reggie grumbles. "He didn't even bother to check our Links or scan our implants."

"I feel sorry for him," Ash says. "He looks so lonely."

"We still would've had to go through the other checkpoints," Micah points out. "The ones further south."

"No, I meant we should've gone through the Harlem tunnel instead of the Midtown."

I shudder. We shouldn't have gone in the first place.

"It's more than twice as long," Ashley says.

Reggie shrugs and rotates his shoulders, as if a five-mile dive — there and back — is a challenge he'd be up for. Now there's no chance of it happening, so he's all Mister Macho again. He obviously forgot how hard it was just a couple days before when the distance was less than half.

Remembering this myself makes me start worrying again about Kelly and Jake. I hope they remember to carry extra cartridges on their belts. And knives. And I hope there aren't any blockages.

We continue south. The land grows even swampier. The road is badly in need of repair. Micah doesn't dare go any faster than thirty. "Don't want to blow an axle or a tie rod," he says. The road dips several times; every so often a shallow stream of gray water flows over it. Some parts of the road are covered in undisturbed mud or silt. We leave fresh tire tracks on it, making me worry that someone might follow them.

The empty buildings this close to the river are even more desolate and decrepit than the abandoned ones we saw on Long Island, perhaps because of the repeated flooding and subsequent retreat of waters these have been exposed to. Dried moss and seaweed dangles from eaves and signs. The husks of ancient tree trunks stand stripped and bare, sun-bleached and water-worn. The place makes me think of dead things — not the Undead, but of ancient civilizations and long lost cities and ghosts and haunted places. It gets inside your soul and eats at you from the inside instead of the outside.

We come to a place where a beaten, faded sign points south. It says Locust Point. A hand-carved sign is tacked to it announcing cheap rentals. But there's nothing there to see. The road ends abruptly and the trees clear. The Atlantic opens out in front of us. In the distance, a small rocky island juts out of the water. The stark gray walls of Long Island rise up behind it, looking like a long, low battleship a hundred miles long.

"Now what?" Reggie asks. "It's high tide. We can't get out there to rent a boat."

Micah doesn't answer. He steers the car to the right and follows the road as it heads west through these wastelands.

"There used to be a bridge back there," he says. "The Throng Neck. Two bridges, actually. I remember them from the map."

The three of us strain our necks back to look, but of course we don't see anything. All the bridges were bombed out after the outbreak, after the military went in and evacuated and closed the island off. Nobody thinks to ask why he remembers their names. They would've been gone long before he came from Texas, so there wouldn't be a personal connection.

But that's Micah, I remind myself. His brain works in ways that are mysterious to the rest of us.

We hit the remnants of the Cross-Bronx Highway. If we were heading for lower Manhattan, we would go inland from here, crossing the Hudson into New Jersey before turning south again. Today, however, we stay along the coast. We pass signs for the old towns of Trinity and Castle Hill, Hunts Point-Longwood — where the LaGuardia tunnel is supposed to come out — Foxhurst and Melrose. All neighborhoods that were wiped out by the floods. They're now reefs for the strange fish that have learned to survive with the poisons bleeding out of the ground here.

Finally a sign tells us we are about to cross the Harlem River — though it's impossible to tell where the swamp ends and the river begins. The highway veers right and disappears into the distance, the opposite direction from where we need to go.

The bridge over the Harlem River is gone. A shallow ribbon of gray leads out to where it used to stand, an old road that's barely even there anymore. Our way is blocked by concrete barriers. The surface is too unstable, too broken down to permit automobile traffic. Now only weekend fisherman and checkpoint guards and their nieces and nephews use it.

"I guess we walk from here," Micah says as he turns the car off. "Or swim."

Chapter Twelve

"My new shoes are ruined," Ashley complains as she high-steps over the muddy parts.

I look down at her feet and notice for the first time that she's wearing a new pair of Nike sneakers. I want to ask her how her family can afford them — not to mention the two-hundred dollar Ronnie Marx bikini she wore on Friday for the practice dive — but Micah interrupts the thought.

"There's another rental shack." He points off to the right. "Looks like they've got two-man kayaks."

"Or two-*woman* kayaks," Ashley says.

We head over to it. I've only got a few dollars in my pocket, so I wonder how we're going to pay. Maybe Ash can sell her shoes.

"I'll talk to the owner," Micah says. He looks at Reg when he says this. Everyone knows Reggie doesn't do tact. He's not the subtlest guy in the world. "I'll see what I can negotiate. Just wait here."

We watch as he walks over. He has to take a winding course, since there are puddles everywhere and sinkholes that could swallow him up in an instant. The shack stands on the edge of an expanse of water that stretches out beyond it. Several hundred feet away, a line of crumbling buildings rise, the tops of second-floor windows peeking up a few feet above the water, one foot below the high-water mark. Micah disappears around the corner of the shack.

I turn my gaze to Reg and Ash. I have so many questions I want to ask, but I need to get each of them alone and that's not going to happen here.

"Freaking hot out here," Reggie mumbles. He turns and wipes away a bead of sweat on his face and adds that he wishes he'd worn a hat. He rests a hand on Ashley's shoulder for a moment before dropping it. His thumb catches on where her knotted-up tee shirt bunches up at the middle of her back. Her skin's bronze, making the few wisps of hair I can see back there look blond like mine, rather than red. Her hand twitches reflexively at the touch. She curls her pinky around his for just a moment. Then the moment passes.

Careless gestures, completely natural and completely unnoticed by either of them. I can't help but feel a twinge of jealousy. They've grown so comfortable around each other, even as Kelly and I seem to be drifting apart.

It never used to be like this with them. The first few years I knew Reggie and Ash, they were constantly clashing with each other. Two insecure kids thrust into adolescence, both overwhelmed by new feelings, both helplessly attracted to the other, neither wanting to be the first to admit it. A sign of weakness. They were like magnets on strings, bumping into one another, repelling and spinning and finally aligning. Finally attracting each other.

Then, at some point — probably within the past few weeks — they started aligning. I guess it was inevitable, two people as passionate as they are. They were bound to end up together.

Ashley grabs Reggie's elbow and points past the line of buildings. "What's that?"

He shields his eyes against the glare of the sun off the water. I squint to see what they're looking at. There's a tiny spot in the air, way off in the distance, a glint of something shiny hovering over the edge of the wall surrounding Long Island.

"Is that an airplane?"

"Looks like it, but I thought that was supposed to be a no-fly zone."

We watch as the dot slowly moves. It appears to be circling. At some point we realize it's not actually out over Long Island, but over southern Manhattan.

Micah returns with a pair of old wooden oars. The paint has long since worn off of them and the wood appears brittle with age and dry rot. "I got us a rowboat," he announces. "It's not the greatest, but it'll get us out to where we need to go. Told you I'd think of something. Although, we might have to bail."

Nobody answers. He turns and follows the direction of our gazes. "What are you looking at?"

"Plane," Reggie says.

Micah finally spots it. "Strange."

"It looks like it's circling over lower Manhattan," Ashley says. She turns toward me. Micah and Reggie follow suit, all of them waiting as if I've got the answer.

"A surveillance plane?" I guess.

"It might have something to do with the zombies," Ashley says.

"Hey!" Micah hisses, pushing his palms down. "Keep it quiet. Our voices carry out here. Now let's get that rowboat and head over to where we're supposed to be."

Reggie drops his hand, immediately losing interest in the airplane. "Just paddles? No fishing gear, brah? I was so looking forward to trying those bloodworms."

Ashley laughs and slaps his arm. "That's my Reggie, always thinking about his stomach."

He smiles and nods, then frowns. "Hey."

We all laugh as we pass the shack. I notice it's built on plastic pontoons, presumably so it'll rise during high tides. It's attached to the cement by a long thick chain, which is crusted with dried moss. I glance back, but there's not much to see. The door's closed and the dark glass in the window is shuttered against the heat and glare. But I feel like whoever's inside is watching us.

We reach the bridge abutment and find a boat tied up to it with a frayed piece of twine. It leans against a cement block. Reggie tries to untie it, but the rope is hard, stiff. It refuses to come undone. Finally he just grabs the ends and snaps it apart. He tilts the boat over into the water with a splash, where it settles onto its bottom, rocking. We watch it for a few minutes to make sure it doesn't sink.

"Well, if there's a leak, it's not a bad one," Micah finally says. He hands the oars to Reggie. It's understood who's going to row.

While he climbs in and seats himself at the front, I notice a bronze placard embedded in the cement next to us. It reads, "Willis Avenue Bridge, Opened 2010." Of course the bridge is no longer there. Presumably not a victim of the bombing campaign, since it doesn't lead to Long Island. More likely a victim of the floods.

The rowboat is barely large enough to hold the four of us, and it makes me wonder how on earth it'll ever fit six. Micah assures us that it will, so Ash and I clamber aboard while Reggie holds it steady with his hand. He's the last one in and he seats himself in the middle. Ash pushes us off.

"This must be for bailing," she says, pulling a squared-off scoop from its cubby under the seat. I look down and see a thin line of water bleed across the bottom of the boat. The leak looks like it's coming from the front.

Micah doesn't look concerned though. He pulls the old computer tablet out of his pack and turns it on so he can more accurately locate our end of the Harlem tunnel. "Just head in that direction," he says after a minute passes. He points without looking up. Reggie angles us in that direction.

Then Micah's arm swings south like a compass, past the stumps of several buildings, past a line of red buoys to where a point of land rises in the distance. "That's Randall Island. Keep us away from there. It's probably mined."

Reggie has to strain to keep us on course. He guesses we're passing over the old Harlem channel connecting the East and Hudson Rivers. He points the boat toward the shell of the tallest building a few hundred feet away. The corners look like someone took a giant sledgehammer and chipped away at them. The façade is pocked by holes.

"Welcome to East Harlem," he says. "Keep your eyes open for street signs."

"Can you see the guys on your Link?" I ask. Ash looks up from where she's playing with the ribbon of water below her feet. Micah's got his face down near the screen of the tablet, trying to block out the glare. He reaches absently into his pocket and extracts his Link and hands it over. Reggie grabs it and passes it back to me. I start scrolling through to find the tracking app while Ash glances over my shoulder.

"Okay," Micah says, turning around. "According to this, we're a couple thousand feet from the tunnel opening. Take that passageway between those buildings there, Reg."

Reggie puffs from the exertion and the heat. I reach into my pack and grab one of the waters Micah gave me and hand it over to Ash so she can help him drink. Then I turn my attention back to the Link. He's got it all set up weird and I can't seem to find the tracking app.

A shadow overtakes us as we pass between buildings, blocking out the sun. The air is still hot, but I can't help shivering a little as the blank, dark windows drift by just out of arm's reach. Reggie keeps us close to take advantage of the shade, but far enough away so the oars don't hit. He's already dripping with sweat.

The buildings act like a wind funnel. It's a wet wind, humid and laden with decay. It pushes and pulls us in every direction but the one we want to go in.

"Did you hear that?" Reggie suddenly asks. He stops rowing for a moment, docking the oars. We all listen, but nothing comes to us but the wind, the dripping of water from the paddles, and the cries of gulls.

"What soun—"

But then we do hear it: a low rumble, like thunder. Actually, we feel it rather than hear it.

"What the hell is that?" Reggie says. "A storm?" He looks up at the drab gray, cloudless sky.

"Sounded more like an explosion," I say. "But it was too far away."

"A mine on the river? They sometimes go off, if there's a school of fish or a shark or something."

"There's no sharks here."

"Are too," Ashley says. "My cousin said he saw—"

There's another low rumble, this one more distinct. Ashley looks up in alarm. The noise gives me the creeps. I'd once read in a banned book — *Tom Sawyer* — that they used to bomb the Mississippi River to bring up dead bodies. I always wondered if it really worked.

"Let's just keep going," Micah murmurs. He turns his attention back to the tablet. I try and turn mine back to his Link, but my mind keeps drifting back to that book.

I finally give up after cycling through all the menus. "This thing's a disaster, Micah. I can't find it."

I tap Reggie on the shoulder to hand it forward, but Ash says she wants to give it a try, so I give it to her instead. She passes me the scoop. There's barely a quarter inch of water in the bottom of the boat. Not enough to bail out yet.

"Looks like the opening comes out on East One-Twentieth Street," Micah announces. We all look up. "Where are we?"

"One-Twenty-Fifth. Have we passed it?"

Micah shakes his head. "The numbers go down. Head left the next chance you've got. The tunnel opening is about three blocks inland."

Reggie snorts. "Inland from what?" He lets go of the oars and shakes the strain out of his hands.

Micah grins. "If you see a sign for First Avenue, take a right."

"Should I use my blinker?"

Ash and I laugh. Micah's driving habits are more insane than my road instructor's last summer. He not only follows all the rules, but with a wide margin of safety to boot.

We pass a massive storage tank of some sort. It was once painted white but is now mostly rust-red and black. Beyond it, several cross-shaped buildings break the surface of the water.

"First Ave," Reggie announces.

We pass through the buildings. They remind me of the pictures of old cemeteries that Ash's G-ma Junie once showed us. "We used to bury our dead," she'd once told us.

"Buried? In the ground? That's disgusting," Ash and I had both exclaimed. Incineration is so much more tidy. A guarantee that the dead will never come back.

"East One-Twentieth," Ash says. She points to where a moss-covered streetlamp arches out of the water. The green sign that hangs from it barely reaches above the surface.

"This should be it, then. Reggie, let's tie up to the sign. Ash, let me have my Link back, please."

"Fine, I couldn't find it either. This thing's as messy as your house is."

Micah grins. He reaches over the side and splashes us with water.

"Hey! Yuck!"

But she reciprocates. Pretty soon the three of us are splashing each other while Reggie yells at us to stop. "I'm trying to row here!" But we keep it up until the front of the rowboat bumps into the sign. Micah ties what's left of the rope to it and we rest for a moment drinking water from our packets. There's no respite from the glaring sun.

"What'd you do to this thing?" Micah complains after a moment. He looks up from his Link.

"I didn't do anything," I say.

"I might've moved a few things around," Ashley confesses.

Micah makes a sour face. "I can't find anything now."

"Yeah, well, I couldn't find anything before."

"Yeah, but—"

"Hey, guys," Reggie interrupts. He gestures south. "I don't think those are surveillance planes."

The tiny dot circling over lower Manhattan has now split into three separate dots. We watch as one dips and disappears past the edge of a building in our way. A moment later, it appears around the side and begins rising up again. The water underneath it seems to reach a finger up toward the sky.

"What the fuck is that?"

A second plane dips down like the first. Then the dull sound of the explosion reaches us.

"Holy shit," Reggie exclaims, laughing in amazement. "They're bombing the goddamn city!"

"Not the city," Micah says after a moment. The sound of another explosion rolls past us. We expect the third plane to follow its companions, but it doesn't. Instead, the other two planes line up behind it and together they turn away. "I think they're bombing the river."

"Dead bodies," I murmur.

They all turn and look at me. I shrug.

"What are they doing now?" Ash says. Her eyes grow large in her face. "Are they getting closer? I think they're heading this way!"

"Don't worry, Ash," Reggie says. But our fascination soon turns to concern as the dots grow larger. They do appear to be heading straight for us.

"Just act natural, guys," Micah advises us. "Remember, we're just out for a day of fishing. We're not doing anything illegal."

But we can't help but stare with dread and fascination as the planes come ever closer. Somewhere in the back of my mind, I'm aware that my toes are wet inside my shoes. I've forgotten to check the leak. Ash even says something about the wetness, but neither of these things seems to register as all that important right now.

It's only when the first plane descends and heads straight for us that our concern morphs into terror. Micah reaches around to untie us from the sign, but by then it's already too late.

The plane is over us in an instant. We watch with horror as an object disengages from its belly and falls toward the water.

Part Two

That's Why We Have Contingencies

Chapter Thirteen

Awareness comes so abruptly that I feel like I've been startled awake from a deep sleep.

But I don't feel rested. I don't feel like I've been asleep. I'm bone tired and hurting all over.

I don't open my eyes. I'm lying on my back and I can feel sunlight searing my face. The light presses against my eyelids. They glow a deep, fiery red. But the air is cold, frigid, colder than I'm used to. My skin stings. Without moving, I know I'm naked.

I try to move — a finger at first, then a hand — but it hurts so badly that I have to stop. Everything about me hurts: my shoulders scream out in agony and my spine has been replaced with a hot steel rod. Even my eyelids hurt.

Hours pass, but the pain never ends.

Finally I crack open an eyelid. My need to know where I am wins out. White light scorches my brain. I close my eyes, then open them again. Slowly. Just a slit. Then a little wider.

A hospital lamp materializes from the blur. It's the only thing I can see above me. I try to look around, but new pain shoots through my neck. It reaches down my back and squeezes my lungs until breathing itself becomes a wish to die. But death doesn't come, and I keep on breathing and hurting. I lie as still as death and stare at the light until it no longer blinds me. Until the agony is no longer the biggest part of me.

I raise a hand to my face. There's a sound. I don't know how long it's been there, but I hear it now. Buzzing. A million tiny angry wasps. They're stinging me. The sheet covering me slips off, tearing mercilessly at my skin, shredding it. My skin flows like hot oil to the floor. The wasps settle down after a while, crawling all over me.

Later, I move a leg. This angers the wasps so that they buzz and sting me some more, but not nearly as much as before.

Kwanjangnim Rupert's words come to me: *Don't fight your enemy's strength; use it. Flow with it; yield to it or it will break you.*

Pain is my enemy right now.

So I yield to it. I close my eyes and focus on breathing.

I slowly edge to the side of the bed, letting the pain flow through me and over me. I learn to use it, the pain, to move with it, to let it carry me like a current. My feet drop over the side and the pain flows freely past me and onto the floor. An endless tide of agony bearing me from unknown seas to unknown shores.

I'm in a hospital room. The décor is spartan, a few older-style instruments, bare walls, no clock. Just a barred window and sunlight passing through it. One of the public hospitals, nothing fancy.

Am I back home?

Something ropy caresses my thigh. I look down and nearly scream seeing the snake in my bed. I reach down and grab it and try to hurl it away, but it's latched onto me — attached *inside* of me! I feel it tug at my belly, see the bag of golden fluid it drains from my body. My fingers trace it to where it enters me.

Then I really do scream.

I tumble out of the bed and scream and scream until the pain consumes me and I flee from the hoard of angry wasps until I leave it so far behind that I know they will never find me again.

But they flow with the tide of pain.

They find me.

And they sting.

† † †

The second time I'm aware of waking, it's dark. My body tells me it's nighttime, but I have no way of confirming this. I'm back in bed and covered, though still naked underneath. The buzzing is gone and the silence is blissful. The cold is gone. So is much of the pain.

The tube still penetrates me between my legs. I try to pull on it, sobbing drily, but it refuses to let go.

Everything's so quiet that I can almost believe I'm totally alone in the world. I peer at the darkness above me until details emerge: shadows cast on the ceiling, the faint reflection of instrument lights around me. The hospital lamp above me is gone, replaced by the stained tiles of a drop-ceiling. It's a different room than before. The walls are even barer than the other. There's no window.

Where am I? What happened? Why am I here?

The pain awakens deep inside of me, so I know I'm still alive. It tells me I haven't died. I haven't reanimated.

I think I haven't, anyway. Are zombies self-aware?

I lift my arms and stare at them. They're covered in dark spots, days-old bruises and half-healed scrapes.

Why can't I remember?

I groan as I rotate my head all the way to the left. There's an IV machine, blinking away, dripping liquid into a tube that snakes its way beneath the sheet, but not into my arms.

I reach up and find it sunken into my neck. I want to rip it out, but as my fingers dance carefully over the tape that binds the needle to me, something inside of me warns me to wait.

I call out.

My throat is dry and it comes out as a low moan.

"Can someone help me?"

Nobody answers. Nothing moves.

I give up. I let myself slip back into the darkness.

To sleep.

Chapter Fourteen

I awaken to the sound of a female voice:
 . . . *updated implant* . . .
 . . . *stable and fully functional* . . .
 . . . *ready . . . treatments . . . stable vital signs* . . .

It fades in and out until awareness finally kicks in and I drag myself to the surface of the black pit of unconsciousness where I've been floating for who-knows how long. I still can't remember what happened to bring me here. I don't recall a thing beyond sitting in Micah's basement and the boys playing *Zpocalypto*.

The boys. Alarm bells inside my head. *Where's Kelly?*

I open my eyes. The room is dark, but light spills in through the cracked door from the hallway. I tip my chin down the tiniest fraction of an inch and I see a hand resting on the knob.

Kelly?

I almost call out.

"I'm still not sure I understand what her connection is to the Corben boy," a man says. The hand repositions on the knob.

Corben boy?

They're talking about Kelly.

"We had forensics go through the Stream records," the female voice says. "The girl popped up because she tried pinging him after he vanished from our tracers. That's all we could find."

"Well, as long as she's a good candidate for the treatment, I won't complain."

"She's young and strong. Records show she spends almost twenty hours a week invested in the game. A big fan. She'll make an excellent player."

Player? I wish I knew what they were talking about.

"Well, she's still a bit of an unknown variable, as far as I'm concerned. Give her tonight to recover from the immune suppressant. I've scheduled to have the prep nurse take the six AM shuttle to arrive at seven o'clock sharp tomorrow morning. Would you help get her ready for the initial Alpha injection? Good. But hold off on the rest of the procedure until I arrive. I'll be on the next shuttle out. Got some early business in the city. Expect to be here by nine thirty at the latest. I want to supervise the entire metamorphosis, understood?"

"Yes, sir."

What treatment? What metamorphosis?

"As this is our first try with the new batch of virus, we've got no baseline for how long it'll take for the infection to carry through to completion. Make sure the remaining contingencies are all in place. Oh, and I want a full live video and audio recording of the entire process. We'll send them to Hadley for analysis."

"I understand."

I frown now, disturbed by what I'm hearing. Virus? Infection? Contingencies? What the hell are they planning to do to me?

"Where are we on Miss Daniels? Still unconscious?"

Wait. They're talking about me now. Who were they talking about before? Ashley? Is the injection meant for her?

"Yes, sir. She's been unresponsive to anything but pain stimulus since they brought her in from New York Medical. It's not a deep coma. Very active brainwaves."

"And the new implant? Still showing signs of rejection?"

"Over thirty percent of the neural connections have degenerated. The decay rate is steady. We're losing between twelve and eighteen percent every twenty four hours."

"It's possible that it'll reverse; we've seen it happen."

"Yes, sir, but unless it does, the new implant will become completely detached in less than six days."

"Might be the new materials. Are we sure it's not a software glitch?"

"Maybe. I can't get a handle on the new program. I tried adjusting one or two of the interface parameters, but the system hung on me. I had to reboot."

"No, don't mess with it anymore, Mabel. Too risky. If something happens while the system's down, we could completely lose her. Keep her stable; a shock to the system could trigger a total rejection. Then we'd be back to square one."

"But the coder's going to be out for at least another couple more days. Isn't there anyone else who can do the programming? I'm a bit lost here. I do better with people than machines."

"You're doing fine, Mabel. Just keep following the protocols until the coder's online again. Besides, it'd take us at least a week to get another engineer up to speed, and this is just too sensitive to give to anyone else. It's a risk, but I don't we should bring in another ArcWare engineer."

ArcWare!

"We'll know for sure for before then anyway, sir."

"Yes, either the new L.I.N.C. will fully anneal to her cerebral cortex or it won't. We can always go back to the old one."

"Without the failsafe in place? Is that wise?"

"Like I said, that's why we have a backup, Mabel. I'm sure you can appreciate that fact more than anyone else right now. You checked her vitals this evening?"

"Half an hour ago. She's stable. She was lucky. The blast could've done a lot more damage— "

Blast? What blast?

" —in the water. There was only minor internal bleeding. The laparoscopic surgeon at NYMC repaired any leaks before your guys extracted her. Everything seems fine now — her fluid input and output, vitals — she just hasn't come out of the coma."

"She will when her body's ready. I don't want to rush it. Have we figured out why the kids were even there in the first place?"

"The other girl, Miss Evans, said something about the tunnel before she clammed up."

So Ashley is here! But what does she mean by tunnel?

"She's refused to say anything more. Keeps insisting on seeing her parents. She's trouble, that one. I just know it. She filed a report a couple weeks ago on her grandmother's conscription."

G-ma Junie?

The man chuckles. "She's smart is all. They all are. That's why we recruited them."

"She tried to escape last night, so I put her in restraints. But I had to sedate her when I found she'd gotten out of them this morning."

"That's fine."

The alarm bells already jangling inside my head are now going crazy. *Ashley escape? Sedated? What the hell is going on?*

My mind goes back to what she said about the tunnel. It niggles at me until I manage to coax an image from somewhere deep down inside of my head: a memory of swimming in darkness. More like a dream than anything real. Then, being attacked, needing to escape. Kelly's there, too. I'm choking.

What the hell did we do?

Reggie's voice echoes inside my head: *We should break into Gameland.*

Did we?

"No doubt they were trying to go back," the man says, as if he'd somehow heard my thoughts. It confirms my fears: we did break in. The man makes a whooshing sound as he breathes. "And now that whole business in lower Manhattan. They must've figured they could to go back in through a different tunnel."

And then it all comes back to me in a sudden rush: the maps and the preparation to go, the practice dive at the reservoir, the actual dive to LI through the Midtown tunnel, the narrow escape coming back. The blockage. I remember we had to leave Jake behind. And I remember Kelly telling me I was not to go back.

Kelly.

Except he did exactly that. He went back. Without me.

Did the rest of us try going back?

Finally the panic that my mind has been damming gushes forth. Kelly never did come back.

No! He was trying to get out. We were going to meet him.

Whoever the man is standing out there in the hall, he's wrong. We weren't going back to LI, we were waiting for Kelly to return with Jake.

But something's still missing, some vital piece that my mind refuses to yield. I squeeze my eyes shut and try to remember. It doesn't come.

"I thought the Harlem tunnel was cemented in years ago," Mabel says.

The Harlem tunnel?

There's a bang as the man slaps the wall, making me jump. "It was! That's what angers me about it! The coder knew that! Those kids weren't supposed to be there! They were supposed to stay on the island the first time! Why else would our guys go down there and block the tunnel? But not only did they come back, but they also brought the whole god damn zombie horde with them!" He growls with frustration.

"What's the latest on the outbreak?" Mabel asks, clearly eager to change the subject.

"You know I can't say anything about that, Mabel."

"And you know I'm stuck here. Who am I going to blab to?"

The man sighs. "Ironic isn't it? This'll probably be the safest place to be once the outbreak takes hold. And it will. Fine. I guess you deserve to know. The New Merican Air Defense went in this afternoon and napalmed the shit out of everything. Media's still in blackout. Jackers are posting every kind of conspiracy theory they can come up with. We shut down the black streams as soon as we can find them, but new ones pop up somewhere else just as quickly. Ask me, the bombing of the tunnels was too public. It was completely mishandled. And it places our entire operation in jeopardy. I told Padraig he should've had better control of the operation from the beginning. Logistics is his bailiwick. He was supposed to be our mole in the government. He dropped the ball."

The hand on the knob rises halfway up the door. A finger with a large ring on it taps the wood. I can almost see the man thinking. The crack shrinks to a finger's width, letting in less light.

"Should I put her in restraints, just in case?" Mabel asks.

"No, just keep the motion detectors on the floor around the bed. That should be enough to alert you if she wakes and tries to get up again. But keep a close watch. I don't want to lose another one."

"Maybe if I had some assistance— "

"Soon, Mabel. Patience. Once I get the committee fully on board, I'll bring in some more help. Not everyone understands the delicacy of this situation, much less the importance, as you do. We don't get very many . . . volunteers, such as you."

"Thank you, sir."

"Okay. I'm going home. Been a long day. I'll be here in . . . twelve hours. Keep monitoring her. Miss Daniels is our best hope for success. And our biggest risk. I don't want to think about what will happen if she ends up being our biggest failure, too."

"We still have the other girl. Her new implant is a hundred percent annealed."

"Yeah, but her connection to the target is still unclear. And unless she's also related to the good father . . . ." He chuckles. "Anyway, everyone's expendable. It'd be better to just terminate— "

A door slams closed further down the hall, followed by the sound of approaching footsteps.

"Speaking of expendable, there's Padraig now. Why is he never on time?"

The fingers slip off the door. It clicks shut. Darkness and silence envelop the room.

Chapter Fifteen

Terminate what? *The project? Me? And who's the target? Or, for that matter, the good father? Is it Dad?*

I reach my hand up to the back of my neck. There's a bandage there, stiff and crinkly. Why would they replace my implant? What's the new one for? What does it do?

And why is my body rejecting it?

An inch above the edge of the bandage, my hair has been shaved away. From the feel of the new bristles coming in, the surgery couldn't have been more than a couple days ago.

The questions flood into me, foremost among them: What is the alpha injection? Is it anything like the Zulu Process?

I shiver, dreading that it might be.

Back when reanimation was first discovered, living humans were turned into zombies to create an army of the Undead for national defense purposes. The process was codenamed Zulu. Back then, only Death Row prisoners were conscripted. The program was so successful that the murder rate dropped like a rock. Then, when the military started running out of suitable candidates, they began taking life-without-parole inmates. They said it solved two problems with one stroke: it beefed up our security forces — depleted after the Middle East conflicts of the first two decades of the century — and eased prison overcrowding.

Of course, Zuluization generated new problems for the country. Intended to stop global strife, the program only brought it home to us. The Southern States Coalition demanded that they have more say in which citizens could be turned into Zulus and how they were to be used. When the federal government refused, the SSC seceded. A civil war followed. The remaining thirty-six states became New Merica, isolating itself from the rest of the world.

After the Life Service Law passed eleven years ago, the government finally dropped the term Zulu and began formerly calling them conscriptees. There were the Omegamen, placed into the military to fight and protect against our enemies. Then there were all the rest, the Controlled Undead. CUs. These do the jobs nobody else wants. But no matter what they do, most people just call them what they are: zombies.

Then Arc properties entered the picture. They wanted access to CUs for a wholly new purpose — entertainment — and they were willing to pay well for them.

Is that what they're doing to us? Are we to become Players in *The Game?*

I lower my hand and slip it back under the covers just as the lock clicks and the door opens. I shut my eyes and pretend to be asleep, but my heart is hammering inside my chest, threatening to give me away.

The nurse — Mabel, I remind myself — comes in and slips a cuff on my arm to check my blood pressure and pulse. As she works, she talks to herself. She says my name once or twice. I don't respond. I pretend to be unconscious. I try to lie still and impassive. I force myself to sink away into the deepest part of me.

But then she runs something hard along the sole of my foot. The sensation is almost too much to bear and I draw it away, curling my toes and nearly yelping with pain. I bite my tongue. She appears to be satisfied that this is a normal reflex, even for someone unconscious, as she doesn't make any remark.

She returns to the head of the bed and gently lifts my left eyelid open. I'm barely able to brace myself before she shines a harsh light into my eye. I try not to flinch or pull away. She repeats this with the other eye.

Finally, she draws the sheet completely off my body. The air is cool, but not cold. Still, I shiver and become aware of my nakedness. I stiffen. I sense her hesitate, as if she notices something's amiss. I sense her eyes on me, judging me, inspecting my every movement, from the flutter of my eyelids to the rise and fall of my chest.

"Jessica?" she says, testing. "Miss Daniels?"

I don't answer.

"Are you there? Can you hear me, honey? It's okay. I'm here to help you."

I'm so tempted to respond, to plead with her to help me. But I don't.

She sighs and pulls on my right shoulder and leg, rolling me toward her. She checks the sheets beneath me. I'm so ashamed, so embarrassed for anyone to see me like this, that I want to tell her to stop. But I remind myself that I'm a prisoner here, a guinea pig, and that it's not just me. My friends are also in danger. Letting Nurse Mabel know I'm awake will undoubtedly only make things worse for all of us.

She rolls me back. I let my arm and leg flop back to the bed. The bone in my wrist hits the metal rail on the side of the bed and I wince. Thankfully, she's not looking at my face.

"Changing your catheter, honey," she murmurs. "This won't hurt a bit." She apparently talks just to hear herself speak. From what I can gather, she's the only one on duty here. She must be lonely. I almost feel sorry for her.

She doesn't deserve your sympathy.

I crack open my eyelids and watch as she pulls a syringe out of her smock pocket. She turns her back so I can't see what she's doing. I feel her reach down and draw my knees apart. I feel the tube wiggle against my skin. It makes my skin crawl.

When she straightens again a moment later I can see that the syringe is full of some kind of clear liquid, presumably withdrawn from whatever is inside of me. She sets this onto the table beside me. I then feel her tug on the tube. It slips easily out of me, but the sensation makes me want to pee so badly that I almost whimper.

She reaches over and slips a new tube from a plastic package and lets it unfurl like a dead snake.

"Okay, young lady. This might hurt a little going in."

And I swear I'm not imagining it, but there seems to be the faintest hint of a smile in her voice when she says it.

Chapter Sixteen

I have to get the hell out of here.

I have no clue where I am and why I'm here. I don't even know who my captors are. I just know I need to escape.

I need to find Ashley. I need to save her.

I wonder if any of the others are here, too. How can I save us all?

The man said they lost one of us already. What did he mean by that? And which one was it? Reggie? Micah?

Please, God. Make it not be Kelly.

I wish I could remember more. I wish I knew what they meant by the blast.

But remembering is a luxury that I just can't afford right now. I don't need to know what happened to bring me here in order to escape. I only need to know that I have to get away.

I wait until Mabel leaves the room, watching her carefully through slitted eyes as she inserts the cardkey attached to her belt into a slot above the doorknob. There's a beep when the release activates. She exits and the door clicks shut behind her. Then I wait some more, just in case she's forgotten something and decides to come back in.

Move! my mind screams.

But my body refuses to obey. I know the longer I wait, the more likely it is that she'll return, but I'm suddenly paralyzed with fear. I don't even let myself cry, though I want to. I want to break down and give up. I want to crawl into a corner and roll up into a ball and cry. Let someone else take care of me for once.

But there isn't anyone to do that. There never has been.

I bite away the tears. It's better that way. If she sees them on my cheeks, she'll know I'm awake. She'll tie me to the bed. She'll sedate me and inject me with whatever they're planning on giving to Ash. I can't let that happen to either of us.

So why aren't I moving? Why do I just lie here, frozen, choking on sobs my body doesn't seem to remember how to let out?

Finally, just when I've managed to push the fear far enough away that I can move, the door opens again and Mabel comes in. The terror I've so desperately pushed away comes flooding back in again.

"Don't know why I have do this every hour," she mumbles unhappily to herself.

She goes through the same routine, all the while talking to herself. Despite my panic and loathing for her, I find myself drifting in the sound of her voice. She checks my blood pressure and eyes, stimulates my foot, takes my temperature. It's easier this time to keep still, now that I know what to expect.

I watch her between the slit of my eyelids as she bends down out of sight. She talks to the catheter bag as she measures and empties it. She moves to the head of the bed and does something to my IV. I hear the rustle of her clothes, smell the soap on her skin and the slight tang of body odor. Then she goes and stands at the foot of the bed and records her findings on the medical Link. She clicks it back to the bed frame when she's done.

"Back in another hour, honey." Then, with a dry chuckle, she adds: "Don't go anywhere."

Finally she leaves.

Don't go anywhere?

I want to throttle her.

I try to remember Kwanjangnim Rupert's wise advice. Patience and pliability. Strength in waiting for just the right moment to act. *A skilled hapkido expert will always bend to adapt to his situation.*

So I lie in the darkness for several more minutes, thinking about my situation — what little I know about it. I consider my enemy's skills and strengths — not just hers, but who I assume she works for: ArcWare. I assess their known and presumed disadvantages. I strain my ears for any hint of a sound outside the room.

But there's nothing, just the quiet clicks of the IV drip and the occasional ticks and creaks of the bed as I breathe.

Fifteen minutes have passed since she came in. I measure this by the digital readout on the instruments beside me.

Ever so slowly, I sit up. I reach down and find the Link and turn the screen to me and wake it. It tells me it's Friday, eleven twenty three in the evening. Almost a week has passed since we first broke into LI, probably three days that I've been in this place. Eric must be going frantic by now — assuming he doesn't know.

He doesn't. That's what my instincts tell me.

I wonder if Grandpa knows.

My instincts remain silent on that one, as they do regarding whether Mom has realized I'm gone.

I want to apologize to her. I want to tell her she's not as bad of a mother as I always believed. It's me who's bad.

I scroll through the Link, blinking away tears that aren't there, and find the initial admittance report. The basic information is there: my name and age, height and weight, blood type, viral infection status (clean), implant status (version 4a, intact, latent), and life expectancy. Then there's the triage nurse's report at the emergency room at the New York Medical Center:

<< 17Y/O F ADMITTED POST TRAUMA (EXPLOSION) >>

<< UNCONC >>

<< H2O INHAL ASPHYXIA W/RESUSC BY EMS EN-ROUTE >>

<< PER EMS: BLEEDING FR L EAR, NOSE, MULT ABR TO LIMBS, TRUNK, HEAD. ABD SWELLING >>

<< NML EKG. BAGGED W/100% O2, SALINE DRIP >>

<< CXR, ABD/NECK/HD CT SCANS, IV RINGERS. CBC, TYPE & CROSS. 3 UNITS. >>

Most of this is incomprehensible to me, just a bunch of medical mumbo jumbo, but I get the basic gist of it. There was an explosion, just as the man and nurse said there was. The cuts and bruises all over my body are proof enough of that.

Why can't I remember?

I look, but there's no mention of any of my friends.

No mention of us being in East Harlem.

Third tunnel.

Kelly and Jake were coming back. We were going to meet up with them. That's it. They were trying a different way back to avoid the zombies around the midtown. That's why we were there, to meet them, not to go through ourselves. We were in a boat. Reggie was rowing. And then . . . .

Something happened. Planes. Flying over us. A bomb. *Napalmed the shit out of everything.* That's what the man had said. A sob escapes from my throat. Kelly and Jake had been in the tunnel when it was bombed. *Already lost one subject.*

Who died?

No! I can't let this stop me.

I glance over the side of the bed at the floor, looking for the motion sensors. I do see something there in the darkness: four small pods at the corners of the bed, red eyes in the shadows staring at each other. They're directly in line with where a person getting up would set their feet. Easy enough to avoid now that I know about them.

First, though, I need to take care of these damn tubes in my body.

The IV turns out to be harder than I thought. I waste precious minutes trying to loosen a corner of the tape holding the needle in my neck. I finally manage to peel a little away. It sticks like glue and feels like I'm ripping ten layers of skin off. I give it a hard yank and the needle comes out. Blood leaks out of the hole and drips down my neck. I feel it pool in my collar before spilling down my chest. I dab at it with the sheet, but I can't bother with stopping it right now. It'll have to clot on its own.

Blood all over the bed. No way to hide it now. No going back.

Another ten minutes have passed. Nurse Mabel will be returning in another twenty. I need to hurry.

I lift the sheet off my legs and look down between them at the urinary catheter. Just the sight of it makes me shake with fury. My hands tremble as I give it a tug. It doesn't move. A crazy thought enters my head: maybe they sewed it in. But then I remember Mabel and her syringe.

About a foot past the point where the yellow tube comes out of me, there's a Y. One arm connects to a clear rubber tubing that snakes off the side of the bed. I watch that line for a moment, fascinated as several teaspoons of pale yellow urine leak out of me and run down the tube.

The other arm of the tubing ends in some kind of adapter. It looks like it would fit a syringe. After inspecting it more closely, I guess that it must be where the nurse extracted the liquid earlier. There must be some kind of balloon inside of me that holds the catheter in place. But without a syringe to empty it, how am I supposed to get it out? I can't very well escape dragging a bag of pee around with me.

I check the time. Fifteen minutes before she's back.

I could disconnect the catheter from the bag. It looks like it'd just pull apart. But then what? I'd still have the tube inside of me and I'd leak all over the place.

Pop the balloon.

Minutes tick by and panic rises up inside of me as I consider this. How the hell am I supposed to pop it?

Finally I bend down as far as I can and stretch the tubing until it reaches my face. I stick it between my teeth and try to bite through it just below the syringe adapter, grimacing. My stomach revolts. Then my teeth pierce the soft rubber and a warm gush of liquid spurts into my mouth. I immediately spit it out onto the bed before realizing it's just water. I give the balloon an experimental tub, but it still won't budge.

"Fuck," I whisper.

Ten minutes.

I bend down one more time. This time I try and suck out the remaining water. My mouth fills. I spit that out, too. Finally the tube slides out.

Five minutes.

I make my way to the foot of the bed, then slowly and carefully crawl over it, avoiding the motion detectors. My head swims and the room spins, but I blink and force myself to focus. I'd puke, but there's nothing in my stomach. I haven't eaten in days and my body shakes from weakness. I don't know how I'm ever going to overpower anyone, much less free Ashley and any of the others and escape.

Two minutes.

My feet hit the floor. I'm completely naked, but I don't feel the cold. Blood drips down my chest, splattering on the floor. My vision swims before my eyes. I'm barely able to stand upright.

One minute.

I lean on the bed frame and wait for Nurse Mabel to walk in, not a clue what I'm going to do, not caring anymore. The minute passes and the door remains closed. I breathe deeply, hoping to clear my head.

My strength slowly returns. I'm still shaking, but it feels good to stand. I bend down, carefully, wobblingly, then straighten back up again. Every muscle sings out at me. My stomach actually grumbles. And still she doesn't come.

"Little Miss Mabel must have fallen asleep," I whisper.

I make my way over to the IV and yank the tubing free from the bag and wrap it around my fist. I can use it to choke her if I have to.

"Let's get things moving," I whisper, and I kick the motion detector across the floor.

Within moments, footsteps sound on the other side of the door. My heart pounds in my ears and my skin tingles. Now I'm ready.

I'm behind her as she comes through the door.

" —ways happens when I'm sound asleep." She's already halfway across the room before it registers I'm not in the bed. It's empty and covered in blood, my blood. "What the— "

"Looking for me?"

She spins around, but I'm ready for her. I grab her arm and yank as she turns. She's off-balance, completely unprepared. The motion jolts her off her feet and she slams to the floor with a loud cry of pain and alarm. I hear a crack — probably her elbow — but I'm on her in an instant. I yank her arm up her back, past the point of resistance. She screams.

"Shut up!" I tell her, growling to keep the weakness from my voice.

She keeps right on screaming. I yank even harder, then realize she's in agony, so I yield a little.

"Shut the fuck up, you bitch," I breathe into her ear, "or I'll rip your arm out of your socket."

She snaps her mouth closed but continues to struggle a little. Tears fall from her eyes. It just pisses me off all the more seeing them.

"Who else is here?"

She doesn't answer. I twist her arm and she yelps.

"Who else is here?"

"The guards."

"Don't you fucking lie to me, you little shit!"

"I'm not. I'm— Fuck! Okay, okay. It's . . . just me."

I place my knee on her arm and lean all my weight onto it. She grunts but I don't let up. I unwind the plastic IV tubing from my fist and grab her other hand and pull it behind her and up against the other.

"You're hurting me."

"I told you to shut up."

Once I've got her wrists tied, I loop it around her neck so she can't pull them down. Then, standing up with my foot on her neck, I reach over and grab the catheter off the bed.

"I should shove this down your throat, you sick bitch." Instead, I tie up her feet with it. It stretches even more than the IV line, but it's stronger. It won't break.

She doesn't move. She's stopped struggling and now just lies on the floor with her cheek pressed against the linoleum. Her eyes follow me as I search for my clothes.

"Where's the alarm for the motion detectors?" I demand.

She doesn't answer.

I take a step toward her and she flinches.

"Where?"

"In my pocket. It's in my pocket!"

I reach under her and find her Link. The screen is already awake, flashing. I thumb it off. I bend down and place my lips up next to her ear.

"Now, where are my clothes?"

"Burnt, torn. I don't—"

"Where can I get some?"

"I . . . in the supply closet, I think. I don't know." Then she half-laughs, half-coughs.

"What's so funny?"

"Nothing."

Blood trickles from a cut on her scalp. I reach up and pull the sheet from the bed and use the corner of it to dab it away. She winces.

"Just a cut. You'll live. Too bad. Now, tell me: where are we? What is this place?"

"You're choking me."

"You can breathe just fine. Where are we? Answer my questions if you want to live."

"You wouldn't kill—"

"I don't think you want to find out. One last time, then I really am going to hurt you: Where the fuck am I?"

"Someplace you'll never escape from."

I grab a handful of her hair and yank. Her head whips up. She inhales sharply.

"You'll never get out of here alive," she says. "You or your friends."

"Bonus question. Answer this and I might let you live: Where is my friend Ashley?"

She doesn't answer.

"I know what you plan on doing to her. I know about the new implants and the injections. Who else is here?"

"Fuck you."

"Brave words coming from someone in your position," I spit. "You should be begging for your life."

"You're just a kid. You won't hurt me. You can't. You need me."

Doubt begins to trickle in. I don't know if she's right about me needing her — maybe I do — but now that she's got me thinking about it, I realize she's right about the rest. I'm not a killer.

"You don't know who you're dealing with."

"I know you're with Arc. What do they want with us?"

She laughs again. "Arc? You just don't get it, do you?"

"Then explain it to me."

"Maybe you should ask your grandfather. He's the one responsible for all this."

This shocks me for a moment. "I've heard that all my life, bitch. It's nothing I haven't heard before. Tell me where my friends are."

"It's too late for them," she says, wheezing as she cough-laughs. "They're already dead. Just like you."

"Oh, I'm very much alive."

"No, you're not."

Something happens to me then. Rage swallows me. Fear overwhelms me. I don't know where it comes from, but when it does, it consumes me.

I pull her head up. "I told you that you didn't want to find out what I'm capable of."

I rocket my arm straight down, shooting my hand toward the floor. Her head hits with a loud, sickening *crack!* I can feel the jolt all the way up into my shoulder. She gurgles once, then her chest collapses beneath me.

And doesn't rise again.

Chapter Seventeen

I don't know how long I sit in shock on Nurse Mabel before I realize something is dripping down my arm, something warm and sticky. Slowly, my eyes tilt down. I don't see anything there at first, but then there's the faintest glistening on my skin. I'm crying. I'm actually crying.

Except my cheeks are dry.

I stumble to my feet, gasping, reeling backwards until I hit the bed. It moves out from behind me and rolls away, throwing me onto the floor on my ass. I sit there for several more minutes staring at what I've just done.

I killed someone.

But I'm not a killer!

And it's not tears on my arm, it's my blood.

Zombies don't cry, and they don't bleed.

The lying bitch. Why'd she have to lie like that?

Finally my body begins to react to the knowledge of what it did. It starts to shake with the truth — not the panic or the remorse, but the pleasure. I liked doing it. I just killed someone and I enjoyed the thrill it gave me. What the hell kind of monster have I become?

Not become, my mind whispers. *It's what you've always been.*

Eric knew what I was capable of. That's why he had me take hapkido. He knew I had a violent streak inside of me. He knew about the pain and the fury I've always kept bottled up inside of me.

Maybe yoga would have been a better choice.

I let my head drop into my hands. "This is not me," I moan. "I'm not like this. I'm not a killer."

But the proof is lying in a pool of blood in front of me. I let my rage get the better of me and now a woman lies dead on the floor. I can't stop staring at her. But neither can I bring myself to wish her back to life. I want her dead. I want her to pay for what she's done to me.

She doesn't move.

I can't look at her anymore. I bury my head in my arms and focus instead on my breathing techniques instead.

Eventually I realize I should be moving. The time on the nurse's Link tells me it's past two in the morning. Only a few more hours before dawn and the prep nurse from ArcWare and that man return. I need to find my friends and get away before they do.

I raise my head.

Mabel's head rests in the middle of her congealing blood. Her eyes staring glassily at me, filming over.

Her jaw twitches.

It startles me. I stare harder at her face, paralyzed with a mixture of both fear and hope. But it's just my imagination. She really is dead. She didn't move. Or, if she did, it's just her muscles relaxing.

I get up and untie the bindings from her hands and feet. I can't stand seeing her like this, her body twisted and drawn to itself, an unnatural pantomime of agony. The IV tubing has sliced into her fat wrists, leaving purple ligature marks that will never heal, not like my own bruises, given time. The catheter I've tied around her ankles is stiff and taut, refusing to untie. It reminds me of the zombie fingers that grabbed me in the Midtown tunnel on the way to LI. I shiver and yank on it until it snaps free of her heels. Her feet fall back to the floor with a *thuh-thunk*. I toss the tubing to the side.

My neck itches where the hole from my IV has finally clotted. It feels sore, hot. I scrape the dried blood off with my fingernail and glance at the door. I need clothes. Nurse Mabel's would be both too short and too husky for me. And I don't want to undress her just so I can be dressed. I need to find the storage closet where she said there'd be clothes.

I step over the body and bend down to grab the sheet off the floor. It's covered in blood — some hers, some mine — but it's better than going out there naked. I shake open it and wrap it around me. The feel of the cold, partially stiffened, blood-soaked fabric makes my skin crawl, but I try not to think about it. Instead, I tuck the corner in under my arm, then tie the IV line around my waist and cinch it snug so I'm not flapping in the breeze.

I freeze when the whisper of a sound comes from behind me, a wet, sticky noise that sounds like rubber tires peeling slowly off the hot pavement. I whirl around.

Nurse Mabel is on her knees, her head hanging down between her arms, blood and saliva dripping from her lips. Her hair is plastered against the side of her face. She wobbles a moment, her arms shaking. For a moment I'm not certain of what I'm seeing. Joy courses through me knowing she's not dead. Joy and anger. She's supposed to be dead. How am I supposed to leave her now?

Tie her up. She'll only cause problems and get in your way.

But she also needs medical attention. I really did a number on her head. She'll be lucky if she doesn't have a concussion. Or worse.

She doesn't move, just hovers there on the floor on her hands and knees, looking like she's trying not to puke.

"This is fucked," I mutter.

Her head snaps up. She bares her teeth and hisses. There's nothing in her eyes, not a shred of light or life. They're as black as night and as soulless as a grave. The side of her head is sickeningly flattened. Her mouth gapes open and her tongue lolls out.

That's why we have contingencies. I'm sure you can appreciate that more than anyone else, Mabel.

"Oh, god," I whisper. "Please, no."

She moans her first death moan and I know it's true. It's a sound I'll never forget from LI, the sound of death and hunger and desire. Cold fingers sweep up my spine and twine around my neck, choking the air from my lungs.

"You're not supposed to come back," I tell her, as if speaking one truth will somehow negate another. The dead do not come back on their own. They either have to be infected by another zombie, or they have to be reanimated by injection with the government's virus. They don't just happen.

That's why we have contingencies.

We don't get very many volunteers, such as you.

She moans again and lurches unsteadily to her feet. Her body lists to one side and crashes into the blood pressure machine. They both slam into the wall. She recovers too quickly — frightfully so — and moves toward me.

I manage to step to the side just as her arms reach into the space I'd just occupied. She crashes to the floor again. This time, she lies there without moving for several seconds.

Get out of here! my mind screams, but all I do is stand there staring, wasting precious moments.

She moans again and begins to contract, pulling her arms and legs beneath her. This time she's quicker. It seems impossible, but it's like her body is readjusting to its new life-in-death state. Before I have a chance to react, she's on her knees and gotten a foot under her, ready to launch herself at me.

I spin around and grab the closest thing to me — the IV stand — and lift it above my head. I try to swing it down on her, but the base wedges itself into the ceiling and stops. I lose my balance and slip on the bloody floor. Only my grip on the pole keeps me from breaking my arm.

Nurse Mabel — or whatever she's become — advances while I scramble away. My back hits the wall. She lunges forward, groaning and hissing. Her hands reach out at me. Her head tilts unnaturally toward the side I crushed. She looks like she's suffered a massive stroke. I guess she has.

I skitter to my left. Her fingers reach for and catch my hair. I kick out with my foot, connecting with her knees, but it only pushes her legs out from under her. She falls directly onto me, her mouthful of teeth and infected saliva barely missing my knee. Instead, her chin hits my kneecap, knocking her head back. I hear a crack as her neck snaps. She rolls off me but immediately begins to move forward again, her head at an even more awkward angle.

I lash out again with another kick, this time to her neck, spinning her away. I scramble to my feet and my hurt knee gives beneath me. The door's further away to my left. I slide over, hands behind me on the wall, helping me stand, feeling for the handle. I keep my eyes on her as she gets clumsily back to her feet.

I turn the knob and, just as she charges, twist the handle and yank on the door.

But it doesn't open! My fingers slip away and I lose my balance and tumble to the floor. I need the cardkey, but it's on her belt!

Her momentum slams her into the wall. Just as gracelessly, she turns around and finds me. I scramble to the far side of the small room, putting the bed between us. It's the only thing I can use to protect myself.

With the bed in her way, I gain a few seconds. I look frantically for something to use as a weapon, anything that'll help me get that cardkey off her belt. But there's nothing on this side of the room for me to use.

I move behind the foot of the bed, keeping it between us. Mabel circles toward me in the same direction. I wait until she's square at the head before shoving all my weight into the bed frame. It lurches forward and pins her to the wall with a loud bang. Her elbow sinks into the drywall. She moans and waves her hands longingly at me, but she can't get free.

Still leaning onto the bed, I check the wheels and find a lever. I push it down until I feel it lock into place. Then, ever so slowly, I let up. The bed stays put despite Mabel's attempts to push it out of her way.

I move quickly now. The bed won't hold her for long. I reach up and yank the IV pole down from its place in the ceiling. A tile falls, showering me with dusty bits and cobwebs and mouse droppings. I lift the pole to my side and take aim at Mabel's neck, angling one of the pole's feet forward. Then, with a grunt I swing it at her. She doesn't duck or try to move out of the way. Zombies don't duck.

The foot of the IV stand sinks deep into the wall two feet past her head. I lever the pole over her neck and shove the top against the wall on this side until the bag holder penetrates the drywall. It sinks all the way in and the hook acts like an anchor. She thrashes against it, but the pole stays put.

Now I circle around the bed one last time. She watches me with those dead black eyes, hissing and writhing. I lean down beneath her flailing arms and snatch the lanyard off her belt. It snaps free just as the IV pole explodes from the wall. Mabel bends down and reaches for me.

But I'm already around the bed again and back to the door. I hear the bed frame groan and the wheels squeal against the floor.

I slip the key into the slot just as she slips from her trap.

The lock doesn't release.

She steps toward me, her shoes making sticky sounds on the tacky blood.

I try again.

Still nothing.

"What the fu— "

Another step, a quick glance back to see her jersey caught on the bed. A rip and another step. The hair on the back of my head moves. I duck. My skin prickles.

I turn the key around and shove it back into the slot. The tiny red light on the locking mechanism turns green.

I yank the handle just as Mabel's fingers grab the sheet wrapped around me.

I don't even look. I just lean into the wall and do a back kick. My heel buries itself into her stomach. A puff of stale air escapes her dead lungs and she stumbles back. I plunge through the opening, turning to pull the door closed. It resists, hissing on its safety hinges.

And then it clicks shut.

I can hear her on the other side, moaning, scratching. She can't get to me now. I'm safe.

At least for the moment.

Finally, once I've finally gathered myself, I raise my head and look around.

I'm not in a hospital at all.

Chapter Eighteen

The hallway is short and dimly lit. The floor is carpeted. Several rooms open out into it, but the doors are all closed. All except one, anyway.

I turn back to the door I just came through. The words on the sign make no sense to me at first:

> DEPARTMENT OF HOMELAND SECURITY
> PRIVATE SCREENING ROOM 3
> AUTHORIZED PERSONNEL ONLY

It's an airport. Got to be.

The Teterboro?

The lights in the hallway flicker once, fast, bringing me back to reality. I step away from the room that was my cell and step to another door. The sign says the same thing, except that it's numbered 2. I skip this and go onto the next room down, number 1, where the door is propped open.

The room is sparsely furnished. The light flickers on when I walk in. There's a low cot made up with white sheets and a green blanket. It looks recently slept in. I guess that it belongs — *belonged* — to Nurse Mabel. Well, she won't be sleeping ever again.

There's a medical cart with dozens of drawers filled with needles and syringes and ampoules of drugs with names I don't recognize.

There's also a small desk. A few items sit on top: a lamp, a personal Link, a coffee mug, a cold half-eaten Insta-Meal. A folding metal chair sits behind the desk.

A backpack leans against the wall in the corner, and I go over and search through it for clothes. There's two outfits. The pants won't fit me, but I manage to score a pair of panties and socks, which I put on immediately. I don't even bother with the bra; I'd need more socks than she has to fill it out. I finish with a new tee-shirt that advertises the TV program *Survivalist*. She probably gets these for free just for working at Arc.

I personally never got into the show. I much preferred to play *Zpocalypto* rather than sitting passively by and watching what happens in Gameland when other people play *The Game*. Besides, Eric always gives me grief whenever the guys come over to watch it.

Thinking about Eric makes me angry again. Anger sets me back into motion.

Beyond this room, the hallway ends at another security door, an unlit EXIT sign above it. I place my ear against the panel for several moments. When I'm convinced no one is on the other side, I try the cardkey. The red light turns green.

Slowly, carefully, I turn the handle and push the door open. But it's too dark, hiding whatever is out there, and all that greets my ears is the low grind of a motor running in some room somewhere. The sound wavers and the lights on my side of the door flicker. Electrical generator.

I let the door slide closed and turn around. I need to find pants and a shirt. Then my friends.

As I pass each closed door, I stop for a moment and press my ear against it and listen. I hear nothing, no indication that anyone else is here. I begin to wonder if maybe it's just me and Mabel.

The supply closet turns out to be the sixth door down the hall. This room is unlocked. When I open it, a light blinks on. There's a motion sensor above me, winking its tiny orange light. Mouse droppings litter the floor. Leaning against a wall is a petrified mop. Next to it, a bucket on wheels.

I move the mop and something small and brown scurries out from under the bucket and into a back corner. Mice used to terrify me, but this one barely even registers. I just murdered someone, and that someone tried to eat me. A little mouse isn't going to do a fucking thing to hurt me.

Shelves line the back wall, stacked with well-gnawed rolls of toilet paper and ancient bottles of cleaning supplies, the liquids inside oxidized brown, the chemicals settled to the bottom. There's a half-eaten bar of soap and some dry-rotted rubber gloves. No clothes though.

As I close the door, I hear something brush against the other side. I glance around the edge and spot a pair of blue overalls hanging on a hook there. They smell of mice pee, but otherwise appear okay. They'll do for now. I slip them off the hook and shimmy my way into them, kicking the bed sheet into the closet. The zipper catches halfway up. I give it a tug and the fabric tears a little before it reaches my chin. They're not overly long in the legs and arms, though they are baggy, so I use the IV tubing once more to cinch it around my waist.

I guess it was too much to hope for shoes. Nurse Mabel can keep the ones she's got on.

Before shutting the door again, I grab the mop to use as a weapon. The head sticks to the floor, crackling stiffly. It's not exactly a bo staff, but once I break the mop part off, it'll do just fine. With it in one hand and the cardkey in the other, I make my way back up the hall.

I stop and listen at the door to my room. Mabel has settled down now. I wonder what she's doing. I picture her standing on the other side, staring at the door with those sightless eyes. I wonder how long she'll stand there in the darkness like that. Weeks? Years? The zoms on LI have been there for over a decade. They took a little time to get moving again, but they did . . . .

Maybe Mabel will be there until the end of time. I wonder what the end of the world will look like. I have a feeling I already know.

But then I realize she won't be there very long at all. Someone'll come in the morning and find her.

I decide not to leave a warning note. Arc did this to themselves. They can deal with the consequences, too.

I tap quietly on the door, suddenly sure she's not there anymore. Maybe she got out when I wasn't looking.

A faint scratching comes to me. Then a low moan.

I stop at a room marked INTERVIEW 1. Once more I listen for signs of anything living — or otherwise — but there's not a sound. After unlocking the door, I turn the handle as quietly as I can and open it a crack. The lights come on.

A single stainless steel table sits in the middle of the floor. It looks like an autopsy table except for the pair of heavy nylon straps dangling on either side. Medical-looking equipment surrounds it. A hospital light hangs overhead. At the head is a strange looking contraption, a frame rising to the ceiling, where a long heavy blade has been elevated.

I realize with a jolt that it's a guillotine.

It's where they planned to inject Ashley. The guillotine must be in case something goes wrong.

One wall is entirely covered in black glass. When I open the next door down the hall, OBSERVATION 1, I see the same glass on the adjoining wall. This room is empty, except for a row of chairs facing the window.

I want to supervise the entire metamorphosis.

"Too bad," I say to the empty room, and close the door. "There won't be a show today."

Behind PRIVATE SCREENING ROOM 1 is where I find Ashley.

Chapter Nineteen

I say her name, quietly at first. Then louder.

She just lies there looking lifeless, her skin pale, the mound under the sheet seemingly too small to be all of her. Her trademark auburn hair — always her pride and her spirit, as well as her biggest enemy at times — is a flat, drab mess of tangles. It spreads like a dying fire across her pillow and falls across her face likes flakes of rust. It doesn't hide the bruises. One eye is puffy and has a halo of black and purple around it. Her cheek is scraped. The scab looks several days old.

"Ashley?"

I swoop over to the bed and shake her shoulder, but she doesn't respond. Her eyes remain closed and her head rolls loosely to the side. Her skin feels too cold to be healthy.

Holding my breath, I press the back of my hand to her cheek: the skin there is a little warmer. The soft whisper of her breaths reaches my ears.

She's alive.

"Ashley, can you hear me?"

She moans, but doesn't wake.

I call her name again, louder this time, and move the hair from her face. A faint smell rises from her, body odor and the metallic scent of blood. There's something else, something mediciny. A bandage covers the left side of her neck and reaches around to the back. An IV line drips through a tube that passes beneath the sheet and into her arm.

I decide to try doing the foot thing that Nurse Mabel did to me. I move to the foot of the bed and lift the sheet.

That's when I notice the restraints. They're around her ankles and her wrists.

... she tried to escape ... put restraints on her ... sedated her.

I flash of anger pulses through me, directed at Nurse Mabel and the mysterious man she was talking to. Anger at Arc.

I find the point where the IV enters her arm and remove the tape. Then I pull the needle free. I clamp the tubing then. No sense to letting the rest of the sedative drip onto the floor. Something tells me I might need it.

I turn my attention to the restraints. They're simple fabric cuffs, padded to prevent Ashley from cutting herself. They're connected with simple metal loop and Velcro fasteners, easy to undo. I free her limbs, then peek even further under the sheet to see if she has a catheter. She doesn't, but she's just as naked as I was. Nurse Mabel's clothes will fit her better than they would have me.

I hurry back and gather a full set of clothes from the bitch's backpack and return to Ash's room with them. I do my best to get her dressed. Urgency forces me to hurry; embarrassment holds me back.

It's not an easy task getting someone dressed without their assistance. It eats up a lot of time and makes me want to scream out of frustration. There were countless times I got my mother undressed and into bed after a night of drinking. That was easy compared to this. Physically, anyway. Emotionally . . . .

When I finish, I'm panting and shivering from the exertion. I notice I've put the shirt on inside out, but I don't bother fixing it. I really need to eat.

The combination of jostling and the removal of the sedative seems to be working. Ash is mumbling and moving her arms. But she still won't respond when I call her name. I need her to recover if we're going to get out of here, and soon. It's already a quarter past three.

I prop the door open with the IV stand, but leave Ash in bed with the side rails up in case she wakes and tries to get up. I need to find the others. I pray they haven't been sedated, too.

If they're naked . . . I'm not sure what I'll do then. Although I'd love to see the look on Reggie's face if he were to wake up wearing Mabel's bra. That would be worth the price of admission.

I stop for a few minutes to finish Mabel's half-eaten Insta-Meal. It's bland, and it barely takes the edge off my hunger. I also find a package of cookies, which I wolf down, washing their dryness down with a water packet. After a few minutes of alternating between looking for something else to eat and wanting to puke it all up again, I get up and go back out into the hall.

I swipe the cardkey at the next door. The release clicks and I quickly enter without bothering to check inside first. I know I'm being reckless, but desperation is getting the better of me. Time seems to be flying by.

The light flickers on and the room comes into view. Beneath the fringe of a drawn privacy curtain, I see the wheels of another bed.

"Jesus, lady." Reggie's voice comes to me from the other side. He groans. "Dim the freaking lights, will ya? And why can't you just let me get a little sleep? Just a few hours uninterrupted is all I ask."

"No time for sleeping, *brah*," I say, grinning to myself.

"Jessie?" The bed creaks. "Jessie, is that you?"

I yank the curtain back before remembering he might be naked. Reggie's lying there, propped up by pillows, thankfully covered with a sheet. He looks as bad as Ashley did — pale and bruised and scraped and shrunken. His arm is in a sling.

He smiles when he sees me. Then it fades and is replaced with a look of suspicion.

"Please tell me you're not with *them*."

"Them who?"

"Why are you dressed like that?"

I look down and realize it's not a janitor's outfit at all but a jumpsuit. A patch on the arm says Security.

He sees the cardkey in my hand and says, "Oh. You are." He lets his head sink back onto the pillow and closes his eyes.

My own smile falters. "I'm not with anyone, Reg. It's just me. I escaped."

He lifts his head again and frowns at me. I can see the struggle in his face, the wanting to believe me and the doubt. Another wave of hatred comes over me for Arc. Look what they've done to us, made us all suspicious of each other.

I flash the cardkey at him so he can see that it's Mabel's picture on it and not mine.

"If I get my hands on that bitch," he snarls, "I won't—"

"It's cool, Reg. Don't worry. I took care of her."

"Do you know what she did to me?" He sputters as he tries not to say words he knows I hate hearing. "I hope you fucking killed her. I hate that bitch."

He must see the look on my face. He must know what it means, because he stops and his eyes widen.

"Did you?"

I wince. "She's dead. Except.... Fuck, how do I explain this? I'm not even sure about it myself. She's not dead."

"What? She's either dead or she's not, right?"

"She's neither."

"You're not making any sense."

I shake my head and sigh. "Look, there's no time to explain. Just get your lazy, fat ass out of that bed and come with me."

"I would, except...." He tries to lift his good arm. The sheet slips off it and I see that he's handcuffed to the rail. "I know this has always been one of your fantasies, to get me handcuffed in bed."

"Really?" I chuff. "You're going to go there? Because I'll just leave your ass here."

"Okay, okay." He laughs. "The key's on that chain you're carrying."

He gestures at the cardkey.

I hold up the tiny metal rod. I'd thought it was some kind of trinket. "So that's what this is. I was wondering."

I move over to the other side of the bed. "Promise, no more bad jokes."

"What bad jokes? They're all gems. Now unlock the cuffs. Pretty please."

I roll my eyes but go ahead. Too much time is passing to argue.

Reggie immediately tries to swing his legs over the edge of the bed. He winces in pain.

"You broke your arm?"

"Dislocated." He rotates his shoulder to show me and I see a flicker of pain cross his face. He tries to mask it. "Still a little sore. I can feel it clicking or something inside." He waves my hand away. "Where's Ash?"

"Next door. She's . . . okay. Sort of."

"Tell me the truth." There's that look of fear in his eyes.

"She's alive. But she's drugged. Look, we need to find everyone else and get out of here."

I check the time. It's almost four already.

Reggie nods. He starts to stand up, then abruptly sits back down again. "Um . . . . Would you mind turning around?"

"Oh, Jesus, Reg! Really? A moment ago you were joking about handcuffs, and now you're suddenly Mr. Modesty?"

"Well?"

"Just wrap a sheet around yourself and come on. I still haven't found Micah yet. Or our clothes."

I grab his pillow and shove it between the door and the jamb to keep it from shutting all the way and locking, then I leave him to figure out how to manage the sheet on his own.

"Let's go, Reg," I yell, as I'm opening the door to the next room. "Any day now."

A faint voice calls from inside the room: "Jessie, is that you?" It's familiar, and for a moment I think it's Micah. But then I know it's not. It's a voice I hadn't expected to hear in here.

If ever again.

Chapter Twenty

"Jake?"
What's he doing in here? How?
I hear him laugh with relief. "Yeah, it's me, Jessie." Something rattles, metal on metal, another handcuff. "Sorry if I don't get up, but I'm a little— "

But I don't wait for him to finish. I spin around and whirl back out into the hallway.

"Hey!" he cries. "Where are you— "

The door closes, cutting him off.

Jake's alive. He's here. I don't know how that's possible, but it also means Kelly's alive and here, too.

Don't get your hopes up, girl.

We've already lost one. Don't want to lose another.

Who did he mean? Kelly or Micah?

They're the only ones left. And there's only one more room I haven't checked: the one marked CENTRAL COMMUN-ICATIONS.

I stand in front of the door, unwilling and unable to move. If Kelly's alive, he has to be behind this last door. But if I find Micah instead, then . . . .

I lower my head and lean it against the door. I don't want to think about either of those scenarios. I don't want either of them to be true. I just want them both to be alive and safe and all of us back home.

Maybe they're both in there.

Somehow I know they won't be.

I slip the cardkey into the slot. Out of the corner of my eye, I see Reggie coming out of his room. The sheet is wrapped around him toga-style and he's using his good hand to hold it closed. He's not doing a completely effective job at it. I get a flash of skin I'd rather not have.

I gesture at the door between us. "Jake's in there."

"Jake's here? But how? Where's . . . ." I can almost hear what's going through his mind. Where's Kelly. That's what he was going to say.

I shake my head. "This is the last room. They've got to be in here."

They. Not he.

Micah and Kelly.

Or maybe just Kelly.

But not just Micah.

Please God, let it be both.

A thump comes from my room. Reggie spins and takes a step toward it.

"Don't go in there!" I yell, startling him. It's unnecessary for me to shout. Without the cardkey, nobody can open that door.

"Nurse Bitch?" he says.

Something scratches on the other side of the door, as if she recognizes her name. Then there's a low moan, almost inaudible. I feel it more than actually hear it. The hair on my scalp rises. Reggie looks at me in alarm.

I nod. "I told you it was complicated."

He hurries over to me, his mouth working overtime but not saying anything. I can almost see the questions piling up inside his head, all vying to get out, all at the same time. Unfortunately, I don't have answers to any of them.

Contingencies. That's what they'd said. How can anyone volunteer for something like this?

I pull the key from the lock, turn the handle, and push against the door. But it doesn't yield. I try the key again. The little red light doesn't change to green.

"What the hell?"

"Backwards?" Reggie suggests.

I turn it around and retry the lock. Still nothing.

"Damn it!" I cry, slapping the door in frustration. Three more attempts yield the same result. Now I'm positive Kelly's on the other side of that door. I can almost taste it in the back of my mouth. He's there and I can't get to him. It's fate getting back at me for killing Mabel. "God damn it!"

Reggie gently pulls me away. "Let me try." But then he points out the keypad beside the door. I'd totally missed it.

"Don't suppose you know the code?" he asks. I shake my head and he says, "Didn't think so. Just when we could use Micah to hack something, turns out we have to hack it to find him."

I don't say anything. I don't want him to know my thoughts, that I hope and pray it's not Micah on the other side of that door.

"Which room is Ashley's?" Reggie asks. "She might be able to crack this fucker."

"She won't be hacking anything for a while. She's too out of it."

He sighs, then tries ramming the door with his good shoulder. After that doesn't work, he kicks viciously at it. But while the door rattles loosely in the frame, it doesn't budge. And the noise is just agitating Zombie Mabel all the more. She's slapping on the door now, clawing, trying to push her way through it. The moaning is even louder.

"Creepy," Reggie says. He gives her door a worried look before returning his gaze to the one before us. "But if I can't bust this door down, we know she won't be coming through hers anytime soon."

"It's not her I'm afraid of getting to us, Reg. It's the people she worked for, Arc. We're running out of time."

"Arc? They're the ones who did all this. Christ, we're fucked. They got their fingers in everything."

I slip down the wall until I'm sitting on the floor. I rest my head in my hands and try to think. Reggie stands in front of me being his usual useless self, waiting for someone else to make the tough decisions. I want to yell at him to do something, but I know it'll only make things worse. Finally, he turns and goes in to check on Ashley. A minute later he comes back out again.

"She's blotto."

He uses the key to go into Jake's room.

I put my head in my arms. "Kelly," I moan. "Kelly."

Mabel calms down again.

Reggie and Jake come out a few minutes later. Jake's sheet is wrapped tightly around his own waist. Unlike Reggie's, it looks pretty secure.

Standing side by side, Jake looks fitter and stronger than Reggie does. Both their faces are a little leaner than they were almost a week ago, but Jake started off heavier than the rest of us and so doesn't look quite so bad.

It's because he doesn't have the bruises.

Jake wasn't anywhere near the explosion. The Harlem tunnel was blocked; they didn't go inside.

So where did they go when their signals disappeared?

"What do you want to do, Jess?" Jake quietly asks. He kneels down, rubbing the soreness from his wrist.

Reggie tosses me the cardkey before heading down the hallway to Ashley's room. He disappears inside.

Now I get up. I've got an idea. It's not totally original, but, hey, it worked once before.

"Fire extinguisher," I say, setting my jaw. I head down the hall past Ashley's room to where an extinguisher sign hangs from the ceiling.

"You're going to burn the door down?"

"I believe I said *extinguisher*, not starter. If we're lucky, there's an axe."

"You and your axes," he says. He was there on LI when I used one to chop a few zoms down to size.

But when I get to the end of the hall, there's no axe, just the extinguisher. I hesitate for half a second before yanking it out of its little glass home. I heft it in my hands and test the weight. It'll have to do. Jake watches me, understanding dawning on his face.

I try hitting the door first, but the wood is too hard and the tank just bounces off. The door doesn't even splinter, though it does dent.

Jake flinches when Mabel starts going apeshit, but he doesn't act surprised. "Reggie told me about her," he explains.

It's strange that they've both accepted what happened to her so readily — and what *I* did to make her that way. Or maybe it's because our whole situation being here in the first place is just so screwed up to begin with.

Even so, people don't just spontaneously turn into zombies when they die. At least, not as far as I've ever been told.

Then again, it wouldn't be the first time we were lied to about Reanimation.

Reggie sticks his head out of Ashley's room to see what the noise is about. "Try the handle," he suggests. Then he goes back inside.

I lift the tank over my shoulder, both hands on the neck like I'm strangling it. I hope and pray the thing doesn't explode on me. Jake must have the same fear, because he raises his arm to protect his face and suggests I empty it first.

"Good idea," I reply. "Maybe later, when there's actually time to think about things."

I bring it down with all my force onto the door handle.

The tank pings off. The handle rattles and bends a little, but it doesn't break. I try again. This time the handle goes flying off across the hall.

I push against the door. It doesn't open.

"I think I just fucked it up."

"Too bad it's not glass," Jake says, as he reaches for the tank. "You were a pro breaking glass back there."

"Shut up." But I gladly let him take over.

He gestures for me to step back, then he puts all of his weight into slamming the bottom corner of the tank straight at the center of the door. He hits it so hard that his sheet nearly falls off. He gives me a sheepish grin and shrugs, his face turning a bright red. It quickly bleeds away when Mabel crashes into her door.

"Christ."

Jake hurriedly lifts the tank and brings it down on the door again. This time a crack appears. He does it two more times and the crack widens and chips of wood begin to fly.

"Kelly!" I shout, mostly so I don't have to listen to that fucked-up moaning. "We're coming in."

But there's no answer from the other side of the door.

Jake rests for a minute and I take his place, but now my efforts seem paltry next to his. I manage to scrape a few more chips off the door, but the crack doesn't get any larger. After two or three more minutes, Jake takes another stab at it.

Reggie comes out with Ash's arm draped across his shoulders. I notice he's abandoned the sling now, though he holds his hurt arm against his chest, favoring his shoulder.

Ashley's feet half drag, half walk along with Reggie, and her head rolls crazily against his chest, but at least she's trying to hold herself up a little. He sets her down on the floor and leans her against the wall. She opens her eyes and blinks a few times, mumbles something incomprehensible, then closes them again.

"Let me try," Reggie tells Jake. Jake gladly agrees. As Reggie whales on the door — his one-armed strikes so much more powerful than Jake's two-handed attempts — Jake carefully kneels down on the other side of Ash and watches me try and revive her.

"Too bad we don't have smelling salts," he says.

"Idiot!" I cry, slapping my forehead. He watches me get up. "I should've thought about that."

I run down the hall to Nurse Mabel's room and start opening the drawers. I finally find what I'm looking for about halfway down: a box of ammonia inhalants. I extract one and run back down the hall squeezing it between my fingers. I feel the glass ampoule inside shatter. A cool liquid soaks the cotton wrapper and the smell of ammonia reaches my nose, making me want to sneeze.

I shove it right up to Ashley's nose and wait. At first she does nothing, then her head snaps back. It lolls to one side. I push the ampoule back into her face.

"Whuh?"

She lifts a hand and swipes weakly at her face.

"You're going to burn her nose hairs off," Jake says, misplaced concern on his face.

"You're worried about nose hairs? She'll grow them back." I practically shove the thing into her nostril on the next try.

"No!" Ashley raises both hands now and pushes. She blinks, her eyes watering. "Whathafug?" she asks. "Jeh?" Her head turns and she sees Jake.

Reggie bends down. "Hey, babe, it's me."

"Reggggsh? Whazgoingon?"

He smiles and nods. "Good thinking, guys." Then he gets back up and starts pounding on the door again, this time with both arms. Ashley winces from the noise. She looks drunk, but it's a definite improvement from where she was just a few minutes earlier.

Finally, there's a splintering sound. Reggie doesn't stop. He just keeps pounding. He winces every time the tank hits, but he's a total maniac now, almost impervious to pain. Every once in a while he glances over at us. At Ashley. My heart skips a beat seeing the worry on his face, and I can't help feeling a little jealous.

The hole in the door widens. Reggie reaches over and rips the wood with his bare hands. Jake gets up and helps.

"I can see a bed," Jake announces, peeking through the opening.

My heart skips, then sinks. *A* bed. Not two.

"No, wait a sec. There's another."

This time my heart takes flight.

I hurry over, but Reggie pushes us both out of the way to tear away at the door some more.

He hammers and pulls and kicks. Then a corner of the door bends in. He pulls it free with a loud ripping sound. The hole's still not large enough for either of them, but I can squeeze through. I do, forcing my way in despite their protests.

"Careful," Jake says. "You'll get splinters."

Reggie snickers. At least they're back to their old selves.

I get back to my feet once I'm fully inside.

Just as with Jake's room, there's a privacy curtain pulled closed, partially obscuring my view of the two beds. I can see that they're both occupied. That's all I need to know.

I barely notice the stuff piled up on the floor around me, the packs and clothes. I barely notice the stacks of old computer servers softly humming away on the left, their lights blinking green. I barely notice how cool it is in here. But I do notice, and causes me to wonder what the hell all this equipment is for.

"Are they there?" Reggie shouts through the opening. He yelps and says something about splinters.

"I told you," Jake says.

I pull the curtain open and find Micah lying in the first bed. He looks like hell. His eyes flutter open and he sees me and whispers my name.

"Sa noise about?" he mumbles. "Thought we were being bomb again."

"Micah's here," I shout excitedly. "He's . . . ." I notice the bandages around his head and the burns on his arms. "He's okay."

Then I turn to the other bed and see the face of the person lying in it, still as death.

And this time I can't stop my heart from breaking.

Chapter Twenty One

"**Jessie?**" Reggie asks. "Is it . . . ?"

"I don't want to talk about it," I say, as I sink to the floor between the beds.

I can hear them quietly murmuring to each other outside the room, trying to decide what to do. They finish clearing away the rest of the door and come in

"I'm sorry, Jess," Reggie tells me. He gives the figure in the other bed a baleful glance but doesn't say anything.

When I don't move, he joins Jake over by our packs and begins sorting our clothes.

"What the hell happened to you guys?" Jake quietly asks. "How'd you end up here?"

"I'd ask the same about you and Kelly."

"Long story."

"So's mine."

"I asked first."

Reggie exhales with a sigh and looks over at me. Then at Micah, who appears to be sleeping again. He shakes his head and rubs his sore shoulder.

"We came down because Micah said you were coming out through the tunnel. He got the hack to work and was tracking you as you moved northeast toward the Harlem tunnel. We were in a boat. The bomb hit about a hundred yards from us."

He holds up a shirt — Micah's, I think. I can't quite remember what Micah was wearing. My mind's a blank. The fabric's all stiff from dried mud and blood. It's torn — even burnt in places.

"Damn blast knocked us all into the water. I saw Micah get thrown. I was sure he was a goner."

I squeeze my eyes closed as the full memory finally comes back to me, the final pieces my mind has been holding back. And as soon as the picture's complete, I wish I could erase it all over again: the bomb hitting the water, the water bulging upward, shattering into a billion pieces, the boat lifting, the five of us flying through the air.

The sickening thud as Micah's body hit the sign we were tied up to.

The color of the water.

So much blood.

"God, we were so stupid!" Reggie cries. "Right from the god damn beginning."

"Bomb?" Jake asks.

"The planes were dropping them. We didn't know they were targeting the tunnels, collapsing them. First the Brooklyn Battery. We heard the explosions but didn't know what they were at the time. Then the Midtown. Those we saw, but even then it was too far away to know. We didn't even guess what the hell was happening until it was too late. Then those god damn planes were right over us, dropping the bombs."

He pauses and turns his head and gives Jake a strange look. "What I can't figure is how the hell you survived? You were supposed to be inside the tunnel. How'd you get out?"

Jake frowns. "We weren't in any tunnel. We planned to go through the Battery further south, but.... Why would you think we were in the Harlem tunnel?"

Reggie looks over at me. I don't move. I'm still trying to understand how it could be Kelly we've lost.

"It's like I said. We were tracking you. Well, Micah was, on his Link. He and Ash cracked the codex. Your signal was moving north before it disappeared. He said it was because you were inside the Harlem tunnel by then, underneath the EM barrier. The signal was blocked."

Jake shakes his head. "The Harlem wouldn't have been my next choice. After the Midtown tunnel collapsed and separated us, I came back. I just holed up for the night. I mean, I barely even managed to get out of the water — those zombies were everywhere. But then I found this drainage pipe and went through it. I came out in this access shaft and climbed up, but the opening was covered by a metal plate. I thought I was trapped. I finally managed to get it off and climb out before the zoms heard me."

"How did Kelly find you?"

"I didn't sleep a wink all night worrying about where those things might be and if they were going to find me. When the sun came up, I was shocked to find the place deserted again. It was like they'd never been there, except for the few bodies still lying around, the ones we'd managed to kill."

We? I think. He'd been too panicked to even get his wetsuit on right. He didn't kill any.

"Gone?" Reggie asks. "Where'd they go?"

"Back into hiding, I guess."

I remember how I thought the zombies had been hiding, how ridiculous that seemed. It doesn't seem so ridiculous now.

"I don't know what freaks me out more," Jake says, "knowing they can show up so quickly, or not knowing where they've disappeared to. The island's got to be crawling with the Undead, but we just can't find them."

"Zombies don't hide," Reggie insists. He holds up Micah's old tablet computer and inspects it for damage before shoving it into the backpack. He comes over to me and asks, "What do you want to do with Micah? I don't think we should move him."

I lean my head against the wall and stare straight ahead of me.

"Jessie? Come on."

I blink. I hear Kelly telling me, *I need you, Jessie.*

"Jessie?"

"Go away."

"We need you."

"No, Reg, you don't. Leave me alone."

"You're wrong. We do need you. We all do."

You're our rock.

Kelly was my rock, and now he's gone.

"Please, Jess. There's not much time."

I push him away. He clenches his jaw and makes to say something. I shake my head. I turn to Jake. I'm ready.

"I need to know what happened to Kelly."

Chapter Twenty Two

Jake nods.

"I was going back to where we'd stashed the bags the day before," he says. "I needed to get some fresh cartridges. I was going to try the other bore of the Midtown tunnel. I was out in the open when I saw something moving by the car where we'd stashed everything. Scared the crap out of me, at least until I realized it was Kelly. I don't know how long he'd been there, but he'd already gathered up some of the equipment. He told me there was no way we were going back through the Midtown tunnel. It was too active with IUs. Both sides."

"When exactly did you guys decide to try the Harlem tunnel?"

"Like I said, that wasn't the plan. We were heading south toward the Battery when those two guys found us."

"What two guys?" Reggie asks. "Zombies?"

"No. Warm bloods."

I give him a strange look, and he shrugs. "Better than calling them 'The Living.' Anyway, they claimed to be Arc employees. Said they were surveying the island. They had all this survival gear with them, EM guns, shotguns, machetes, body armor."

"Civilians don't get issued EM guns," I say.

Jake shrugs. "Kelly thought that was strange, too, but what could we say? These guys promised to get us off the island. I didn't like the idea of going further inland, but Kelly said we'd be better off just going along with it. When we asked why we were going by foot, they said they didn't use cars or motorbikes. They said the first teams did, the ones that didn't come back. Apparently the zombies have become supersensitive to sounds."

"They weren't surprised to see you here?" I ask.

"Not really. That was a little suspicious, too. They seemed bothered only when we confessed to having come through the tunnels to get here. One guy got on his Link and sent a few messages, but then he came back and thanked us and said they'd be taking care of that."

"Who was he pinging?" I ask, starting to worry. There are too many inconsistencies in Jake's story. I'm not sure if he's telling the truth or not. "The EM barrier would block them from pinging anyone outside."

"I don't know. I never got a chance to find out, because after that, they pretty much ran us hard. There wasn't much opportunity to talk. But the further we went, the more of a bad feeling I got. I mentioned this to Kelly. He said not to worry, but I could see he was starting to have serious doubts, too. Later, he told me to be prepared."

"For what?"

"To escape, I guess. He didn't say. They brought us both into the terminal here and they said everything would be okay. They promised us food and water. But it was a trap. Kelly must've known because he suddenly punched one of the guys in the face and shouted at me to run. But I wasn't prepared. They were on me in a second. They grabbed me. I heard a gunshot. I'm sorry, Jessie."

Reggie stands from where he's crouching, sifting through the last of our stuff. "I knew this was an airport. I was hoping it was Teterboro, though. So you're telling me we're back on the island again?"

Jake and I glance at each other. Jake nods. "We're at LaGuardia, not Teterboro."

I can see the line of Reggie's jaw tighten. The news comes as no surprise to me. I'd been hoping and praying I was wrong about being back on LI, but somehow I knew that's exactly where we were.

"It's all my fault." Reggie murmurs.

"It's not your fault," I tell him. "We all agreed to come. We all wanted to come."

"All except Kelly," Reggie says. He sort of shrinks a little when he says this and gives me a nervous look. "We should've listened to him. I was such an asshole."

"You're not an asshole," I tell him. "A prick, maybe. A jerk, definitely. An arrogant son-of-a— "

"All right already," he protests. But I think I see the hint of a smile touch his lips. If I'd known he liked this kind of abuse, I would've piled it on more often.

"So, where's Kelly now?" I ask Jake. "What happened to him?"

"I don't know," he replies. "Those two guys drugged me. The next thing I knew, I woke up handcuffed to a bed with a bandage on the back of my neck. I think they did something to my implant. I think they might've removed it."

"They messed with all of our implants," Reggie says, turning his neck to show his bandage.

"They didn't remove them, but I think you're going to wish they had." I quickly explain what I'd overheard Nurse Mabel and the mysterious man talking about. "I think they've replaced them. With what, I don't know, but I have a bad feeling about it."

"Why the hell would they replace them?"

"I wish I knew." I shake my head to clear it and stand up and look at the figure in the second bed. She hasn't said a word to any of us. "Kelly's out there somewhere. That's all I need to know. I need to find him."

"First we get out of here," Reggie says.

I nod. "And before the prep nurse comes at seven."

Jake gives me a curious look. I haven't explained the rest to them. I wave it off. "Later."

I go over and unlock the girl's handcuff and tell her to get up, but she doesn't move. I hand her the clothes Reggie and Jake found mixed in with ours. Reggie's already packed mine away for later. Hers are the only ones besides Jake's that aren't filthy and bloody. "You need to come with us," I tell her.

But she just sits there. She doesn't make a move to help or even stand. She's been lying there staring at us, flinching whenever any of us make a sudden move or even look at her. She has this wild look about her, like she's in shell shock and might at any moment suddenly start screaming. But she hasn't made a single sound.

Like us, she's got a bandage on the back of her neck.

I wonder if maybe they've already done something more to her, something bad.

"Come on, Tanya," I beg her. "Get up or we're leaving you here."

"Tanya? You know who she is?" Reggie whispers. "Is she slow or something?"

I give him a dirty look and tell him to go and get another ammonia inhalant from Nurse Mabel's room. The one I'd used on Ashley is dried out and useless.

After he returns with it, I crush it and pass it under Micah's nose. He quickly comes to. At first, he's more disoriented than Ashley had been. He pushes my hands away as I try to get him ready to move. He mumbles and thrashes out, and this quickly devolves into a shouting and shoving match. He doesn't even seem to recognize me. I try talking to him in a quiet voice and this seems to calm him.

Jake gathers up our packs. Reggie hands me my Link — the temp I got at the Citizen Registration office — along with my inhaler. "Found it in the medicine cart," he says. I quickly pocket the Link, but I take a blast from the inhaler. Reggie shakes his head. I know they all think I don't need it. They constantly tease me about it. Maybe it's psychological, but taking it does make me feel better, despite what I might've said to Grandpa.

"So, who is she?" he whispers.

"Her name's Tanya," I say, watching her face for any sign of recognition. She cringes, as if I've just exposed her deepest secret. "I met her on the bus coming back from Hartford the day I reported my Link missing."

"That's a strange coincidence," Jake says. But the look on his face tells me he doesn't think it's a coincidence at all. Thing is, it's not. I know it's not.

"She said she worked for Arc as a recording clerk."

"Another Arc connection. But why would they do something like this to one of their own?"

I think about Mabel and how she volunteered. "I don't know."

But the truth of the matter, I do know. She wasn't a volunteer. She's here because of me.

We had forensics go through the Stream records. She popped up because she tried pinging the Corben boy.

Kelly. She'd tried pinging Kelly and, whoever these people are, they discovered that.

Except she didn't try pinging him. I did. I'd just used her Link. She's just an innocent bystander.

And she's a good candidate for the treatment?

Young, Mabel had said. *Strong... invested in the game. She'll make an excellent player.*

Not just any game. *The Game*. They were planning on turning her into a CU and selling her as a volunteer Player. I'm sure of it now. That's what the alpha treatment is. It was for her, not Ashley.

"We need to go!" Reggie reminds me.

"She's coming with us. Micah, too."

"But—"

I throw Jake the cardkey. "See if you can find a wheelchair. These places always seem to have one. Bring it back here for Micah. And don't go too far."

Jake runs off without a word.

"Jessie," Reggie says, "listen to me. We're already in over our heads. We don't know who she is. Think about what you're doing, dragging her in—"

I whirl around to face him. "She's already dragged in! Can't you see that?" Tanya whimpers at my shouting.

"I... I know, but this girl—"

"Tanya, Reggie. Her name is Tanya."

"Fine. Tanya."

"You wanted me to tell you what to do, so shut up and let me do it." I push him aside and head over to her bed. "Can you walk, Tanya? Look, I'm not going to hurt you. Do you understand what I'm saying?"

"You're the girl from the bus," she stammers.

I nod impatiently, though I'm grateful to hear her speak. "Yes. Now, can you walk?"

She nods. "I... I think so."

"Good. Get dressed." I stop and look her straight in the eye so she knows exactly how serious this is. "We need to get the hell out of here soon or else we're all dead. Are you ready?" She nods again.

I go back to Micah's bed. He's got an IV dripping into his arm, a urinary catheter coming from . . . underneath, and oxygen going into his nose.

"How're we going to take him with us, Jessie?" Reggie asks. "He's unconscious."

"Damn it, Reggie! Stop telling me what I already know and start figuring out— "

But then Micah startles me by reaching up and grabbing my arm. "I'm not . . . going, Jesss . . . ."

"Shut up. Yes, you are."

He coughs. "Won't get . . . very far."

"You're as bad as he is." I smile at him. "Maybe worse."

"You don't understand. I'm— "

"He'll die," Reggie argues. "Can't you see how bad he is?"

"He's not dying. Otherwise he'd be in the hospital. He just needs time to recover." I don't know if this is true, but it seems reasonable. Besides, I know what'll happen to him if he stays: something much worse than dying.

"No!" Micah says. He coughs. "Please."

"You're upsetting him."

"He's delirious, Reg." I wait until Micah stops coughing. He leans over and spits. I expect to see blood, but there isn't any. For whatever reason, he seems to think he'd be better off staying, but he's wrong. He just doesn't understand how serious the situation is. And I don't have the time to explain it to him. It's just burning precious minutes we don't have.

"Stay here with him," I instruct Reggie.

"Where are you going?"

I ignore the question. Tanya's managed to stand up, but she clutches her sheet around herself and doesn't move.

"You need to get dressed," I tell her. I point to her clothes, then at Reggie. "He's going to help you, okay?"

She nods slowly, but doubt still clouds her eyes.

"Don't frighten her," I warn him.

I pass Ashley as I step out into the hallway past the remains of the demolished door. She's still groggy. She calls my name as I hurry past, but I ignore her, too, and instead head for her room.

By the time I return, Tanya's dressed — thank God for small favors — though still just standing there. Ash has made her way into the room. She's crying, holding Micah's hand. He's telling her he's staying and trying to tell her she needs to stay, too. It's crazy talk. I pull her out of the way. She protests weakly and tries to move back. I don't let her. I tell Reggie to take her out of the room.

"What are you doing?" Reggie asks, when he sees me switching out Micah's IV bag. "Do you know what that is?"

"Sedative. You wanted me to take charge, so I am."

Micah glances up and frowns. He tries to protest. He reaches out at me and grabs my arm, but I open the drip all the way and within moments his hand falls back to the bed. His eyes droop. Half a minute later he's asleep.

"That's some powerful shit," Jake says.

I turn the drip rate down. I don't want to kill him.

I pull the wheelchair to the side of the bed and instruct Jake to help me get Micah into it.

When we're done and the IV and catheter are repositioned, I check the time on Mabel's Link. It's almost six thirty. I toss the Link into the corner of the room. I don't want them to track us through it.

"Half an hour before the prep nurse shows up."

I push Micah out into the hallway.

"Once we find the shuttle they're coming on, you guys are leaving."

"Us?" Jake says. "You're coming with us, aren't you?"

"Kelly's still here," I say. "I can't go home until I find him."

Chapter Twenty Three

The sound of the generator grows loud when we push through the door. We all hesitate for a moment so our eyes can adjust to the gloom. Our nerves are on edge.

From what I can see, we're standing inside the international terminal, the abandoned kiosks and stainless steel counters and conveyor belts twinkling dully in the dim light of morning. The high windows across the empty room are so dirty that very little light manages to filter through. If it wasn't for the sun shining low on the horizon, it'd be hard to know if it was morning or the middle of the day.

Ash shuffles over to me. She's almost fully recovered from the sedative by now. "You can't stay."

"Recognize anything?" I ask Jake, pushing her to the side.

He shakes his head. "I remember seeing the control tower as we came in, but from in here I can't tell which direction that was."

"That's probably behind us," I say. "Out by the runways."

We keep walking, not sure which direction to take but feeling better just to be moving.

We reach an escalator. It's not moving, of course, so Reggie and Jake lower Micah down it a step at a time.

Ash goes ahead of us to scout for food and water. She returns just as we reach the bottom. She's got a bagful of old candy bars and sodas.

"Junk food," Jake says, making a face. "*Twelve-year-old* junk food."

"Fine," Ashley says, swiping the Milky Way with the faded wrapper out of his hand. "I'll eat it. I'm starving."

"I didn't say I wouldn't eat it."

"No Red Bulls?" I joke.

"How much time we got?" Reggie asks.

I check my Link. "Quarter to seven. The shuttle should be here any minute now, and we still have no idea where it is."

"I do," says a voice from the gloom.

We turn as one — all except Micah, of course. He's passed out cold in the chair, his elbows dangling off the armrests and his head flopping to his chest. Reggie's tied him in with a sheet so he doesn't fall out.

A figure materializes from behind a coffee cart, cobwebs tenting the ancient urns and the display of teas beside the cash register.

It's Kelly.

I drop the backpack I've been carrying and run over to him. He throws his arms wide and I launch myself into them. And now — now when I finally see him standing there, when his arms wrap around me and hold me like a promise to never let me go — only then do I finally let myself collapse. Only then do I let myself let go of the belief that I was never going to see him again.

He waits a moment before speaking. Everyone has gathered around, clamoring for information.

"There's a shuttle arriving at seven," I tell him.

"I know. And I know where it comes in — down in baggage claim — but we need to hurry if we're going to get there in time."

"How do you know where it is?" I ask.

"Been watching for days now. They bring meals and supplies each morning. This is a minimal operation here. Always the same two or three people."

He gives Ashley a quick hug and nods to Jake and Reg. They both exclaim how glad they are to see him, but already his gaze has passed from them to Micah and finally to Tanya. I can see the questions in his eyes, the sudden suspicion of this stranger in our midst.

"She's not a part of this," I hurriedly say. "But she needs our help." I don't mention how it's my fault she's here.

Kelly leads us through the darkened terminal, deep into the bowels of the airport and into places that were once off limits to the public. We probably would have figured out where to go ourselves by following the doors which have been propped open or whose locking mechanisms have been disengaged. If we were thinking clearly. If we had time.

"After I escaped, I hid out here for a while and kept watch, trying to figure out what they were doing. Trying to figure out how to rescue Jake." He glances over. "I wanted to try and get you, but I never got the chance with the door locks. I considered destroying the generator, but I didn't know if it might do more harm than not. Then I saw them wheel the rest of you in a few days ago. I didn't realize it was you at first — everyone was covered up — but then I overheard this one guy talking, some guy named Harrison, Padraig Harrison. He was talking to this other guy about doing some experiments on a bunch of kids. He mentioned that you were all gamers and hackers, so I knew it had to be you."

"It's Arc," I tell him. "I don't know what they're planning." I gesture at Tanya's back and whisper, "I think they were going to volunteer her."

Kelly's jaw clenches. "Fuckers," he spits. "I didn't want to believe it was. How could they do this? God damn liars. 'We serve the people' my ass."

I frown at him. He shakes his head bitterly.

"What do you mean? What did they lie about?"

"Nothing, Jess." He sighs. "Everything. ArcWare, Arc Entertainment, ArcTech. They've been fucking lying to us since day one. They're just out to make money. They don't care who they screw to do it!"

"Tanya works for Arc," I whisper.

Kelly's eyes narrow again as he stares at her back. "Remind me again who the hell she is."

I quickly tell him about my bus ride to Hartford to get the replacement Link. When he hears this, he reaches into his pocket and pulls out my lost Link and hands it over. I thought I'd be glad to see it, but suddenly it feels dangerous, like a ticking time bomb, no longer a part of me but rather a part of this place. I cradle it in my hands, expecting it to suddenly bite me or something, but it just sits there.

He reaches over and wakes it. The screen brightens and I see the picture Kelly had sent to me just moments before the zombies attacked us at the fueling station, when I'd lost the Link in the first place.

I quickly close it. He tries to grab it away again, but I pull away, crossing my arms around my chest.

"Jessie."

"Not now, Kel. Please."

"I need to know!"

"You left me!"

"I had to."

Everyone stops and turns around to stare at us. I keep walking, passing them. We've reached the carousels and I have to admit that I don't know which way to go next. I spy a door standing open across the room, so I head for it.

"Jessie, please."

"Can we talk about this later?"

"This is our future we're talking about, Jessie."

I stop and slowly turn. "You're worried about our future? How about worrying about our present?"

He catches up with me and takes my arm. "Just tell me why not then."

I sigh and look around at the others. All of them look back at me — all except Micah, who's still out cold, and Tanya, whose face looks as blank as if she'd had a lobotomy. Do they all know? Do they expect me to answer Kelly's question? We're standing in the middle of an abandoned airport in the middle of the Forbidden Zones on Long Island with an Undead nurse upstairs and people trying to kill us so they can reanimate us. And they all want to know if I'm ready to get married?

It's too surreal for me to even contemplate.

"Kelly, I—"

But then there's a heavy clang coming through the open door, a hiss of iron wheels on steel tracks. There's a squeal and another release of compressed air. We all look at each other. Then we hear the voices.

"Hide!" I whisper.

But too late we realize that there's no place to hide in the baggage claim's wide open space. And once again, we don't have a plan.

Chapter Twenty Four

Reggie runs straight toward the door, grabbing Jake and Kelly as he goes. Jake nearly trips over his own feet. The scuffles sound loud in my ears and I can't believe anyone on the other side of that door didn't hear it. But the voices — a man's and a woman's — don't stop.

I hurry over to Micah's wheelchair and gesture to Ash to grab Tanya. Together, we quickly move to one side, out of direct line of sight of the door. There's no place to conceal ourselves, not here, but from the way Reggie and the others are crouched against the wall, it doesn't look like they intend to remain hidden for long anyway.

We wait, but our captors don't come through right away. Snatches of conversation reach our ears:

[Female voice]: " —surance the coder will be ready in time? CUs are dangerous enough . . . three times as potent."

[Male voice, louder, clearer]: "Potency's not the issue, Novak. We've been through this. It's the ability to maintain more than just basal functions. This is the breakthrough the boss has been aiming for since the first Zulu."

[Female voice]: "I'm worried about transmissibility."

[Male voice]: " . . . worry."

"What are they talking about?" Ashley whispers to me.

I gesture for her to be quiet. My guess is they're talking about the alpha treatment. Tanya stands with her back against the wall, her eyes staring out into the gloom. She has no affect on her face at all. It's like she's really not there at all.

And I don't like it.

"Hurry up with that cart!" the male voice suddenly shouts. A second male voice responds from deeper inside the room.

A shadow falls across the doorway and a moment later a woman walks through, completely absorbed on her Link. She's followed immediately by a man carrying a small, black case. Jake and Reggie are on them before they know what's hit them. Kelly slips into the room. I hear him shout at someone inside: "Get your hands up where I can see them. I said up, asshole!"

A moment later, a young man stumbles out through the doorway, tripping over his own feet. He lands on the floor before Kelly steps through holding a pistol directed at the man's head. It appears to be the same gun I'd found inside the fueling station in Long Island City. I'm actually glad to see it again.

Reggie has Miss Novak's arm wrenched behind her back. He's holding her up against a column. I can see from the look on her face that she's not used to this sort of treatment. There's no fire at all in her eyes, no fight. She gives up too easily.

The man, however, struggles with Jake. He manages to slip from his grip and spins around with the case, aiming for Jake's head. The sound of it hitting reverberates across the empty room. Jake staggers backward several steps and trips over the luggage carousel.

He quickly recovers though, and lunges at the man. But the man's ready and steps away. Jake stumbles past, looking like an amateur instead of the green belt he really is.

"How did you boys get out?" the man demands. He grabs a luggage cart and thrusts it at Jake, who deflects it. He's puffing, whereas the man looks like he's barely exerting himself. "Ah, Mister Corben," he says, spotting Kelly. "We thought we'd lost you."

"Shut up!"

"Why the hell were we being kept prisoner?" Reggie demands.

"Prisoner?" The man laughs and jockeys himself around a set of chairs. He still hasn't seen the four of us huddled in the shadows. "You're not prisoners. You're *pioneers*, the lucky chosen ones in a grand new world order." His laughter crackles against the walls and makes my ears hurt.

"I don't remember signing up for anything, asshole," Reggie growls. "And I've already seen the new world order. It's no better than the old one. In fact, I think it stinks."

"This is your chance to change it, Mister Casey. Soon you'll see. You'll be heroes."

Kelly's kneeling on the other guy's back. I get a good look at his face. He doesn't appear to be much older than the rest of us. Tanya's age, maybe. He looks terrified.

I edge my way around behind the man. I know Jake can see me, because he moves in such a way so that he keeps the man's back to us.

"What do you know about heroes, old man?" Reggie spits, also making sure the man doesn't see me as I slip from the shadows.

"I know a lot about them, son. I helped create them."

"I'm not your son, so stop calling me that."

"Listen to me, boys. I think maybe there's been a misunderstanding. Let's start— "

"Shut the hell up!" Jake suddenly screams.

The man lunges. He moves so quickly that I barely have a chance to react. I kick out with my foot just as the young man beneath Kelly shouts a warning. My toe manages to catch the other man's ankle, but it's enough to throw him off balance. He crashes to the floor and I'm on him in a flash. Jake steps in and begins whaling on the man, kicking him in the side and face. I can feel his foot hitting beneath me, can hear the man's grunts of pain keeping time with Jake's grunts of effort.

"How's— " *huhn* " —this— " *huhn* " —for a— " *HUHN* " —misunderstanding, asshole?"

"Stop it!" I scream. I glare at him in shock. Where did this violent streak come from? "Stop!"

He staggers away.

"You've got it all wrong, son," the man coughs. He turns his head and when he sees me he smiles. "So, the gang's all here. Nice to see you again, Miss Daniels. I trust you've been keeping well since the last time we spoke."

Everyone looks at me, shock on their faces, shock and suspicion.

"What does he mean, Jess?" Kelly asks. "Do you know his guy?"

I yank the man's head up by the hair, the same way I'd done to Nurse Mabel. I'm totally ready to slam his head into the floor, just like I did—

No!

It's the image of that woman, Mabel — that monster I turned her into — that stops me.

"I don't know what you're talking about, asshole. I've never met you before in my life. I've never spoken to you."

He laugh-coughs, but doesn't correct me. Instead he asks about my grandfather. "I hope he's doing well in his old age. One of the fortunate few who'll never be conscripted."

"You look like you might be about conscription age," I say.

"Oh, I'm not, really."

"Ignore him," Kelly says.

Jake appears with some coiled flexible wire that he ripped out of some ancient device. It's coated in brittle rubber that rubs off on his skin, turning it bright red. He binds the man's wrists with it, and not very gently either. The wire cuts into the man's skin.

I look over and see the young man kneeling now, his hands clasped behind his head. Kelly's standing behind him. Reggie's still got the woman shoved against the column.

"What should we do with them?" Jake asks.

"Tie her up," I tell Reggie. "We'll leave them here."

"We should take them back with us."

"Actually," Jake says, "we should kill them."

"No," I say, "I don't need that on my conscience."

There's already enough weighing it down.

Theoretically.

A vision of Mabel comes to me. I want to feel guilt for what I did, but somehow it's just not there. Maybe it'll come later. I doubt it. And maybe that's why I decide to let these two live, so I won't have to ask myself to feel guilty about doing to them what I did to Mabel. Because I know I won't be able to. I can't live like this, torn between how I should feel, and how I actually do feel.

"We'll take him," I say, gesturing to the boy. "For insurance."

"You can't leave," the man says. It's not an order or a warning. He says it like he's simply stating a fact.

"Shut up," Jake tells him. "Or I'll kick your sorry, puny, wimp-shit ass again. And this time I won't stop until you're bleeding from every orifice you've got, including a few new ones. Do you understand me?"

I stare at Jake in shock.

Back when I first met him at the dojang — God, was it only a week ago? — he'd confessed that his previous trainer emphasized brutality and aggression. It was the reason he left his studio for Rupert's. It looks like that training is kicking in, and it scares the hell out of me.

"He's right," Miss Novak says. "It'll only make things worse if you leave."

"Nothing could be worse than this, lady."

Reggie's still holding her arm behind her back. He looks uncomfortable, like he doesn't want to hurt her.

Jake turns to her and says, sneering, "Maybe he won't kick your ass up through your neck, but I wouldn't think twice about doing it."

"That's enough!" I gasp.

"You can't leave," she repeats, daring Jake to act on his threat.

He looks at me, grunts once and turns away.

I stand up quick and get in her face. "I'm going home," I tell her, snapping my words. She doesn't even flinch. "We all are. You can too, when you get yourself free. If I weren't so forgiving, I'd have you all killed and stuffed."

"Tell us how the shuttle works," Jake demands. "Tell us and we won't hurt you."

I narrow my eyes at him. Since when does he make the rules?

"It's a simple switch," the young man answers. "The tram rides a track through a tunnel under the East River. Push the lever one way and the tram moves in that direction; push it the other and it goes in the opposite direction. In the middle it stops. But— "

"What's on the other side?"

"The tunnel opens up in a warehouse in Hunts Point. It's abandoned now, of course."

"Is it guarded?"

"No," the woman says.

"Don't you fucking lie to me." I walk over to Kelly and grab the gun away from him and point it at her head. She still doesn't flinch. Now I realize what I'd mistaken for fright is just composure.

I swing it over to the young man's head instead. "Is it guarded?"

"N-no," he answers. "It's not. Honestly."

"Gather everything up," I tell Kelly. I glance over at the man still lying on the floor. "I don't know what the hell you people are doing, but we're going home. Leave us alone! Understand? If I ever see any of you again, I won't hesitate to kill you."

The man just stares.

"Are we ready?" I ask everyone. Jake nods grimly. So do Kelly and Reg.

"But you can't go," Miss Novak insists, as Reggie ties her up.

"Miss Novak," the man grunts. He chuckles. "Let them go. It's not the end of the world for us. There's always the backup plan."

"What does he mean by that?" Jake asks. "What the fuck do you mean backup plan?"

"Nothing, Jake. He's just screwing with your mind."

I go over and kick the man in the kidney. Then I lean down so my mouth is inches from his ear. I want to tell him he's an asshole. I want to say he has no right to live.

Instead, I just say: "You'll find Mabel in Room Three. I think she'll be happy to see you."

Chapter Twenty Five

"Tie up his hands, but not his feet," I say, pointing at the man kneeling on the floor. "Let's get out of this pit."

Kelly bends down and grabs his arm and yanks him upright. The guy starts to protest, but Jake glares at him and he quickly quiets down.

I march through the doorway into the dimly lit room beyond. It must've been an old transportation link for airport employees. Railcars sit on tracks that lead into several different tunnels. A colorful map on the wall shows lines connecting the various concourses and terminals. I wonder if they all still work.

"What's your name?" I demand.

"S-stephen," the man answers.

"Well, Stephen, which one gets us out of here?"

He gestures with his bound hands to a two-car tram along the far wall. The door to the engineer's compartment stands open. I walk over and look inside. The controls are lit up with a faint green glow.

"Can someone call this remotely from the other end?"

He shakes his head.

"How about from this end?" Another shake. "Good."

I instruct Jake to grab the cart that Stephen was pushing in when we ambushed them. The smell of Insta-Meals wafts from inside and my stomach grumbles. My knees shake, but I ignore them. We need to get on the train car and get moving first. I'll think about my own personal needs once we're on our way.

A black satchel sits on top of the cart. A stethoscope dangles out. The bag probably holds the injection Miss Novak had been planning to give to Tanya. I wonder if they intended the same injection for any of the rest of us or if we were going to be used for some other plan.

We have our backup.

If there were more time, I'd tell him to explain. I'm even having second thoughts about leaving them behind, but now's not the time to be second guessing my own decisions.

I watch Jake roll the cart toward the tram. I have to resist the urge to get the injection out and administer it to one of them instead. But who knows what horror that would unleash. I doubt that Stephen is completely aware of what Arc is doing. He must think he's in over his head by now, wondering what nasty shit he's gotten into. I wish I knew, too.

Once we get back to the mainland, I'll turn him over to the cops. He's weak. He'll give up Arc. Hopefully, it'll be enough to put them permanently out of business.

Reggie comes through the door pushing Micah. Tanya follows behind him like a drone, blinking and shuffling. I wish I knew what they've done to her. She should've gotten over her shock by now. She's nothing like the bubbly woman I briefly met on the bus.

"I'll drive," Reggie volunteers. He's back to his old self, that's for sure.

I shrug, and no one argues with him. They all make their way to the open car. Everyone just wants to get back home.

I take Micah's wheelchair from Reggie and enter the car, finding a space that's not in the way. Jake brings the cart in and positions it next to Micah. Then he settles himself down in the adjacent seat, smoldering. I wait until Ashley brings Tanya in, leading her by the elbow. They sit down across the aisle from the boys. Jake watches them both for a moment, rubbing the bandage on the back of his neck. He suddenly looks completely depleted. They all do, especially Kelly.

Stephen stumbles in, Kelly poking him in the back with the pistol. "Sit down and don't move!" he snarls. But even I can tell it's more bark than bite.

Stephen just lowers his head into his hands and tries to wrap himself up. He looks like a man condemned to early conscription. A bubble of sympathy floats through me before I remember what he's a party to. Even if not entirely aware of all the details, he's still guilty of some complicity.

I join Reggie in the engineer's compartment and tell him we're ready to go. I watch him as he turns a key. Dials spring to life. A half dozen gauges do their brief jiggity electrical dances before steadying. We have power and brake pressure and who knows what else. It's old tech and I don't really understand much of it. It reminds me a lot of Micah's old Ford. All I know it that it still works, so somebody must've been maintaining it all this time.

A low hum vibrates the air.

"I guess that means everything's good," Reggie says. "No red flashing lights or alarm bells. No sirens. No explosions." He gives me little shrug and grins.

The word 'explosion' sets me on edge again. "Let's go then," I say impatiently.

I know it's just nerves, but I can't shake the feeling that something's not right. It's been troubling me ever since I broke out of my room. Maybe I'm just being extra paranoid, but ever since finding out that our 'impromptu' plan to break into LI was really part of a larger scheme involving Arc, I've been second guessing everything, every decision, every move.

How did they know? Who could've told them? Jake? Grandpa?

God, we thought we were being clever and secretive, a bunch of juveniles getting away with random crap that we really had no business messing around in. The only part of our excursion that was truly our own decision and not Arc's was when we came back. And we screwed that up.

Who can I trust? Who *can't* I?

It makes me suspect everything that happened, starting with Reggie's suggestion to come here in the first place.

Was our earlier attempt to hack *The Game* some kind of trigger that set our path?

What about when we hacked the old government computers for the maps?

And my faulty rebreather in the tunnel. Accidental or intentional?

How about the sudden appearance of the zombies on LI?

Was meeting Tanya on the bus part of the plan?

Reggie curls his fingers over a control lever and slowly pulls it down. The external doors close. A bell chimes and a female voice announces that we'll be moving soon. There's a chuff of air as the brakes release. I brace myself, but we don't move.

"What's going on? Why aren't we going?"

He shakes his head and studies the control panel. The he reaches over and pushes a red button with the palm of his hand. The train car lurches. We begin to move.

"Seems our friend was holding out on us. It's not just a lever. It's a lever *and* a button."

I hope it's the last surprise.

"Let's go home, Reg."

"I'm with you on that one, girl," he replies. "And never come back, neither."

ACKNOWLEDGEMENTS

As always, my *undying* thanks to all of the devoted staff of Brinestone Press for their keen eye and gentle but firm touch in helping me bring these stories to life, for believing every step of the way that I could speak with and for the dead.

To my devoted fans and followers on Twitter, especially the zombie apocalypse junkies. Everything's better with the #zombie hashtag.

http://twitter.com/saultanpepper

And to my faithful friends and fans on Facebook.

http://facebook.com/saul.tanpepper

‡ ‡

My deepest gratitude goes to my family for their unflagging support, especially my beautiful children.

‡ ‡ ‡

ABOUT THE AUTHOR

‡

Saul Tanpepper is a writer of speculative fiction for teens and adults. A former molecular geneticist originally from Upstate New York, he now calls Northern California home.

If you enjoyed GAMELAND Episodes One & Two, please check out the rest of the series, as well as the companion books, available in digital and paperback formats.

For more information about the author and his writings, please check out his website:
http://www.tanpepperwrites.com.

‡ ‡ ‡

Made in the USA
Middletown, DE
15 December 2014